a weekend at
BLENHEIM

J. P. MORRISSEY

Thomas Dunne Books

a weekend at

BLENHEIM

St. Martin's Press ⚓ New York

THOMAS DUNNE BOOKS.
An imprint of St. Martin's Press.

www.stmartins.com

Designed by Lorelle Graffeo

Library of Congress Cataloging-in-Publication Data

Morrissey, J. P.
    A weekend at Blenheim: a novel / J. P. Morrissey.—1st ed.
      p. cm.
    ISBN 0-312-28268-0
    1. Blenheim Palace (England)—Fiction.   2. Balsan, Consuelo Vanderbilt—Fiction.   3. Americans—England—Fiction.   4. Country homes—Fiction.   5. Architects—Fiction.   6. Vendetta—Fiction.   I. Title.

PS3613.O68 W44 2002
813'.6—dc21

                         2001042381

First Edition: March 2002

10 9 8 7 6 5 4 3 2 1

This book is for Rula

ACKNOWLEDGMENTS

I am exeedingly grateful to the following people:

—Luke Cyphers, Patricia Eisemann, Nan Graham, Susan Moldow, Charles Scribner III, Susanne Kirk, Gary Larson, Dorothy McCarthy, Ruth Pomerance, and Bill Watterson, for their wise counsel and extraordinary efforts on my behalf.

—Suzanne Gluck, whose intelligence and sound judgment made finding the home for this book seem simple.

—Sean Desmond, for his graceful editing and unending good humor. All authors should be so fortunate.

—Ezra Fitz, Elizabeth Catalano, Ragnhild Hagen, and David Rotstein at St. Martin's Press, for their exemplary attention to this book. It is immeasurably improved by their efforts.

—Jean, Emma, and Charlotte Morrissey, for their unending patience and interest in seeing this project through. They'll never know how much they helped.

While all excesses are hurtful,
the most dangerous is unlimited good fortune.

—SENECA

THE MARLBOROUGH (SPENCER-CHURCHILL) LINE OF DESCENT

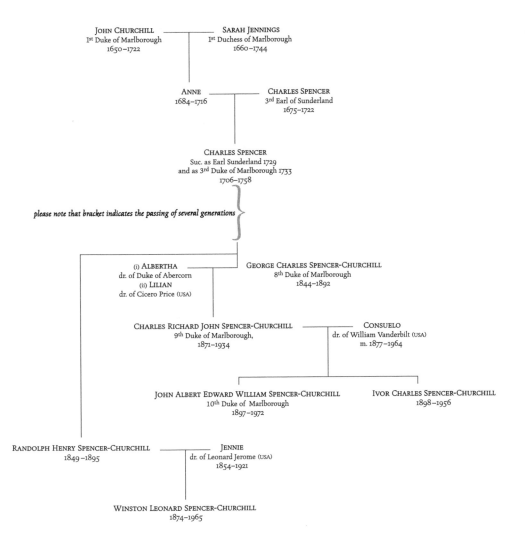

JOHN CHURCHILL
1st Duke of Marlborough
1650–1722

SARAH JENNINGS
1st Duchess of Marlborough
1660–1744

ANNE
1684–1716

CHARLES SPENCER
3rd Earl of Sunderland
1675–1722

CHARLES SPENCER
Suc. as Earl Sunderland 1729
and as 3rd Duke of Marlborough 1733
1706–1758

please note that bracket indicates the passing of several generations

(i) ALBERTHA
dr. of Duke of Abercorn
(ii) LILIAN
dr. of Cicero Price (USA)

GEORGE CHARLES SPENCER-CHURCHILL
8th Duke of Marlborough
1844–1892

CHARLES RICHARD JOHN SPENCER-CHURCHILL
9th Duke of Marlborough,
1871–1934

CONSUELO
dr. of William Vanderbilt (USA)
m. 1877–1964

JOHN ALBERT EDWARD WILLIAM SPENCER-CHURCHILL
10th Duke of Marlborough
1897–1972

IVOR CHARLES SPENCER-CHURCHILL
1898–1956

RANDOLPH HENRY SPENCER-CHURCHILL
1849–1895

JENNIE
dr. of Leonard Jerome (USA)
1854–1921

WINSTON LEONARD SPENCER-CHURCHILL
1874–1965

prologue

SUMMER 1933

In a word, the whole is a most expensive absurdity; and the Duke of Shrewsbury gave a true character of it when he said it was a great Quarry of Stones above Ground.
—ALEXANDER POPE ON BLENHEIM PALACE

THE château at Saint-Georges-Motel sits in a peaceful glade of high trees near the forest of Dreaux in Normandy. Built of pink brick and topped by a steep roof of blue slate, it is tall and stately, elegant without being haughty. Its most notable features are the two square towers that frame the château's center. The house is ringed by a moat, devised more for decoration than defense. It is spanned by a low bridge of buff-colored stone, which connects the house to the forecourt, a correct rectangle of raked gravel bordered by manicured shrubs. A wide avenue of chestnut and linden trees links the house to the village. In the gardens, long shaded alleys lead to hidden groves; down them one can glimpse sculpture from another time: a wild boar and a leaping stag, both caught forever in stone.

This is a place of quiet contentment born of the confidence that springs from a life well lived. The light is welcoming here, the breezes soft. Laughter springs forth more easily than it seems to in England, which lingers in the half-light of unanswered questions.

I stood in the forecourt by the bridge, my parcel secure in hand, and gazed at the château's façade, calculating. It is a habit I have, engendered more by my profession than by personal interest, but one I nevertheless find difficult to ignore, even when I am not working. I have become as skilled at estimating the amount of raw materials needed for a particular project as a politician is at predicting the impact of a speech or a portraitist the number of colors needed for that day's sitting. I have become the Churchill of architects, the Sargent of engineers. It is only after the stone or iron or steel has been put to its intended use that I am at a loss. I can plan and build well enough; it is what to do afterward that baffles me.

I must have stood there longer than I had thought, for when I approached the heavy front doors a servant opened one of them, as if he had been waiting for me.

In my correct if academic French, I said, "I would appreciate a brief interview with Madame."

"Madame is not receiving this morning," the servant said.

I shifted the parcel to my other arm and extracted a card from my jacket pocket. "I believe she will see me," I said. "Please tell Madame it concerns a personal matter."

He glanced at the card, then at me. After a moment he opened the door a little wider and beckoned me into the hall. "If Monsieur will wait a moment...," he murmured and then disappeared.

The hall was a deep, two-storied room with a worn stone floor, thick beams, well-rubbed paneling the color of molasses, and a huge wrought-iron chandelier hanging from the center of the ceiling. A second-floor balcony cantilevered off the walls and made the room seem narrower than it actually was. The furniture, large and comfortable, was arranged on a faded but still attractive Oriental rug and in front of a fireplace tall enough for a man to walk into. At either end of the fireplace were two attenuated statues, carved in agonized profile and facing each other. They looked terrified—frightened, perhaps, that they were not strong enough to hold up the heavy mantel they had been created to support. On both sides of the fireplace large French windows were open. Through them I could see a terrace that overlooked the rear moat and the gardens beyond.

The servant returned quickly. "If you will follow me, Monsieur," he said.

He led me to a small corner room that was cool and feminine. The lady of the house was at her writing desk, an impossibly fragile-looking Louis XV *escritoire,* and looked up from what she was doing when we entered. After a moment she stood up. Though past fifty, she was still handsome, but was not as willowy, as ethereal, as she once had been. Her famous swanlike neck was still smooth and was circled by her trademark choker of pearls. She was dressed in a simple lavender-colored dress of a subtle, subdued pattern which even I, no expert in haute couture, knew was expensively made. Her dark hair, which when she was young was worn long and piled high on her head, was now streaked with gray and cut short around her delicate ears. But her appraising eyes and upturned nose still made her look inquisitive, and perhaps a little mischievous.

"Monsieur Vanbrugh," the servant announced.

The lady took my hand. Her skin was still soft, her grip firm. "Your . . . Madame," I said in English, bowing slightly.

"Mr. Vanbrugh," Madame Balsan said. "I am surprised and pleased to see you after all this time." Her voice was low, with only a hint of her native accent.

"I promised myself that I would come if ever I had news," I said.

"And do you?" she asked, looking at my parcel.

I did not reply immediately. "You have an impressive home. Louis the Thirteenth?"

Madame nodded. "So you have become a student of architectural history. After all this time."

The comment stung, but I tried not to let it show. "I have learned quite a bit since we last met," I said. "I have become educated."

"Really. How astonishing. What have you learned?"

I smiled. "May we sit down?"

Madame frowned, as two narrow furrows appeared above her eyebrows. "Of course." She indicated two settees, upholstered in a soft fabric the color of butter, facing each other near the windows. As we sat she asked, "Would you like some tea? Oh, of course not. How stupid of me. You prefer coffee."

"Yes," I said, placing my parcel carefully in my lap.

"Coffee for Mr. Vanbrugh," Madame said. The servant nodded and left. The lady smiled and relaxed a little. "I am always struck by how Americans adapt to living abroad. Some of us absorb the world, like a sponge. Some of us retreat from it, like a turtle into its shell. We become more American when we live in a foreign country, not less."

The parcel in my lap suddenly felt very heavy.

"I am trying to determine how you look after all this time," Madame said after a moment. "There is something changed in you."

3

"Undoubtedly," I said. "I have grown old. One of the many trage-
dies I've endured."

Madame Balsan's cheeks colored. "No, that is not what I mean. I
cannot think . . ." She frowned again, as her hand distractedly reached
for her pearls and she tapped one delicately. "Do you still live in London? Does it still agree with you?"

"I am leaving London," I said.

"Leaving London?" She seemed taken aback. "After all this time?
Why?"

"I am returning to America. For good."

"I must say, I am surprised."

"Why does that surprise you?" I asked.

"I would have thought that America would hold little appeal for
you."

"Even turtles can be unpredictable," I said.

Balsan smiled slightly and arranged the drape of her skirt over her
knee. "I was in America for my mother's memorial service," she said.

"I read of her death," I said quietly, careful not to express any
sorrow. I would not be a hypocrite, even now. "She was a most unusual
woman."

Madame tilted her head. " 'A force of nature,' my father used to call
her. Her service was just like her: bold and brash. Suffragette societies
from all over the country sent delegations. The ladies carried their
banners into St. Thomas's church as they marched up the aisle. The
choir sung a hymn my mother had composed."

"A hymn? I was not aware your mother was musical."

"She was not, I am sorry to say. My mother was a better architect
than she was a composer."

I thought about this for a moment. "So she arranged her own funeral."

"That should not come as a shock." Madame looked at me deliberately, and sat up straighter. "But I assume that you did not travel all
the way from London to discuss my mother, Mr. Vanbrugh," she said.

"No. I came to give you this." I handed her the parcel. "I did not
trust the post for such a package."

Her large brown eyes took in the package greedily, almost hungrily.

She held it tentatively, as if it were a piece of Meissen too fragile even to hold. "Is this it?" she asked.

"Yes," I said.

"Then it is done," she said quietly. "At long last."

"Yes," I said. "It is done. At long last."

chapter

1

SUMMER 1905

I was in a foul temper the afternoon the letter came. London had been hellishly hot the entire month of June—a hazy, oppressive, provoking heat that seemed to enervate the city and everyone in it. It was all but impossible to work, or even to keep drafting paper dry enough to draw upon. Every time I rested my hand on a sheet for longer than a moment, my palm would cling to the paper, dampening it so badly that it was difficult to draw on with either pencil or ink. I was forced to redraw the elevation of a small villa the firm had been commissioned to design three times before I finished a fair copy.

At home, life was almost as difficult. My wife, Margaret, was not sleeping well, which made her fretful and churlish. Her pregnancy had not been an easy one, and as she neared the end of its third month, she had become decidedly ill-tempered. The quick, assured woman I married had become testy and impossible to please. Our rooms off Baker Street, which she had thought delightful only a few weeks ago, were now a torture to her. She found them cramped and inhospitable, and complained bitterly that she could hear rats nesting inside the walls—defects I had not detected, vermin I had neither seen nor heard.

"At least, Van, you can *see* the river from your office," Margaret complained over a dinner of overcooked chops and soggy carrots—as if glimpsing a dirty river through grimy windows soothed the soul. "The only thing I can see is the milliner's across the street."

"The milliner's smells appreciably better than rotting fish," I said as I poked at my food. "And if you find it agreeable to lean over a drafting table while sweat pours down your aching back, by all means come to the office."

I realized instantly that I had been too harsh; Margaret pressed her lips together and, holding her stomach, broke into deep, heaving sobs. I sat across from her in resigned silence, waiting for the squall to abate. My strategy for withstanding these outbursts—the only one that I had found to work—was to remain silent for a few minutes and then to surrender unequivocally.

Eventually Margaret managed, "What a despicable thing to suggest, Van—to me, to your *wife*..."

"You are right," I agreed, defeated. "I am sorry. It is this damn heat that is making all of us short-tempered."

Margaret looked at me in surprise. "I am not short-tempered," she said indignantly through her tears. "I am as calm and as dignified as I can be, under extremely trying circumstances." Her hands fluttered up to indicate the room and then settled back into her lap. "But it has not been easy." She leaned against the chair back and settled into a renewed bout of tears.

"What about a visit to your father?" I said when it appeared that the worst of her temper had passed. "It must be cooler in Long Hanborough than it is in London." Margaret's father, the Reverend John Barton, was the vicar at Christ Church in Long Hanborough, a village a few miles northwest of Oxford. He was a good-hearted if slightly befuddled cleric who yearned to do good for others. I had met him a year ago when he and Margaret traveled to America, to Boston and New York, to raise money for a children's charity he was involved with. My sister, Ann, who was a member of one of the churches in Boston that welcomed Reverend Barton, introduced us at a small reception, proclaiming, "Reverend Barton, Miss Barton, this is my heathen brother John Vanbrugh. He is an architect."

"A struggling one," I amended.

"Ah, at long last," Mr. Barton said, shaking my hand vigorously. "Delighted, delighted."

"So you eschew belief for bas-relief," Margaret said smiling, her eyebrows raised. "How brave you are."

Her father chuckled and said, "My dear Margaret, do not poke fun at Mr. Vanbrugh."

"It is no trouble, I assure you," I said, grinning at the plump, dark-haired woman before me who was dressed in a dark blue gown of a European cut and matching hat. "I believe in the Almighty, but I suppose it is true that I am more interested in the certainty of this world than what I can hope for in the next."

"True faith is the ultimate certainty, Mr. Vanbrugh," she said. "For myself, I cannot imagine anything more certain than the Absolute. Would you agree?"

I did not reply, for I had noticed her eyes. They were easily the most remarkable parts of her face. Almond-shaped, they were a deep blue with flecks of gold and were set wide over a prominent nose. The rest of her face was not what one would call handsome: Her mouth was a little too broad, her lips fuller than they should have been, and her complexion tended toward the sallow. But there was a commendable air of intelligence about her that was pleasant enough.

"Absolutely," I said after a moment.

Miss Barton looked abashed as her father laughed. "Touché, Mr. Vanbrugh," he said.

The Bartons spent several weeks in New England, traveling to Providence, to Newport, and up the Maine coast as far as Brunswick. During their visit I came to know them well—so well, in fact, that when Mr. Barton sailed for England, I accompanied him and my bride, Mrs. John Vanbrugh, née Margaret Barton of Long Hanborough, Oxfordshire. I own that our courtship was brief, and that she and I did not transport each other into the sweet garden of transcendent love that the lady novelists write about. But we were compatible enough, each willing to overlook the limitations of the other in the interest of harmony, and we were agreeably disposed toward each other in nearly every way.

Mr. Barton was pleased at our engagement—more than I had expected. "You two will do well together, my boy," he said to me one evening at my sister's house after he had drunk too much cider. "Neither one of you expects too much of the other. You are not children, either of you: Margaret, good heavens, is nearly twenty-seven! Imagine—still a maid!" He shook his head in wonder. "It is time for her life to begin."

As we left Boston Harbor, on that cold, clear evening in February, I turned back toward America for a final look. I was not sorry to leave the city, although I would miss my sister and her family. But it had long been apparent that some change would have to be made: I had not secured a suitable position at any of the city's architectural firms. Since I was not trained in the classical traditions of the craft and the history of structure and design was not known to me, I was destined to remain a journeyman—a draftsman for hire. For a man of ambition, that was a bitter brew. I knew that I was a man of ability and imagination, and as my courting of Margaret took its course, the idea of going to England with them took root. I flirted briefly with the idea of moving to the Continent, to Paris, but the happy accident of my encounter with the Bartons proved too persuasive. And while there were moments when I regretted not settling in the French capital, I came to appreciate the simple lines of London's buildings and its reassuring domesticity.

Despite the dire warnings of my acquaintances in America about the difficulties of establishing myself in a foreign country, my drafting proved well received in London, and thanks to an introduction provided by my new father-in-law, I was offered a position at Burlington and Kent, a small but highly regarded firm in the City. I settled quickly into the position and to my new role as an interested observer of that extraordinary but puzzling race, the English. And to our surprise and delight, Margaret soon learned she was to have a child—news which made my father-in-law glow with happiness. Since then, he had been imploring Margaret to visit him, and even suggested that the baby be born in Long Hanborough.

Margaret seemed to consider the idea of traveling: Her sniffling slowed. "What would you do if I went to Long Hanborough?" she asked.

"I would be fine. Mrs. Meaghan would look after me."

"Mrs. Meaghan would drink herself insensible, drop her teeth into your dinner, and then rob you blind on her way out," Margaret said of the woman who came in to do for us. She removed a fresh handkerchief from her sleeve and dabbed at her nose.

"I am fully capable of taking care of myself," I said. "Even when it comes to Mrs. Meaghan."

Margaret laughed and said, "Men. Such children."

"We are nothing of the kind," I said in defense of my sex. "Our wives just treat us as if we are."

Margaret smiled as she removed a speck of dust from her skirt. "It is so easy to take advantage of you," she said, "you are so willing to be duped by a female."

I reached for the *Morning Post* and made a conspicuous display of reading an account in it of the visit by the king of Portugal to Windsor Castle. "That is too ridiculous even to reply to," I said, "so I will not."

Margaret was silent a moment. "I suppose a short visit to Long Hanborough might be all right," she said. "No more than a few days."

"Of course not," I said, peering over my newspaper. "No one would expect you to stay longer."

"I would be gone just long enough for the city to cool down," Margaret said, more to herself than to me.

"I am sure the heat will break very soon," I agreed.

"And Father has sounded increasingly melancholy in his letters," Margaret said. "Poor man. He is growing lonely."

"He misses you," I said.

"He has never lived in that house alone," Margaret said. "He wants company. I think a short visit would be better for all. A week at the most." The decision made, her tears gone, Margaret stood up. "There will be much to do there, I expect. The house will be a sight. The whole place will need a good airing-out, and Mrs. Coggins is far too old to do it properly. The mattresses will have to be turned, the rugs cleaned, and everything will have to be dusted—oh, the dust!"

"The weather will be much cooler in a week," I said.

She laughed and kissed me on the head as she walked by. "My dear, as if anyone could predict the weather."

The emotional storm had passed; her sea of tears had calmed. She was composed now, her course set. Margaret went to her writing desk, which snuggled into the corner of the sitting room like a plump cat before the fire. "I will write to Father, to ask him when I should come to him," Margaret said with decision. She glanced at me. "Perhaps I can drive him to distraction, too."

This time I had the sagacity to stay silent.

*   *   *

"Is that your real name? John?" Davy, the Burlington and Kent office boy, asked early one morning three days later as he threw a letter onto my drafting table.

"Mind the ink," I said irritably, shooing the letter to one side. "It is not dry yet."

Short, thin, and surpassingly stupid, Davy glanced incuriously at what I was working on, an elevation for a new bank in Bristol. "Nearly," he said.

"Nearly is not good enough," I said.

The boy ignored me. "Why they call you Van then?"

His obtuseness was remarkable. "I am called that because the name Victoria was already taken."

Davy frowned, mumbled something incomprehensible, and shuffled back to his desk across the room, shooting me occasional dark, puzzled looks.

The envelope was small and neat, and made of thick, good-quality paper. It was addressed only to "Mr. John Vanbrugh."

"Who delivered this?" I asked.

"Dunno." Davy shrugged. "Ned brought it up, from downstairs."

I opened it. The letterhead read in small, raised letters "Blenheim Palace." Above it was a small ducal coronet.

The message was brief.

> Dear Mr. Vanbrugh,
>
> Your father-in-law, Mr. Barton, mentioned you to me, and naturally your name and nationality piqued my interest. I wonder if you would mind calling on me at Blenheim soonest?
>
> Consuelo
> Duchess of Marlborough

I chuckled.

"What's it then?" Davy asked.

"Someone is having a bit of fun. It is supposed to be a letter from someone important."

I had heard of the Duchess of Marlborough, of course. It was almost impossible not to. She was the only daughter of William K. Vanderbilt, the American millionaire, and had come to England a decade ago when she married Charles Spencer-Churchill, the ninth Duke of Marlborough. I had never seen her in person, though I had seen her photograph in the newspapers. She was tall and possessed the arrogant beauty of the rich, which, I surmised, sprang more from a languorous life of idleness than it did from any inner fire. She and her husband, who had been undersecretary for the Colonies in the government, lived idly at Blenheim Palace, a large estate near Long Hanborough. I had never visited the place, but my father-in-law was eager for me to see it. "It is magnificent, my boy, a house fit for God himself." If that were the case, why was the lady of the manor inviting me?

The letter was obviously a prank. The Duchess of Marlborough had no more need of me than she did of another million dollars. The two of us existed on different planes; the paths of our lives would never intersect. I was not the kind of architect she would employ: I was not famous, I had not designed any fashionable, overdecorated houses in London or in the countryside. I had not studied in Paris or visited the ruins of Greece and Rome. My name, which I own was a little unusual, was simply what I was called; it held no other meaning for me. The fact that I was an American by birth was more interesting than important. Everything about this letter was so puzzling, in fact, that I was convinced it must be a prank—some nonsense cooked up by a wag. Perhaps Mr. Hodges, one of our surveyors, was the culprit, or Edward Williams, a draftsman I sometimes met for a pint at the Fox and Vixen. Whoever the prankster was, he apparently enjoyed the thought of my presenting myself at the door of Blenheim Palace, panting at the prospect of working for a duchess. The whole thing was so patently ridiculous that I did what any rational man would do in my situation. I tossed the letter away.

The elevation was finally dry. As I was readying it for Davy to deliver to the bank's London office, I heard a thin voice on the stairs. "I wonder, is John Vanbrugh up there?"

Davy went to the top of the stairs and asked self-importantly, "Who wants to know?"

"Oh, my boy, is he up there? If he is, please tell him his father-in-law wishes to speak to him."

I went to the top of the stairs and saw Mr. Barton peering up at me, his face crinkled in nearsighted concentration. "Ah, *there* you are," he said in relief. "I was beginning to think that I had come to the wrong office."

"What on earth are you doing here?" I asked, walking down the stairs to greet him. "You are supposed to be in Long Hanborough."

"And so I was, so I was." Mr. Barton nodded eagerly. "And so I will be." He smiled benignly, his pudgy cheeks ruddy with excitement. Reverend Barton was a short, cheerful man with the same intelligent eyes his daughter inherited. He had a thin, horseshoe-shaped arc of wild white hair, but the crown of his head was as pink as his face. Befitting his role of a clergyman, he dressed in black, but inevitably there was some part of his toilet that was askew: Today he was missing a button on his coat.

"But Margaret wants to come to you in Long Hanborough," I said. "We were to leave in a few days."

"Yes, I know, I know, I have come to escort both of you. To Long Hanborough."

Inwardly I groaned: Our rooms were not ready for visitors. "So you will be staying with us?" I asked.

Barton looked confused. "Did you not receive the letter this morning?"

I shook my head. "I got no letter today."

Davy, who had been listening to every word at the top of the stairs, interrupted us. "Yeah, you did. Just now, it was. That letter you tossed."

"That was a stunt," I said. Turning to Barton, I explained. "Someone was trying to make me think that the Duchess of Marlborough wanted me to call on her."

Barton clutched my forearm, fairly bursting with glee. "But that is why I am here, my boy, she *does* want to see you," he said with enthusiasm. "I came for you myself."

"That cannot be. She has no idea who I am."

"Oh, she does, my boy," Barton said. He leaned toward me and lowered his voice. "I told her about you."

"You? Why?"

Barton grinned and almost danced with excitement. "She has been *very* generous indeed toward my orphan school project, and after our last meeting she mentioned . . . well, I will let her tell all. But let us hurry, we may still be able to make the train."

"What? Go now?" I asked, flummoxed at the suggestion.

"She's a duchess, isn't she," Davy said, as if it were necessary to remind me of the obvious.

"A duchess is not to be kept waiting," Barton said.

"But I must speak to Mr. Kent first," I protested.

"Leave him to me," Davy said. He retrieved the letter from the trash and waved it at me with every indication that he heartily disapproved of my lack of respect toward my betters. "I'll show him this. Pleased as punch, he'll be, one of his own staff meeting the Duchess of Marlborough. He knows what's important, even if others don't."

"Come along, Van," Barton urged. "We have a great deal to do."

When we arrived home Margaret was packed and waiting; her father had obviously stopped at our rooms first. We arrived at Paddington in good time to make the train to Long Hanborough, and during the journey Margaret divided her time between bombarding her father with questions about why the duchess wanted to see me and upbraiding me for my cavalier attitude toward a peeress's correspondence. My father-in-law refused to answer any question Margaret posed about the duchess, and I kept silent because her chattering relieved me from having to distract her from her condition and how she was feeling.

We arrived in Long Hanborough to find that Margaret had been correct in her estimation of Mrs. Coggins: The house was cluttered with papers and books and was dustier than usual, but was otherwise in good order. Margaret would have just enough work to make her feel she was accomplishing something without exhausting her.

As I brought in her last parcel, Margaret kissed me. "Now pay attention to *everything*," she admonished. "I understand she is transforming the palace."

Barton bustled into the hall, his coat still on. "She is, my dear. Slowly but surely." He kissed her lightly on the forehead. "Now, are we ready?"

"But I was just about to eat something," I said.

"I am certain the duchess will offer you something," Barton said. "Her hospitality is well known, well known, indeed. So hurry along, there's a good boy."

He and I piled back into his carriage and as we rode the few miles from Long Hanborough to Woodstock, I pondered once again the eccentricities of the English. The two Bartons, whose family had lived in Oxfordshire for as long as people could remember, were excited at the prospect that I, who had been born in America, was to meet an English duchess, also born in America. Both the duchess and I had come to England because that was where our spouses lived, and we had found places for ourselves in a culture that was not known to embrace foreigners, particularly Americans. Yet we had been accepted by the English and by all appearances had settled into comfortable respectability.

Just before we reached Woodstock, we passed on our left a huge, ornate arch of stone that dwarfed a pair of black iron gates, its spears tipped in brilliant gold. The gates were closed and there was no one about to unlock them. My father-in-law was not in the least bothered by this. He drove his horse through the village confidently, passing the town hall, a stolid, square building of golden stone, an ancient coaching inn crowded with men and horses, a small Gothic church settled snugly on its plot of green, and a string of well-tended houses, their neatly planted window boxes overflowing with summer blossoms. At the end of the road, we veered to the left around a small guesthouse that advertised "Views of Blenheim" and came upon another heavy stone archway, a twin to the one we had passed earlier. A gatekeeper, holding a silver staff with a scarlet tassel hanging from it, stood at firm attention when we passed from the village onto the estate.

Instantly the scenery changed. To our right, sheep grazed along the gentle grassy hill that sloped down to a broad, placid lake, as white swans skimmed the surface of the green water. In front of us, towering trees, grouped in dark clusters, obscured a full view of the house. All that I could make out clearly from a distance was a flag flying from a thin pole.

"There," Barton said, pointing toward the house. "That is Blenheim."

He guided the carriage down the drive, and we turned right onto a broader avenue planted on either side with small, sickly trees, which ended before another enormous stone arch, standing bluntly in the middle of the thick-set wall. The arch was covered with garlands of stone while classical figures stood in niches fifteen feet above us, below oddly shaped stone finials, which stood atop the arch itself. The gates themselves consisted of tall metal spears, each painted black and its point tipped with gold. Gold medallions of animal heads, florets, intertwined letters, and a lion holding a flag in one paw, his tail curved merrily, decorated each side.

From this prospect, I could not see Blenheim clearly, but I was struck by how impressive it was. Assembled across the crest of a low hill was a startling array of architectural elements: massive wings topped with stone pinnacles thirty feet high which looked poised to shoot into the sky, curving arcades of narrow stone columns, hundreds of blank, black windows, stone roof urns supporting golden orbs that caught the sun. The palace looked monumental, immense—a home for giants.

As we drew nearer, I could see that the palace was built of roan-colored stone which over the years had aged and blackened, giving the house a forbidding, even sinister cast. Four thick towers anchored each corner of the main house, with a square arcade of chimneys rising from the center of each one. The central section, all weighty porticos and broken pediments, lurched up out of the house, as if thrust through the roof, a golden orb atop its highest point. The entire effect was of a jumble of stone thrown together in a cataclysm. It was a far cry from the elegant mansions I saw in London: There was none of the comfortable domesticity one saw along Park Lane, or even at the Queen's House at Greenwich. This house put me in mind of the Tower of London. It had the same feel: heavy, warlike, unbreachable. It did not look like a country house but a citadel, the seat of a medieval despot set among the gentle hills of Oxfordshire.

Barton directed the carriage toward the arch. As we drew closer to the house, I noticed that it was impossible to discern anything beyond the tall, gaunt windows: They turned a blank cheerless aspect to the world.

We passed through the narrow, elaborately decorated entry, while three nearly nude female statues looked away, as if embarrassed; above them, three horrified, openmouthed stone faces stared down in dismay. The Marlborough arms were hung prominently from each side of the gate. Though I was no student of heraldry, I knew the coat of arms was impressive. Its shield was divided into quarters, with a fifth smaller shield in the middle of the top half. Two lions, one each in the upper left and lower right quadrants, faced left and stood on their hind legs, holding military flags. Four strong, square buckles, linked up from the bottom left to the upper right, were balanced by two narrower strips of seashells that slashed down from the upper left to the lower right quadrants. The entire shield was protected by two ferocious dragons and a large, two-headed eagle which peered from behind a ducal coronet. At the bottom of the coat of arms was a foreign phrase I was not familiar with: *"Fiel Pero Desdichado."* The effect of the arch had a disconcerting feel to it, as if it were a portal to something unpleasant.

"This is the East Gate," Barton said above the clatter of the horse's hoofs on the cobblestones. "Did you read the inscription?"

"What inscription?"

"The one above the archway."

"No," I admitted.

"Never mind. The duke added it very recently. We will read it on the way out."

"What is the flag?" I asked.

"The duke's standard," Barton said. "It always flies whenever His Grace is in residence."

We drove across a large court cluttered with wagons, ladders, and piles of wood and dirt. It was ringed by a series of stocky archways, behind which long arcades ran into heavy shadows. We did not pause, but passed through another archway with a large clock above it and came finally to a magnificent central court, around three sides of which the palace was arranged. Unlike the cobblestones in the courtyard, much of the central court was grass, though it was in the process of being recobbled with what looked like granite. Neat pyramids of stones, like fires at a military encampment, had been placed at intervals around the court and groups of men were laying them.

Barton pulled up to a sweeping set of stairs that led to the main entrance and stopped. "Well, here we are, then," he said brightly.

Almost immediately a servant appeared to tend to the horse. Barton handed him the reins and we climbed out of the carriage.

As Barton gave instructions to the servant, I took stock of Blenheim from between two decorative cannons, each six feet long, which displayed the same coat of arms I had seen on the gate. Above the enormous front doors, which were taller than three grown men, an intricately carved pediment was supported by six cumbrous pillars. Even up close, Blenheim looked as if it had just been heaved out of the earth.

Barton turned to me and began to climb the stairs. "You will, I am sure, find Blenheim magnificent," Barton said. "Visitors usually do."

"How do the residents find it?" I asked jokingly.

Barton did not reply.

As we entered the hall, a soaring cube of limestone, I understood why my father-in-law had used the term "magnificent." The space clearly had been designed to overwhelm. Three tall tiers of arches—some of them windows, some of them doorways, some of them recesses displaying sculpture or statuary—climbed up the walls to the immense oval mural that dominated the ceiling and depicted a Roman soldier kneeling before a woman holding a spear. The expansive floor, decorated in a pattern of white marble alternating with smaller inlays of black, was covered by two faded carpets of an Oriental pattern. At the end of the hall, directly across from the front doors, was another, flatter stone arch, supported on both sides by heavy pillars. An elaborate coat of arms of fleur-de-lis and lions topped by a crown—similar to the one I saw on the gate and cannons—was carved into the keystone of the arch; two stone cherubs blowing trumpets and carrying curving branches of leaves proclaimed its uniqueness. Beneath the arch and above a doorway of sumptuous white marble hung three faded flags of gold, white, and red. The room was indeed stately, but the effect was more funereal than triumphant. Despite its cavernous height—surely more than sixty feet—and the windows that lighted it, the hall was dim and airless, like a mausoleum.

Two women emerged from one set of shadows, talking earnestly.

Both were young, and both wore aprons. The one on the right—a tall, fragile-looking creature with a heart-shaped face, thick, dark hair piled high upon her head, an upturned nose, and a long, elegant neck—was speaking intently to the smaller woman, a housemaid, who was holding a square package wrapped in brown paper and frowning. The taller lady was wearing gardening gloves and held a beautiful array of brightly colored flowers. She placed the flowers on a large marble table near the wall and whispered to the housemaid. The younger girl nodded quickly, and with an abrupt curtsy departed, hurrying up the stairway that was just visible through the outsized arcade on one side of the Great Hall.

The woman smiled when she noticed my father-in-law, revealing a small dimple. She removed her gloves as she walked toward us, and extended her thin, elegant hand to my father-in-law. "Mr. Barton, I am so sorry that I was not here to greet you. As you can see, you have caught me impromptu." Her smile was warm and playful.

My father-in-law bowed and took her hand gently. "But you are here now, Your Grace. That is pleasure enough for an old man."

The lady smiled and turned to me. "But perhaps not enough for a younger one?"

"I expect that it depends on the pleasure," I said. "And the man."

The duchess gazed at me and arched a well-formed eyebrow as my father-in-law said, "Your Grace, may I present to you my son-in-law, John Vanbrugh. John, this is the Duchess of Marlborough."

The duchess gazed at me with kind, heavily lidded eyes. "I am always pleased to meet a fellow American," she said, offering me her hand. Her grip was cool and firm, but her skin was soft as the petal of a flower. Her head cocked slightly to one side, as a bird's might to listen to the song of its mate. Her dark brown eyes were large and full of barely concealed mischief, as if she expected a joke at any moment.

"And I am always surprised to encounter an American duchess," I said, bowing my head. "You are indeed a rarity."

"Oh, yes, I am a hothouse flower, locked in a conservatory of stone," the duchess said dryly. "But that is not why I imposed upon your father-in-law to meet you." She checked a tiny watch that was pinned to her blouse beneath her apron. "Would you care for some refreshment? We always have something for guests a little bit before luncheon."

"That would be delightful," Barton said, looking at me.

She removed her apron, revealing that she was attired in a soft, flowing dress of summer green with a lacy, tight-fitting jacket over it. The dress's collar covered her fantastically long neck, but over it she wore a wide choker of magnificent pearls; I made a mental note to remember these details for Margaret. We followed the duchess across the hall and into the Saloon, a room that was almost as large as the hall itself. It was wider than it was deep, with a narrow, oval dining table at its center, ringed by a tight complement of crimson chairs set on gilded legs. On all four walls a huge mural had been painted, depicting dozens of figures I did not recognize. They peered down at us from a series of balconies between towering pillars as heavy curtains were pulled back to reveal Arcadian scenes. Their stern, stately gazes made me feel as if I were a jester who had failed to amuse them sufficiently.

The duchess took no notice of the room. Instead, she walked toward an already open set of doors on the left-hand wall. "I understand that this is your first visit to Blenheim, Mr. Vanbrugh," she said.

"Yes, Your Grace," I replied.

"I am sorry that my husband is not here to greet you. He is out on the estate on business. He very much enjoys showing Blenheim to visitors. Particularly visitors who fit in well here, as I am sure you shall." She paused at the doorway. "He is like my mother, you see: always building up and tearing down. Mostly tearing down." For a moment she looked tired. She removed her apron and placed it and her gardening gloves on the weighty serving table next to the door. "I am not as knowledgeable as my husband about the scenery of the palace, Mr. Vanbrugh, but this is my favorite view."

She pointed into the next room. Directly across from us, on the opposite wall, was another set of open doors. Through the doorway I could see into the next room, where another set of doors also lay open, leading the eye into the next room and to the next open doorway. The pattern was repeated through four sets of doors until at last, at the outer wall of the very last room, a tall window let in comforting white light. I could not see much of the rooms themselves, but the vista, the parade through them, looked inviting—full of possibility and surprise.

"Ah, yes," Barton said softly. "Delightful, just delightful."

"Winston tells me that this is called an 'enfilade,' " she said.

"Enfilade?" Barton asked.

"An enfilade is a progression of rooms, one after the other, with parallel sets of doors," the duchess explained. "If one stands in the right place, one can see clearly to the very end."

"If only life were like that," I said.

The duchess looked at me speculatively. "Do you want to see into the future, Mr. Vanbrugh?" she asked. "Do you want to know what is going to happen?"

"No. But sometimes I do feel the need for a little more perspective."

The duchess laughed. "Then we must see what we can do to assist you."

chapter

2

THE duchess avoided the grand public rooms; instead, she guided us through the hidden back corridors of Blenheim, the grim, gloomy anterooms and lobbies that the servants used to navigate the house. They were narrow, mazelike spaces, the gray paint on the walls peeling through inattention, and were stuffed with the detritus of living: empty wooden barrels, piles of cleaning brushes, discarded boots, a worn fire hose, and a row of battered cupboards. As we progressed, meandering around an inner courtyard, the corridor narrowed and felt damper, as if we were heading into some sort of subterranean chamber.

"This is not the route I normally take visitors," the duchess admitted as she held open a narrow door that opened out into the main corridor. "But I feel, Mr. Vanbrugh, as if we are intimates already." She smiled. "Or soon will be."

I was too startled to say anything, but my father-in-law said, "I beg your pardon, Your Grace?"

But the duchess seemed distracted. She opened a door to her right and we entered a large room with a semicircle of three tall arched windows at the far end that looked out onto a tangle of shrubbery.

"This is the family dining room," the duchess said. "Our rooms are in this part of the house."

It was the furthest thing from a family dining room I had encountered. The room was tall and rather narrow, with a rectangular dining table so highly polished that it reflected the silver centerpiece—a man on horseback. Its walls were painted a yellow that brought to mind daffodils. Hung on three of the walls were large tapestries that depicted events from the battlefield, grisly reminders of the brutal outcomes of war. In one tapestry, a dying soldier lay facedown in the road, ignored by the other soldiers around him, blood seeping into the dirt beneath his head. An unsettling tableau, I would imagine, when one looked up from the soup.

Over the fireplace was a broad chimneypiece of white marble, upon which sat several colorful porcelain figures of farm animals—a horse, a milk cow, a ewe and her lamb, a collie leaping mischievously. Above the menagerie was a large portrait of a confident-looking, self-possessed man who gazed smugly down at us. The chair seats were covered in a green silk the color of cool moss, and into the back of each chair was carved a different musical instrument. Floorboards of light oak peeked around the edges of the elegant carpet and fanned out to the windows, which were draped in yellow damask that matched the walls and were open to catch an afternoon breeze. Though the proportions of the room were severe, this was a graceful, commodious room.

"Cleverly done," I said.

The duchess turned and said, "The duke redecorated it himself, just after we were married." She reached up to the chimneypiece and adjusted the figure of the ewe. "I was younger then, and unsure of my taste, so I was not asked to help."

"Why not?"

"My husband, Mr. Vanbrugh, is a man of very definite opinions—as Mr. Barton knows." The duchess reported this as fact, and Mr. Barton nodded.

"It is true, very definite opinions, indeed," he said.

"But you use this room, as well," I said.

"Yes, we have our meals here," the duchess agreed carefully.

"Were you not consulted at all, about the color or the furniture or the window draperies?" I asked.

The duchess laughed. "This is Blenheim," she said, as if that were explanation enough.

"I do not understand."

"This is my husband's house," the duchess said. "His family home. The rest of us who live here, we are merely tenants."

"That hardly seems fair. Or generous," I said.

"True enough, but generosity is not a particularly English attribute." Her brown eyes rested on me. "Except for Mr. Barton. He is extremely generous."

"Your Grace is too kind," my father-in-law said.

"Come, let me show you my rooms."

She opened a door on the far side of the room and we proceeded into a small, vividly decorated bedroom approximately twenty feet square and at least that tall. A wide canopy bed with a white satin spread was placed against the wall it shared with the dining room. On the wall to the right of the bed was an intricately woven tapestry depicting a Roman charioteer entering a fallen city. The tapestry covered the wall opposite the windows and seemed to absorb what little light the windows allowed in: The room, despite its size, felt cramped, constricted. The ceiling was embellished with an expansive, showy molding across which frolicked gilded cupids. Shield-shaped medallions hung from each corner and were festooned with ornate decorations. Two large overstuffed chairs in the French style were placed about the room, and a Chinese desk stood beneath the tapestry, its top edge just touching it. Faded Oriental carpets were scattered about the floor, and in front of the fireplace lay a large white polar-bear rug, its enormous head still attached to the pelt. Faded green velvet hung on three of the walls, while on the fireplace wall thick paneling was painted a muted green. The velvet, I noticed, was somewhat threadbare in spots, particularly near the bell pull, and the paneling looked loose. In fact, there was a disquieting feel to the room, made more so by an inscription directly across from the bed. Carved into the fireplace marble, in deep, precisely etched letters, was the phrase "Dust Ashes Nothing."

My father-in-law came up next to me as I contemplated the words. "A dreary sentiment," I said quietly.

"The old duke, the father of the present duke, was a man much given to melancholy, I believe," Barton said as the duchess joined us.

"Melancholy is the Churchill curse," the duchess said. "A cousin of my husband's calls it 'Black Dog.'"

"It does seem a particularly inopportune place to remind one of the inevitability of death," my father-in-law said.

The duchess smiled. "It cheers me no end to hear you say that. If a clergyman finds it unsuitable, then my husband can have no objection to its removal."

"Oh, no, Your Grace," Barton said, shocked at such an idea. "I would never dispute His Grace."

"But I will," the duchess said playfully. She shepherded us next door to a small, dark sitting room decorated uncomfortably in blue velvet. Even though it was summer, the odor of burned wood lingered in both rooms like an ill-timed remark, and there was a dankness that clung to the furniture and curtains, which made breathing unpleasant. While this suite may have been suitable for the mistress of Blenheim when the house was built, it was clearly unfit for one today. Margaret Vanbrugh had more comforts in our simple rooms in London than the Duchess of Marlborough had at her disposal at Blenheim.

As if she read my mind, the duchess asked, "How do you find my situation here, Mr. Vanbrugh?" We had settled into chairs near a window she had opened to let in the warm, sweet-smelling air. She seemed eager to speak to us in private.

"Most of the rooms face east, I see," I replied, not really answering her question.

The duchess said shrewdly. "You need not be shy, Mr. Vanbrugh. I am well aware that these are the ugliest rooms in the palace."

"Your Grace, that is an exaggeration," my father-in-law remonstrated.

"Mr. Barton is scandalized," the duchess said, patting his freckled hand. "His delicate English sense of honor has been trampled—by a Yankee, no less. Very well, I withdraw my comment, but not my conviction that Mr. Vanbrugh should make these rooms habitable."

I frowned. "Excuse me, ma'am?"

"I beg your pardon, I have not been clear," the duchess said. "Mr. Vanbrugh, I would very much like you to take on the task of redesigning my apartments here at Blenheim. I would like them to be modernized and made more convenient so that I—and the other women who someday find themselves the Duchess of Marlborough—will live here more comfortably than I so far have."

If the duchess had announced that she was returning to America to join the United States Cavalry, she could not have surprised me more.

"Surely you are joking," I said, shifting in my chair, and looked to my father-in-law for support.

"On the contrary. I am quite certain you are the man for this task. You are clearly . . . sympathetic to my needs."

How she had reached such a conclusion was beyond me.

Barton's cheerful face beamed with pride. "When Her Grace has settled on a plan, it is impossible to dissuade her," he said.

"But I must be the most unqualified man in England for such a job," I said. "I am only a draftsman, with no large commissions to recommend me."

"Nonsense," the duchess said. "I have good reports of your abilities. You understand stone, and piping, and plumbing, and electrification. And you will be engaged by me, a client who understands her requirements. We will realize them together. What could be simpler?"

Barton nodded with vigor. "Her Grace is a very easy benefactress, very easy, indeed," he said.

"And you also have two attributes that appeal to me most particularly," the duchess said.

"What would those be?" I asked.

"Surely you can guess."

"I assure you, I cannot," I insisted.

"Why, where you are from and what you are called, of course."

I recalled a fragment of her note: "Your name and your nationality piqued my interest."

"What about them interest you?" I asked.

"I do not come across many Americans of ability in this country, Mr. Vanbrugh. When I encounter them, I like to promote their talents."

"And I am sure they are grateful," my father-in-law said.

The duchess shrugged. "They are usually quite grateful when I sing their praises to others."

"I have no doubt of that," I said. "But what is intriguing about my name?"

The duchess looked surprised at the question and leaned forward. "Do you mean to say that you are not familiar with the history of Blenheim?"

"Why should I be?" I said a bit harshly. "As my father-in-law may have told you—as he *should* have told you—I am not a trained architect. I have not studied architecture formally or attended college. I am just a man who draws up the plans others design so that builders can use them. I am nothing more."

"You are too modest," the duchess said. "We must change that." She leaned back and stretched luxuriantly, like a cat, arching her back and hips so that every curve of her supple form was obvious, apparent even under the modest restraints of her dress. She held herself in a kind of suspension for a long moment, as if willing me to take stock of her body. I must have looked shocked by such a provocation, for the duchess chuckled and repeated, "Too modest, too modest by half." She relaxed her body and returned to normal, only to surprise me further by pulling her right leg up underneath her left so that her shoe, a delicate satin slipper, peeked pertly out from the folds of her dress.

"In fact, you share much in common with the man who designed this estate more than two hundred years ago. Like you, he was not a trained architect. He was a soldier, in fact, and a playwright, and from all accounts a bit of a rake. But he had influential friends who offered him the opportunity to try his hand at a new profession. And he had the ambition to succeed. His name, Mr. John Vanbrugh, was Sir John Vanbrugh."

I must have looked dumbfounded by this unexpected news, for Barton burst into giggles and clapped his hands in pleasure. "My boy, I have waited for this moment," he said, rising to embrace me. "It is delicious, positively delicious."

"That is impossible," I blurted.

"It is the truth, I promise you," the duchess said.

"I ... I am sure that I am no relation to the man who designed this place," I said. "My family has lived in Boston for years."

The duchess' intelligent eyes narrowed and her jaw took on a firmness, a resolve, it did not have before. "Perhaps you are right. But do you not agree that the combination of your name and your occupation make you the ideal man to refurbish my rooms?"

"Unquestionably," Barton said, wiping his face with his handkerchief. "A delightful combination. Even providential, if I may say so."

I gazed at both of them—one serious, the other gleeful—and wondered at their motives for proposing such a suggestion. Surely the duchess did not come to me because of my expertise, as I had never designed anything more elaborate than a cottage on the dunes of Cape Cod, and I had designed nothing at all since moving to England. I had only completed the drawings of the architects at Burlington and Kent. I was an assistant to their imaginations, nothing more. But as I endeavored to convince myself of the preposterousness of this idea, I began to hear a small voice inside me, which grew in volume and intensity. It was the voice of my ambition, shouting over my judgment, insisting that I pay attention to this opportunity, to take this chance as far as I could.

But what was the chance? To transform even a small part of Blenheim, surely, and to work directly for the duchess, whose good opinion could open doors. And there was something else—something that lurked deep within: a glowing ember of my being which she had begun to fan with her smile, her attentiveness, her charm.

"I must admit, I am a bit taken aback by all of this," I said after a moment.

"Of course you are," the duchess agreed. "All of this must be a great shock. But I hope that does not mean that you will decline my request." She lowered her voice. "I sensed from the first that you and I were sympathetic souls who could work together successfully."

"Did you?" I said. "What drew you to such a conclusion?"

The duchess looked out onto the garden and asked in a different tone, "Are you a superstitious man?"

"Not particularly," I admitted.

"Why not?"

"They seem silly to me."

"My husband is superstitious. He believes in visions, and signs from the other side. He thinks he is cursed, that this place is cursed. I must say, there are times when I believe him."

"And there are times when you do not," I said, completing her thought.

"Yes, but I want to break at least one curse at Blenheim while I am here."

"Oh, it is hardly a curse, Your Grace," Barton protested.

"Then what is it?" she asked.

"It is history." My father-in-law turned to me. "Vanbrugh, you see, was chosen to design Blenheim by the first Duke of Marlborough, the famous General John Churchill who defeated the French at the Battle of Blenheim. His portrait hangs in the Third State Room, I believe."

"And everywhere else in the house," the duchess added.

"Yes, quite," Barton agreed, clearing his throat. "But his wife, Duchess Sarah, never liked Vanbrugh, or this house. She thought him extravagant and wasteful and preferred the quieter work of Christopher Wren."

"The duchess and the architect spent the better part of a decade arguing over every detail of the palace, from the stone for the kitchen courtyard to the cost of the ceremonial bridge," the duchess said. "It must have been extremely wearing for them both."

"Why did the duke not intervene?" I asked.

"He was in Europe, commanding the British army," the duchess said. "While Marlborough was fighting the French, his wife and architect were fighting each other. In fact, Sir John eventually quit as surveyor of Blenheim and was banished from the palace forever by the duchess."

"You are very knowledgeable about the history of this house," I said, a touch of grudging admiration in my voice.

The duchess adjusted her choker. "Living here, it is difficult not to be," she said. "You see, Mr. Vanbrugh, Blenheim has more history than comfort. It is an improbable house, more a stage set than a home, designed by a playwright for a general who never lived to see it completed. The general's wife loved her husband as much as she hated his architect, and she spent most of her married life fighting with one to gratify the other. I sometimes think that this is a house that was designed and built for reasons beyond habitability and comfort. It was born breach and has never been right." With long, delicate fingers, she turned an emerald ring on her right hand. "Perhaps it sounds ridiculous, but I think that having a Duchess of Marlborough hire an architect named John Vanbrugh and working with him congenially at Blenheim Palace might restore a little balance to the place, it might right a wrong." she laughed. "How silly that sounds when I say it—how superstitious. But that is what I believe."

She looked at us as if to challenge us to disagree, her eyes resting first on my father-in-law, then on me, trying to gauge our reactions. Although I knew nothing about the history of the place or the people who built it, my American heart—and, I admit, my ambition—had been roused by her words and by the possibility they held tantalizingly before me.

"I think it is an excellent notion, an excellent notion, indeed," Barton said.

"You have always been my champion," the duchess said, squeezing my father-in-law's hand.

"You have always merited it, Your Grace," he replied gallantly.

"And what do you say, Mr. Vanbrugh?" the duchess inquired. "Am I absurd?"

"No, I don't believe so," I said slowly.

"So it is settled, then," the duchess said.

"I cannot say yes right now. I must ask my employer for permission. Mr. Kent has several projects—"

"Surely Burlington and Kent will have no objection to my engaging the firm to renovate my rooms," the duchess said.

"No," I agreed, as the vision of an openmouthed Mr. Kent receiving a note from the duchess danced through my mind.

"Good," the duchess said. "I will have them engaged on Monday for what I hope will be an acceptable sum." She named a figure that was as large as any two commissions of the firm's best architects.

"They would be pleased to have your patronage," I said.

"As I would to have yours," the duchess replied. "Now, given that all of your objections have been overcome, could you start soon, Mr. Vanbrugh? Even tomorrow?"

My head swam at the swiftness at which this was happening, but I managed to reply, "I am staying with Mr. Barton and my wife at Long Hanborough . . ."

The duchess brightened. "I have a marvelous idea," she said.

"Would you and your wife consent to be our guests for a few days here, at Blenheim? I am sure Mr. Barton could spare you. We are a very dull party here—no one but family and a few friends—and would so enjoy having you both."

I looked at Barton, who nodded. "I know my daughter would be delighted," he said. "She has longed to see the real Blenheim."

"I shall happily give her a tour," the duchess said. "So then we are agreed?"

"There . . . there is one point, Your Grace," I said, feeling suddenly embarrassed. "My wife, Mrs. Vanbrugh . . . that is to say, she is, at the present moment, while quite honored by the invitation, I am sure, but she is . . . not herself at the moment because of the . . ." I rambled, stumbling into awkward silence.

The duchess looked perplexed: two small creases appeared about her nose. She turned to my father-in-law, who explained. "Your Grace, my daughter is to be blessed with a child at the end of year."

"What wonderful news, Mr. Barton," she exclaimed, clapping her hands. "And many congratulations, Mr. Vanbrugh. Is she far along?"

"By no means," Barton said. "Three months."

"Then no one but us need know it, and she can spend several days with us perfectly at ease. So that should be no impediment."

"No, it would seem not," I said after a hesitation.

A satisfied smile played about the pert mouth of our hostess. "Excellent. Then shall we go in and meet the others?"

The room Her Grace guided us to was in the southeast tower of the palace, where the suite of rooms occupied by the duke and the state rooms met. It was a lofty apartment nearly thirty feet square but was an idiosyncratic combination of the formal and the haphazard. Six arched windows, topped with gilt cornices and hung with heavy draperies of scarlet velvet, gave out onto the green flatness of the South Lawn and the uninviting garden to the east. Between the windows pier glasses were hung, their frames gilded and mounted with a large decorative shell; matching console tables stood beneath them. They were piled indiscriminately with London newspapers, books, a pair of bedroom slippers, and a shining sword with a large diamond in its hilt. Arranged around the somber fireplace and its mantel of gray stone were too many pieces of dingy, mismatched chairs, settees, footstools, and library tables, the latter nearly invisible beneath dusty photographs, small bronzes of dogs, ceremonial plates, and two sets of antlers. In one corner of the room a pile of clothes—coats, shirts, and cravats—had been tossed atop a shotgun, its muzzle peeking provocatively out from underneath a pair of ripped riding breeches. Several large, rather dispirited portraits of, I presumed, long-dead Churchill family members decorated the walls but brought little cheer to the room. The place was shabby and felt shapeless, like an old cardigan worn more out of habit than for comfort.

One picture, hung above a lumpy French loveseat, caught my eye. Like the others, it was a portrait, but it was much older than the others in the room, and its odd composition arrested my attention. A woman was sumptuously dressed in crimson silk trimmed with gold ribbing and was seated at her dressing table, gazing at her reflection in the mirror. Her reflection was strangely obscured, as if out of focus.

The duchess came up to me. "Are you familiar with portraits of this kind?" she asked.

"No."

"Walk to the right as you look at the painting."

I moved a few steps and noticed nothing until, without warning, the reflection of the woman in the mirror disappeared and in its place appeared the crisp outline of a skull caught in a hideous, painful agony.

My face may have revealed my surprise, for the duchess smiled. "*Sic transit gloria mundi*," she said.

"I beg your pardon?" I said.

"Never mind. My husband uses this room as his study, but it really is more of a catchall. He prefers to have something served in the morning before luncheon." She looked around. "It is a bit of a shambles, I am sorry to say."

"Not at all," I protested, but I agreed completely with her sentiment.

Three people were already in the room, arrayed around an elaborate silver tea service that had been set up between the fireplace and sofa. A plump, older woman, as ugly and smug as a lapdog, was pouring, and she gazed at us with ill-concealed annoyance through her pince-nez, which clung to her broad nose the way a woodpecker does to a tree.

"Hill has gone for more cups, Consuelo," the woman said, her voice authoritative. "Gladys broke hers, so I had to pour her another cup and I used the one I was saving for you."

The young woman sitting next to her, as beautiful and as languid as a slow-moving river, said, "It was completely Winston's fault. In fact, I am sure that he jostled my elbow on purpose. He will do anything he can to ruin this rug. He as much as told me so."

"It will take more than a cup of tea to compel Sunny to replace this carpet," the man at the windows said without looking around. "The rug was a ruin long before you used me as your scapegoat, Gladys." He pronounced the name "Glay-dus."

"Beast." Miss Deacon leaned against the back of the sofa and looked at me appraisingly, her clear blue eyes moving slowly. She was inordinately handsome, with elegant, almost feline features, a fine complexion, firm mouth, and dark hair that swept up from her neck. She was fashionably dressed in a confection of the lightest peach with a short jacket that exactly matched her dress and accentuated her narrow waist as it highlighted her delicate color.

"Winston jostles people for sport. It is how he passes the time in the country," the duchess said as she rang the bell. "Mother, you remember Mr. Barton, the vicar at Long Hanborough. Mr. Vanbrugh, this is my mother, Mrs. Belmont. And this is a friend of ours, Miss Gladys Deacon. Gladys, this is Mr. Barton and his son-in-law, John Vanbrugh."

At the mention of my name, the young man who had been staring out the window turned. He was pale and freckled, with astute eyes deeply set in his broad, fleshy face, a pronounced brow, and a heavy jaw crowned by a head of thinning auburn hair. He slouched, as if he were about to pick up something he had dropped on the carpet, and his hands looked like a child's, fat and pink. He was by no measure handsome, but there was an intensity to him, a thirst for life, that was immediately apparent.

He came toward me. "What did you say your name was?" he asked, his voice a husky bark.

"Vanbrugh," I said. "John Vanbrugh."

"Extraordinary." He peered at me closely. "Are you American?"

"Yes."

"He is married to my daughter, Mr. Churchill," my father-in-law added.

"Winston, you remember Mr. Barton of Christ Church in Long Hanborough," the duchess said. "This is his son-in-law, John Vanbrugh. He is an architect."

"A draftsman," I corrected.

"Good Lord. You are an architect, too," he said in surprise. He stared at me, his widely spaced eyes unblinking. "There is a bit of a resemblance. Do you see it, Consuelo?" he asked. For a moment I felt like a racehorse being inspected for its potential.

"No, but I have not studied his face as thoroughly as you have," the duchess said. "I am intrigued by other aspects of him."

"Are you, Consuelo? You quite startle me," Miss Deacon said.

"What startles you, Gladys, is of constant astonishment to me." The duchess said this lightly, but there was something dark in her tone.

"*Are* you any relation?" Mr. Churchill asked me. "Of the original John Vanbrugh?"

"Not that I know of," I said.

"Yet there is something about the eyes that is familiar. We will ask Sargent if he sees a likeness. Perhaps he will notice something we do not," Mr. Churchill said firmly.

"Mr. Sargent?" I repeated. "Is he another family member?"

Miss Deacon smiled indulgently.

"He is a painter, a very good one," the duchess said. "My husband has hired him to paint a family portrait for one of the drawing rooms, so Mr. Sargent is here this weekend, as well, to sketch us and to scout out likely backgrounds for it."

"That sounds intriguing," I said.

"It isn't a bit," Miss Deacon said. "It is tedious beyond description. Like listening to one of Sunny's endless political speeches."

"Shut up, Gladys, you silly cow," Mr. Churchill said, "You will give Mr. Vanbrugh the wrong impression entirely. "What brings you to Blenheim?" he asked.

I looked to the duchess for guidance. "Mr. Vanbrugh has been engaged to refurbish my rooms," the duchess said.

"About time," Mrs. Belmont said. "They are a scandal."

"They have been suitable for a dozen duchesses and were redecorated by Sunny to receive his bride," Mr. Churchill said.

"And I am sure a dozen duchesses found them about as comfortable as a cave," Mrs. Belmont said.

"But they are rooms of history," Mr. Churchill said. "Remember that, Mr. Vanbrugh, before you plot grand schemes for them."

"Winston, you would live in the stable Jesus himself was born in if you thought it was historic enough," Mrs. Belmont said.

"Mama," the duchess said reproachfully.

"It would depend entirely on the caliber of the wine cellar he kept," Mr. Churchill said as he sat down on the floor next to Miss Deacon and accepted a cup of tea from Mrs. Belmont.

Miss Deacon laughed—a bubbling giggle—and stroked the top of his head playfully, as one might a puppy. "Winston does enjoy his luxuries," she said.

"And I have no intention of forsaking them in the interests of progress or modernity," Mr. Churchill said. "There is no inconvenience at Blenheim that an ample supply of hot water, well-prepared food, and chilled champagne cannot make agreeable."

"You are impossible," Mrs. Belmont said as she offered him a sandwich.

"There is no use arguing with him, Mama, you will never change his mind," the duchess said.

"I can see that," Mrs. Belmont said. "Winston is obsessed with this house. All the Churchills are."

"It is one of our endearing charms," Mr. Churchill said as he bit into his sandwich.

"Enduring, at least," Mrs. Belmont said.

At that moment the servant named Hill arrived with additional teacups, and my father-in-law and I were served tea. Mrs. Belmont was about to pour mine when she paused and asked, "Would you by any chance prefer coffee, Mr. Vanbrugh?"

"Yes, I would," I admitted.

Mrs. Belmont nodded in satisfaction. "I thought so," she said as she picked up a small ceramic pot near her elbow and poured its contents into my cup. "There," she said as she handed it to me.

"Coffee, I understand, was once considered an aphrodisiac by the

Indians of South America. The Incas, I believe. Or was it the Mayans? I cannot say which," Mr. Barton said.

"Mr. Barton, you are full of useful information. Is what he is saying true, Mr. Vanbrugh?" Miss Deacon asked.

"I do not know," I said.

"Of course you do, you must," she pressed.

"Never mind that, Gladys. What are you planning to do with the rooms?" Mr. Churchill asked.

"I have not had much of a chance to think about it," I said as I held the cup nervously. "Her Grace has several ideas, I understand."

"Indeed I do," the duchess said. "Mr. Vanbrugh and I will pore over all of them tomorrow. Today I would like him to get a sense of the rooms and the house. Mrs. Vanbrugh will join us later today, and they will stay the weekend."

"Are you familiar with the history of Blenheim in any detail?" Mr. Churchill asked.

"Hold your tongue, young man, if you know what is good for you," Mrs. Belmont warned me. "No one is as familiar with the history of this place as Winston Churchill."

"You cannot compete, Mr. Vanbrugh," Miss Deacon said. "No one can. Not even the duke."

Mr. Churchill took no notice of these jibes. "The hopes of the future are built upon a solid knowledge of the past," he said placidly. "The more we understand, the stronger the foundation."

"Oh, for heaven's sake, Winston, have a cake and be still," Mrs. Belmont said impatiently. "No one wants to hear your pontificating."

"On the contrary, Mrs. Belmont, I find Mr. Churchill's comments about Blenheim most illuminating," my father-in-law said.

"They are—the first time you hear them," Mrs. Belmont said.

Mr. Churchill replied loudly, "Thank you, Mr. Barton. It is a relief to know that there is at least one civilized person in this room who understands the importance of history, family, and the legacy of tradition."

The duchess put down her teacup. "We all understand the importance of Blenheim, Winston. But the question remains: How do we mere mortals live in a temple fit for gods? The answer is, not very well."

"Exactly," Mrs. Belmont agreed, as she bit into a French éclair with relish.

"That is why Mr. Vanbrugh is here. To help us—*me*—to live more comfortably," the duchess said. Turning to me with an expression I could not read, she asked, "Do you think you can assist me to be more comfortable in my rooms?"

I swallowed a sip of my coffee. "I will do my best," I said.

The duchess looked pleased. "I have no doubt that will be more than satisfactory," she said.

chapter
3

WE left Blenheim shortly thereafter, amid much amity and good-
will, and returned to Long Hanborough. I was concerned about
what reaction Margaret would have to the news of our invitation—
she had been skittish of strangers since her pregnancy was known—
but my father-in-law assured me that all would be well. He was right:
Margaret was by turns delighted and calculating at the prospect of
spending the weekend at the greatest house in the kingdom. Plans and
schemes for what we were to wear at every meal poured from her, and
she blessed Providence that the garnet necklace and ear bobs that she
had inherited from her mother were still at the vicarage and not in
London.

When we returned to Blenheim, I read carefully the inscription
engraved above the arch:

———◄◇►———

UNDER THE AUSPICES OF A MUNIFICENT SOVEREIGN THIS HOUSE
WAS BUILT FOR JOHN DUKE OF MARLBOROUGH, AND HIS DUCHESS
SARAH; BY SIR J. VANBRUGH BETWEEN THE YEARS 1705 AND 1722.
AND THIS ROYAL MANOR OF WOODSTOCK, TOGETHER WITH A
GRANT OF £240,000, TOWARDS THE BUILDING OF BLENHEIM
WAS GIVEN BY HER MAJESTY QUEEN ANNE AND CONFIRMED
BY ACT OF PARLIAMENT [3. & 4. ANNEC. 4.] TO THE SAID JOHN

DUKE OF MARLBOROUGH AND TO ALL HIS ISSUE MALE AND
FEMALE LINEALLY DESCENDING.

———◁◦▷———

"Rather long-winded, the duke," I said.

"It is not every husband, my dear Margaret, whose name is carved above the entrance to a great estate," Barton observed.

"And it is not every husband who is engaged by the Duchess of Marlborough to renovate her rooms," she said, her voice jubilant. "This commission will do a great deal to enhance your career, Van. I know it."

"If it's done properly," I said. "Right now it feels as if I'm swimming in deep water and my foot cannot touch the bottom. I am out of my depth."

"Nonsense," Barton said. "The duchess could not have been kinder to you."

"Or more vague about her plans."

"She will speak to you soon," Margaret said with confidence. "Everything will become clear when you see her again."

"Of course it will," Barton agreed as the carriage pulled up to the steps and stopped. He jumped nimbly from the carriage and assisted Margaret out of it as several servants came forward to fetch our luggage. Turning to us and kissing his daughter good-bye, Barton whispered, "Enjoy yourselves, my dears. And do yourself proud, Van, my boy." With a cheerful wave, he climbed back into the carriage and was off.

I ascended the shallow stone steps, slightly behind Margaret, feeling a bit like another Jack, the one from the tale of the beanstalk as he neared the giant's castle: Blenheim seemed to have grown. But there were no ogres behind these doors. Instead, we were greeted by the butler and were shown upstairs by a discreetly dressed footman. Our rooms were furnished more simply than those downstairs but were comfortable enough and had a marvelous view onto the broad, green lawn and the dramatic lake that curved away from the house.

"If you please, sir, Her Grace asks that I take you to her as soon as your valet unpacks you," the footman, a tall, sturdy young man with an open face and dark curly hair, said.

"I do not have a valet, but if the duchess would give me a few moments, I will be happy to join her," I said.

The footman did not change his expression, but continued, with a careful correctness, "If that is the situation, sir, then Her Grace has asked me to serve you in that capacity. I am Jamison, sir."

"That is thoughtful of Her Grace," I said.

"Yes, sir," the young man said—his expression leaving no doubt that I was to be pitied for not keeping a manservant. He took over my unpacking immediately and made short work of the task, deftly organizing my clothes and toilet while I stood by uneasily, straightening the blotting paper on the writing table that stood between the windows. A small pile of notepaper peeked out from one of the cubbyholes in the desk; I noticed that they had the same heading as the letter I received: "Blenheim Palace."

"Sir, where is your white tie?" Jamison asked.

"I beg your pardon?"

"Your white tie. His Grace insists all of his gentlemen guests wear white tie at table."

"But I do not have a white tie," I said, dismayed.

"Yes, sir," Jamison said, eyeing me with a glance that was equal parts pity and derision. "I will inquire if any can be secured from one of the staff."

From the passage came a voice: "So we are to be neighbors."

I turned and saw Miss Deacon standing in the doorway, dressed for walking in a short, roomy blouse of white linen and a gray skirt of flowing pleats. Upon her head she wore a becoming straw hat with a single white rose pinned to its side and she carried soft white gloves and parasol.

"I will wait outside, if that is convenient, sir," Jamison said.

"Of course, Jamison," I agreed. "Thank you. I will be ready in a moment."

Jamison bowed slightly as Miss Deacon lingered in the doorway, leaning against the door frame.

"Is your room nearby?" I asked.

"Next door," she said, entering my room as the footman passed her. "I am above the room we had tea in." Like the duchess, Miss Deacon had a pleasant voice: distinctly American, but without the brassy twang that characterized the speech of many of my compatriots.

"It must have an excellent view," I said.

"I suppose. But it is a horror," she said, shivering. "Everyone says so. No one understands why Consuelo has not redecorated these guest rooms. They are in a simply shocking state."

"Perhaps she has more pressing concerns," I suggested.

"What could be more important than the comfort of your guests?"

"Your own comfort," I said.

Miss Deacon raised a smooth, well-formed eyebrow. "Perhaps so. But I would never admit that to anyone. It would be vulgar."

Once again, I felt that lady's sting. "I understood that the duke has very particular views about Blenheim," I said carefully.

She suppressed a smile. "Mr. Vanbrugh, you are delicious." She came farther into the room conspiratorially, as if there might be a spy hiding behind the screen in the corner. "This place is still standing because of Consuelo Vanderbilt and her millions. Her millions and *millions*. When the Bad Duke died—"

"The Bad Duke?"

"The father of the current duke. When the present duke inherited the title, Blenheim and a mountain of debt came with it. The future of the Marlboroughs, and of Blenheim itself, had fallen onto the narrow, unpromising shoulders of Sunny Churchill, the Ninth Duke. A *most* disadvantageous place to land."

I felt rather than saw the shadow of the footman just outside the door and lowered my voice. "Surely it is not as bad as all that."

Miss Deacon glanced at the open door and moved to close it. "Oh, it was worse," she said, her voice a whisper. "The duke suffers from the double calamities of being both arrogant and stupid. He cannot help it, I suppose; it is the Churchill way. But he does understand the importance of his family and his title: They must be preserved. When the Bad Duke died, Sunny determined to find a solution to his chronic lack of money. He went searching for a willing girl of marriageable age in robust financial health. And he found one."

"The duchess," I said.

Miss Deacon nodded as if I were a dull-witted schoolboy who had finally mastered his lesson. "Well, not exactly willing. Compliant, perhaps. Mrs. Belmont, back when she was Mrs. William K. Vanderbilt, the richest, most calculating creature of my wide acquaintance, arranged it all."

"So it was not a love match?" I said.

Miss Deacon put on her gloves. "We are talking about something more important than love, Mr. Vanbrugh, The future of Blenheim. Alva Belmont was a mother of surpassing ambition, and Sunny Churchill was a man of desperate need. Her greatest triumph is that she married off her only daughter to the dimmest man in England—a race not known for its intelligence. She has succeeded beyond her wildest dreams. And so, in his way, has he."

Her bluntness took me off guard. I cleared my throat. "You do not seem to be an admirer of the family, Miss Deacon. I wonder you are here at all."

Miss Deacon noticed her reflection in the dressing-table mirror. She adjusted her hat slightly and said, "Do you? Mr. Vanbrugh, you surprise me. I thought it was perfectly clear why."

"Why are you telling me all this?" I asked in exasperation.

The lady looked down at her gloved hands. "I want you to be prepared."

"Prepared for what?"

"For whatever Providence has in store for you. For all of us."

"I pray to Providence I need no such help."

"Oh, you will at Blenheim," she said with certainty. "Providence does not answer prayers from here. If He did, so much would be different. The duke would be rich in his own right, Consuelo would be in America married to that Rutherford fellow, and I—" She stopped abruptly.

"Yes, Miss Deacon? What would be different for you?" My voice was sharp, as my patience for this young, beautiful minx had worn as thin as the rug we stood on.

The lady offered an apologetic smile. "I would learn to hold my tongue," she said. "Perhaps I will by Monday."

"What is to happen on Monday?"

"Nothing. But I have very good reason to hope for pleasant tidings this weekend."

"In that case, I wish you every good luck."

"Oh, luck has nothing to do with it, Mr. Vanbrugh. It is all pre-meditation."

There was a knock at the door that connected my room with the room beyond. Margaret peeked from behind it. "There you are," she said, sounding relieved. "I was beginning to think I had lost you."

"Not yet, but I have every hope," Miss Deacon said brightly. "You must be Mrs. Vanbrugh. How delightful. I am Gladys Deacon, a friend of Their Graces, and I hope, of the Vanbrughs very soon."

"Are you also American?" Margaret asked, taking her hand.

"Alas yes, but I live in Paris in spinster's disgrace with my mother and sisters."

"Surely it is no disgrace to be unmarried," Margaret said, "even in Paris."

Miss Deacon laughed. "The only disgrace worse than not marrying, Mrs. Vanbrugh, is not marrying well. Tell me, how do you find the duchess?"

"I have not yet made her acquaintance, but my husband tells me she is very handsome."

"Oh, yes, she is, very. She is quite the most beautiful duchess in the land—a delicate flower of American womanhood. Of course, most of the other duchesses are forty years older, stone-deaf, and have teeth the color of rotting leaves. Consuelo may have her faults, heaven knows, but she has a superb set of teeth."

Margaret and I looked at each other, surprised and confused. What were we to make of this cultivated woman who spat venom as she chattered so beguilingly?

Miss Deacon turned to face me. "And what do you think of the duke?"

"I have not yet met him, either," I said.

"Goodness, the manners of the Marlboroughs," Miss Deacon said, shaking her head in mock dismay. "It is a wonder that you poor mice found your rooms at all."

"But we did," I said—and felt as if I had just admitted something I should not.

Miss Deacon looked at me inquiringly, her head tilted to one side.

"Well, enough of this tittle," she said after a moment. "I shall see you both soon, I am sure. Good-bye." Smiling, she walked from the room.

"My goodness," Margaret said after I closed the door to the hallway and indicated to Jamison that I would not be long. "What an extraordinary woman."

"Why did I think she was laughing at us?"

"Because she was," Margaret said. "The nerve. And I did not appreciate her remark about you—not at all. That she was trying to steal you away."

"There is no danger of that," I said.

"Oh, I *know*," Margaret said, dismissing such a notion. "It is that she is so composed about it. As if it were expected."

"I must go," I said.

"What for?"

"There is a footman waiting outside to take me to the duchess."

Margaret smiled, her face shimmering with excitement. "You must not keep the duchess waiting."

"I will not," I said, putting on my coat. "How is your room?"

"I came in to tell you. I have been given a housemaid to wait upon me."

"A fine lady, you," I said, grinning at her evident satisfaction.

"Her name is Emily, and she is quite..." She paused.

"Yes?"

Margaret lowered her voice. "She hinted that she is sweet on one of the footmen. I think it might be yours, Van."

"Jamison? What of it?"

Margaret flushed. "I know, it is only that, you see..." She sighed. "Oh, never mind," she said, suddenly angry.

"What is wrong *now*?"

"Nothing. Go to the duchess. I am sure it will go *splendidly*." She ran to her room and slammed the door.

In silence, Jamison led me downstairs to the family quarters and directed me not to the sitting room but to the bedroom.

"Mr. Vanbrugh, hello," the duchess said as I entered. "Please join us." A settee and two chairs had been arranged around a delicate-looking mahogany table in front of one of the open windows. The duchess occupied one, and in another sat a man I assumed was the Duke. He appeared to be in his middle years, prosperous and self-possessed, and was dressed for the morning in a well-made suit of charcoal wool; a sleek silver cravat, a discreet diamond pin holding its elegant folds in place, peeked out from underneath his vest. His well-shaped face was mature, but there was a vigor to its aspect, even though it was partially concealed by a full, well-trimmed beard and moustache that had no trace of gray. His dark green eyes, appraising and expressive at the same time, were discerning, and when I arrived they turned to me with interest, even affability. In his right hand a pencil was poised above a blank folio in a large, thick sketchbook, which sat comfortably upon his lap like a well-loved child used to such privilege.

"Do you know Mr. Sargent? John, this is Mr. Vanbrugh, whom I was telling you about. Mr. Vanbrugh, this is John Singer Sargent, the painter."

Mr. Sargent stood up stiffly and took my hand. "How do you do," he said, his voice quiet but amiable.

"A pleasure, sir," I said.

"Mr. Sargent is to paint us, as I told you," the duchess said.

"That will be a great honor for you both," I said, as I sat down in the empty chair.

"Ah, a diplomat," Mr. Sargent said, as he opened his cigarette case and extracted a small brown cigarette of the Turkish variety. "This will be droll."

"Mr. Sargent has determined to paint us in the Great Hall between two columns," the duchess said.

"Between two pillars of wisdom," he said, his lips pursed in a wry grin.

"I am to stand on a step, and the duke will be to my right," the duchess said. "It is the most advantageous positioning."

"Advantageous?"

"My husband is shorter than I, Mr. Vanbrugh," the duchess explained. "This arrangement sidesteps the . . . asymmetry, wouldn't you agree?"

"It sounds suitable enough," I said.

"It must be a great deal more than that," Mr. Sargent said. "The painting is to be a complement to the portrait of the fourth duke and his family that hangs in the Red Drawing Room. Can you imagine? That Reynolds portrait has eight people and three dogs in it. How I am to fill a canvas of that size with only you, the duke, and your two sons is a quandary His Grace has not chosen to address," Sargent said, smiling at the Duchess.

"It has been my experience that the artist is the best judge of his own medium," I said.

Sargent looked me in the eye. "You obviously are of an artistic temperament yourself," he said.

"Hardly," I admitted.

"There is art in architecture," he pressed.

"But in very little of what I have done."

Sargent began to sketch. "Sometimes the artist is not the best judge of his own work," he said as his hand skittered across the page.

We sat quietly for some moments, the attention of all three of us on the pencil Mr. Sargent held in his hand, which was skimming the paper like a dragonfly over a pool. From his short, jerky strokes a study began to emerge. It was rough, and some of the details were unformed, but it became clear that Sargent was drawing my face, an expression of puzzled discomfort on it.

My cheeks felt hot suddenly as the duchess said, "You have been immortalized, Mr. Vanbrugh."

"Surely Mr. Sargent can find a worthier subject," I said.

Sargent looked startled and abruptly closed his sketchbook. He stood up and gazed the window. "You have work to do here," he said awkwardly. "I am in the way. Mr. Vanbrugh, I hope we have an opportunity to become better acquainted this weekend." He nodded to the duchess and left the room.

"I am sorry, I had no intention to offend," I said.

The duchess shook her head. "Mr. Sargent has not taken offense, I assure you. He is a very private man. He means no umbrage."

"None was taken," I replied.

"Thank you. Now shall we begin?" She walked over to her desk and returned with two sheets of paper and several pieces of fabric. She arranged them in a semicircle around the perimeter of the table. "I have sketched some ideas for rearranging the rooms, and I have some thoughts about colors and design." She handed several sketches to me, and as I glanced through them, I grasped that her ideas were modern but cultivated, elegant but practical—full of strong lines, bright colors, and comfortable fabrics.

"I want these rooms to be private but to feel welcoming," the duchess said. "I want the people who are invited here to feel at ease, that they can be natural. I have spent my life in rooms that others believe to be beautiful or commodious. It is time for me to exercise my own preferences." She looked over at the fireplace, which reminded her of another objection. "And I will not be preached to. I suffer that indignity enough in the rest of the house." She shook her head and leaned over the table, fingering a piece of fabric. "I want no gaudy wall coverings or showy boiserie. They are for Blenheim's public rooms. Here, I want quiet, beauty, repose."

"Rather a tall order," I said as I stood to hand the sketches back.

The duchess made no attempt to take the sketches. Instead, she looked at me for a long moment, her eyes reaching down into my soul, and rose from her chair. She came around the table and pulled me out of my chair, standing directly in front of me. She was so close I could smell her eau de cologne: The scent of gardenia was intoxicating, rousing.

"But not impossible to a man of your attributes. I would say that nothing can be denied a man who knows what he wants."

I scarcely breathed, and I felt my body tense. "You cannot be serious," I said nervously.

"I am."

It was as if there were nothing else in Blenheim but the two of us. The duchess stood before me frankly and demanded that I drink her in: her soft skin, her delicate neck, her upturned nose. Slowly, almost imperceptibly, I leaned toward her full lips just as she asked, "What color would you say this is?"

I sprang back, startled, and struggled to regain my composure. I looked down at the fabric she was holding. It was a soft, muted hue, at once pink and peach, and reminded me of the warm days I spent as a child at the seaside.

"What color?" the duchess repeated, an edge to her voice.

"I would call it 'seashell,' Your Grace. It reminds me of the inside of the shells that my uncle and I used to collect. He was a fisherman who lived out on Cape Cod."

She relaxed. "How clever you are. That is it," she said.

"It is not cleverness, just a memory for color," I said.

"An excellent attribute for an architect," she said. She returned the fabric to the table. "Now that you have heard my ideas, I am eager to hear yours."

"I have several," I said. "I suggest investigating to see if the fireplace wall could be pushed several feet into the next room, or better yet removed altogether, to widen the room. I recommend that the wall facing the windows be brought forward a dozen feet closer to the windows. That will allow a series of wardrobes or a even small dressing room to be fitted out between the new wall and the corridor to gain you more storage, since two of the smaller wardrobes in the next room can be fitted up as a bathroom. But above all, I wonder if you know what condition the walls are in, underneath the paneling and wall covering? I should like to see what sort of trouble we will encounter with them."

As I spoke, I was surprised at the confidence of my words, as if the duchess hadn't disconcerted me by her strange behavior. But she gave no indication that anything was amiss.

"I am sorry to say that I do not, but I have no objection to your attempting some exploratory surgery on the patient," she said. She consulted her watch which today was pinned to the lapel of her dress. "I must meet my husband and his steward in a few minutes, so if you would like to remove some of the paneling or wall covering now, you have my permission." She went to a delicate-looking cabinet to the right of the fireplace and opened one of its doors, removing a short wedge and small hammer. "In fact, I was going to attempt the very thing myself, but I was certain that I would break my thumb or something equally ridiculous."

I took the tools. "I will be very careful," I promised.

"Thank you. Of course you will. I shall return as soon as I can, for I am quite curious to see what you discover." With that, the duchess departed, leaving behind only the lingering scent of gardenias.

I surveyed the room for the most likely place to begin my exploration and settled on the paneling above the chimneypiece. Reaching up to its right side, I inched my index finger between it and the wall and shook it slightly. It moved quite easily—so effortlessly, in fact, that the painting hanging on it—a portrait of a young woman holding a laughing child—was in danger of pulling the paneling off the wall of its own accord.

I moved a low footstool to the fireplace and stood up on it. It was just high enough for me to reach up to remove the painting and several small decorative items from the chimneypiece. I placed the wedge into the space between the paneling and the plaster and tapped it gingerly with the hammer. I worked my way quickly around the bottom half of the panel—which was roughly six feet wide—and discovered that, with just a little effort, I could pry the entire piece off the wall.

But I had misjudged the weight of the paneling: It was unexpectedly heavy. As the last nail at the top gave way, the panel fell on top of me and struck me square in the face, throwing me back against the end of the duchess's bed.

For a moment I lay there, pinned beneath the panel, the wind knocked out of me, certain that I had broken my back. But panic can be a useful emotion, and even before my breathing returned to normal I struggled out from underneath the large piece of wood.

As I steadied myself, shaken and embarrassed at the impropriety of my unintended forwardness, something on the back of the panel caught my attention. It was a series of scrawls. At first I thought they were nothing more than scratchings—the instructions from laborers. But when I paid closer attention, I noticed that it was, in fact, a message, written upside down. I righted the panel and leaned it against the fireplace so that its upper extremity covered the marble lament the duchess found objectionable. Written in black, in a huge, erratic hand, were the words: *"All is lost—the world will know—we are undone. Silence is the only hope."*

I wiped my eyes with my sleeve, sure I was seeing things. I turned the panel to the windows and held the message toward the light, peering at the words closely, then at each letter in turn. This forced me to conclude that I had read the message correctly. Though one or two of the letters had been smudged, there was no mistaking the meaning.

I stood there, bewildered. The words made me feel as if the writer had opened his soul and given vent to an unspeakable despair. But who had written them? And what was the cause of such dismay? And why commit this sentiment to a tablet that would never be read.

Gooseflesh prickled up my spine. I could have sworn that someone whispered in my ear, but the voice was so low I could not hear clearly.

From behind me a harsh voice demanded: "Who the devil are you?"

I looked back and said, "I am so sorry."

"Sorry about what?" the man demanded. "What is going on in here? Where is my wife?"

Standing in the doorway was a man who could only be the Duke of Marlborough. He was short and slightly built, and his face was thin and tense, with a provocative jaw, a long nose, small bulging blue eyes set too close together, and lips that were full but chapped and cracked. But there was an air of elegance about him, thanks to the excellent ministrations of a skillful tailor, barber, and valet. His sand-colored hair and moustache were neatly trimmed, his doe-colored summer suit crisp and well fitted, and his leather shoes the color of caramel. He had the cocksure air of the men I used to see parading along Beacon Hill, whose whims are always acceded to because that was the way of their well-ordered world. He put me in mind of a sleek, well-tended ferret, more rodent than human, and he was obviously displeased at the sight of an unknown man standing in his wife's bedroom.

"I believe she is looking for you, Your Grace," I said. "She indicated that she had an appointment with you and your steward."

"Oh, she did, did she?" He sounded irritated. He turned to leave but stopped and looked at me again. "What *is* going on in here?"

"I was examining the wall . . . for the duchess," I said uncertainly. "That is, she asked me to."

"What on earth is Consuelo doing that for?" he demanded.

"I believe she is—" I stopped, wondering if the duchess had alerted the duke to her plans for these rooms.

"Out with it, man, I do not have all day," the duke snapped.

"My name is John Vanbrugh," I blurted. "I am an architect."

The duke's jaw went slack in surprise. "The devil you say," he said. Then more loudly, he continued: "Did Winston put you up to this? Or is this one of the practical jokes Alva is so fond of?"

"No, Your Grace. My given name is John Vanbrugh, and I am an architect," I repeated, feeling foolish. "I understand that is a name that is familiar here."

The duke laughed. "It is much more than that. Are you a descendant of our John Vanbrugh?" he asked.

"Not as far as I know, Your Grace. I am an American," I added irrelevantly.

"And your name really is Vanbrugh? And you are an architect? Are you sure?"

"Yes, sir," I said. I recalled the views of Miss Deacon on the intellectual prowess of my host.

The duke frowned. "I'll be damned," he said.

The duchess appeared behind him. "There you are. Stevens and I have been looking for you."

"Consuelo, this man says his name is Vanbrugh," the duke said, pointing to me as if I were a curiosity he had encountered in Hyde Park on a Sunday morning.

"It is Vanbrugh," the duchess said. "Mr. Vanbrugh, this is my husband, the duke. My dear, this is Mr. Vanbrugh, an architect from America. I have engaged him to refurbish my rooms."

"Have you? Did you know his name before you hired him?"

"Of course," the duchess said.

The duke shook his head in wonder. "Extraordinary." His expression darkened suddenly. "And what is wrong with these rooms?"

"I am having them modernized," the duchess said. "To suit my taste."

"On whose authority?" the duke demanded.

The duchess looked at me, then at her husband. She took his elbow. "Perhaps we could discuss this on the way to Stevens's office," she said.

"I want to discuss this here," the duke said, scowling at me.

"I thought you told Stevens that you wanted to see him before you met with the mayor," the duchess said.

The duke did not reply, but he threw one more sullen glare at me before he and the duchess departed. As he turned to follow his wife, the duke said in a petulant, disagreeable tone, "And just *how* were you planning to keep this project from me?"

Relieved I had not been asked about the paneling that leaned against the wall, I replaced it over the fireplace, taking pains not to smudge the words, and pondered what I should do with this intelligence. I winced at the prospect of bringing it to the attention of the duke, although by rights I should have: He was the master of Blenheim. On the other hand, the duchess employed me, and since the message had been found in her room, I determined that the best course of action would be to inform her immediately. I dashed off a short note to her, apologizing for leaving her room in such disarray but requesting an interview at her earliest convenience, and left it on her desk. With that, I headed for my room.

As I departed, I looked about and for the second time I had the distinct sense that someone—something—was whispering to me.

"What is it you want?" I demanded. "Tell me."

But I heard nothing.

chapter

4

THE route from the family suite to the stairway up to my room was a circuitous one, full of echoing corridors, unexpected shadows, and silences heavy enough to crush all sound. I had much on my mind, and soon lost my way. So it was with considerable relief that, upon opening a door I hoped led to a back hallway, I encountered Mr. Churchill. He was alone and was slouched deep in a dark leather chair in the middle of a cluttered room that was shaped like a slice of pie. It was clear he had been here for some time. He was frowning deeply, his lips pursed in thought. The lapels of his charcoal-gray suit were sprinkled liberally with ash that had fallen from the preposterously large cigar he held between two of his plump fingers. The smoke lingered balefully above him. Papers were strewn about the floor amid piles of thick books, open boxes of old letters, and briefcases brimming with other documents and portfolios. His red hair was askew and he looked weary, even defeated, and barely noticed my interruption.

"I beg your pardon," I said, retreating.

"On the contrary, Mr. Vanbrugh," he said, rousing himself slowly, his voice a bluff combination of a growl and a whine. "You are a welcome distraction." He rose and came toward me, walking across his papers without concern. "The past is too much with me. I am eager to renew my acquaintance with the present. I believe it can be a most congenial companion." He smiled, and it lightened his appearance. For although Mr. Churchill was a young man—he could not have been more than thirty years of age—his wide forehead, pallid complexion, and lowering brow gave him the appearance of an older man, one used to the weight of responsibility and duty.

"Are you a historian?" I asked as he threw books off the only other seat in the room, a small oak chair with a rounded back and a faded embroidered decoration of flowers on the seat, and gestured for me to sit.

"A historian? No such luck."

"Then what do you do?"

He frowned, looking displeased. "I am in Parliament. And I write for the newspapers."

"I do not follow politics, or read those rags," I said.

Mr. Churchill looked amazed. "You should. These are great times. Great ideas are about."

"Perhaps, but they are never *about* anything," I said.

"They are about the future of the Empire," he said. "India, Australia, the Colonies."

"So you find public life stimulating."

"I am stimulated by the possibilities." He grinned, and his face became boyish.

I remembered something about Mr. Churchill I had heard a while back. "Politics always seem to be more about ambition than about the future," I said. "Did you not used to be a member of the Conservative party, and then you became a Liberal? You crossed the aisle, I think the term was."

His heavy cheeks colored and for a few moments I thought I had angered him. But he shook his head. "You Americans. My mother says things like that. But she is much prettier than you, so she can get away with it. Champagne?" He reached for a bottle that stood on the floor next to him. He did not wait for my answer, having secured an empty glass of questionable cleanliness from a portable lap desk next to him. He poured the liquid into it and handed the glass to me.

"So tell me, Mr. Vanbrugh," he said, drawing out my name speculatively, tasting it on his tongue as he might a particular vintage. "You clearly know nothing of British politics. What do you know of your distinguished namesake?"

"Not much," I admitted, taking a sip. "So little, in fact, that I do not even know if he and I are related."

"Nonsense." Churchill waved his glass dismissively. "Of course you are. You must be. I will not have it otherwise. It is ridiculous to allow that a coincidence this extraordinary is not in some sense providential. You must be his descendant; it is simply too astonishing for you *not* to be." He puffed on his cigar combatively. "In fact, at times I have wondered just how chaotic chaos really *is*. There seems to be an unbending logic to it, even at its most uncontrollable." He shifted his weight, leaning toward me as he warmed to his point. "Take a waterfall—your Niagara Falls, say. Millions—billions of drops of water tumble into its pools each second, roiling about in whirlpools and eddies. It is nature at its most wild, we might say, its most tempestuous. But why do the drops always fall into the same pools?"

I shrugged. "Gravity, I suppose."

"Yes, but *why* is gravity so unyielding? Why does the water insist on dropping in the same place time after time after time? Nothing else in the universe seems to be so absolute. Not even God." He smiled, and for a moment I wondered if he expected me to reply. "The truth of the matter is, no one really knows for certain. But this order in the chaos of cataclysm, it fascinates me."

Mystified, all I could utter was, "It is puzzling."

Churchill chuckled. "I am completely off the point, of course, and you are too polite to reprove me. Damn polite race, you Americans. Except my mother, of course. She can be a brute. Lovely, but a brute nonetheless. I doubt your ancestor was ever as polite to John Duke. Certainly not to Duchess Sarah."

I was relieved to return to a subject I had a chance of understanding. I asked, "Do you know much about Sir John Vanbrugh, Mr. Churchill?"

He shrugged his sloping shoulders indifferently, the way a dog might shake off a leaf. "As much as anyone, I suppose," he said without bravado. "From all accounts Sir John was an exceptional man in an exceptional age. He was born in London of Dutch parents in the late seventeenth century, and entered the army. He was captured by the French and was thrown into prison—Vincennes, I believe—on charges that he was a spy."

"Was he?"

"That is hard to say," Mr. Churchill said. "But I would say that it was possible. He was released eventually and made his way back to England."

"Was he an architect while in the army?"

"Good Lord, no," Churchill said, as if such a suggestion were ridiculous. "When he returned to this country, he took to playwrighting." Churchill took a healthy sip of his champagne. "He was quite good at it, too. Ever heard of *The Provok'd Wife*? A delightful bit of fluff; I saw it last year with Consuelo." He burped appreciatively and indicated the room with a theatrical flourish. "Only a playwright could concoct this preposterous stage set of a house and call it a place fit for human habitation."

"So you are not an admirer of Blenheim."

He looked astonished at such a suggestion. "On the contrary," he said. "I believe it to be the most remarkable house in Europe." He removed the cigar from his mouth. "My mother tells of the day that my father brought her here and she caught sight of this house for the very first time. It was summer, with the trees in full leaf and the lake shimmering under the cerulean sky. She felt, she said, as if she were driving into a Turner landscape. My father said to her, 'There, my girl, is the finest view in England.' She did not say anything then, but she told me that she felt as if she had just received the finest gift a husband could bestow."

"But surely it was a stretch for Vanbrugh to become a playwright and then an architect," I said.

"The eighteenth century was a time of dilettantes, Mr. Vanbrugh. Sir John was a successful playwright and a member of the Kit-Kat Club, a society of the ablest Whigs in England. They would meet in London to gossip and plot their way to power. John Duke was a Kit-Kat, as well as being the queen's commander in chief and the finest general since Alexander. It was inevitable that the two should meet. So when John Duke crushed Marshal Tallard and his French troops at Blenheim and Queen Anne presented this land and palace to him as a gift from a grateful nation, whom should he turn to for his architect but a fellow Kit-Kat?"

" 'Under the auspices of a munificent sovereign,' " I mumbled.

"What? Oh, you read the new inscription over the gate. Sunny will be pleased. Terribly proud of this place, of course."

"The duke has much to be proud of," I said.

Churchill looked around the small, oddly shaped room, as if my comment had never occurred to him. "I suppose you are right. He is the head of this family and well deserves the respect due him," he said gravely.

"Of course," I said.

Churchill finished the remainder of his champagne in one gulp and stood up suddenly. "Shall we go in?"

"In?" I asked.

"To luncheon," Churchill said.

I followed him out the door and expected that we would return to the dining room. Instead, Churchill headed toward a wing of the house I had not yet visited. "We collect before luncheon and dinner in the Long Library," Churchill explained as we walked along the vaulted passage. "It has been a tradition ever since my grandfather was duke."

We walked in silence along a fraying, plum-colored carpet. After a time I prompted, "You were telling me, Mr. Churchill, about how Sir John came to design this house."

"Ah, yes. No doubt you have observed that when two men of talent become acquainted amid sympathetic circumstances, a casual comment leads to a question, an answer leads to a confidence, and a bond is formed. That is what occurred between the duke and Sir John. They became friends, and the result is that the duke asked Sir John to design him a house."

"It sounds quite simple when you say it," I remarked.

Churchill, his hands clasped behind him, his head bowed, thought for a moment. "It has been my experience that a simple thing and a complex thing begin exactly the same way. It is only when the simple thing feels unfinished that it becomes a complex thing. This house, this entire estate, began as a simple gift from a queen to her victorious general and dear friend. It ended, nearly a decade later, in disappointment for three people. John Duke wanted a finished house. Sir John wanted an impressive house. Duchess Sarah wanted an economical house. None of them got what they most desired."

Churchill stopped at a small passage just off the Great Hall, where a large painting hung along an otherwise empty wall. It was a formal portrait of the first duke and duchess surrounded by their children. The duke was on the left, proud and haughty in expensive-looking clothes and a luxuriant wig, while the duchess, attired in a gown of blue satin, sat erect and confident on a carved chair in the middle of the canvas. Her left hand fondled a piece of fruit from a basket held by one of her daughters.

"I am surprised to hear that, Mr. Churchill," I said. "This strikes me as a most impressive house."

Churchill said, "Follow me."

I accompanied him down a passage, past an oval basin of white marble full of freshly cut flowers to a set of doors made of excellent mahogany. Churchill opened them and we stepped into the library, an exaggeratedly long room painted a soothing shade of the lightest yellow. Two tiers of tall windows faced us, and they looked out onto a tangle of shrubbery and old-fashioned garden that once had been well maintained but had been let go. At either end of the room were two broad arches, supported by square white pillars. Low domes and emblems, painted white and outlined in beautiful stucco florets and leaves, decorated the ceiling. The floor was of a light oak, with large rugs placed in front of the two imposing marble fireplaces; around them were arranged a collection of lumpy looking sofas and chairs. Next to the fireplaces, and across the room from the windows, were a series of impressive wooden bookcases painted the same yellow and white as the room, but with delicate golden lattice work on the doors. Even in the midst of summer, the room smelled slightly of wood smoke, as if a fire had just been extinguished.

Churchill turned to the right and walked to the end of the room, very nearly to the enormous pipe organ that lurked like a watchful dragon in its lair. He reached a long, broad oak library table and from one of the low shelves under it extracted a large volume. He laid the book on the table and opened it.

The book was some sort of architectural survey, being an extensive series of plans and elevations of English estates. With a small grunt of satisfaction Mr. Churchill stopped at a page and pointed. "There," he said.

The engraving was an old-fashioned presentation rendering of the entrance front of Blenheim as drawn by the architect, along with el-evations for the garden front and a plan of the house. While they were similar in many particulars to the palace as it was built, there were deviations. The entrance court as built did not have the complex walls and gates that the engraving indicated it should have, fireplaces had been placed along different walls, staircases had not been erected, and the stable and kitchen wings were not nearly as extensive or as sym-metrical as they were planned to be.

Mr. Churchill pointed to the family wing of Blenheim on the plan. "Many of these rooms were rearranged during construction," he said. "Staircases that had been planned were not built, walls were not put up. And the stableyard," he said, pointing to the wing outside the library windows, "was not built as Sir John designed it. Duchess Sarah thought it too immoderate." He looked up from his book to the ceiling above us. "The ceiling in this library was to have been painted by James Thornhill, the same artist who painted the ceiling in the Great Hall. But by the time this wing was completed, the duchess and Sir John were no longer speaking."

"What happened?" I asked.

Mr. Churchill looked wistful, as if this memory of Blenheim sad-dened him. "Everything ran out. The duchess ran out of money. Sir John ran out of patience. And John Duke ran out of time: He died three years before this room was finished."

He closed the book carefully. "This house is an exacting burden—a noble misery, my father called it. It demands much of the people who live here; I suspect it always has. Some of the Churchills have risen to the challenge. Some of us have not. Duchess Sarah thought this place too large, too costly, and too inconvenient—she saw it as a triumph of drama over domesticity. But the duke loved this place, and she loved him. She lived here for years after his death and completed it as a memorial to him. She battled with Vanbrugh over every detail of this house, from the stone for the kitchen courtyard to the design of the stairway balusters. There was constant bickering over the years until finally, in frustration, Sir John quit, telling the duchess, 'You have your end, madam, for I will never trouble you again.' "

"You speak eloquently of Blenheim," I said. "But I suppose it is easy to be eloquent about something you love."

"You are an observant fellow," Mr. Churchill said, "That is it exactly."

"I can understand why you admire it," I said.

Churchill shook his head slightly. "Ah, but there is a sea of difference between the two. This is a house that is easy to admire but difficult to love. The only other man who loves this place as ardently as I do is my cousin. The duke would do anything to preserve this house."

The door we had entered by opened again, and the rest of the luncheon party appeared. The duke was at its vanguard, frowning and arguing loudly: "That is a lie, Gladys." My wife and Mr. Sargent were at the end of the procession. They looked like silent, awkward mourners at a funeral for a notable they did not know well. Mr. Sargent was carrying the same black sketchbook he had with him earlier. Two footmen appeared from another doorway, bearing trays of glasses filled with champagne.

"Winston," Miss Deacon said, catching sight of us, "Sunny just said the most amusing thing."

"I did nothing of the sort," the duke said, taking a glass and falling into a chair.

"You did—you said that your toothbrush was broken." Miss Deacon, champagne glass in hand, sat familiarly on the arm of the chair the duke was occupying and straightened the dress she had changed into, an attractive vanilla-colored confection of moiré silk.

"And so it was," the duke said. "The damn thing would not work."

"Only because his valet had neglected to put any tooth powder on it," Miss Deacon giggled. "He was so irritated with it that he threw it across the room."

Churchill began to laugh, a throaty rumble that shook his whole body. "Good Lord, Sunny, is that true?"

"How was I to know that the thing does not come with powder? What am I, a mind reader?" the duke demanded.

"Certainly not," the duchess said, as she handed Margaret a glass of champagne.

"There. Consuelo agrees with me," the duke said.

"But that does not alter the fact of what you did," Miss Deacon said.

"How do you know what he did?" Mrs. Belmont said. "Were you spying on him?"

"Of course not," Miss Deacon said, coloring slightly. "But I have this information on the highest authority."

His Grace frowned, and for a moment he looked like Mr. Churchill: The family resemblance was clear. He turned to a man I had not seen before, a distinguished-looking priest, dark-eyed with a mane of well-tended gray hair, dressed in a violet cassock, who stood near the fireplace. "Who is she talking about, Monsignor?" he asked.

"With Miss Deacon, I could not even begin to hazard a conjecture," the man said quietly, a slight Germanic accent attaching itself to his words.

"Mrs. Vanbrugh, Mr. Vanbrugh, are you acquainted with Monsignor Vay de Vaya? He is the apostolic protonotary and a dear friend."

We nodded to the man, who acknowledged us perfunctorily. The monsignor stood very straight, as if at attention, and he held in his right hand the large jeweled crucifix that hung from his neck. He had a sharp, aquiline nose and thin lips, which did not seem to move when he spoke. His face was disapproving: There was an unwavering certainty in his own righteousness that was perturbing.

"Yes, but what do you mean, the highest authority?" the duke insisted. "What does the king have to do with this?"

Miss Deacon laughed. "No, not the king. Never the king."

"Be careful, Gladys," the duchess warned.

"Tell me who this authority of yours is," the duke demanded. "And we shall see who is passing about these stories."

"Never," Miss Deacon said. "I will take this secret with me to my grave."

The duke scowled, and with a sudden shove of his shoulder pushed Miss Deacon off the arm of his chair. She managed to catch herself from falling to the floor but could not keep from spilling her champagne.

"Oh, no," my wife said quickly, pulling out a handkerchief and blotting the stain. "Such a lovely dress."

"It is nothing, I am fine," Miss Deacon said, her voice tight. She took the cloth from Margaret and turned away from the group. There was an uncomfortable silence as she wiped the front of her dress. The duke ignored her and with great deliberateness stood up and walked to a window, taking his champagne with him.

"There," Miss Deacon said as she turned back to us. Her voice was low, and though her cheeks were dry, her eyes were ringed in red. "That is better." The stain was still there—a long, dagger-shaped mark that extended from her waist to her knees—but it seemed lighter.

"It looks much better," Margaret offered.

"I am certain it will be all right," Mr. Sargent said.

"That was uncalled for," the duchess said to her husband.

"What? What are you talking about?" the duke demanded.

"You know what I mean," the duchess said.

"The girl lost her balance," the duke said. He turned from the window and glared at Miss Deacon. "She cannot hold her bubbly." He giggled, revealing small, yellowed teeth. "That's rather good. Did you hear that?"

"Yes, Your Grace," the monsignor said.

"Besides, what was she doing perched on the arm of my chair, like a canary?" the duke continued. "There are plenty of other places in this bloody room for her to sit than right on top of me."

The duchess looked at the duke and said, after a pause, "That never seemed to have bothered you before."

Miss Deacon gasped, and the duke glared at his wife.

"For heaven's sake, Consuelo, ring the bell for luncheon," Mrs. Belmont demanded.

Her Grace turned to one of the footmen. "Is luncheon ready yet, Jamison?" the duchess asked.

"In a moment, Your Grace," Jamison murmured.

"Hurry it along, please. His Grace is ready to sit down. But not with Miss Deacon on top of him."

"At once, Your Grace," Jamison said and bowed. As he left I thought I caught a slight smile slide across his face.

There was an uncomfortable silence as we watched Jamison leave the room.

"Mr. Vanbrugh," the duke said a bit too loudly, "do you know anything about central heating?"

"A little. That is not my area of expertise."

But the duke was undeterred. "What do you suggest I do to keep this wing heated in the winter? My father installed central heating, but it has never worked properly. My rooms get quite chilly, and I am always after the servants to keep the doors closed. But the Great Hall seems to suck every ounce of heat we can produce. I'll wager that the only person warm enough in this house at Christmas is John Duke himself, on the hall ceiling." He chuckled. "Winston, did you hear what I said?"

"I did indeed, Sunny," Churchill said, smiling. "We all did."

"Another good one," the duke said, nodding to us. "Did you not think so, Monsignor?"

"Most amusing, Your Grace," the monsignor agreed, his expression implacable. He took a sip of his champagne as his gaze fell first on Mr. Sargent then on the duchess. "I am always struck by irony when one visits Blenheim. Aren't you, Mr. Sargent?"

"Irony? There is precious little at Blenheim to be ironic about," Mrs. Belmont said bluntly.

The monsignor dabbed the side of his mouth with a pinkie. "Precisely, Mrs. Belmont. Blenheim is a very serious place."

Mrs. Belmont frowned and removed her pince-nez from her broad nose. "You Catholics can be so tiresome. You never say what you really mean."

"On the contrary, Alva. The monsignor is saying exactly what he does mean," Mr. Sargent said.

"And just what is that?" the old lady demanded.

"It is not for me to say," Mr. Sargent answered. He traced the rim of his champagne flute with his thumb. "Perhaps the monsignor would elaborate?"

A soft, emphatic "No" escaped from Miss Deacon's lips.

"Winston knows what the winters here are like," the duke blurted, as if the conversation had never left the subject of heating. "It can get as cold as hell here."

"I did not think that was possible, Your Grace, either spiritually or meteorologically," the monsignor said mildly.

"What?" the duke asked. "What do you mean?"

"He means that hell is thought to be too hot, not too cold," Winston said.

"Oh." The duke sat for a moment, looking puzzled. "Well, you

know what I mean. Good heavens, you are not all cretins, are you?"
He laughed, a short bark of mirthless sound that echoed off the walls.

"Indeed, we are not," Mr. Sargent said.

The butler, with Jamison hovering behind him, appeared and
announced that luncheon was served. With considerable relief our
party left the library and paraded down the corridor to the family dining room.

We settled ourselves at the table, which had been simply but at-
tractively set. The duke and duchess sat across from each other at the
center of the table, and the rest of us were placed around them. My
seat faced the bleak tapestry of the dying, bloody soldier, while Margaret, who was seated on the opposite side of the table, had the rather
more pleasant prospect of gazing upon the portrait above the fireplace.

"I never can get used to those tapestries," Miss Deacon, seated next
to me, said with a shudder.

"I understand they are called *The Arts of War*," Mr. Sargent said.
"Rather an unfortunate name for something so magnificently done."

"I do not care. They have ruined my digestion, I cannot abide
them," Mrs. Belmont proclaimed. "Hideous, ugly things. Blood and gore
everywhere."

"Good art should provoke as well as celebrate," Mr. Sargent said.

"But not during meals," Mrs. Belmont said.

"You are one of the moderns, John," Mr. Churchill said.

"More of an agitator, I think," Mr. Sargent replied.

" 'Master' is a better word for him," the duchess said.

"Hardly that," Mr. Sargent said.

"Your portraits are all right," the duke said. "As long as they're of
good-looking women."

"As long as they are flattering, in other words," the monsignor said.

"No use looking at ugly women on your wall," the duke said.

"War is ugly," Mrs. Belmont said.

"Horror and glory, that is what war is," Churchill said. "When I
was in South Africa, I encountered much worse."

"The battlefield is the only place in civilized society where savagery
is still acceptable," the monsignor said as the servant ladled an appe-
tizing cold consommé into the bowl in front of me.

"Oh, I can think of several other places," the duchess said.

"As can I," Mrs. Belmont said.

"Really?" Churchill said, his spoon hovering above his soup. "Enlighten us, ladies."

"Prisons," Mrs. Belmont said with alacrity.

"Slums," the duchess said.

"The boudoir," Miss Deacon said.

"Oh, my goodness," Margaret said, shocked.

"You are all very cruel," the monsignor said.

"Of course we are. Women are much crueler than men," Mrs. Belmont said. "Surely you know that by now, Monsignor. We have to be. We must be."

"Must be? Why?" Churchill asked. The duke, I noticed, was following the conversation closely.

"You men have many more acceptable places to vent your cruelty than we do," Mrs. Belmont said. "The city. Your club. Your sport. And you have more weapons. Money. The law. The vote. We women have fewer choices, and our only weapons are our minds and our bodies."

"Alva, enough," the duke said sputtering. "I will not have this, this *prurience* at table. It is disgusting."

"Ignoring injustice between the sexes will not make it disappear, Sunny," Mrs. Belmont said.

"It will when I am eating," the duke snapped.

The table fell into another uneasy silence that was finally broken by the duchess. "Mrs. Vanbrugh, your father tells me that you enjoyed visiting America."

"Yes, very much."

"Where did you go?"

"Boston, Newport, and some smaller towns along the Atlantic coast," she said.

"Newport?" Mrs. Belmont said. "When were you in Newport?"

"Several months ago," Margaret said, glancing at me. "I met Mr. Vanbrugh while I was there."

"A pleasant trip, then," Mr. Sargent said.

"I understand that Newport is a rather daunting place," the monsignor said.

Margaret smiled at the memory. "I thought it was lovely."

"Damn silly place, Newport," the duke said.

"Silly?" Mrs. Belmont repeated.

The duke waved his spoon in the air for emphasis. "Too much money and too little taste," he said. "All those preening Americans dashing about, trying to outdo each other by building bigger, grander houses. They pile abomination upon abomination—it is practically a mortal sin."

"Hardly that," the monsignor murmured.

"There is not a square foot in the entire town where the eye can rest. There is no quiet you can look upon. That is the appalling thing about Americans: They have no restraint. They can never buy enough gold and silver and marble and paintings and sculpture. The place looks more like a coolie fortress than a place fit for polite society. It is . . ." He paused. "Vulgar."

Mrs. Belmont started. "Vulgar? Newport has more elegance and grace in its buildings than even London. You are being absurd."

"I am not being absurd, I am being perfectly frank," the duke said, warming to his theme. "Newport is a very vulgar place. Did you not find it so, Mrs. Vanbrugh?"

Margaret blushed, and looked at me in silent appeal. She had no wish to offend the Americans at the table by endorsing the extraordinary remarks the duke had made, but the thought of disagreeing with him in his own home was more than her British sense of propriety could bear.

"Do you not agree, Mrs. Vanbrugh?" the duke repeated. "As an Englishwoman, did you not find it vulgar?"

The duchess said suddenly: "Mr. Vanbrugh, my husband asked you earlier about central heating."

"Yes?" I said.

"The duke is contemplating fitting a set of doors between the Great Hall and the family wing so that we might keep the heat in this side of the house. Something in the style of the other doors, of course, which could be kept open during the summer. Do you think that might be a workable solution?"

"I do, yes, that is certainly an idea," I agreed readily, grateful to the duchess for diverting the conversation from Margaret. "That is quite a resourceful idea on Your Grace's part," I said, turning to the duke.

"Did I suggest that?" the duke asked. "When?"

"When we were in London," the duchess replied. "You were speaking about the improvements to Blenheim you would be willing to make and you mentioned adding a set of doors. You said someone you knew had tried it successfully."

The duke put down his spoon. "I wonder who it could have been," he said, a finger tracing the line of his heavy jaw. "Was it you, Winston?"

"No, but it seems a reasonable suggestion," Churchill said.

"And when the doors are open, the vista along the corridor will be maintained," Mr. Sargent said. "When all the doors are open, you will still be able to see from one set of windows to the other."

The duchess smiled. "Mr. Sargent is quite captivated by our vistas."

Mr. Sargent smiled, his thick moustache curling at the sides of his mouth like a happy caterpillar. "It is a captivating house," he said. His gaze rested on the duchess and then on the duke. "One of the finest I have worked in."

"That is high praise from Mr. Sargent," the monsignor said.

Miss Deacon added, "It is said in Paris that John found fault with just about every room he was asked to paint in. 'Is there not one room in Paris worth preserving on canvas?' he asked. 'Must the Louvre be stormed again?'"

The table laughed, both at Miss Deacon's apt mimicry and the improbability of such a pronouncement. For Mr. John Singer Sargent, it was plain, was a quiet man who kept much of what he thought to himself. Even his pince-nez, which sat delicately on the bridge of his nose, did its best to conceal his eyes. But their shrewdness could not be hidden: Though he said little, Mr. Sargent noticed much.

The laughter seemed to distract the duke, who moved on to other topics. Margaret, relieved, smiled at me from across the table before turning to answer a question put to her by Mr. Churchill. My glance then fell on the duchess. She had eased herself out of the conversation like a tired foot from a dancing slipper. She looked weary, depleted, as she idly turned the glass of water in front of her. She stared into it intently, as if she expected secrets to be revealed in it. She then looked up slowly at the portrait of Louis XIV that hung above the fireplace, and her eyes widened in sudden alarm. She jerked her gaze away from the portrait, as if cowed by what she had seen, and shivered, though it was not cold in the room.

chapter
5

AFTER luncheon, the party dispersed to its various afternoon pursuits: the duke to his garden, Mr. Churchill to his books, Mr. Sargent to his inspirations. Miss Deacon announced that she was withdrawing to her room, while Mrs. Belmont indicated that her plans were to travel to Oxford in a motor car to attend a debate on women's suffrage. The duchess had no fixed appointment, and I was eager to communicate my discovery to her at the earliest opportunity. I was about to ask if she had found my note when the housekeeper appeared, and in a wounded whisper demanded an immediate audience with her mistress. With a resigned smile of apology, the duchess led the housekeeper, Mrs. Andrews, out of the dining room to her sitting room.

Margaret and I were surprised to find ourselves alone. "We have been abandoned, thank heaven," Margaret said, relieved.

"Lunch was rather trying," I admitted. I told her of the message I had discovered.

"How strange," she said. "What can it mean?"

"It could mean anything," I said.

"I suppose it could be some sort of trick, a game," Margaret suggested.

"What would be the point of that?" I asked. "It is not often that someone removes paneling from a wall for sport."

"That is true," Margaret agreed. We left the dining room and wandered the corridor in silence. She paused a moment before a bust of the duke that stood on a pedestal in a niche. It was carved of an ivory-colored marble that had been polished and smoothed so that it gleamed, even in the sad, strange gloom of the passage. But the likeness itself was uncomplimentary. The sculptor had rendered the duke with his head tilted up, his chin thrust forward, and his protuberant eyes narrowing, It was a pose that was meant to suggest confidence and ambition; instead, the bust had a petulant, complaining aspect, which did nothing to flatter the duke's features. He looked as if he were about to stamp his foot in irritation. Even more disquieting, the bust sat on a base supported by four carved dragons, which snarled at the subject.

Even at the height of the day, the light was so undependable in the corridor that it took us a moment to notice, huddling in the niche behind the bust, the young maid I had seen with the duchess in the Great Hall during my first visit. She was crying softly.

"Why, what is the matter?" Margaret inquired. "Are you unwell?"

As soon as she was noticed, the maid stopped crying and wiped her eyes. She eased herself out from behind the sculpture and straightened her apron. "No," she said, twirling a thin silver ring on her finger. "I am waiting for Mrs. Andrews."

"Why, it is Emily," Margaret said carefully.

"Yes . . . ma'am," the girl replied, looking away.

Margaret took her hand. "What has happened?" she asked.

"Mrs. Andrews is with the duchess," I said.

"Yes, sir," the maid said. She was young, about the same age as Margaret, and attractive in a fading way, her prettiness a mist that evaporates as soon as the sun shines upon it. She was of medium height and sturdily built, with capable hands. Her dark eyes were red and puffy, but her complexion had a robust, healthful hue, her light blond hair was curly and neatly arranged under a crisp cap, and she spoke in an honest country accent.

"Emily, is there anything we can do? Margaret asked. "What does Mrs. Andrews want to see you about?"

Emily looked down at her hands. "She wants what don't belong to her."

Margaret puckered her lips and looked at me. "May I inquire what the object might be?" she asked. "Is it fragile?"

Emily looked at Margaret in alarm, her eyes wide. "I never took it,

I swear, it was given to me," Emily said, her voice rising. "For safe-keeping, it was."

"Of course you did not steal anything," I said soothingly. "We are not accusing you. Mrs. Vanbrugh was simply wondering if it was something that could be replaced."

Emily shook her head. In a quieter voice she said, "It is of a private nature, sir."

"A private nature," I repeated.

"Yes." She swallowed hard and stood up straighter. "I made a promise to keep it away from prying eyes. And I will." There was a note of defiance, a resolve to her voice that had not been there before. The young woman was about to say more when a door to the sitting room was thrown open and Mrs. Andrews, severe and magnificent in her disapproval, stood before us in her long black dress "Come in, my girl," she said, her tone dreadful.

Emily composed herself and with a self-possession fit for one of her betters, she walked past the housekeeper into the room. Mrs. Andrews glanced at us briefly but said nothing as she closed the door firmly behind her.

"Oh, the poor girl," Margaret said. "I hope everything will be all right."

Down the corridor a door from the duke's rooms opened and Miss Deacon appeared.

"She is down from her room quickly," Margaret said.

Miss Deacon looked startled to see us and made a motion to return to the room she had just quitted. But she seemed to think better of that notion, for she made her way toward us. "Mrs. Vanbrugh, at last I have found you," she said, scurrying to us. "What do you think of our little party?"

"Everyone has been very pleasant to me," Margaret said cautiously.

"And well they should, a little lamb like you." Miss Deacon patted her forearm. "Tell me, what do you think of the monsignor? I have heard that he has his vestments made by a Paris couturier. I must admit, they are magnificent, so perhaps he does. He has the right coloring for purple, the lucky man." She sighed. "Do you think what everyone says about Mr. Sargent could be true? I, for one, do not believe it for a minute."

"What do they say about him, Miss Deacon?" I asked.

She looked startled by the question, as if this were common knowledge. "Why, that he's a sodomite." She lowered her voice and looked behind her. "They say he hires young men, art students, to pose for him. It's wicked—completely false, of course, but there are stories. . . ."

Margaret closed her eyes tight and shivered, as if to squeeze the image of Mr. Sargent from her.

"Oh, never mind all that," Miss Deacon said, suddenly bright. "I wonder, would you be kind enough to take a stroll with me? I am *desperate* for companionship." Taking both of our elbows, she guided us down to the furthest reaches of the corridor, into a round, belve-derelike space in which two enormous elephant tusks, their tips curving toward each other, were displayed on either side of a tall, arched window that looked out onto the Great Court. "You do not mind my kidnapping your wife for a walk, do you, Mr. Vanbrugh? You can always spend time with her. We have her here so little."

"Of course I do not mind," I said, turning to face Miss Deacon. But the lady insisted on holding my elbow. "As long as my wife is not otherwise engaged. Or too tired."

Miss Deacon looked dismayed. "How stupid of me. Do you have another appointment, Mrs. Vanbrugh? Or are you too tired? Say you are not."

I half hoped that Margaret might invent an excuse to stave off such an invitation, but she is the daughter of a clergyman and was taught to tell the truth in all things—it was as unconscious now to her as breathing. "No," she said, a trace of regret in her voice. "I have no fixed engagement and I am not too tired, if we do not go too far."

Miss Deacon clapped her hands. "How enchanting," she said. "We must leave at once. We will walk toward the cascade, Mrs. Vanbrugh, and you will divulge all about yourself. I am simply mad for new acquaintances. And such an impressive one, with a duchess for a patroness." The two turned to go and nearly ran into the monsignor.

"My goodness, you gave me a start," Miss Deacon said.

"That was not my intent," the monsignor said, his voice solemn.

"Of course you did not. I never thought you did," Miss Deacon said—though she looked as if that was exactly what she did think.

The monsignor stood before them, stiff and judgmental, his unsettling gaze falling first on Miss Deacon, then on Margaret. Nothing moved on his gaunt, somber face except his eyes, which shifted from one woman to the other speculatively, unhurriedly, as if he were deciding between bouquets of flowers.

After an awkward moment, Miss Deacon demanded, her voice querulous, "What is it? What are you looking at?" Her hand moved to smooth the skin beneath her eyes.

"It is nothing," the monsignor said.

Miss Deacon offered a bleak laugh. "It must be something, since you stare so definitely." She leaned into Margaret and said in a mock whisper, "Perhaps he is trying to convert you."

"That would be a presumption," the monsignor said. He stared at Margaret without blinking, and she returned his look fearfully, like a timorous mouse who did not have the strength to look away from a coiling snake.

"I wonder, Mrs. Vanbrugh, if you would be so kind as to give me one of your hands," he said.

Hesitantly, Margaret settled her hand into the monsignor's outstretched grasp. With a deliberate gravity, he straightened her index finger and drew it slowly toward his face. Miss Deacon's icy blue eyes widened, but she did not utter a sound as the monsignor slowly placed Margaret's finger directly in front of his open, staring right eye. After the hint of a pause, the monsignor placed the soft pad of Margaret's finger directly onto his unflinching eye and held it there, as if to challenge her to snatch it away.

Margaret went very white but did not cry out. She stood transfixed, as if she could not believe what she was witnessing. Then, just as deliberately as he had placed it there, the monsignor removed the finger from his eye and held Margaret's hand in both of his. It was only then that he blinked. As he did, the tiniest of smiles curled over his colorless lips. "God sees everything that we do; his eye is unblinking."

Margaret nodded and pulled her hand away.

"What a peculiar man you are, Monsignor," Miss Deacon said, clearly shaken. "Come, Mrs. Vanbrugh."

The monsignor moved aside to let them pass, but as Margaret walked by him, he laid a thin hand on her forearm and said in a low voice, "Do not be deceived, Mrs. Vanbrugh."

Margaret looked stricken. She was about to say something when Miss Deacon urged her again to come along.

The two walked down the passage, Miss Deacon chattering all the while.

The monsignor observed them depart and came toward me.

"What did you mean by those words?" I asked. "By what you said."

"Your wife understands," he said.

"I am not sure she does."

The monsignor bowed his head slightly at that. "What sort of buildings do you design, Mr. Vanbrugh?"

"Whatever anyone pays me to," I said.

"Of course. But you must have a preference."

"My preference is for a simple design built with care and honesty."

The monsignor straightened the crucifix around his neck. "And yet you are here. Life is full of surprises," he said, "Good afternoon." He turned and walked away.

I stood for a moment between the tusks, perplexed. I was not at all sure what to make of what had happened to us at Blenheim. It seemed that the more I learned of the place, the less I understood it. It unsettled me in ways I could not explain. I did not know what to make of the people: They were insubstantial somehow—inconsistent and unreliable. They reminded me of the woman in the painting, gazing at herself in the mirror: What one expected to see there wasn't what one actually saw. I shuddered and turned my attention to the window, hoping for a distraction. The Great Court was a hive of bustle and commotion. Dozens of men were organized around the courtyard in groups, toiling with great energy and purpose as they removed the green turf and replaced it with the gray stones of quarried granite. Occasionally one band of workers halted to wait for two men and a boy who pushed a large, old-fashioned wheelbarrow full of stones to the work areas that required them.

At first this scene appeared to be one of disorder. But after some minutes of observation, I noted a certain rhythm, a definable logic, to the action. Though the afternoon sun was well settled in the sky, the men displayed no diminution of purpose: Each seemed to understand his place in the larger venture, and each continued upon the task he was assigned to capably and with good humor. From the foreman to the water boy, every soul worked in harmony with the others. No doubt the work would consume many days, but these men did not seem to be daunted by the monumental task before them. They pressed on, carrying out the orders of the man at whose table I had only recently eaten. I wondered what these men really thought of the Duke of Marlborough. Did they despise him? Were they proud to work for him? Did he treat them well?

I turned away and noticed that the sitting room door was ajar; I had not heard Mrs. Andrews and Emily leave. I moved toward it and stood before it a moment, listening. Hearing no sound from within, I nudged the door open a little wider and saw the duchess sitting across the room in a delicate gilded chair that stood in front of a window, staring off into space. Although her manner was composed, her face was pale and she wore an expression of such profound desolation, such inescapable loneliness, that I thought she might collapse into tears. But she did not. She sat there, immobile in her sadness, her eyes wide, her mouth anxious, her long fingers playing restlessly with her pearl choker.

I hesitated to interrupt her; my presence could be of no comfort. But I was determined to alert her to my discovery. I knocked quietly on the door. She turned toward me and after a moment smiled—a slight, shy smile.

"Mr. Vanbrugh, come in. I was just about to call for you," she said, beckoning me into the room. "You will take me away from my troubles." She said this lightly, but there was an undercurrent to her tone.

"If I can be of any help, I will."

"Oh, it is only my husband. He has accused a servant of stealing a little box from the Green Writing Room. My housekeeper has determined that it was one of the housemaids, a girl she dislikes. The girl denies it, and oh, it is a terrible tangle." She sighed and indicated a chair next to her. "Such are the pleasures of a duchess."

"This girl, is she the one who has been waiting on my wife?" I asked.

"Yes, she is," the duchess said. "How does Mrs. Vanbrugh find Emily?"

"I have heard no complaints from her," I said.

"Good. Emily is an able girl. She is willing enough, but a trifle headstrong. And that is a distinct liability in a servant. And a woman." The duchess looked out the window. Below us in the garden was a series of carefully trimmed dwarf box hedges planted in a formal style, all flourishes and superfluities. In the middle of the garden was an ornate stone fountain, topped by a nude woman, a gilded cape around her shoulders, holding a crown of gold above her head. The fountain was empty, and the duke himself was standing on its rim, directing the assembled workmen on how to clean the topmost pool.

I said: "I think a liability is nothing more than a possibility in the wrong place."

The duchess looked at me. "Mr. Vanbrugh, you are a philosopher."

"No, ma'am. I just have a different perspective."

"You see things in elevation," she suggested, smiling.

I shrugged. "If you like."

She leaned toward me suddenly and straightened the cuffs of my shirt. When she was finished, her hand lingered a moment on my wrist, and she traced a delicate line down across the top of my hand to my knuckles.

"Why, you are trembling," she said, surprised. "Whatever for?"

"Nothing. That is, I am not trembling." I said.

The duchess looked amused. "There is nothing to be afraid of. I will not bite you. At least, unless you would find that pleasant."

"Of course," I agreed quickly, and regretted instantly such a comment.

"We are making progress," the duchess said. She settled herself back against her seat.

I changed the subject. "Your Grace, I have some news about your rooms that is rather startling." I recounted how I had taken down the panel and come upon the message, which the duchess immediately demanded to see. We returned to her bedroom and I removed the paneling. It came down more easily than it had the first time, and I was prepared for its weight, so I did not repeat my ignominious fall onto her bed.

The duchess studied the words carefully. " 'All is lost—the world will know.' How queer." She frowned.

"I had hoped that you might know what to make of it," I said.

"I? Why would I?"

"It was found in your room."

"I am sorry, I do not. But still, it is rather alarming."

"It is always disturbing to have one's property defaced," I agreed.

"You misunderstand," the duchess said. "What alarms me is the hopelessness." She studied the words carefully. "Who in this house would be so despairing and yet so fearful of being discovered?"

I began to understand. "Yes, I see. It is horrible enough to be afraid. But to be afraid of voicing that fear, that must be . . ." I searched for a word.

"Suffocating," the duchess said definitely. "It must be like drowning in an ocean of silence. Who else have you told about this?"

"No one," I said.

"Good. I would appreciate your not saying anything to anyone else." She looked around the room. "That is, until we know what we have."

"We have a message."

"Yes, but what else do you think it might mean?" She crossed her arms, pressing her palms tightly against her. "I wish I knew. It is odd, but it feels as if . . ." She stopped and her voice drifted off.

"Yes?" I prompted.

"Oh, it is preposterous. But the oddest feeling has come over me. I have the distinct impression this house is trying to tell me, to tell *us,* something." She looked embarrassed. "Do you think you could continue to explore this room? Quietly? Without being discovered?"

"I suppose so," I said. "At least I could try, if I had the proper tools. And if you do not object to my moving the furniture."

"I welcome it." The duchess moved to ring the bell, and a footman appeared almost immediately. "Please tell my maid to move my things to the North Apartment at once. Mr. Vanbrugh will be working in here. He is not to be disturbed. And please tell Baines to bring Mr. Vanbrugh his tools." The footman bowed and disappeared.

The duchess turned to me. "Baines is the oddman."

"What is wrong with him?"

"Nothing. That is what we call the man at Blenheim who performs the odd tasks here."

"I have never heard the word before," I said.

"There is much about Blenheim that is singular," she admitted. Her complexion, which had once been pale, was now pink, and her eyes were animated. "I will leave you to your adventure, then. Do tell me the moment you discover anything, Mr. Vanbrugh. And remember, I am relying on your discretion."

"You have that, Your Grace," I said.

"You are very kind," she said, and departed.

I looked around the room to determine where I should begin. Though the room was of modest proportions by the standards of Blenheim, it nonetheless seemed to me a formidable assignment to search for... well, what *was* I trying to find? Directions to a trove of jewels? Amulets for a forgotten rite? Talismans of a lost civilization? I felt preposterous suddenly, as if I had been sent on a fool's errand. But I could not rid myself of the gnawing sense that there was a grim reason for the message on the panel.

The maid arrived in a few moments, along with Baines, who brought with him a stepladder and a canvas sack full of clanking tools. Courteous and affable, he agreed to remove the tapestry from the back wall and took it down with great gentleness. Together we rolled it carefully and set it aside near the bed. The maid, a dour, old-fashioned matron of pitiless Swiss efficiency, observed us in aggrieved silence. She made no secret of her displeasure at my presence in the bedroom of her mistress. As Baines and I worked, she removed anything she thought might tempt my unsavory inclinations: silver picture frames, porcelain figurines from a table beside the bed, a gold carriage clock, an engraved brush and comb set, and, inexplicably, a silk shawl of vivid peacock blue that had been draped over a chair. As Baines departed, she turned to me, her jaw set and her arms full, and asked, "Will that be all?"

"Yes, thank you," I said, to which she sniffed and withdrew in a huff of censure.

After they had left, I took a moment to determine what should be my first task. I settled on the green wallcovering.

I inspected the fabric carefully and discovered that it was being held in place by a single line of tiny brass nails concealed near the edges of the paneling, the crown molding, and the wainscoting. Using my pocket knife, I pried the nails loose from the backing so that, one by one, they popped out into my hand. Working down from the ceiling, I extracted each nail carefully without damaging the silk, just as a dressmaker might remove pins from a gown on a mannequin. It was tedious work, but I did not know how else to carry out my task—or truly even what my task was.

The fabric and backing smelled stale, and the velvet was frayed in a great many more spots than I had originally estimated. The walls underneath the backing were rough, cracked, and stained in a thousand different places. They looked every day of the two hundred years they had been standing. With each section of bare wall I uncovered, the elaborately embellished ceiling seemed immodest, almost ridiculous, like a courtesan caught in the unforgiving light of morning.

There was a pronounced sag to the middle of the fabric, and as I worked toward it, it became clear that some thing was pulling it down. With each nail I extracted, the fabric slumped down a bit more, forming a long, graceful arc of cloth. Halfway along the wall, the velvet fell more abruptly. The culprit was, in fact, a small pouch, long and thin, which had been sewn haphazardly onto the back side of the silk.

I extracted the contents of the pouch with care. It appeared to be a letter, and it was folded in on itself. There was no address anywhere, though there was the unmistakable stain of a wax seal. The contents were penned in a broad, spiky, antiquated hand and read:

My dear Lord R.—

> *I dare not expres to you, at these, many miles' distanse, how ardently I long for yr return. I was Disconsolate at yr leave-taking this morn, and Mr. F. wonder'd at my Melancholy— which he sirmised was due to th poor cold breakfast we Ate in Silence. I console myself with this, our Great Jest, and how the world mistakes us for our true aspect and sentiments! It is ere more than I cn bear, as my heart burns for yr caresses. O, when shall you return to me? Wherever you are whilst I have life my soul shall follow you—and wherever I am I shall only kill the time, wish for night that I may sleep and hope the next day to hear from you.*
>
> *I fly—Mrs. Morley commands. Her eyes, they are ill—they water so. She demands my presense—it soothes her. To ne'r see Court again, with its triflings and petty blandishments, is my*

most fervent prair. To dwell with you, Sir Knight, in the bower
of our Most Perfect Love—that would be My Perticular Bliss. I
hpe. You will send me word that you wll see me this nighte.
Hurry back to me—I care only for yr kisses.

As ever S
Mrs. F.

The letter was signed with a large, florid initial—S. Under it, in capital letters, was written "Mrs. F.," followed by a small flourish. Nowhere was the letter dated.

I was of two minds about the communiqué. I felt as if I had interrupted a tête-à-tête, or eavesdropped on a conversation, and shrank from that discourtesy. But a kind of disquiet began to seep into my veins—like tea in boiling water, its darkening strands curling slowly around my organs—until I was suffocated with . . . what? I did not really know. Some deception was being proposed—even carried out— but what was its purpose? And what had it achieved? Were the two correspondents ever punished for their actions? I bristled at the thought that their adultery—for it was clear that they were lovers— might never have been detected and that their dishonesty not brought to justice. I hoped that it had, and that I was exercised over nothing, but I honestly did not know. So much was ambiguous.

The duchess must see this, that much was clear. But a wiser course might be to continue to search for other clues, to identify Mrs. F., so I returned to the task of removing the fabric.

I worked more deliberately, taking care to examine carefully every yard of fabric. The undertaking proved to be trying work: The fabric had collected vast amounts of grime and dust over the years, and every time I moved it, I brought down a shower of fine gray grit, which smelled both rank and acrid, as if a firecracker had been set off in a mausoleum.

I am not usually affected by the unexpected ordeals of renovation— in my profession, they are a matter of course—but this particular soot brought on a sneezing fit, one so fierce I could scarcely regain my breath. The only remedy that worked was to abandon the fabric in a heap on the floor and rush to the open windows, where I spent some minutes recovering. The fresh air helped, and my sneezing eased. But as soon as I returned to work, I was immobilized again by another sneezing spasm, this time accompanied by a dry, choking cough. The dust had gotten into my throat and had settled there, burrowing in my insides like a tick.

I was at a loss on how to proceed until I remembered how American cowboys kept dust from their mouths by tying neckerchiefs around them. My handkerchief was too small for this purpose, and a quick search of the room revealed nothing suitable. But in the dining room I found a linen napkin that had not yet been reclaimed by a footman. I dipped the napkin into a nearby vase of flowers and tied it around my face so that the wettest part of the napkin hung in front of my nose and mouth. Thus fortified, I turned my attention to the wall. Several minutes later, I came across another pouch. It was smaller than the first, and was placed higher up on the same wall but was more loosely sewn onto the fabric, thereby making it more difficult to notice when the fabric fell away from the wall.

The letter also was not addressed and, though it was by the same person, the hand was more deliberate than the first missive. There was no date, but there was an indication where the letter had been written.

> *Oxford*
> *My Lord Rake—*
>   *I am got this far on my way to the Manor when Yr Agreable letter came to me ere I was to enter the Coach, & I was much pleas'd with it. I put it near my heart & the longing for you was soothed, but only for a moment. As for the perticulars of its Sentiments, I own I esteem them as grately I admire their Master— & I wish for our reunion all the more.*
>   *'Tis later this day. The house continews well; You have conjured wondrous things from the hill. Mr. F. is wll pleased by it, tho I mock it to the world. And what a great joke I have contrivid—I shal inquire Sir Chris. if he would put up a Habitation in London for us. That surely wil amuse ye, the master plotter!*
>   *All is quiet and ful of ease here. The Apothocary, Cowp'r, has ben to me, and his potions have aid'd me e'er wel. And so I to return to London in a Fortnight.*

It was signed "Mrs. Freeman."

Well, I thought, at least we know the names of the two correspondents. But who the devil are Lord Rake and Mrs. Freeman? The
names meant nothing to me, but perhaps they would to the duchess.

But the more I pondered the letter, the more uneasy it made me.
There was something odd about it, something different from the first
note I had found, which kept me from simply folding it and squirreling
it away in my pocket. Rather than return to my work, I sat on the
floor amid the piles of musty fabric and reread the letter several times.
Each time I did, my agitation grew. While I could not identify precisely
what it was about this letter that had taken hold of me so insistently,
I began to feel certain that these letters were dangerous.

I was more attentive to my task when I returned to it, and was
rewarded twenty minutes later by uncovering another pouch near the
corner. It was written by the same person, but the handwriting and
tone this time were much more agitated, the hand was hasty, jittery:

> *I hav suf'r'd more than any one can bear. You undo me—Anne
> has reveal'd all. She says that you love her and that the Earl of S.
> wil ne'r know of it. But I wil, and I do, and it is my own hell,
> never to avow it.*
>
> *To think that I have thrown myself in yr pow'r and into yr
> hands—you, who profess'd yr undy'ng love, have condemned me
> to a living death. How can I stand to think of thes last months?
> How can I ever look upon this child—Anne wants to name him
> after yu if tis a boy, but she says you insist on Charles—oh, the
> gall!*
>
> *I rage against you and the pile of stones that is your incon-
> stant heart. Every day I die a litle more. But Beware, my Soul wil
> rise up against you—you, who have driven me to this hate. It
> consumes my love like fire arownd a piece of coal. In you I found
> myself; in you I have lost myself; I am doomed.*

The tone in each letter was different, even wildly so. The first one was
both ardent and almost childishly conspiratorial, as if the writer relished the secrecy of their liaison. The second was more businesslike,
mentioning the house and others—Sir Chris and Cowper the apoth-

ecary. In the third, however, the writer, Mrs. Freeman, sounded devastated, angry, and overwhelmed by the news that Anne was pregnant by the recipient of this letter. Lord Rake indeed—the man seemed to have toyed with the affections of Mrs. Freeman, only to be undone by an admission from another woman, this Anne.

The letters were a fascinating glimpse into a love triangle, but there was so much unknown. Perhaps Margaret might have an insight into the meaning of these letters. I copied them as quickly as I could and finished the task just as the door from the dining room opened and Mr. Sargent appeared, looking distracted. His face was white and drawn, and his fastidious appearance was disheveled.

"Mr. Vanbrugh, is the duchess about?" he asked.

"No," I said as I placed my copies into an inner pocket of my jacket. "I do not know where she is."

His eyes darted about the room. "Have you come across a sketchbook? I fear I have lost one of mine."

"No, I have not." If Mr. Sargent noticed that the wall coverings and paneling had been removed and that the room was a jumbled pile of discolored silk, he gave no outward indication. He was in search of his sketchbook and made no effort to attend to his surroundings.

"Perhaps it is in this room somewhere," he said, scanning the floor quickly. "Did you encounter anything under the chairs, or perhaps behind the settee or desk?"

"I have not seen anything like a sketchbook," I admitted.

But he seemed not to hear me. His forehead was deeply creased, his dark eyebrows furrowed, and his shrewd green eyes were in constant motion, darting from one part of the room to another. He began a strange search, lighting on individual pieces of furniture and scrutinizing them in minute detail. First he examined a mahogany chest that sat behind the door to the dining room. He spent nearly ten minutes inspecting it inside and out, and found nothing. He replaced the chest and turned his attention to the fireplace. He approached it carefully, and after adjusting his pince-nez and peering closely at the stone, he ran his fingers across the marble, as a blind man might who is struggling to recognize a place he once had visited. I watched in silent fascination as his frown deepened and his back tensed: it was plain Mr. Sargent had not found what he was searching for.

Next he turned his attention to the thick white bear rug in the center of the room.

"Is there something I can help you with?" I ventured as Mr. Sargent peered down at the enormous pelt.

"Where can it be?" he asked himself, his voice taut. He threw the rug to one side and stared insistently at the Oriental carpet beneath it. But he found nothing.

He moved over to the bed next and, crouching low beside it, pulled aside the bedskirt and poked his head into the darkness beneath the mattress.

"Do you recall what the sketchbook looks like?" he asked, his voice muffled.

"I saw it when you sketched me," I said.

Unsuccessful, Mr. Sargent emerged from under the bed, his hair tousled and his lapels dusty. He remained crouched for a moment, a look of anxious concern on his face. "It *must* be here. I am certain I had it with me the last time I was with Consuelo," he said. "Where can it be?"

The familiarity with which he used the first name of the duchess jarred my ear, I did not know that the two of them were on such terms. "Where do you last remember seeing it?" I asked.

He stood up and dusted off his coat and trousers. "Two days ago, I left it in her sitting room before luncheon."

"Have you looked there?"

Mr. Sargent appeared annoyed. "Of course."

"Perhaps one of the servants returned it to your room," I suggested.

Sargent shook his head and fell into a chair. "I have already searched my room," he said. "I questioned my man about it. He has not seen it. Nor have the other servants. No one has. But someone must. I must have it back. It contains some extremely important sketches."

"For the portrait?" I asked.

Sargent, who was staring at the fireplace, said nothing. But after a moment he roused himself and said, "What? Oh. No. Well, yes, certainly there were sketches for the portrait in it." He looked at me as he struggled to refocus his attention. "What do you think of this portrait idea?" he asked suddenly.

"Me? I am no art expert," I said.

"But you are an architect," Mr. Sargent said.

"Not much of one," I said. "I have never designed anything note-worthy."

Mr. Sargent's eyes narrowed and he pursed his lips. "Accomplishment has nothing to do with it. It is desire that makes one an artist."

I paused, absorbing his words. I must have looked puzzled, as Mr. Sargent chuckled and said, "What an American you are, Mr. Vanbrugh."

The dismissiveness in his tone was an affront to my country. "What do you mean?" I demanded, my voice rising.

"Only that you allow others to judge you. Or rather, you allow the judgment of others to influence how you judge yourself."

"I do nothing of the kind," I protested.

"Yet you insist you are not an architect." He cocked his head. "I am convinced that success in life has less to do with talent than it does with discipline and self-confidence. If one is disciplined and believes he can achieve his goals, he will—whether or not he truly has the talent." He ran his hand down one side of his beard. "Though it is true, talent does help."

I could scarcely believe what I was hearing. "You do not mean to tell me that you would rather have self-discipline than talent," I said.

"Of course not."

"I am glad to hear it," I said.

"Only that if I had to choose and wanted a fighting chance at success, I would opt for discipline over talent. Talent without discipline is nothing more than laziness." He rested his chin on his hand. "Are you happy with what you do?" he asked suddenly.

I shrugged. "Happy enough, I suppose."

Mr. Sargent looked dubious, and then glanced around the room, for the first time noticing that the tapestry had been taken down and that much of the silk had been stripped from the wall. "What are you attempting here?"

"I am charged with carrying out a task for the duchess," I said carefully.

"She asked you to remove the wall covering?" Mr. Sargent asked in surprise.

"No, not exactly," I said.

Sargent sat up straighter. "Then why on earth *are* you?"

"I am looking..." I began, then thought better of it. "I am sorry, but I am really not at liberty to say," I said.

Mr. Sargent studied me in silence, his eyes appraising. It was clear I interested him, but there was a reticence about his aspect, an unwillingness to reveal what he truly thought, that put me on my guard. "Why not?" he asked.

I tried to fashion a response but failed; I was never particularly good at thinking on the spot. "Perhaps you would like to take it up with the duchess."

He shook his head. "You, too?" He sighed. "I will *never* give in to this again," he said. With that, the quiet, unassuming artist stood up and without a word left the room.

After a moment I rang for a servant, who arrived quickly. It was Jamison, who did not look surprised at finding me in his mistress's room amid a mountain of debris and clutter.

"Jamison, do you know where Her Grace is?"

"I believe she is in the chapel, attending to some business. Some earthly business, sir." The hint of a smile played about his lips.

I grinned. "Thank you, Jamison," I said. "I wonder, could you direct me to the chapel?"

Jamison glanced around the room, as if to calculate the amount of time that would be required to clean it. "Of course, sir," he said. "If you will follow me."

"Oh, and please instruct the others to leave this room just as it is," I said.

"Yes, sir."

chapter
6

JAMISON walked slightly ahead and to one side as he led the way to the chapel, glancing back on occasion to ensure that I was following him. We were not far from the family rooms when we passed a set of windows that gave out onto an internal courtyard. The windows had been opened to lure into the house any breeze capricious enough to find itself marooned in the unwelcoming confines of the courtyard. But the occasional summer draft did little to dispel the cheerless damp that gripped Blenheim, even in June.

There was no one about, and the household seemed to welcome the brooding lull of an empty afternoon. The entire place had fallen into a sluggish rhythm, but behind such lethargy I felt the early stirrings of something else, something untoward and disturbing, as conscious and contrived as any I'd yet experienced here. But who was the contriver?

As I pondered this, a growing alarm began to take hold of me, distracting me from my surroundings, so it was a bit of luck that I heard the argument at all. If the windows had been closed, if there had been others guests about, and if I had not been in a heightened state of excitement, I might have passed by.

But that is not what occurred.

What both Jamison and I noticed first as a series of low murmurs accelerated into a disjointed argument of shouts and whispers.

We both stopped, halted by the tone more than the words' meaning.

"Did you hear that?" I whispered, going to the window.

"Yes, sir," Jamison replied, his voice also low.

"Where is it coming from?" I asked.

"Upstairs." He pointed to three windows that were in an apartment just at the top of the stairs.

"Whose rooms are those?" I asked.

"No one's, sir."

A voice, choked with anger, said from above, "Great Christ, tell me."

A woman replied, "Leave me alone. I don't know, I swear it."

Jamison looked surprised. "My God, that's Emily," he said.

We heard a door open and the man say, "Not so fast," The door slammed and we heard feet running above us.

We hurried down the corridor and dashed up the stairway, our attention directed to the floor above, to see if Emily needed our help. On the landing we encountered the duke, who was adjusting his tie.

"Are you all right, Your Grace?" I asked.

The duke flushed. "I am perfectly fine. Why would I not be?" he demanded.

"We heard an argument of some sort," I said.

The duke stiffened and thrust out his lower jaw. "You most certainly did not."

"But we did," I pressed. "Up here."

"I did not hear anything," the duke said gruffly. "And I was upstairs."

Jamison was staring at the duke with ill-concealed distrust. "In the empty apartment that overlooks the courtyard, Your Grace. That was where the argument come from. We heard it, Mr. Vanbrugh and me."

The duke glared at him. "I told you I did not hear anything," he repeated. It was clear, at least at Blenheim, that if the Duke of Marlborough did not hear anything—or if the duke *said* he did not hear anything—then no one did.

I did not know what to say. I could not precisely make out who the voices belonged to, but Jamison believed one of them was Emily, and I suspected that the other one was the duke himself. But why were they arguing in a room neither occupied?

"May I ask, Your Grace, what were you doing upstairs?" I said.

"What an impertinent question," the duke said, pulling at his shirt cuffs in irritation. "I cannot believe that I am being hounded in my own house by a guest and a servant." The duke looked at Jamison. "What are you doing, lolling about? Go back to work," he said.

Jamison bowed to the duke and retreated down the stairs, disappearing into the shadows of the main floor.

The duke brushed past me and followed Jamison. "Where are you going? To your room, I suppose," he said. "Have you finished your work already?"

"No, Your Grace. I am still . . ." I paused for the right word. "Investigating."

The duke turned and looked up at me, his face a scowl of impatience. "Well, hurry it along. I am sure Consuelo is anxious for you to be finished. I know I am."

"Yes, sir." I looked down at him, and a question occurred to me that was so presumptuous, so rash, that I hesitated to pose it, even though I very much wanted to know its answer.

The duke noticed my hesitancy. "Why do you look at me like that? What is wrong?"

"I was . . ." I faltered.

"Oh, get on with it," he said.

"I was wondering if you liked living here, Your Grace. At Blenheim."

The duke looked at me oddly—taken aback, I suppose, by both my question and my impertinence in asking it. But after a moment his face relaxed, his expression softening to something more charitable, and his drooping moustache twitched.

"You want to know if I like living at Blenheim," the duke said in a speculative tone. "May I ask what prompts such a question?"

"I assure you, sir, I am no gossip," I said, descending the stairway slowly.

"That remains to be seen," the duke said. "But you did not answer me."

"I am interested in what it is like to live amid such magnificence."

The duke chuckled. "There's a word." He peered along the main floor passage, which even on a bright afternoon was in the grips of a lowering gloom. "Come with me a moment," he said suddenly. "I want to show you something."

He led me down the corridor past the Saloon, where several servants, their livery covered by long aprons, were methodically polishing the dining table. Selecting a door beyond it on the left, he opened it and directed me into the room.

We entered a spacious chamber of considerable splendor. It was roughly thirty feet square, and almost as high, its white ceiling ornamented with curling wooden garlands gilded in the French style, which adorned the molding in each corner of the ceiling and where the chains of the two large chandeliers hung down. The settees and furniture, upholstered in damask of gold and aquamarine, were low but comfortable-looking and were arrayed irregularly about the room on a sizable though faded French carpet of a floral design, which once had been bright blue and deep red. Arranged between the chandeliers in the center of the room was an ornately carved table of green marble with sturdy gilded legs, upon which stood a bronze sculpture of a small baby lying on its stomach, reaching toward the sun with its left hand. Above the flamboyant marble chimneypiece of veined brown and white marble—which looked like smoke captured in stone—was an imposing portrait of a man whose proud bearing, red satin robes, ermine-fringed cape, staff of state, and haughty expression signified that the subject could only be a king.

But what commanded my attention were the two tapestries that hung on either side of the fireplace. They were so large that one wall could not display them: They continued around the corners to the adjacent walls. They were similar to the wall hangings in the family dining room—they were also of military themes, just as intricate, just as detailed—but these depicted far less grisly events. In one of them, a group of men on horseback had gathered under a large shade tree at the top of a hill, and as the others looked on, one of the generals dispatched a messenger. In the background were meticulous renderings of the surrounding countryside, complete with meandering rivers, tiny villages surrounded by copses of trees, military encampments, and the lingering smoke of battle.

"This is one of the state rooms," the duke said. "I had it redecorated just after I inherited the dukedom."

"It is grand," I said.

The duke nodded. "The chap above the fireplace is Louis the Four-teenth, of course, whose armies got the stuffing knocked out of them when John Duke beat them on the battlefield. These"—he pointed to the tapestries—"commemorate the moment when the duke sent news that the French had been vanquished again, this time at Bouchain." The duke fell silent, pondering what was before him, his lower jaw thrust out. He licked his dry lips several times before continuing. "John Duke is the chap in the scarlet coat on the white charger. The blue ribbon around him is the Garter, you see. After all his triumphs, par-ticularly his victory at Blenheim, the queen was willing to give him anything. She gave him the Royal Manor at Woodstock and promised to build him a house here. At government expense."

"Generous," I said.

"The duke had beaten back the French and saved Europe. He was a hero. People lighted bonfires all over the country for him. Medals were struck with his profile on them. He was as great as Alexander, as Charlemagne. No tribute was too much."

"Of course. I meant no disrespect—" I said.

"Do you see that dog down there?" the duke asked, interrupting me. He pointed to a barking dog at the bottom of one of the tapestries, which seemed to be chasing after a soldier on horseback who was departing the scene. "Look at his feet. He has hooves instead of paws." His expression softened. "The weavers made a mistake. They had wo-ven so many horses in these tapestries that they forget they were weaving a dog until it was too late. How I laughed at this when I was a boy. But now there are times when I feel like that dog: running after a man on horseback, with clumsy hooves instead of paws, never catch-ing him." He reached over and gently touched a back leg. "No Churchill has ever had as illustrious a career as John Duke, did you know? And no Churchill ever will. My job, my *duty*, is to tend to his memory. We live here at Blenheim, but this house is not really ours. It belongs to a man I never knew, as repayment for accomplishments few remember today. My charge is simply to keep Blenheim intact so that I can pass it along to Bert. That little boy in the sculpture over there. He and his brother are up in London, you know. Consuelo spoils them, you see, shamelessly—especially Ivor, the younger one. I used to call her 'Nanny,' since she spent so much time in the nursery."

The duke related this without bitterness or rancor, as if the sentiments the words expressed had been long accepted. But from that gesture, that admission, I began to have an inkling of what the duke was trying to say. As a descendant of the first Duke of Marlborough, he was destined to chase his memory clumsily—like a dog with hooves, never quite catching it. I felt a glimmer of sympathy for the man.

The duke continued in a quieter voice, his tone wistful. "Did you know that I have been criticized for insisting that my guests wear white tie at table here? And that I sign my name 'Marlborough,' even in notes to my closest friends? I know people laugh at me. But they do not understand that we in certain stations must maintain the proper degree of dignity." He adjusted the fall of one of the draperies. "Sometimes that is all there is.

"The only other person who appreciates Blenheim the way I do is Winston. That is why he and I get on. He understands. But I am not clever like Winston, or Sargent. I am a plodder—a blockhead, my father called me. But I can bring Blenheim back to glory. I know it." There was a conviction to his voice that was impressive.

"If this room is any guide, you have succeeded," I said.

The duke looked about appraisingly. "It is gratifying work, but it is a damned expensive place to bring back. My father let everything go, you see, so I have had much to do. That, really, is why I married Consuelo. To shore up the foundations, as it were. What is the matter?"

I must have looked shocked at his frankness, for the duke emitted a shrill laugh. "Do not look so scandalized, man. Neither Consuelo nor I labor under the pretense that we married for anything but expediency. I needed capital, she needed to escape from her mother, so we each of us mortgaged our future for our immediate present."

I swallowed. "I must confess that I am a little taken aback by what you say."

The duke patted my shoulder. "There, there, old man, buck up. She and I are both quite forthright about it, I assure you. Do not concern yourself: We will all muddle through. It is what we do, you know." Whether the duke was referring to his family, his class, or his countrymen, I could not tell.

He displayed no embarrassment at his revelations; on the contrary, they seemed to propel him into the happiest frame of mind I had seen in him since we arrived. Far from dismissing me from his presence, he entreated me to remain: "You have not seen the other treasures in this room," he said. He walked over to a low chest with a curved front that stood to the left of the fireplace and looked as if its two drawers were about to explode. The warm honey-colored front was complemented by complex inlays of both darker and lighter woods that formed a diamond pattern on each side. "They are French commodes. Rather magnificent examples, I understand. Have two of them." He indicated its twin against the far wall. "The old bitch, Duchess Lily, used to leave the bottom drawer of this one open so her damned spaniels could nap there." The duke shook his head in disgust.

I frowned. "Was Duchess Lily your mother?"

"Good Lord, no. She was my father's second wife. An American. Only thing heavier than her moustache was her purse." He laughed unpleasantly. "Worth a fortune," he said.

It took a moment for me to regain my voice, as my throat had seized in indignation at his insensitive remark. "Not all American women are so ill-favored," I said.

"Of course not," the duke said, waving one small hand at me with impatience. But his denial was hollow, as he next words revealed. "But the truth is the truth. She would never be a true duchess or a true Churchill."

It was then that I realized that the duke's true love, his enduring passion, was not for any one person—certainly not for the duchess— but for this house, this dark, brooding quarry of stone. I smiled at the thought, and my heart beat more quickly. I was ashamed to admit my relief, even to myself, but my feelings would not be denied. They were too strong; they lingered so enticingly. I was glad the duke did not love his wife.

"And you must see what has been done in here." He pushed his hand firmly against my back and guided me into the next room, which was smaller than the others and served as a lobby to the Long Library beyond. It was an ornate, garish chamber, the decoration overpowering its relative compactness. The paneled walls were painted a dusky green and were edged with gilded garlands and cherub faces, a pattern that was continued up into the moldings, at the corners of the coved ceiling, and on the ceiling itself. The room was full of elaborately ornamental furniture, including two ebony chests, which stood before a large tapestry commemorating another Marlborough victory. The chests were adorned with three solemn faces affixed to their fronts and were bound into a complex design wrought in gold metal work. Each chest was displayed on its own stand, also decorated in a fussy French style, the four legs curving in wavelike arcs to the parquet floor.

"I call this the Boulle Room, because of the furniture, of course," the duke said with obvious pride. He did not elaborate on what "Boulle" was. "When my father was duke, this room was a complete muddle. It was one of the first rooms I changed after I married."

He cast an eye toward the carpet and his attention was caught by a faded rosette. He traced the small flower with the toe of a well-polished shoe. "Grandfather used this room only at Christmas, for the children to unwrap their gifts in, away from the tree in the Hall and the adults. He said it was the easiest room to tidy up, as it was the smallest state room." He frowned. When he spoke again, his voice was quieter, as if he were far away.

"There is a story that my father once struck Duchess Lily. They were in the Long Library talking—you could see them through the open doors—but they were too far away for anyone to hear. She said something to him, and he just slapped her face. He walked away without saying anything, right past me." He paused, and his eyes misted. "Odd, isn't it? I never saw him express anything more than indifference toward anyone else—except his old mistress, of course. Lady Colen Campbell. She could always make him smile. But he was wrapped up inside himself completely. He paid no attention to anyone or to anything except his own desires. Extraordinary, really."

I hardly knew what to say. "I suppose," I said.

My voice startled the duke back to the present. He looked at me in surprise, his expression anxious.

"What's that? What are you saying?"

"Nothing," I replied as a small idea was taking root in my mind. "I suspect these rooms are beautiful when you entertain," I said.

"Splendid," he said with satisfaction. "There is a good promenade between the library and the Saloon. What Winston calls an enfilade. That is French." He almost preened in satisfaction.

"How many people can you entertain here?"

"No idea, really. Hundreds, I suppose. Never counted them. Consuelo knows all that. She is the one who organizes all the parties, once I have determined when they will be."

"Tell me," I said, "has Lord Rake ever been to Blenheim?"

"Who?" the duke asked.

"Lord Rake."

The duke did not answer my question directly. "What makes you ask of him?"

"I came across his name recently."

"Well, he does not travel in my circle, of that there is no doubt," the duke said. A clock in the next room struck the hour. "Good Lord, is that the time?" he said suddenly. "I am to meet—"

He looked up to see the butler announce, "Your Grace, Her Grace wishes to see you, in the chapel, on a matter of some urgency."

"Urgency? What urgency? We have had prayers already."

"Yes, Your Grace," the butler said with practiced gravity. "But I believe that there is a matter of an odor."

"An odor?" the duke repeated.

"Yes, Your Grace."

"Where the hell is it coming from?"

"I understand that the likely source is the crypt, Your Grace." The butler, a man of profound fastidiousness, clearly was distressed to be the bearer of such information.

"The crypt?" the duke said. "I do not understand."

"No, Your Grace," the butler said.

"What the devil can I do?" the duke asked.

"I cannot say, Your Grace," the butler said. He stood his ground, his very presence an unspoken reminder of the request the duchess had made to her husband.

And after a moment the duke relented. "Oh, very well," he said. "I suppose I will go see what the devil is going on. Tell Her Grace I will be there presently."

"Very good, Your Grace," the butler said, withdrawing.

As soon as I heard this, I resolved to find the room in which the duke and Emily had argued. With the duke occupied at the other end of the palace, I knew I would have ample time to search it thoroughly. I had grown more troubled as I pondered the letters, a suspicion I could not name taking root and spreading like a weed, fertilized by the disconcerting sense that the duke was up to something. I was confused and uncertain, but I was determined to bring to light the truth, for I was convinced that it was the only way to protect the duchess. Each guest I met, each discovery I came upon, bewildered me further, just as the shadows that hung about Blenheim grew darker and the slanting light weakened. I needed some time alone to arrange my thoughts.

But the duke had other plans for me. "Come along, Vanbrugh," he said. "This might be just your thing."

"But Your Grace—"

"Nonsense, you can go to your room in a few minutes. You might be useful in the chapel. Architecture is your line, after all."

"But I am not an expert at that kind of work, if there really is an odor." I stopped, unsure what I was saying.

The duke frowned. "Oh, come, come. It will not take long. And besides, your duchess needs you." He forced a laugh, and I felt my cheeks suddenly get hot.

I blurted out, "She is not my duchess, she is yours."

The duke stopped laughing. "Of course she is not your duchess," he snapped. "She never will be. Now come along."

I looked at him, shocked, and tried to keep the revulsion from my face. His tone, his bearing, his very *being,* proclaimed that he thought my comment foolish, even puerile—the protest of a mouse in a land of giants. His certainty that he *possessed* his wife—nicely mounted and framed for all the world to see, like the duchess in Browning's poem— was appalling. I wanted to tell him that he did not own Her Grace, but he had the same heady arrogance of the poetic duke. I felt a sharp and pointed hatred for this unworthy man.

We walked to the chapel in silence, traversing first the Long Library, past the enormous pipe organ that dominated the north end, and then along an open colonnade arcade that overlooked the Great Court and all of its disorder. The chapel door was the first door along the wall to our left, and it was open to the narrow landing from which two gray stone stairways, mirror images of each other, snaked down to the chapel below.

It was a high, constraining room whose walls, painted a dingy yellow, were decorated with narrow white pilasters topped by flamboyant Corinthian capitals. The tall, clear windows, nearly twenty feet high and at the level of the door we entered, had been opened as wide as possible, and the chirping of birds and the occasional bleat of a lamb could be heard through them. The floor, like that of the Great Hall, was a series of white marble octagons with small black marble diamonds inlaid between them. Against the wall to our right, in a shallow niche, stood a mammoth, heavy memorial to the first duke and duchess. Carved in white marble and carrying a baton, the duke was depicted as a Roman general, while the duchess, seated beside him to his left, gazed up at him for eternity. Two cherubic boys attended them. The entire group perched precariously on a tapered ledge of white marble in front of a triangular backdrop of veined black marble. Two angels, one holding a quill pen, the other a trumpet, sat at the feet of the duke and duchess upon a dark stone sarcophagus too small to hold the cumbersome figures above it. Trapped below the sarcophagus, nearly crushed by it, was a winged dragon with a forked tongue that gazed up in envy. Seated in a pew across from this overpowering piece of funereal excess, looking insignificant by comparison, were the duchess and Mr. Churchill.

The room smelled acrid and sour, but as we climbed down the stairs the scent altered into something stronger, deeper, more noxious.

"What the devil is that smell?" the duke demanded.

"That is exactly what we are trying to find out," the duchess said, dabbing a handkerchief to her nose.

"I brought Vanbrugh along," the duke said. "Thought he could sort it out."

"You need an undertaker rather than an architect, Sunny," Mr. Churchill said.

"Why?" the duke asked.

"Putrefaction," Mr. Churchill replied with gusto.

"Winston thinks the bodies in the crypt have somehow been corrupted," the duchess said.

The duke looked aghast. "Corrupted? Impossible. Who has been mucking about down there?"

"No one has," the duchess said.

"Sometimes, Sunny, this sort of thing happens without human intervention," Mr. Churchill said.

"They cannot just pop out of a coffin," the duke scoffed.

"That is precisely what they can do," Mr. Churchill said. "If the bodies are not properly contained at the time of burial, gases build up."

"Gases?" the duke demanded. "There are no gases in the crypt. My father had this entire place electrified years ago."

Mr. Churchill and the duchess exchanged a look. "When a body decomposes, it emits certain gases," Mr. Churchill explained.

"There was a strange odor this morning at prayers, but nothing like this," the duchess said.

"This odor is coming from somewhere, and in all likelihood it will get worse unless we—unless you—do something, my lord." Mr. Churchill walked over to the far corner of the room, where a small trapdoor in the floor was located. It was unobtrusive, its top having been painted to match the rest of the floor. "Shall I?" he asked. Without waiting for either our approval or our censure, he bent down and with an energetic heave pulled at the door.

It did not move.

"Vanbrugh, your assistance, please," Mr. Churchill said.

I joined him, and together we managed to open the heavy trapdoor and were immediately accosted by a stench of such overpowering corrosion and decay that the four of us, as one, recoiled. Mr. Churchill gasped, and the duchess looked as if she might be overcome. Only the duke maintained his composure, choosing to cover his nose and mouth with his hand, rather than a kerchief.

For a terrible moment there was silence as the horror of decomposition overcame us. Finally, Mr. Churchill, with an effort, slammed the trapdoor closed. The bang sounded like a clap of thunder, and the echo reverberated around the room, momentarily smashing the odor out of our senses. With the cloth still at his nose Mr. Churchill returned to the group, his eyes red but merry. He sat down next to the duchess and said, "Rather a lesson in the impermanence of mankind."

With the trapdoor closed, the odor was a bit less repulsive, so after a moment we were able to converse again without the need for masks.

"Did you see anything, Winston?" the duchess asked.

"It was too dark and I was not inclined to linger," Mr. Churchill said. "It could be any one of them, I suppose."

"Never mind that," the duke said. "Who should we get to sort this out?"

"Hanson from Oxford, I think," Mr. Churchill said. "He is quite the hand at this sort of thing, having confronted the inconvenient return of the collegial dead with some regularity."

The duke pursed his lips. "Hanson? Never heard of him. Expensive chap, is he?"

The duchess said, "I would have thought that speed is more important here than economy. The prime minister is coming in a week."

"I am well aware of my calendar," the duke snapped.

"Perhaps Barton knows Hanson," Mr. Churchill suggested.

"Mr. Barton will be at dinner tonight. You can ask him then," the duchess said.

The duke frowned. "He will be at dinner *again*? The man *lives* here."

The duchess offered me a small smile of apology. "I thought it might be pleasant for our guests," she said. "Mrs. Vanbrugh is Mr. Barton's daughter."

"What? Oh, all right. Barton. Yes. I will inquire of him." The duke consulted his watch. "Is that all? I am off." And without further comment, he departed.

As the sound of the duke's footsteps faded, Mr. Churchill stood up and turned to the duchess. "I am sorry about the stench, old girl. I had no idea that it would be so strong." He helped the duchess to her feet.

The duchess rose. "Oh, that is all right," she said, looking pale. "I am far too squeamish for my own good."

"You do all right for yourself." He smiled.

"With your help from time to time," the duchess said in an indulgent tone. "I did not know the mortal residue of death could startle me so much."

"It would startle anyone," I said.

"No, I am too shielded from the world," the duchess replied. "I need to confront unpleasantness more often."

"I would say you confront more than your share of unpleasantness, my dear," Mr. Churchill said quietly.

The duchess looked grateful, but said nothing. Then with a courtly gentleness, Mr. Churchill offered the duchess his arm. She took it gratefully, and gently leaned her head against his. With his free hand he stroked her cheek, just once. She closed her eyes, as if remembering, as Mr. Churchill guided her up the stairway, I followed close behind, troubled by this unexpected display of affection for Mr. Churchill.

We returned to the house along the route the duke had taken me, Mr. Churchill and the duchess conversing amiably about this and that. I said nothing but noted the sympathy each had for the other; they seemed to like each other genuinely. The duchess, with her long, graceful neck and natural charm, was a far cry from the hunched shoulders and chafing intensity of Mr. Churchill. But each took pleasure in the other, and I found myself jealous of him.

During a pause in their conversation the duchess turned to me. "And how have your endeavors been progressing, Mr. Vanbrugh?"

"I have made significant progress, Your Grace," I said.

She cocked her head, as a bird might. "Really. So quickly?"

"What renovations are you proposing?" Mr. Churchill asked.

"I hardly know. I have scarcely begun," I said.

Mr. Churchill looked puzzled. "But you just said you have made progress."

Quick to deflect his inquiries, the duchess said, "What Mr. Vanbrugh means, Winston, is that he has begun the process of pulling down."

"It has been my experience with architects that they plan first, then pull down," Mr. Churchill said.

"That is normally true, but not this time," I said.

"Why not?"

I turned to the duchess for help.

"Because I asked him to," she said. "I could not stand that wallcovering one moment more. It made me positively bilious."

Mr. Churchill chuckled—a low, throaty rumbling. "Tell Sunny that. He was of the opinion that green flattered beautiful women."

"If that is the case, then I am most definitely not in that category," the duchess said.

We had arrived at the Great Hall, where the duchess removed a wilted flower from the center of the flower arrangement that stood on one of the tables. "I have always understood that beauty is in the eye of the beholder, not the upholsterer," she said.

"I agree," Mr. Churchill said. "I hope, Mr. Vanbrugh, that you will make Her Grace as lovely in her rooms as she is in the world."

"Winston, you are being absurd," the duchess said.

"Certainly I will try my best," I said.

"Capital," Mr. Churchill said.

"Mr. Vanbrugh has done wonders already, even by just removing the wallcovering," the duchess said.

"Is that all you have done?" Mr. Churchill said. "From all of your talk, I had visions of scaffolding everywhere and Mr. Vanbrugh lying on his back under the ceiling, madly painting frescoes of divinities, cursing the Catholic pope."

The duchess puckered her lips. "It is not the ceiling I am concerned about. Winston. It is down where we Protestants dwell."

"Of course," Mr. Churchill said. "Tell me, Vanbrugh, how do you find the rooms?"

"They have a great deal of potential," I replied.

"Do they, indeed? How marvelous for you, Consuelo," Mr. Churchill said.

"I think this will prove to be a very rewarding task," I said.

Mr. Churchill eyed me speculatively. "Rewarding. Yes, I see," He glanced at the duchess.

I understood the implication of his comment, and I replied quickly. "Mr. Churchill, I was not speaking of monetary rewards. I have no plans to make my fortune here at Blenheim. For me, much of the reward is the work. To modernize such a piece of history—"

"Which your ancestor designed so excellently," Mr. Churchill interjected.

"If you like," I agreed. "That is a rare pleasure for any architect."

"I have long been fascinated by architecture—especially here at Blenheim," Mr. Churchill said. "It is a happy marriage of art and engineering that improves as it endures."

"Though it has too few bathrooms, the central heating cannot begin to ease the chill, and the girls in Housemaids' Heights have no running water," the duchess said.

"Progress takes time, Consuelo," Mr. Churchill said. "Minds have to come around to new ideas."

"Where is Housemaids' Heights?" I asked.

"In the attic, above the family wing," the duchess replied. "My husband refuses to let me modernize the servants' quarters. So the maids live much as they did in the eighteenth century. It is unconscionable."

"They are used to it," Mr. Churchill said.

"They should not have to be," the duchess said.

Mr. Churchill shrugged. "Perhaps."

"Your Grace," I said, as we reached the door to the family dining room, "if I might ask you to take a look at one or two items in your rooms that are of interest..."

The duchess looked inquiringly at Mr. Churchill, who gazed at me with renewed interest. "What did you come across in your labors?" he asked.

"I...really think that the duchess should see it first," I said.

"A mysterious discovery," Mr. Churchill said. "The intrigue deepens." He said this lightly, but there was curiosity behind it.

"Winston, do you mind?" the duchess asked.

"Not at all, you two go along," he said. He cast a long look at me before he lumbered down the hall, pulling out a cigar as he did.

"What have you discovered?" she asked as we settled into two chairs at the window. I handed her the letters, which she took and read them quickly.

"They appear to be love letters," I said.

"They certainly are," the duchess replied, folding them up.

"Do you know Lord Rake or Mrs. Freeman?" I asked.

The duchess shook her head. "No." She thought for a moment. "Mr. Vanbrugh, could you show me where you found these?"

I unrolled the fabric so that the duchess could see the pouches in which the letters had been stored.

"There is a premeditation to this that is rather extraordinary," the duchess said.

"Maybe knowing who Mrs. Freeman and Lord Rake are will help," I offered.

She studied the fabric again and fingered one of the pouches.

"I did notice that the pouches seem to be sewn differently," I said.

"What do you mean?" she asked.

I indicated the first pouch I had discovered. "Here. This one is sewn tightly, but the second one I came across is sewn more loosely, and on the third the stitches are even more slapdash."

The duchess examined each pouch carefully, fingering the stitches. "That is very observant of you, Mr. Vanbrugh," she said, a note of respect in her voice.

"I am a draftsman, Your Grace. My livelihood is to attend to the details. Though I wish I knew why the letter was there in the first place."

The duchess turned to face me. "Why, to conceal them," she said.

"Why not just burn them?" I asked. "Surely that is the easiest way to keep a secret."

She nodded and with the letters still in her hand walked back to the chairs by the window. "Whom have you told about these?" she asked.

"No one," I said, sitting down.

The duchess reopened one of the letters and scanned it. She sighed and threw it onto the table. "I suppose I must tell my husband about them."

My heart sank a little at this, but I did not reply—though my face must have expressed my regret because the duchess said: "You object to that, I see."

"It is not for me to object to anything," I said. "The letters are not mine."

"True, but you did discover them," she said. "You should have a say in how they are dealt with. I must admit, Mr. Vanbrugh, I did not expect you to discover anything like this when I asked you to continue your search. I do not know what I expected, but certainly not these." She held up the letters. "I have an idea. Someone should make a copy of each letter to prevent something untoward from happening."

"I already have," I said, taking out the copies I had made.

The duchess looked surprised. "Mr. Vanbrugh, you are a man of imagination." She paused. "I very much want to know more about them before I do anything. Perhaps they reveal something about the past that will be useful." A low gong sounded and the duchess reached for her watch brooch. "It is time for tea," she said. "We are in the Saloon today."

"What? That is all?" I asked. "Shouldn't we decide on a course of action?"

"I will preside over tea and think carefully about what you have discovered," the duchess said. "I must have a definite idea of what I— we—should do." At that, she leaned toward me unexpectedly and kissed me—a light sweet kiss that sent my heart racing. "To battle, Sir Knight," she whispered, pulling me toward the door.

chapter

7

THE kiss—that startling kiss—had roused in me emotions I could not ignore. I was both bewildered and delighted; the kiss had stirred feelings in me I never knew I had. It was as if a dam had ruptured, flooding me with relief, fear, and an unexpected passion. I reveled in this emotional liberty, and the more I did, the greater was my desire to pursue the duchess. I knew this giddiness was wrong, but it seemed natural to acknowledge it and I did not want to resist it. But the hectoring specter of Margaret, my *wife*, could not be banished for long. She was as omnipresent—and as increasingly unwelcome—in my thoughts as she had been lately in our flat, and as I moved along the corridor with the duchess, I felt a growing distaste for Margaret and her selfish, narrow-minded attitudes. Something would have to be done.

Tea was served in the tall Saloon, but it was an unwelcoming apartment, austere despite its opulence. The long table, polished to a deep sheen, was bare, as if no one were expected, and the marble, gilt-legged serving tables near the windows held two large arrangements of flowers—though the apron and gardening gloves the duchess had left on one of them had been removed. A small tea table was arranged in front of one of the fireplaces. It was a simple, even meager tea: finger sandwiches and a collection of confections from the kitchens. There were several silver teapots near the cups. Jamison, frowning, stood in one corner near a nervous-looking housemaid, who was whispering madly at him. When the duchess entered, the maid rushed toward her, curtsied, and whispered something.

"Not again," the duchess said, irritated. The maid nodded, and Jamison stiffened. "His Grace will have none of it. He made a special point of asking for Emily. Tell her to pull herself together and come down."

The maid looked at Jamison and was about to say something more but thought better of it. Curtseying quickly, she murmured, "Yes, Your Grace," and left the room.

The duchess motioned for me to sit down in one of the chairs, which was uncomfortable and creaked when I settled into it. Picking up one of the teapots, to my surprise she poured out a cup of coffee, handing it to me.

"Is Emily ill?" I asked.

"I do not understand what has come over her. She is usually a steady, reliable girl. But lately she has been prone to hysterics for no reason she can give."

At that moment Miss Deacon and Margaret appeared on the terrace, having returned from their walk. The exercise had done Miss Deacon much good: Her cheeks were pink, and there was a new sparkle to her eyes. But Margaret looked pale and agitated, and she reached for my hand to steady herself as she sat down next to me.

"What is wrong?" I asked as I tried to pull away my hand.

"Nothing," Margaret said in a hoarse whisper, clutching my hand more tightly. "Everything."

"How was your walk?" the duchess asked Miss Deacon, as Jamison reappeared with another maid who was not Emily.

"Marvelous," Miss Deacon replied with enthusiasm. "We walked to the Grand Cascade and got to know one another."

"Tea, Mrs. Vanbrugh?" the duchess asked.

"Please," Margaret said quietly, her voice shaky. She let go of my hand and held out both of hers to take the thin saucer, as if she mistrusted her grip on it.

"We have become intimates, Mr. Vanbrugh, your wife and I," Miss Deacon said, settling into her chair and smiling. "She now knows all of my secrets and I know all of hers."

Margaret sat motionless, gazing down at the teacup in her lap.

"It must have been a disturbing conversation for you, Mrs. Van-brugh," the duchess said after a moment. "Pay no attention to Miss Deacon. She fabricates most of what she says and does not believe the rest herself."

Margaret looked at the duchess quizzically, as if she did not quite understand what had been said.

"Oh, never mind that," Miss Deacon said impatiently. "I have discovered something quite extraordinary, Consuelo. Mrs. Vanbrugh is satisfactorily married."

The duchess blinked in surprise. "That is indeed an unusual bit of news," she said dryly. "Would you care for a sandwich, Mrs. Van-brugh?"

Margaret shook her head.

Miss Deacon selected a small biscuit from a plate and nibbled at it daintily, as a dove might pick at the remains of a goldfish. "You will never guess where she revealed such heresy."

"No doubt you will tell us, Gladys," the duchess said.

"She told me at the most romantic spot at Blenheim."

"Rosamond's Well," the Duchess said.

"The Temple of Diana, of course. Is that not perfect?" Miss Deacon beamed, and the three of us turned to Margaret. Her head was still bowed, her attention directed at her tea.

Mr. Churchill and Mr. Sargent both joined the party at that moment. Their presence agitated Margaret further. She set her teacup down on the table and rose unsteadily to her feet. "Van, I am unwell. Would you take me to my room?"

"If you like," I said, as eager to be done with this conversation as she was.

"Your walk was too rigorous," the duchess said. "Gladys has over-exerted you."

Margaret nodded and leaned against me as we moved slowly out of the room. As we went out into the hall the duchess said, "Gladys, for heaven's sake, show some compassion. The poor woman has never met the likes of you."

"And I have never met the likes of her, I assure you." She laughed. "I do so enjoy being wicked."

Margaret and I proceeded slowly up the shallow stairs, pausing at each landing to make sure that Margaret could continue. We did not speak, allowing the somber silence of the house to engulf us. The voices in the Saloon below grew faint as we climbed; soon all we could hear was the occasional laugh of Mr. Churchill as he responded to some unheard riposte.

When we gained the bedroom floor, Margaret seemed to deflate: The control she had exhibited evaporated, and the nearer we came to our rooms, the less strength she had. Halfway down the passage she collapsed, and I had to carry her the rest of the way. She leaned her head into my shoulder and gave way to her anguish, sobbing uncontrollably. I opened the door and whisked her into her room, laying her onto her bed. I loosened her clothing and poured water into the basin, dipping a cloth into some water and placing it on her forehead. I said nothing, feeling that it would be better for Margaret to cry a little than to struggle to control. I rang for Emily; I hoped a few sips of strong tea or brandy might soothe Margaret. After several minutes, Margaret regained enough of her composure to speak.

"Oh, Van, it was terrible. Dreadful."

I kneeled down next to the bed and took her hand. "What was?" I asked.

"She is a devil, Van. A demon. I cannot bear to see her again."

"What happened?"

"I do not know," she moaned. "We started out well enough. She suggested that we walk to the lake, that there was a pretty prospect, a cascade of some sort. I was willing enough, I suppose, fool that I was. As she walked, she took my arm and began asking me questions about—well, about everything, I suppose, but mostly about you. At least at first. How long had I known you before we married, how had you adapted to living in England, what were my ambitions for you and your career."

"How did you reply?" •

"I said that you are a fine architect whose talents and abilities are more highly valued here in England than they were in America, and that we were well pleased with your prospects and our situation. She said that it was a very great coup for you to become acquainted with the duchess, that her patronage would guarantee you success. Then she asked me if it disturbed me that the duchess has taken such an interest in you."

"I would hardly call it an interest," I said, biting my lip.

"I told her that I was flattered the duchess had engaged you," Margaret continued. "She nodded and said that flattery was always the first step."

"The first step to what?"

"She did not say, not then. She then asked me about Father. How long had he had the living at Long Hanborough, how had he become acquainted with the duchess, did he find her to be a woman of upstanding reputation. Really, most disquieting questions."

"They sound more than disquieting. They sound presumptuous. What could have been her purpose?"

"I asked her why she wanted to know all this. She said that the duchess had been her friend for many years and that she was very interested in her welfare."

"I do not think that Miss Deacon needs to concern herself with the welfare of the Duchess of Marlborough," I said.

"Then she said that it was her belief that Father . . . improper thoughts about the duchess," Margaret said haltingly and burst into a new round of weeping.

I was outraged—as angered by the grotesque impertinence of Miss Deacon as I was shamed by my own indiscretion. I did not know a man of higher moral reputation or honesty than my father-in-law; he was the least likely man in England to commit adultery. Why she should put forth such an insolent idea to the daughter of a respectable clergyman, a woman whose acquaintance she only recently made, I could only speculate. It certainly did not reflect well on the character or the manners of Miss Deacon; her comment about the enjoyment she drew from being wicked seemed all too apt.

As I calmed Margaret, the shock I felt dissipated somewhat as my anger grew—a fury at Miss Deacon and her willful rudeness.

"I hope you told her exactly what you thought of her and her question," I said fiercely.

Margaret shook her head. "I was so surprised I did not know what to say. I replied that my father was a man of rigorous character, and that he would never entertain such thoughts toward a married woman, least of all the duchess."

"Good."

"But Miss Deacon laughed at that. Surely, she said, I knew that all men were weak when it came to the female sex, and it was that knowledge that was the greatest weapon we woman possessed."

"Weapon?"

"For luring men."

"The woman is preposterous," I cried in indignation. "The duchess would no more lure your father into an entanglement than she would . . ." I paused to think of an unlikely example.

"You?" Margaret asked in a soft voice.

"Me? What are you talking about?"

"Miss Deacon said that the duchess has designs on you. She said that can be the only explanation for her hiring an architect of no reputation to remodel Blenheim unless she had a secret motive. She said the duchess is falling in love with you."

I could not reply immediately. My vision had blurred, and there was a tremendous roar in my ears, like the burst of laughter from a thousand throats. Margaret seemed very far away suddenly, receding from me as if she had fallen into a deep hole. But I didn't care. My heart leapt in exultation. Improper and improbable though it was, I liked the idea that the Duchess of Marlborough was in love with me. And I returned her affection.

Absently I smoothed a section of the bedspread, a rich emerald-green cover embroidered with golden fleurs-de-lys that felt a trifle damp. "What a thing to say," I replied, my voice hoarse. "How completely ridiculous."

Margaret looked relieved. "I know. But Miss Deacon insisted it was true. She said she had never seen the duchess so taken with a man. Not even with the duke."

I blushed. "It is not our business how the duchess regards the duke. Miss Deacon is being very forward."

"She became even more so," Margaret said, sitting up a little. She had stopped crying and some of her color had returned. "She inquired if she could reveal a confidence to me. We had come to that temple building and were sitting on the stone bench there, watching the swans on the lake. It was very peaceful, but her request made me uneasy, so I did not answer. That was of no importance, for in her next breath she asked me if I thought that desire was at the core of our humanity. Such a question! I told her I thought that goodness, not desire, was the essence of man. She smiled at that and said that it had been her experience we humans always long for what we do not have."

Margaret stopped and put her hand in mine, which trembled like a frightened sparrow. "And then...and then she admitted that she had long resolved to marry only a nobleman. No one else would do. 'A great English lord,' she said. That was why she had not yet married. She said that she had finally enticed a man from a great family with a large estate, and that this man had fallen in love with her and wanted to marry her."

"She should marry this doddering fool and disappear into the countryside immediately so we can forget all about her."

"But as she spoke, she had the oddest expression on her face," Margaret continued. "I think she wanted me to understand something more than just the words she was saying, that they had a deeper meaning."

"She should have told you outright."

"I think she wanted me to draw a conclusion, Van—something even she could not admit out loud. When I congratulated her on finding her ideal mate she said, 'But it is not settled. He is definitely not ideal, and there is an impediment to my marrying him.'"

"What kind of impediment?" I asked.

"It seems he is already married. To one of her friends."

"Good Lord," I exclaimed. "The fool."

Margaret, more composed, now relished the telling of her story. "You do not understand. I think Miss Deacon was trying to tell me that the Duke of Marlborough wants to marry her."

It took a moment for me to digest such a revolting suggestion. "That is impossible," I said. "Miss Deacon is too clever to admit such a thing to a complete stranger."

"That does not matter to Miss Deacon. She said that she would cheerfully bear anything to marry this man."

"And to become Duchess of Marlborough. Her audacity is without equal. The woman is a virago."

Margaret nodded and leaned back against the pillow. "I think I would like to sleep a little now," she said quietly.

"Good girl," I said, relieved. I covered her with a light shawl. "I will go and see if I can find out what has become of Emily. I rang for her ages ago."

As I rose to go Margaret asked, "Van, are all American girls as forward as Miss Deacon?"

"No. Most American girls are not like that at all. Look at the Duchess," I said.

"Yes," Margaret said, satisfied.

Smiling to myself, I reached the door and ventured into the passage, which was quiet. The available light was waning, and the growing afternoon shadows crept along the walls like roots burrowing into the soil. I went and stood on the main stairway and then the service stair, hoping to catch a glimpse of Emily. But I saw no one. The only sound I could make out was the low hum of tea in the Saloon.

I turned and passed the door to the room in which I suspected Emily and the Duke had argued. The door was not closed tightly, I noticed; a slim sliver of light escaped from the room. I pushed it open and entered.

The room, furnished as a bedroom, was empty, though it was definitely being employed—as a painting studio, from the looks of it. The bed and its accompanying furniture had been moved to the far wall and had been covered by large tarpaulins. To the right was the wall of three windows, their draperies having been removed and folded haphazardly and placed on the floor next to the bed. They were replaced by diaphanous white gauze, which allowed light to filter through but prevented anyone from seeing into the room from the other three sides of the courtyard. At the far end of the room next to the windows a dais had been assembled. It was a raised platform covered by a dark carpet upon which a settee upholstered in a velvet of deep purple had been positioned to take advantage of the light. A silk robe of vivid aqua and yellow lay discarded across one arm of the settee. In front of the dais, standing on the floor, was a portable easel; attached to it were large pieces of coarse paper. Piled around the low stool that stood in front of it were dozens of black sketchbooks of varying sizes and thicknesses. There were no paints, but strewn about were a great many pencils, pieces of charcoal, and gum erasers. The room smelled slightly of wood smoke and linseed oil. There were sketches everywhere—most of them nothing more than a jumbled series of curving lines. However, when I opened a sketchbook at random, I encountered more considered studies of shape and shadow, culminating in a series of studies of the duke and his two young children, both boys.

This room, it was apparent, was employed by Mr. Sargent as a makeshift studio, and he had settled in comfortably enough. I looked about the room as a breeze feathered the curtains and fluttered some of the papers. As I moved to retrieve them, my eye caught a small pile of paper peeking out from under the folded curtains. Intrigued, I pulled them out. They were also sketches, but were more finished renderings, and were a series of a reclining, unclad female form. These drawings of a torso, legs, and arms—no head had been included—were of such gorgeous detail and delicate sophistication that they could have been drawn only from life. There was a tranquil beauty to them, a dreamy femininity unhindered by modesty or propriety; these were sketches of a woman who felt at ease with herself—and with the artist. I wondered who among the acquaintances of Mr. Sargent would have the composure to sit for what most people would think of as a very shocking series of studies. Perhaps he had employed a young woman whose own artistic enthusiasms would abet such an abandonment of decorum. But any surcease of virtue had not been in vain: The drawings were exquisite. In them, he had captured the sensual nature and appealing roundness of the womanly form, and had imbued the sketches with a warmth for the subject that was quite personal and very provocative. I gazed at them without embarrassment, for they did not incite it: They were a celebration of the body, rather than an invitation to depravity. If Mr. Sargent preferred the company of young men, these were truly extraordinary—a gift from an artist to his subject.

I was not looking long at the sketches before I began to hear fragments of an argument nearby. I replaced the drawings quickly and, opening the door, peered out into the corridor. I saw no one, but from the passage the argument was more distinct. I walked toward the noise, careful to keep myself hidden as best I could, until I reached the landing of the back stairway. The argument, it was clear, was taking place above me, on the servants' floor.

"How thoroughly have you searched?" the duke demanded, agitated.

"I didn't see it, I swear," Emily said, her voice cracking. I climbed a few steps, and by leaning gently over the balustrade and looking up, I was able to see them both without them being aware of my presence. The duke looked flushed; Emily defeated.

"Did you look in his bedroom?" the duke asked.

"And his studio. There was nothing. I promise you."

"Damn him. They must be somewhere. You have not taken them, have you?"

"No," Emily wailed. "I told you, I've never seen them. Never."

"Keep your voice down," the duke ordered, "or you will be in as much trouble as your mistress is if those pictures are not recovered."

"Her Grace never mentioned no pictures," Emily managed before she began to cry.

"Stop it, you little fool," the duke demanded, his voice terrifying in its intensity. He pushed her down onto a step and leaned over her menacingly. "Get hold of yourself."

Emily fell silent, struggling to regain control as she hiccuped between her sniffles.

"Now listen to me very carefully," the duke said. "Sargent is tearing this place apart to find his sketchbook. I want to know why. I *must* know why. So keep looking, and come to me, not Her Grace, the instant you find it—or remember where it is. And if I find out you have breathed a word of this to the duchess or to anyone else, I will sack you and that worthless beau of yours with no references. Do you understand? Good. Now stand up and get back to work. Remember, search everywhere. In all the bedrooms. Perhaps he gave it to that fool Vanbrugh. That would be typical of Sargent."

I crept down the stairs as quietly as I could and headed back to my room.

That the duke was so anxious, even desperate, to locate the sketchbook was evident. That he was willing to go to any lengths, to ignore morality and judgment, to possess it was frightening. He was consumed by a desire to procure the sketchbook. Why? What was in it? What did he plan to do with it?

I heard a chuckle behind me, and I whirled around. But there was no one there. The corridor was empty, silent once again.

MARGARET was still asleep when I returned to our rooms. Watching her steady, peaceful breathing made me realize how drained I felt, and the thought of slumber was powerfully appealing. I lay down on the bed in my room and willed myself to relax. But sleep would not come; the events of the day were too disturbing. So after several minutes of struggling to clear my mind and failing, I rose and fell into a chair. A maid earlier had opened one of the windows nearby, and a light breeze teased the draperies, rippling them into a lively undulation.

The sun was easing over the western paddocks, casting lazy rays on the fields. The only sounds that reached me were the questioning bleat of a lost lamb searching for its mother and the occasional shouts of the workmen in the Great Court on the other side of the palace. Evening was approaching slowly, as it does in England in summer, and the countryside slipped into the soothing rhythms of the night.

Despite the tranquillity around me, I was agitated; I could not understand the events of the day. The discovery of the letters and the identity of Lord Rake and Mrs. Freeman. The missing sketchbook and Mr. Sargent's distress. The duke and his behavior toward Emily. Miss Deacon and her inexpressible rudeness. And finally my triumph with a willing duchess.

The one thought I kept returning to, with a growing sense of anger and guilt, was the promise of the duchess's kiss. The thought that she found me appealing was powerfully flattering, beyond my wildest hopes. But coupled with this elation was a growing irritation at Margaret and her difficult personality. I wondered if she could ever make me truly happy.

I succumbed to the whirlpool of disturbing images and conversations of the past twenty-four hours, which rushed about me with a violence I could not escape. I knew I could not vanquish these thoughts, or even hope to make sense of them; I could only let them overwhelm me, drown me in their inevitability.

A duke with designs on a missing sketchbook owned by a famous painter, one of his houseguests. The duchess, *my* duchess, caught in a loveless marriage. Mysterious letters uncovered beneath wallcovering. A family friend with a waspish tongue who had her eye on the duke. The duchess's mother, who understood more about her daughter's marriage than she would admit. A Catholic priest whose actions intentionally struck fear in others. And Margaret, the querulous girl, an unknowing victim.

It was all a hopeless muddle, bemusing and frightening and glorious in equal parts.

The one detail I kept returning to was not a person or a situation but a name: my own. The presence of Sir John Vanbrugh at Blenheim was pervasive. Everyone at Blenheim were actors who moved across a stage concocted by Sir John, each player strutting and fretting and conniving as called for.

I was startled back to consciousness when a yawning Margaret asked from the doorway how long she had been asleep. To my surprise, it was almost seven o'clock—time to dress for dinner.

Margaret summoned Emily while I rang for Jamison, who arrived, dressed in formal Blenheim livery: white silk stockings, highly polished black shoes, and a powdered wig. With a quiet efficiency he arranged my toilet and assisted with my dinner clothes.

"Are any other guests expected tonight?" I asked as he helped straighten the white tie he had borrowed for me.

"Reverend Barton, sir," he said. He sounded distracted.

"Good," I said. "Mrs. Vanbrugh will be happy to see him. I think she is a little homesick already for Long Hanborough."

"Yes, sir," Jamison said, glancing at the now-closed door to Margaret's room as he helped me on with my dinner jacket.

At that moment Margaret, still in her dressing gown, flew into my room. "Van, I have rung and rung, but Emily is nowhere to be found." Jamison visibly stiffened, but he said nothing. Margaret turned to him. "Jamison, do you know where she could be? I am frantic. I will never be ready in time."

"I will inquire, ma'am," he said, turning to me as if to ask for permission to leave.

"By all means," I said. Jamison nodded and left.

"What an odd man," I said, more to myself than to Margaret.

"Why do you say that?" Margaret asked.

"He keeps so much inside," I said.

"He is a servant," Margaret said, as if that ended the discussion. She gazed at herself in my shaving mirror and rearranged her hair.

"He is clearly worried about Emily," I said.

"Is he?" she said, uninterested.

"Margaret," I admonished.

"I believe I shall wear my hair up this evening. To show off my neck. I have brought along the cameo you like so much, so that will be all right."

There was a knock at the door and a young servant I had not yet seen appeared. Poking her head into my room, she said, "Begging your pardon, ma'am, but I was sent to help you dress."

Margaret stared at her in surprise. "But I rang for Emily." The girl, who was plump and red-cheeked, could not have been more than seventeen.

"Dunno, madam," the girl said, curtseying slightly. "I was told to come."

"Is Emily all right?" I asked.

"Dunno, sir. No one knows where she is," the girl said.

"You mean she is lost?" I asked.

"Dunno, sir," the girl repeated.

"What is your name?" Margaret asked.

"Annie, ma'am."

I turned to Margaret and by a look asked if Annie would be an acceptable substitute for Emily. Margaret frowned as she tried to determine if she could tolerate the ministrations of an obviously untrained youngster for her first dinner at Blenheim.

"I cannot believe that Emily would just disappear," Margaret said. "Has anyone looked for her?"

"Yes, ma'am, Jamison, too. Even he couldna find her. He always knows where she is."

Margaret sighed as she left the room. "Oh, all right," she said. "Let us see how handy you are with a brush." Annie nodded and closed the door behind Margaret.

When Margaret returned half an hour later, she had been transformed. Her hair was adroitly arranged, and a small wreath of white roses circled a tight bun at the back of her head. The cameo decorated her neck to advantage, and its muted blue color complemented nicely the elegant white organdy gown with an overlay of Belgian lace along its square neckline and around her waist. A deep red shawl of moiré silk slipped off her shoulders and set off the bobs at her ears nicely, adding just the right touch of evening elegance.

"You are a confection," I said admiringly.

Margaret giggled. "Thank you."

The guests had gathered in the great bay of windows at the center of the library. The slanting light had recast the west-facing windows into panels of gold, dazzling the eye with an otherworldly shimmer. After a moment my eyes adjusted to the light, and to my pleasure the first face I settled on was that of my father-in-law, who embraced his daughter with as much affection as if he had not seen her for months instead of hours.

"How delightful, delightful to see you both, my dears," Barton said to us without artifice or embarrassment. "I am sure your stay has been agreeable." He lowered his voice. "Such an honor."

"An honor," I agreed. Margaret smiled but said nothing.

"Her Grace has just been telling me how pleased she is to have you both here," he said happily. "She has been full of compliments."

"She is most gracious," Margaret said.

"Splendid," Barton said. "Tell me, Van, how is the work coming? Your ideas have excited speculation, yes?" He looked at me with such faith that I almost laughed.

"It is early yet," I said. "Right now I am just trying to figure out what I have to work with."

The duchess must have heard me, for she came toward us. She looked enchanting, attired in a gown of ivory satin with a low neckline, high shoulders, and sleeves of delicate voile. The skirt was smooth with small butterflies delicately sewn through it, the ends of their antennae accented with tiny gemstones that caught the light. Around her neck was a flawless sapphire surrounded by diamonds. In her gloved hands she carried a fan of peacock feathers. "Mr. Vanbrugh has been working all day, removing the wall coverings so he can determine if the walls are still true."

"I am sure they are, they must be," Barton said with feeling. "This house was built to last forever."

"I thought only God was forever, Mr. Barton," the monsignor said, walking toward us.

"You play with me, Monsignor," Barton said.

"I do," he agreed, pressing his lips into a grudging smile. "You take it with such good humor that I cannot resist." The two men shook hands as the monsignor turned to Margaret. "Your hair is lovely tonight, Mrs. Vanbrugh."

"Emily has worked her magic again," the duchess said.

"Thank you, Monsignor," Margaret said, patting a curl near her ear. "Annie is not quite as experienced as Emily, but she managed."

"Did Annie assist you?" the duchess asked, surprised. "Where was Emily?"

"She never appeared, Your Grace," I said. "Annie indicated that no one could find her."

"I am not sure I understand," the duchess said slowly.

"That is what we were told," I said.

The duchess frowned and said, "You were? How strange. Would you excuse me a moment?"

She left our group and turned to the duke, who was standing with Mr. Sargent, who looked troubled. She whispered something to the duke, and a flash of irritation crossed his face. At that moment the butler announced dinner, and as a group we proceeded to the dining room, which had been simply but exquisitely arranged: A crisp linen tablecloth, two silver vases spilling over with white orchids; two tall bronze candelabra, their red candles covered with small opaque shades; the china rimmed in scarlet, turquoise, and gold; the myriad crystal wine glasses and sparkling silverware—all contributed to the beauty of the table.

As the footmen began to serve, Mr. Barton addressed the duke down the table by asking, with no trace of irony, "May I say grace, Your Grace?" Miss Deacon giggled at the naïve construction, and the Duke glowered at the suggestion.

"Monsignor, you do it," the duke said abruptly.

"Of course, I am so sorry, so sorry," Mr. Barton said, bowing his head as the monsignor murmured a prayer in Latin.

The meal was excellent, one of the best I have ever eaten. It began with a subtle but flavorful asparagus soup, was followed by a tender chicken supreme in a white wine sauce, a fresh salad of greens flavored with a tart vinaigrette, Russian charlotte served with perfectly ripe English strawberries, several excellent French cheeses, and was closed by delectable peaches and grapes newly picked from the Blenheim greenhouses. It was well served by the footmen who, like Jamison, were dressed in their more formal evening livery: maroon coats, silver-braided waistcoats, maroon plush breeches, flesh-colored stockings, silver-buckled shoes, and powdered wigs. The conversation, though congenial, was strained; I think we all sensed that our hosts were preoccupied. The duchess in particular had a distracted air, as if she were trying to eavesdrop on a conversation in another room. The duke barely touched his food; he sat in his chair across from his wife, scowling into his plate and twisting the small gold ring on his pinkie. He contributed to the conversation only briefly and at odd moments.

Both Mr. Churchill and Miss Deacon assumed the burden of amusing the table, relating stories of life in Paris. Miss Deacon—glittering in a gown of peach organza, with a low neckline that exposed her delicate shoulders and highlighted her exquisite complexion and lively eyes—asked if Mr. Sargent did not agree that life along the Seine was infinitely more congenial than life along the Thames.

"I am afraid I cannot agree," the painter said, dabbing his moustache with his napkin.

"Oh, surely you can be more forgiving now about your time in Paris," Mr. Churchill said. "Your mêlée was a thousand years ago."

Mr. Sargent looked at Mr. Churchill, his jaw set and his dark eyes firm. "I was denounced for painting the truth and was asked to corrupt my art in order to satisfy an insipid morality. That I can never forgive," he said with fervor.

"Oh, for heaven's sake, John," Mrs. Belmont said. "A painting is only as moral as the fool who pays for it."

"That, Mrs. Belmont, is where you are wrong," Mr. Sargent said. "You are confusing morality with value. The value of art—of fine art—lies solely in its *being*. Art moves the viewer—to joy, to melancholy, to love, even to hate. A painting by Velázquez is a priceless piece of art because it has stirred multitudes, not because a collector is willing to pay ten thousand pounds for it." He paused. "This is something that the French simply do not understand. They have too many preconceptions about what art is supposed to look like to be truly sympathetic." He smiled slightly. "At least the French of my acquaintance."

"What prompted you to reach such a conviction?" Margaret asked.

"A portrait I painted of a young woman was censured for being immoral," Sargent explained.

"*Madame X,*" Miss Deacon murmured.

"And was it? Immoral, I mean," Margaret pressed.

"The truth is never immoral, Mrs. Vanbrugh," Mr. Churchill said.

"Thank you," Mr. Sargent said.

"The portrait is quite remarkable, as I recollect," Mrs. Belmont said as a servant removed her plate. "But the reputation of the woman was simply ruined. As I recall, her mother begged John to remove the painting from the Salon. John refused. It was a scandal."

"Scandal?" the duke said, pulling himself from his brown study. "What scandal?"

"Madame Gautreau," Miss Deacon said. "The lady John painted in Paris."

"Ah," the duke said.

"Take care, Sunny, that he does not provoke the same sort of reaction when he paints you and Consuelo," Mr. Churchill said.

The duke frowned and with a good deal of bitterness replied, "He will do no such thing. Not in my house and not while I have a breath in my body."

Mr. Churchill looked surprised but said only, "Why, of course he won't."

"Winston was only joking," the duchess added.

"A reputation is not a toy," the duke said. "It is not something to treat carelessly by anyone—least of all by anyone in this household. Is that clear?" He looked about the room in cold defiance, like a bully spoiling for a showdown.

There was an uneasy lull in the conversation, as none of us knew how to react. I glanced across the table at Margaret, who was equally bewildered, and then at the duchess, who was eating a peach calmly.

After a moment Miss Deacon turned to me. "Tell me, Mr. Van-brugh, are you as uncompromising about your art as Mr. Sargent is about his?"

I shook my head. "I am not an artist, Miss Deacon."

"You are too modest, Van," my father-in-law said. "I have seen many of his renderings, and they are very fine. Very fine, indeed."

"I am sure that they are very fine, indeed," Miss Deacon said, and I flushed in anger at her mocking my father-in-law. She had the aggravating talent of being able to infuse her unobjectionable comments with a pointed, disagreeable meaning that just skirted the boundary of good manners.

"No architect can afford to be as uncompromising about his art as a painter or a poet can about his," I said.

"What do you mean?" the duke asked.

"I mean, Your Grace, that the work of an architect is public. It must exist in the world. A painter can paint in his studio or a poet can write in his garret and never let another person see his work. That is his choice. An architect"—I looked briefly at the duchess—"does not have that luxury. In order to create, an architect must adopt his taste to that of his client and of society. To compromise, if you will. It is the compromise that can be the difficulty."

"But it is necessary," Miss Deacon said. "If the first duchess had not compromised, we would not have Blenheim."

"What do you mean, Gladys?" the monsignor asked.

"Sarah hated this place," she said.

"That's true," Mr. Churchill said. "When the breach came between Vanbrugh and the first Churchills, Vanbrugh reserved all of his censure for the duchess." Changing his voice slightly, he quoted Vanbrugh: " 'You have your end, Madam, for I will never trouble you more unless the Duke of Marlborough recovers so far as to shelter me from such intolerable treatment.' "

"Winston, you should go on the stage," Mrs. Belmont said.

"I would have thought the House of Commons was a grand enough stage for anyone," the monsignor said.

"The only one greater is the Vatican eh, Monsignor?" Mr. Churchill said.

"Winston has his eye on a far juicier plum," the Duchess said.

"The Cabinet?" the monsignor asked.

"Chancellor of the Exchequer," Mrs. Belmont said.

"Ah, just like his father," Mr. Barton said. "A very lofty goal, sir."

Winston nodded. "I can think of no higher honor than to strive for the post so ably held by a most accomplished member of the Churchill family. If I serve my country half as well as my father did, I shall be greatly satisfied."

"A heavy task," Mr. Sargent said.

"But he'll succeed," the duchess said. "We all have great faith in Winston."

"Winston has a great deal of faith in himself," Miss Deacon said, smiling.

"Because I have never felt the need to rely on others to advance in this world," Mr. Churchill said.

There was a moment of uncomfortable silence broken by my father-in-law. "I have often thought that to be great, men must believe in themselves absolutely," Mr. Barton said. "Self-doubt should never be allowed to flower if a man is to achieve great things."

The duchess laughed. "There is no need to worry about that with Winston," she said. "That weed will never take root in his garden."

"But surely a man requires more than just self-possession to succeed," Margaret said.

"You are correct, Mrs. Vanbrugh," Mr. Churchill. "They require something more."

"What? What do they need?" Mr. Barton asked.

"Yes, tell us, Winston," Miss Deacon said.

"Oh, come now," Mrs. Belmont said.

"Unquestioning support from his family."

"I am perfectly serious. I do not think John Duke would have succeeded without the support and comfort of Sarah. He relied on her absolutely. By all accounts she was a fascinating creature, almost as lovely as the present duchess, but not nearly as brilliant."

The duchess made a face at Mr. Churchill, who said, "Every word I utter, ma'am, is the God's truth." He leaned into the table. "Duchess Sarah was an intimate of Queen Anne, and promoted the interests of her husband at court, which must have been difficult, as the queen was . . . uninviting."

"Uninviting?" Mr. Barton repeated.

"Not the loveliest flower in the Stuart garden," Mr. Sargent explained. "The statue of her in the Long Library is extremely flattering, I understand."

"Stinkweed instead of a rose," Miss Deacon offered.

"Indeed," Mr. Churchill agreed. "Still, she and Sarah were thick as thieves for years. Sarah was constantly at court when John Duke was off at battle. Some say she and the queen were lovers. They exchanged letters constantly in which they addressed each other by pet names."

Mrs. Belmont said, "I have never heard anything so ridiculous."

"It may sound ludicrous to us now, but such a contrivance offered the prospect of a more relaxed correspondence," Mr. Churchill said. "The two could chatter away about this and that, forgetting for the length of the letter that one lady was the queen of England and the other was her most loyal subject. They each addressed the other with a simple 'Mrs.,' without affixing the 'Your Majestys' or 'Your Graces' that were usually a part of such communication."

"It sounds democratic, if an American can make such an observation," the duchess said. Her eyes sought mine as she reached for a small, plump strawberry and popped it into her mouth.

I grinned and met her gaze. I could not believe her boldness—at her own table, no less, with her husband sitting across from her. It was at once alarming and enchanting.

"It may have been democratic, but it was hardly informal," Mr. Churchill said. "As I recall, the queen was Mrs. Morley and Duchess Sarah was something else. Liberty. No, it was Freeman. Rather prosaic, in fact."

I was still daydreaming about the duchess and was only half listening to the conversation, so I did not catch the significance of what Mr. Churchill had put forth so unknowingly until I glanced at the duchess, whose face had frozen in astonishment.

"Does something alarm you, Your Grace?" the monsignor asked.

The duchess put her napkin to her mouth. "No. I...I was a bit surprised by what Winston said, that is all," she said.

"Surprised?" Mr. Sargent asked.

"It is silly, of course. But I was a little taken aback when I heard the name Mrs. Freeman. I came across that name myself quite recently."

Mr. Churchill raised his glass in salute. "There, Mr. Vanbrugh. My chaotic theory has been proven."

"It would appear so," I agreed, but my attention was elsewhere. It was fixed on the duchess and what this discovery suggested. For if what Mr. Churchill said was true, Duchess Sarah must be the Mrs. Freeman who wrote the letters I uncovered this morning. But to whom was she writing? Surely the queen was not Lord Rake. Who would be close enough to the duchess to use the same pet name that the queen herself used? It was clear from the letters and the use of "Mrs. Freeman" that the duchess was very fond of the writer, and that the letter writer had somehow betrayed her trust. What was even more troubling was the thought that "Mr. F." might be the duke himself. I recalled a phrase from one of the letters: "In you I found myself; in you I have lost myself." I shivered, and the room seemed to darken.

I tried to recall other details from the letters. For the thousandth time I chastised myself silently for my inadequate education and my lack of knowledge of the world. If only I had been better trained as a youth, if only I was better read as a man! Mrs. Freeman wrote of "our Great Jest" in one of the letters. Perhaps that referred to a political intrigue at court since Duchess Sarah was obviously with Queen Anne when she wrote the letter. But who was Lord Rake? And what about him appealed to Duchess Sarah?

The duchess seemed to read my thoughts by attempting an unexpected gambit. As a footman poured more wine for her, the duchess said in a casual tone, "I ran into Lord Rake last week."

The duke came alive at the mention of the name. "Who the devil is he? I just heard about him," he said.

"Lord Rake. Of course you know him," the duchess said, her tone one of sweet certitude.

"I have never heard of this person," the duke replied. "Where did we meet him?"

The duchess cocked her head and turned to Mr. Sargent. "John, have you encountered Lord Rake?"

Mr. Sargent frowned. "I have not, but I admit, the name sounds familiar."

"Surely you, Gladys, have come across Lord Rake in your rambles about town," the duchess said.

Miss Deacon raised an eyebrow at that but was silent. She looked down at her hands, which were covered in long gloves of peach satin, and delicately played with the fingers of one glove.

"Winston, do you know this man?" the duke asked his cousin.

Mr. Churchill signaled for more wine. As the footman served it, he leaned back in his chair and pondered the ceiling. "Lord Rake," he said deliberately. "Lord Rake. The only Lord Rake I am familiar with is that character from the stage."

Mr. Sargent said: "Of course. I knew that the name sounded familiar."

"The stage?" the duke snorted. "Good Lord. A peer on the stage. His family must be apoplectic."

"No, I mean a *character* named Lord Rake," Mr. Churchill said, turning to me. "In one of the plays written by your ancestor, Mr. Vanbrugh."

"*The Provok'd Wife*," Mr. Sargent added as he turned his wine glass.

"I saw that play," Mrs. Belmont said suddenly. "Did you, Monsignor?"

"Yes. Rather devoid of anything approaching morality, I thought," he said.

I coughed; my throat had gone very dry. "What kind of character is Lord Rake?" I asked.

"A bit of a bounder, as you might expect with a name like that," Mr. Churchill explained cheerfully. "He carries on a rather public assignation with Lady Brute."

"Well, then, who are you talking about, Conseulo?" Miss Deacon asked.

The duchess laughed, her chuckle as lively as a brook after a spring rain. "It certainly could not have been Lord Rake," she said. "I do not know what I could have been thinking." But despite this protest, she looked triumphant—well pleased at her artfulness.

"Perhaps it was Lord Ravenscroft," the duke said.

"Yes, that must have been who I saw," the duchess agreed. She signaled to the ladies that she was about to rise when the duke, who had ignored his meal suddenly began to eat, slowly and methodically. The rest of us settled back in to wait for our host, who muttered to himself, "Cold, too cold."

"I wonder if anyone has come across my sketchbook," Mr. Sargent said, his voice measured. "One seems to have disappeared from my room."

"Well, that is a shame," the monsignor said.

"There is some delicate work in it that I am most eager to have back," he said slowly.

The duke looked up from his meal, his face hard, his moustache quivering. "If you please, sir, not at my table," the duke said in a low, dreadful voice. With that, he tossed his napkin onto his plate and, rising, headed to the door, threw it open, and headed out into silent shadows toward the Great Hall.

The duchess flinched at the duke's sudden display, but she did not speak. The other guests, notably Mr. Churchill and Miss Deacon, who were perhaps used to this kind of behavior, seemed unmoved by this outburst. Margaret and my father-in-law, however, were flabbergasted by such a display, as was I. No doubt my face reflected the combination of wonder, incredulity, and fear that I felt, for the duchess smiled ruefully and said, "It is a lovely evening. I thought we would take coffee on the terrace."

chapter
9

THE evening had cooled pleasantly, and the stars had begun to appear—almost as tentatively as Margaret, her father, and I settled into the chairs that had been arranged around one small table on the Saloon Terrace, an avenue of well-tended gravel thirty feet wide, which stretched the entire length of the south front of the palace. Whether by accident or intent, the other guests clustered themselves around another small table and chatted amiably, Mr. Churchill smoking a cigar, Mr. Sargent a short Turkish cigarette. They took little notice of us. The duke was conspicuously absent.

Coffee was served by Jamison, assorted sweets and fruits were presented by other footmen and pressed upon us by the duchess, who indicated that if we did not appreciate the genius of the dessert chef, the guests of the Duke of Manchester surely would, as he had been trying for months to lure him from Blenheim. She stood near the doors to the Saloon when she announced this, and in the soft light from the glowing lamps set out upon the terrace, she looked like a princess dipped in gold.

The duchess came over to us. "I wonder, Mr. Vanbrugh, if you could assist me inside the house for a moment," she said.

"Of course, ma'am," I replied, rising.

"I shall not keep him long, Mrs. Vanbrugh," she said to Margaret.

I felt a bit as if I were abandoning Margaret and Mr. Barton, but I followed the duchess into the Saloon eagerly. The large murals in the room, which in the light had seemed grandiose if dull, took on an ominous, unsettled aspect in the growing darkness, as if the subjects were conspiring among themselves. The shadows of the people on the terrace shifted across them in arrhythmic waves, like ants over a twig. The room was very quiet; the only sound I could make out was the hum of voices from the terrace and the occasional passing of a footman making his taciturn way to the back stairs.

The duchess stopped at one end of the long table and said, "I apologize for pulling you away from your wife and your father-in-law, but given the behavior of my husband at dinner, I think it wise to reveal everything to him about the letters."

"If that is what you think best," I said.

The duchess looked at the table's centerpiece, a large silver rendering of John Duke on horseback, which in the dark looked menacing. "What I think best may have nothing to do with it," she said. "But perhaps he will surprise us both."

We proceeded through the grave, gloomy penumbra of the state rooms. The darkness deepened as we went, as if we were walking deep into a cave. The thick draperies had been pulled tight across the windows, preventing the meager twilight from aiding us. But the state rooms were sun-drenched when compared with the Grand Cabinet. Here the darkness was complete; it was simply impossible to see anything at all.

We hesitated in the doorway as our eyes tried to adjust to the lack of light. There must have been enough light behind us, however dim, to identify who we were, for after a time a voice said, "Close the door."

The duke's voice was thin, severe in its tone. The duchess took no notice of it. "Why on earth are you wallowing in the dark?" she asked, and turned on a small lamp on a heavy marble table near the door.

"Turn that light off," the duke demanded. He was in the far corner of the cluttered room, slumped in a chair, a leg over one arm, one hand in front of his eyes to shield them from the sudden illumination, the other cradling a snifter of brandy. There was a lingering aroma of cigar smoke.

"I will do no such thing," the duchess said, moving toward him. "And may I remind you that we have a houseful of guests."

"At your invitation," the duke said.

"At your insistence," the duchess said.

"I did not want the monsignor here," the duke said.

"I did not want Gladys here," the duchess rejoined.

The duke scowled but did not reply.

The duchess stood in front of her husband, and after a moment sat down upon a low stool in front of the chair. She motioned me to be seated, as well. I found a small wooden chair a few feet away and obliged.

"There is something you should know," the duchess said.

The duke took a sip of his brandy. "There are many things I should know. And quite a few I probably shouldn't but do."

The duchess shook her head irritably. "Do listen. Mr. Vanbrugh has made a discovery that you should be aware of."

"A discovery." The duke laughed.

"Yes. Quite an important one, I think."

"It would not, I suppose, be about you and those Sargent sketches?"

The duchess adjusted one of her bracelets before replying. "No," she said. "It is about what Mr. Vanbrugh has found in my room. He has discovered something about the Churchills that is quite important."

"You have mentioned that already," the duke said.

"Oh, I cannot abide you when you are like this," she said. She rose and turned away.

"How annoying for you," the duke said. He took a sip of brandy.

"We only have a moment before we—or at least I—have to return to our guests. So here it is. This afternoon, when Mr. Vanbrugh removed the wall covering from my rooms, he found several letters."

The duke cocked his head. "Letters."

"Yes," the duchess said. "They had been hidden on the back of the fabric, next to the wall."

"What purpose could that serve?" he asked.

"Someone wanted them hidden," the duchess said.

"Hidden from you?"

"No, of course not from me," the duchess said, angry.

"Then from whom?" the duke asked, a satisfied smirk playing about his lips.

"I do not know from whom. From everyone, I suppose. The letters were from Duchess Sarah," she said.

"There are mountains of those," the duke said. "All over the house."

"Not really quite like these," the duchess said seriously.

The duke caught the changed tone in her voice. "And just what does that mean?" he asked.

"They are love letters," she said. "To Sir John Vanbrugh."

The duke laughed long and loud, nearly spilling his brandy. "How ridiculous."

"It is true, I assure you."

"But the two despised each other. With a passion," the duke said. "That is as well known as ... well, as Blenheim itself."

"According to these letters, that was artifice, nothing but a sham. Like one of the plays of Sir John."

The Provok'd Wife," I muttered.

The duchess nodded. "They used pet names for each other in the letters."

"Hah!" the duke said, suddenly animated. "Then how do you know that the people in the letters are the duchess and the architect?"

"She uses the name Mrs. Freeman."

For the first time in the conversation, the duke looked startled. "But that is the name she used when she wrote to the queen."

"Yes. Apparently she used it when writing to Sir John, as well. At least in her *unofficial* communication," the duchess said. Now it was her turn to look smug.

"But it cannot be Sir John," the duke said. "You do not know that definitively."

"No," the duchess admitted. "But all of the hints point to her correspondent being Sir John."

"And how, pray, do they do that?" the duke asked, his tone once again derisive as his confidence returned.

"He used the name Lord Rake," the duchess said.

"Good Lord," the duke said. "From the play."

"There are other indications," the duchess said. "Mrs. Freeman has seen the house as it was being built, and that it is progressing well, and that Mr. F. is well pleased with it. And she says she will ask Christopher Wren to design her London house so everyone will conclude that she and Lord Rake are at odds. She called him . . . what was it, Mr. Vanbrugh?"

" 'The Master Plotter,' " I said.

"That is it," the duchess said.

"What—he has read them, these letters?" the duke asked, pointing at me.

"Of course he has read them. He found them. How would he know what they were if he hadn't?"

"But this does not make any sense at all," the duke said, forlorn.

"It makes sense if you accept the idea that the two were lovers," the duchess said.

"I cannot understand this," the duke said. Then suddenly, "Show me."

"I do not have them," the duchess said. "I have put them away."

"Then go get them," the duke said impatiently.

I smarted at his discourteous treatment of his wife and itched to come to her aid, but I did not know how or what to say. The duchess bore his bad behavior composedly, only saying after a moment, "If you like," and left the room.

We sat in an uneasy silence, the duke and I. He made no effort to engage me in conversation or to put me at ease—in fact, he stared at me in pop-eyed derision, as if he could not abide being in the same room with me, a lowly American commoner. This rankled me more than I was willing to admit, but I said nothing: It has been my experience that the wisest tactic when dealing with difficult men is to hold your tongue unless you have something worth saying. And at this moment, I clearly did not. So I remained silent and still, waiting for the duchess to return.

She was gone longer than I expected, and when she returned she was frowning.

"I cannot find them," she said.

"Where did they go?" the duke said.

"I have no idea. They are missing. I put them in the drawer next to the bed before dinner and they are not there now."

"That cannot be," the duke said. "Hill must have taken them."

"Hill does not know anything about them," the duchess said. "No one does."

"Well, someone must," the duke said, his voice rising in vexation. "They cannot have just disappeared."

"Excuse me, Your Grace," I said to the duke, "but when I found the letters, I copied the contents. In case the originals were lost." I retrieved them from my pocket and offered them to the duchess.

The duke yanked them from my hand and muttered, "What bloody cheek. When were you planning on telling us *that*?"

It was then that the Duke of Marlborough tried my patience to the breaking point. I could no longer endure his callous, high-handed manner without reply; I had withstood his arrogant condescension long enough. Seething with an anger I could barely control, I snatched my letters back from him and said icily: "I beg your pardon, Your Grace. I was under the impression that I was assisting you. Apparently I am not. So I will take these and myself away. Good evening."

I bowed and turned to leave. The duke gaped at me—bewildered at my unwillingness to endure his behavior. His heavy jaw went slack, as if his face did not know how to reply to such a remark, and his eyes widened in surprise.

"Please do not leave, Van," the duchess said. "I need you here."

I stopped, startled by the use of my nickname. "I should not be here at all," I said.

The duchess turned to her husband, and seemed to will him to say something. After a long moment, he complied. "Of course it is true," he muttered. "We do need you here. I . . . would like to read the letters now. Please."

I smiled. No apology had been proffered, but the duke, in his way, had admitted his error. I felt giddy with defiance as the American patriots must have after they had thrown the tea into Boston harbor.

I handed the letters to the duke. He turned on an electric lamp next to him and read them quickly, and as he did, the color drained from his face. He seemed to diminish in size as he read, to shrink into the shadows of the room. His hand shaking perceptibly, he read the letters again, more deliberately this time, as if he wanted to commit their contents to memory. When he had finished, he handed them back to me and rubbed his eyes.

"They are rubbish, of course," he said without conviction, for it was obvious that he believed our interpretation of the letters. "Utter rubbish." He massaged his temples for a while, as if he had fallen ill suddenly. "I assume they are fair copies?" he asked.

"They are word for word," I said.

The duchess nodded. "Yes. Mr. Vanbrugh has done an excellent job."

"That is it, then," the duke said, his voice heavy and sad. "Congratulations, Mr. Vanbrugh."

"What are you talking about?" the duchess asked.

"You read the letter. We are doomed."

The duchess looked puzzled. "Of course not. This will not become known. Mr. Vanbrugh will be discreet."

The duke laughed. "My dear, that is the one thing you can guarantee Mr. Vanbrugh need *never* be."

I had half a mind to snap back at him, but a glance at the duchess made plain that she had no wish for me to engage the duke.

"Mr. Vanbrugh does not want to divulge the contents of these letters," she said.

"Of course not," I said.

The duke looked as if he did not believe any such thing. "I suppose he cannot tell anyone while he is still here," he said under his breath. He rose abruptly from the chair. "Very well. I want to see where you found them," he said.

"Now?" the duchess asked, surprised.

"Yes," he said.

"But our guests—"

The duke ignored her. He turned to a door at the far end of the room, opened it, proceeded into the next room and turned on the electric light. With a good deal of reluctance, we followed him. The next chamber was his bedroom, an apartment of surprising culture, as its main decoration was, instead of tapestries depicting war, three realistic murals of ruined Greek temples. A canopied bed of scarlet velvet faced the windows. On one side was a stand with a small basin and an electric lamp upon it. On the other side of the bed, there was nothing.

We passed through this room quickly and on into his dressing room, which was painted a rosy peach and whose major detail was a large portrait of a tigress, which cast a suspicious, unfriendly gaze down from its place of honor above the fireplace. Eventually we reached the dining room, where we startled the footmen and maids, including Jamison, who were clearing away the remaining dishes, glasses, and plates. I smiled at him but said nothing.

The duke headed for the back wall of the bedroom as I closed the door. "Where did you find these letters?" he asked.

I unrolled a portion of the wall covering, and showed him two of the pockets I had uncovered. The duke held one of the pockets and fingered the seams contemplatively. "Vanbrugh, are these all the letters you have found?"

I nodded. "And this, as well." I showed him the panel.

The duke studied the message carefully, shaking his head in wonder. He thrust his hands in his pockets and looked around the unsettled room. After a moment he turned to me. The harsh light of the electric lamp threw a strong shadow across his face and thickened his brow. "Were you being honest, Mr. Vanbrugh, when you said that you had no intention of divulging the contents of these letters?"

"Yes. They are not the business of anyone but you and your family."

"Ah, my family. Well done. That is almost funny. For a moment I thought you actually did not understand." He handed me back the letters.

"What are you talking about?" the duchess asked.

"Mr. Vanbrugh is toying with us, my dear."

"I am not," I protested.

"Come now, Vanbrugh. There is no need for pretense. We understand each other."

"Then perhaps you could enlighten me," the duchess demanded.

The duke pressed his hands together. "Of course. The third letter, the one in which the writer makes plain that her lover has been making free with a woman named Anne. Tell me, do you know who Anne could be?"

"I have no idea," the duchess said wearily.

"Think, Consuelo. Think of the portrait."

"What portrait? We are drowning in them at Blenheim."

"The family portrait off the Great Hall. It may interest you to know that Duchess Sarah had a daughter named Anne. This very Anne married the Earl of Sunderland."

The duchess gasped. "The Earl of S."

"Indeed. It appears that Anne became pregnant by the person receiving the letter from Duchess Sarah, 'and the Earl of S. need never know of it.' And if you are correct as to the recipient of that letter, that person was Sir John."

"There is no mention in the letter of Anne being pregnant," the duchess said.

"There is mention of a child, whom the letter writer cannot look at without anger and revulsion."

"Perhaps. But I fail to see why you think we are so lost," the duchess said.

"Think. What happened when John Duke died?" the duke asked.

"There were no surviving male heirs, so the line passed by special order of Parliament through the daughters," the duchess said, as if by rote.

"And where did the dukedom end up?"

The duchess thought for a moment. "With the children of Anne, Countess of Sunderland, when her elder sister, Duchess Henrietta, died childless."

"Precisely. We Churchills are all descended from the second son of Anne and her husband, the Earl of Sunderland. Whose first name is ..."

"Charles," the duchess said. Her eyes grew wide as she suddenly understood the portent of what her husband was saying.

The duke continued, spitting out with obvious distaste. "If we are to believe the letter, the letter *you* found, Vanbrugh, the Dukes of Marlborough are descended from Sir John Vanbrugh." His face fell as he muttered, "I knew it. I *knew* it."

Every fiber in my body froze—my breath, my blood, my thoughts were all stunned by what the duke was suggesting. The sound of his words reverberated through me like a tolling church bell. After a time I sputtered, "I am sure that is impossible."

"We both know, Vanbrugh, that it is nothing of the sort," the duke said.

"I promise you, I would never do anything to harm the reputation of your family," I said.

The duke ran his hand across the wall I had not yet investigated. "What did you find on this wall, Mr. Vanbrugh?" he asked.

"I have not searched it yet," I said.

"But you do plan to remove this velvet," the duke said.

"Yes," I said.

The duke stared at me, as if he were calculating. Then without the slightest warning, he threw himself at me viciously, thrusting his small hands toward the pocket that contained the letters and yanking them out. He threw me off balance, and we fell to the ground, wrestling like two boys in the schoolyard.

"Sunny, stop it," the duchess screamed. "Leave him alone. He is mine."

The duke looked frightened at that, and loosened his grip just long enough for me to slip away. I scrambled to my feet and was about to attack him when the duchess said, "Both of you, stop this or, I swear to heaven, I will leave this house with those letters at once."

The threat caught our attention, and the duke rose to his feet. Breathing heavily, he said, "Do not make a threat you cannot keep, Consuelo."

"Watch me," the duchess said with such terrible conviction that we knew she meant every word. "Now let me be very clear. Until I straighten out all of this, there will be no more of this barbarity. There is too much at stake, for all of us. Do you understand?"

"Then I will keep these letters," the duke said.

The duchess nodded.

"Your Grace," I said to the duke, "I promise you, your family reputation will remain unsullied."

"I hope so, Mr. Vanbrugh." His voice was low, but there was a menacing timbre to it that had not been there before. "For your sake, I hope so. "If my family reputation is going to be destroyed, it will not be without retribution."

From far away, we heard the front doors of the palace crash open and a cry so strong, so terrifying in its raw fear, it propelled all of us toward it.

We arrived in the Great Hall after the other guests had entered from the Saloon, and we watched awestruck as Annie, the young maid we had met upstairs, ran about wildly, screaming incoherently, and in a convulsive, shuddering motion pointing to the doors. Her cap was missing and her hair flew about her face, which wore an expression of abject horror; by turns she screamed and cried, her sobs coming in long, inhuman screeches of terrible, unearthly pain as if she were truly out of her wits. She lurched toward the group at the Saloon door, which recoiled from her, but she ignored them, and plunged howling through the open door and through to the darkened state rooms beyond. Her shrieks reverberated along the enfilade; each room magnified the sound of her dread so that when her cries reached our ears they sounded more animal than human, like a terrified fox caught in a trap.

The butler and three footmen followed her, and eventually caught up with her in the Long Library, where she was cornered. As they tried to subdue her, she attacked them with such unexpected ferocity that they had to carry her back, each man taking a limb, through the state rooms and across the Great Hall, their wigs askew. Just as they reached the green baize doors, behind which lay the servants' quarters, the duke caught up to them. He looked down into Annie's face and grabbed her chin brutally—so firmly that for a moment her struggling ceased. He stared at her hard, his face full of a dangerous, undisguised fury. Her eyes grew wide and she emitted a small whimper before the duke released her and signaled the footmen to remove her into the nether regions of the palace. Annie began to scream again, and it was only after the doors closed with a click that the house fell back into an exhausted silence.

WHAT on earth was that?" Mrs. Belmont exclaimed after a moment. "Has the girl completely lost her wits?"

"At the very least," Mr. Churchill said. His remark hung in the strange quiet that had replaced Annie's anguished screams. It had the effect of drawing us together near the open front doors, which no one made any effort to close.

"What was she saying?" Miss Deacon said. There was anxiety in her voice. "She was trying to tell us something."

"No, she wasn't," Mrs. Belmont said. She adjusted her pince-nez and set her jaw, a gesture that called to mind her son-in-law. "The poor creature went off her head and that is the end of it."

"No, Gladys is right, I think," Mr. Sargent said. He walked to the threshold and stared out into the night. Unlike the lamps that had cheered the Saloon terrace on the other side of Blenheim, the moon and stars were a poor match for the murky shadows that consumed the Great Court: In the dim light, the yard had the appearance of a battlefield after a long day of fighting. The lumpy pyramids of paving stones looked like the remains of a village laid to waste. I wondered if this was as the village of Blenheim might have looked the night John Duke triumphed over the French army.

Mr. Sargent lighted another cigarette. "She said she had seen something. Something out there." He exhaled and pointed out into the darkness.

The duchess came to Mr. Sargent and gazed up at him, her face tentative. She reached for one of his hands. "Do you see anything, John?" she asked softly.

He smiled, his dark eyes full of a truth I did not expect, and took her hand. With his free hand he touched her back lightly, knowingly. "No. It is too dark."

In that small, intimate moment, it was as if the cannons in the Great Court had been set off: Mr. Sargent had proclaimed to the world that the duchess was his. She had been hallmarked, like a fine piece of silver.

I turned away; it was all I could do to remain standing. I searched the faces of the others to gauge their reactions to this stupendous disclosure, but I saw no other response. Even Margaret was oblivious: She peered out into the night. Only Mrs. Belmont watched me with an inscrutable expression.

They do not see, I thought, and it resounded through me until my bones quaked. They do not see.

The duke elbowed his way through the group. "Alva is right, there is nothing to see," he said. "Now for God's sake can we get on with it." With a hurried motion he closed the tall doors, securing them shut with an oversized, elaborate lock and key topped by a ducal coronet in gold. The duke turned to the duchess, and I was struck again by their physical incongruity. She was a head taller than he, and her fine, softly sculpted beauty contrasted with his prickly posturing.

"Shall we go back to the terrace?" the duke said. His voice was even, but there was an edge to it; this clearly was not a request. Others noted it, too: Mrs. Belmont and the monsignor exchanged surprised glances.

There was an uncomfortable silence, which Mr. Churchill broke. "This is like the first day of term," Mr. Churchill said. "All orders and awkward pauses. Of course we will return to the terrace, Your Grace," Mr. Churchill said. "We are at your service." Miss Deacon giggled.

"Don't be such an ass, Winston," the duke said. He thrust his hands into his jacket pockets and frowned.

Mr. Churchill chuckled. "I cannot help it, Sunny."

"Certainly you can help it," the duke snapped. "You just refuse to."

His tone prompted Miss Deacon into a further bout of giggling.

Her laugh, charming and unaffected, bubbled out of her like froth from a champagne flute. "Oh, what a fool you are," she said, unthinking.

Perhaps it was hearing her own remark that caused Miss Deacon to grasp its true import. For however disdainful one may be of a duke, in private or among friends, to belittle him in his own house is simply inexcusable. Miss Deacon understood this as soon as she spoke, for she looked at the duke, her face a study in fear and dismay. The duke said nothing to her, but the duchess stared at Miss Deacon in cool condescension and said with great deliberateness, "Thank you, Gladys. That is quite enough."

Miss Deacon's cheeks turned crimson, as if she had just been slapped. Her mouth fell open and without another word she ran from the hall. No one attempted to stop her as she hastened up the stairs. After a few moments a door slammed far away. At the sound, the duchess turned and walked toward the Saloon. Mrs. Belmont said, "I wonder, Consuelo, if that was wise."

The duchess sighed. "Perhaps not. But I cannot worry about that now. Shall we join His Grace on the terrace?"

As the others departed, led by the duke and duchess, I hung back. I could not move. I struggled to clear my head of what I had seen and heard, but the image of Mr. Sargent and the freedom with which he treated the duchess was too recent. I could not banish it from my memory. It twisted my heart so cavalierly that I could scarcely catch my breath. As I struggled to calm myself, I wondered how long they had been this close. Such a gesture as Mr. Sargent's did not arise spontaneously or from a slight acquaintance. These two people, I realized now, shared a secret history that began before this weekend and would continue for only they knew how long. Miss Deacon, I saw, had been correct about the stories about Mr. Sargent.

From far away I felt a tug on my arm. I turned to it and after a moment realized it was Margaret.

"What is it?" I asked, irritated at the interruption of my reverie.

"Van, I saw something," Margaret said in an urgent voice. "In the courtyard." She pulled me toward the gaunt arched window to the right of the front door. I peered out into the night, uncertain of what I was searching for.

"It is too dark to see anything," I said.

Margaret turned to me, her features in the tempered gloom heavy and dull.

"Not if you look in the right place," she said. "When the duke was talking, I saw something behind him. On the ground, near the last mound but one." Through the window she indicated one of the piles of stones. "Mr. Sargent is right: Annie was saying she saw something. We must find out what it is."

"We will, tomorrow," I promised. "Now let us join the others."

"No, tonight," Margaret insisted. "I think something is out there."

"What do you mean—wolves?"

Margaret glanced at the doors of the Saloon through which her father at that moment was passing. The echoes of conversation died out as the party moved onto the terrace; in a moment the hall was again still, empty of sound. Margaret leaned against a pillar in the corner of the hall and traced a groove in it with her finger. "I think Annie was screaming about something she saw," she said.

"She was too busy blathering to see anything," I said.

Margaret shook her head. "Before dinner, when she was helping me dress, she kept saying that she was afraid for poor Emily, that she was certain something had happened. I did not think much of it at the time. Then, when she came into the house just now, she kept pointing out the door. She was crying too hard for people to understand."

"What do you mean she was afraid for Emily?" I asked.

"I cannot say for sure. But I think Annie believes something has happened to Emily. She is not the kind of girl who simply disappears. Particularly while her young man is still at Blenheim."

"Hardly conclusive," I said.

"But enough for us to investigate, surely," Margaret insisted.

"Perhaps when Annie calms down we can speak with her. Tomorrow," I suggested. "Now we should get back."

But Margaret did not move. "No, we must do it now, Van. If we are to be any help at all."

"Margaret, we have an obligation to our hosts."

"We will not be long," she said.

"We will pursue this in the morning, when you are thinking more clearly," I said. "Now come along."

"So you will not help me with this?" Margaret asked.

"There is no problem I can see that cannot wait until the morning," I said.

"Then I will go myself. Alone," she said.

I had half a mind to leave her to her own harebrained ideas, but I knew she would be missed. "Oh, very well," I said in resignation. "But let us at least wait until the others go to bed. We do not need witnesses to our foolishness."

Margaret nodded, and, taking my arm, we returned to the terrace. We were not there long: The incident in the hall had dampened spirits, and there was little interest in conversation. The duke sat to one side, gazing out onto the lawn, smoking. He spoke to no one. Mr. Churchill, the monsignor, and Mrs. Belmont chatted amiably enough— about flowering shrubs, from what I could determine—while the duchess spoke with Mr. Barton. We joined them.

"Not a very gay party," the duchess said after a moment. "Miss Deacon is in her room, Mr. Sargent said he had work he wanted to complete, and my husband . . ."—she looked over at the duke—"is not himself."

"It has been a lovely evening," my father-in-law said with feeling— as if he could will the evening to improve.

The duchess smiled. "Mr. Barton, you are a loyal friend."

"Not at all, not at all—that is, I am, but I am only speaking the truth," my father-in-law said, his pink cheeks shining at the compliment. "This has been a delightful diversion for an old man. But like Mr. Sargent, I too have some work to do." He leaned conspiratorially toward the duchess. "I have often been struck by the amount of work my profession requires of me on the day God set aside for rest. I expend the most effort on the day others expend the least." He laughed good-naturedly as Mrs. Belmont joined us.

"I must be going, Your Grace," he said nervously, offering a weak smile. "I have work to do."

"So do we all," Mrs. Belmont said.

"What are you talking about, Mother?" the duchess asked.

"Nothing. I am an old fool, aren't I, Mr. Barton?" She took a sip of her coffee. "You never finished telling me how you enjoyed America."

"It was most educational, extremely so," my father-in-law said.

"Did you enjoy Boston?" she asked slowly. "Mrs. Remington said you could not have been more delightful."

Mr. Barton looked sheepish. "Ah, Mrs. Remington. I don't believe . . . that is to say . . ."

"I did not know you met Mrs. Remington," I said, surprised. "My mother used to sew for her."

"Did you know that, Mr. Barton?" Mrs. Belmont asked, acid in her voice.

My father-in-law looked panicked but said nothing. "I must hurry back to my sermon," he said, rising quickly.

"Of course," the duchess said. "My dear," she said to the duke, "Mr. Barton is leaving us."

The duke glanced over at Mr. Barton but did not rise from his chair. "Good evening, Mr. Barton," he said absently.

Mr. Barton took a step toward the duke, but when the duke picked up a newspaper that had been lying on one of the tables and began to read—or pretended to, since it was far too dark to properly attend to it—my father-in-law halted. He nodded briskly to himself and mumbled, "Yes, of course, of course." He bowed stiffly to the duke, and without another word departed.

Margaret said nothing about the deplorable manners displayed by the duke toward her father. She seemed distracted, looking past me toward the golden embers of the cigar that Mr. Churchill was holding in his hand. I wondered what she was thinking about so intently.

Mrs. Belmont yawned. "What a dreadful evening," she said.

"You always know just the right thing to say, Mother."

"There is no use ignoring the truth," Mrs. Belmont said. She stood up and, after adjusting her pince-nez, collected her shawl from the chair, and waited expectantly.

"Perhaps not," the duchess agreed. She rose and said to Margaret and me, "I am so sorry. Our evenings . . . well, they usually are not like this."

"I hope not," I said.

Mrs. Belmont barked out a horsy laugh. "That's the spirit, Mr. Vanbrugh. Fight back."

"We enjoyed ourselves so much," Margaret said mechanically. "But I admit, I am rather tired."

"You are not ill, I hope," the duchess said.

"Not a bit," Margaret said, shaking her head. "I think it is all the excitement."

The duchess nodded. "It has been a rather demanding day. No doubt tomorrow will be easier."

"It had better be," Mr. Churchill said, rising. "I am painting tomorrow."

"You, too?" I said.

"Mr. Churchill is the family artist," the duchess explained. "It is a wonder my husband engaged Mr. Sargent at all."

"Sunny seeks the grand canvas. I crave the small moment fully observed," Mr. Churchill said.

"Winston, escort me to my room," Mrs. Belmont demanded. "I want to talk to you."

"It would be an honor, Mrs. Belmont," Mr. Churchill said.

"But first get rid of that foul cigar," she said. "I never could stand a man who smoked a cigar in front of a lady."

Mr. Churchill looked shocked. "Madam, you cut me to the quick."

"I divorced Mr. Vanderbilt for less," Mrs. Belmont said. "Monsignor, will you join us?"

"Thank you, no. I have other business here. I will stay a while longer."

"As you wish," Mrs. Belmont said.

The duchess took Margaret's arm. "Come, let the two of them bicker in peace." She escorted us back through the Saloon to the stairs. "You must remember, Mrs. Vanbrugh, to be as quiet as you can during this time. It is very hard to regain your strength if you overexert yourself."

"Thank you, Your Grace, but I assure you, I feel perfectly well," Margaret said.

"I remember that my first London season exhausted me so completely, after the last party I slept for twenty-fours hours straight. When I awoke, I felt like Rip Van Winkle," the duchess said, smiling.

"Surely Sleeping Beauty is a more apt comparison," I said.

The duchess looked wistful. "Ah, but she lived happily ever after."

"Who is Rip Van Winkle?" Margaret asked as we reached the stairway.

"He is a character in a story American children learn when they are young," the duchess said. Her voice held a trace of regret. "He nodded off under a tree one day and slept for twenty years. When he awoke, he found himself in a world he did not recognize." She looked up toward the ceiling, her gaze seeking the mural of John Duke high above. But it was impossible to discern anything through the dark. The electric torchères along the walls of the hall were weak palliatives; they shed a wan, ineffective light and made the duchess look weary, drained. Her eyes were empty of all delight, her normally erect posture bent with fatigue. She shrugged her shoulders and attempted to stand straighter, but she could not will the life back into her eyes. "Good night. If the weather is fine, we will have breakfast on the terrace."

Without thinking, I asked, "Let me escort you to your room."

The duchess looked taken aback at such a request. "No, thank you," she said. "I can make my way there alone. You should make sure that Mrs. Vanbrugh gets some rest."

With a small nod she left us, heading through the cavernous hall toward her rooms. The shadows quickly engulfed her, much as a wave overwhelms a seashell.

Margaret began to climb the stairs. "Come, we will change quickly and make our way outside."

"Are you certain you feel well enough for this foolishness?" I asked, following her.

"Of course," Margaret said. In fact, she seemed invigorated by the prospect of this adventure; she almost scampered up the stairway. She changed out of her gown quickly and into a dark blue skirt, a simple cotton shirt, and a gray coat long before I had even determined what I should wear. She stood in the doorway and pressed me to hurry several times as I dressed but refused to let me summon Jamison to help. "We do not want to call attention to ourselves," she said.

As I dressed, Margaret commandeered a small oil lantern for our use.

Slowly, deliberately, we slipped into the passage and paused to listen for the footsteps of others; neither one of us heard a sound. The household, it seemed, was asleep. We heard nothing from the room occupied by Miss Deacon, and there was no light peeking out from under her door. We retraced our steps to the stairway as quietly as we could, and we muted our tread as we passed the room Mr. Sargent used as a studio.

We descended the stairway staying close to the wall. When we reached the bright hall, there was a small click, which in the silence sounded like a gunshot, and the room fell into complete darkness. A servant must have extinguished the electric lights in the room. Margaret started but did not cry out.

For a long moment we stood at the bottom of the stair, waiting for our eyes to adjust to the dark. The sudden blackness had the disquieting effect of intensifying the silence; it seemed suddenly a living thing, a corporeal presence released into the night, like a pack of hounds bent on destruction. I felt it lurking in the darkest shadows, watching us, waiting for its chance to overtake us.

Soon enough the lofty tier of windows at the top of the hall allowed in a small amount of moonlight. It turned the statues perched in the arcades high above into ghostly witnesses to our clandestine escapade, but we were able to make our way across the room with some confidence. However, it was still too dark to make sense of the complicated lock on the front door, which the duke had secured earlier in the evening. And to our dismay, we discovered that the Saloon doors communicating to the terrace had been secured as well.

"What should we do?" Margaret asked. Her voice was muted.

"Go upstairs to bed," I replied.

"No." Margaret was firm. "There must be a way to leave the house unobserved. This is not a prison, after all. Perhaps one of the windows in the state rooms is open," she said.

"They are too high off the ground. Even if one is open, we would have to jump down from it, and we would have a devil of a time getting back into the house," I said.

"Yes, I suppose," Margaret agreed reluctantly. "What do you suggest?"

"Let me think." I tried to recall the plan of Blenheim that Mr. Churchill had shown me earlier in the Long Library, with its complex arrangement of chambers, anterooms, service stairs, corridors, and courtyards. Though I remembered many of the details of the plan, I could recollect only few actual entrances to the house. Most of them were belowstairs and were used by the staff. To attempt to leave that way presented too many difficulties, as neither Margaret nor I had been in the Blenheim basement and neither one of us wished to be discovered by a servant.

It was then that I remembered two other doors on the main floor, which gave out onto the tall colonnades that connect the main house with the chapel and the old kitchen.

"As I recall, there is a door at the end of the Long Library that opens out onto the colonnade by the chapel," I said.

"Of course," Margaret said, remembering. "Near the organ. That will give us access to the courtyard."

We made our way quickly across the hall to the library. The bleak light had settled into a grim, sepulchral grayness; the columns and pilasters that lined the hall walls looked like trees left unfinished by a distracted Creator, and the dark, menacing passage was dismal and uninviting. It was a relief to arrive at the library: Its wall of windows made the room seem almost bright by comparison.

The room had been straightened since we assembled earlier in the evening. The glasses and bottles had been removed, the books returned to their appointed places behind the gilded screens, the pillows and cushions straightened. I closed the thick door behind us quietly as Margaret lighted the lamp. She handed it to me and together we proceeded toward far end of the room, where the great hulking pipe organ loomed before us like a greedy, expectant beast. The colonnade door was tucked into an alcove behind and to the left of it, near the outside wall of the room. The lamp illuminated the small area well, but that was small solace to Margaret when she turned the doorknob to the colonnade door and found that it too was locked.

"There," I said, trying to keep the satisfaction from my voice. "We have done our best. Now can we please go to bed?"

"Wait," Margaret said. "When we came in here, I noticed that there was a key in the lock of the main door. Perhaps that key would fit this door." Without waiting, Margaret grabbed the lamp, hurried back to the main door, extracted the key from the lock, and returned. "Try this," she said, slightly out of breath.

The key fit easily into the lock and turned without difficulty. Margaret smiled and opened the door slowly, endeavoring to make as little noise as possible. She stepped gingerly out onto the colonnade, me close behind her.

It was brighter outside than it had been in the Long Library. Though the night was still warm, the cool silver moonlight and stars covered the courtyard with an eerie pall, making the small, rough pyramids of stones look frozen, as if they had been covered in ice. Behind us, Blenheim's bleak, bellicose façade loomed over us like a horrible, sleeping creature whose malevolence could be awakened by a simple misstep.

We stood at the top of the stairway, surveying the Great Courtyard. "What is that smell?" Margaret asked after a moment, her nose wrinkling in protest.

"It is coming from the chapel. Mr. Churchill believes the bodies of the duke and duchess have burst from their coffins."

"How terrible."

"Yes. I think your father is going to help set it right."

Margaret covered her nose and mouth. "I do not believe you could ever get used to that smell," she said.

"You would be surprised what people can get used to," I said. "Come along."

We descended the shallow stone stairway at the end of the colonnade.

"Where should we go?" I asked Margaret.

"There," she said, pointing across the court. "A little to the side of the front steps."

I took the lamp from Margaret and led the way over the jumble of heavy stones and piles of earth that were littered across the court. I offered Margaret my hand to assist her over several piles of dirt and boulders, but she eschewed my aid, preferring to clamber over the untidy heaps on her own. I exhorted her to take care, and it was with some relief that we arrived at the bottom tier of the front steps without incident or injury.

"I do not see a thing," I said.

"No, neither do I," Margaret admitted. "But as I recall, it was over there that I saw something." She pointed to the east, toward the kitchen tower, and without paying heed to the terrain or the lack of light, ventured out toward her object, stumbling over a stray block of granite.

"Take care," I admonished, following her with the lamp. But Margaret ignored my caution; she was resolved to locate the pile of stones that had caught her attention.

She broke into a run over the uneven stones and did not let up until she reached her goal, a mound somewhat lower than the others but wider, which stood at the eastern side of the court.

"Here. This one," she said, out of breath.

I stood over the stones for a moment, uncertain. "I do not see anything."

Margaret looked quickly up at the house and then back to the mound as if to get her bearings. "Down there," she said, indicating the bottom of the pile closest to the palace. She bent down and began methodically pulling stones away from the mound.

"Take care, they are heavy," I said, leaning down to assist her.

We worked for only a minute before Margaret pushed aside one of the larger stones and revealed, peeking out of the bottom between two pieces of granite, a hand. A thin silver ring circled one finger.

"Oh, my God," I whispered.

"There," Margaret said. "I told you." She began to cry softly.

I stared stupefied, aghast at what Margaret had discovered: a dead girl lying under a pyramid of stone in the courtyard of Blenheim Palace. The enormity of what Margaret saw finally overcame her: Her weeping turned to screams—a series of low, insistent cries that were part fright, part despair. I pulled her toward me and tried to turn her gaze from the stones. She resisted fiercely, pushing me away with a strength I did not know she possessed. "I am not a child, Van," she said as she began to weep softly. "I am not a child."

"This is not something anyone should see," I said. "Come inside. We will alert the house and bring back help."

"She could still be alive, Van," Margaret said.

I shook my head. "That is not possible."

Margaret bent down to look more closely at the hand and then looked back at me. She was more composed now. "All right," she said. "But we should at least push these stones aside."

"We will leave everything exactly as it is. We do not know what is beneath these stones or what condition the body is in. Besides, this is a matter for the duchess."

"And the duke," Margaret added.

"Yes. Of course."

I picked up the lantern and we retraced our steps over the uneven terrain, the flame fluttering as I lost my footing. We made it to the colonnade stair without mishap, but before we ascended I held Margaret's arm.

"What is it?" she asked.

I peered through the darkness at her tearstained face and opened my mouth to ask the question that had been gnawing at me ever since she had moved the final stone. But the sounds would not come; I could not form the words. I thought I knew the answer—I hoped I knew the answer—but my body still had doubts.

If I could not see the body as I stood over the stones, how could she have seen it in the dark from inside Blenheim, one hundred fifty feet away?

"Never mind," I said. "Let us go back inside."

As we walked along the colonnade, I gazed across the courtyard and for a moment thought I could see, in the obscurity of the corresponding colonnade, a figure watching our movements. But as soon as my mind registered it, the image was gone, leaving me unsure if I had actually seen it. I had little time to contemplate the trick my eyes played on me, for at that moment Margaret broke into a run and pulled ahead of me. I marveled at her singleness of purpose. After all, Emily—for there could be no doubt that it was she—was dead. She could be saved now by no earthly effort. What, indeed, was the haste?

I struggled to keep pace with Margaret and to keep the lamp lit. Inside Blenheim, we made straight for the family wing.

We stood at the door to the dining room. "You alert the duchess, I will do the same for the duke," I said.

Margaret nodded and turned toward the room that the duchess was temporarily using, while I made straight for the door in the dining room that communicated with the duke's rooms. My repeated knocks upon his bedroom door, which grew louder and more insistent, did not rouse him, so impetuously I opened the door and let myself into the room.

"Your Grace, I beg your pardon for this interruption, but—" The room was very dark, the curtains having been drawn, but the light from the lamp made clear that the room was empty, though the disheveled bedclothes indicated it had been occupied recently.

Margaret appeared at the door with the duchess, who was in her dressing gown. "Where is he?" the duchess asked.

"I do not know, Your Grace," I said. "No one answered my knock."

"No matter," she said. "Call the butler. Tell him to collect some footmen, lamps, and a blanket and to meet us in the courtyard."

"Yes, Your Grace," I said. But the commotion created by alerting the duchess attracted the notice of the servants who were still awake, for at that moment Jamison and several other footmen appeared at the doorway to the dining room.

"Mr. and Mrs. Vanbrugh have discovered a body under one of the stone piles in the Great Court," the duchess told the group. "They will show us where it is." At that moment, Margaret burst into a new round of crying. The duchess put an arm around her and escorted her into her room. "Jamison, would you come with me, please."

Jamison, still in his formal livery but without his wig, looked surprised at the order. He ran a hand through his disheveled hair and followed the duchess.

Later, as we assembled in the hall, one of the footmen murmured, "Allow me to unlock the door, sir." The duchess and I stood at the doors and watched him address the complicated lock as Mr. Churchill, wearing a silk, scarlet-colored dressing gown festooned with Oriental dragons of vivid yellow, padded toward us in elegant slippers of royal blue. "What is happening?" he asked. "You will wake the dead."

"If only we could," I said.

"What are you talking about?" he asked.

"We have found a woman, the *body* of a woman, in the courtyard," I said.

"Good Lord," Mr. Churchill said. "Is she dead?"

"It appears so," I said.

"Who is it?"

"That is what we are about to find out," the duchess said carefully as the footman finally succeeded in unfastening the doors and a line of people snaked out into the night, Mr. Churchill included.

"How did you detect the body?" Mr. Churchill asked at the top of the steps, his white legs creaking slightly as he gingerly made his way down them.

"Margaret said she noticed something earlier, from the window. Just after Annie ... went off."

"Quite," Mr. Churchill said. He looked out into the darkness. "Your wife is commendably observant. With eyesight like that, I would wager she can see into man's very soul."

At that moment Margaret hurried toward us from the house. She again had composed herself, but there was a frenzy to her, a hysteria that she could barely keep in check. She was about to say something when she noted that the servants, who had collected around the spot where we had discovered Emily, turned to us, puzzled. Margaret ran down the steps quickly, Mr. Churchill and I right behind her. Instead of encountering a small pyramid, there was nothing but the bare stone. The blocks that had formed the pile had been pitched about, as if they had been tossed in haste, and the body of the poor girl had been removed.

"She is not here," Margaret said, her voice cracking. "Van, what has happened?"

I looked around the dark, still courtyard for some hint of what had occurred. But there was nothing to see: The shadows concealed everything too well.

"So Emily has disappeared, has she?" Mr. Churchill said. "How exceptional. Are you certain she has been spirited away?"

"Mr. Churchill, this is exactly where we discovered the body not ten minutes ago," Margaret snapped at him.

"Perhaps the Blenheim moonlight is playing tricks on your eyes," he said.

Margaret whirled at him, her eyes narrow. "How many young girls do you know who choose to sleep under a pile of stones, Mr. Churchill? Both Van and I saw a hand right here, beneath these rocks. And these stones were not flung about as they are now. They were in an orderly pile, just like all the others."

"Besides, Mr. Churchill," I said evenly, "I do not recall any of us mentioning that it was Emily who was under these stones."

Mr. Churchill looked flustered at being caught out, but was prevented from replying by the arrival of an agitated Jamison, who burst into the circle. "Where is she?" he demanded.

"She is gone," I said.

Jamison looked wildly at the faces around him. "She is still alive? Where has she got to?"

"No one knows, man," Mr. Churchill said. "It is all a terrible muddle."

"We will organize a search, Jamison," Margaret said with decision.

"No," he said. "I will find her." Before we could stop him, he ran off into the darkness.

I moved to catch him, but Mr. Churchill prevented me. "Leave him be," he said.

"Van," Margaret said, "take half of the men and search the chapel wing. I will take the other half and search the kitchen court."

Mr. Churchill took her hand and smiled. "You go with your husband, my dear. I will take the rest of these men and search the kitchen court."

Margaret looked at him in surprise. "Mr. Churchill, you are in your dressing gown."

"Mrs. Vanbrugh, all of these men are well acquainted with Japanese silk," he said. "Now, assist your husband with the search. Be thorough and look everywhere. Signal if you discover anything of importance, and we will come to your aid." With that, Mr. Churchill, looking oddly commanding in his dressing gown and slippers, motioned his troops toward the kitchen courtyard.

As we turned to the chapel and its surrounding buildings, I happened to look up at the house. There, standing between the two enormous central pillars, his arms crossed, was the monsignor, thin and severe in the moonlight. I was too far away to read his expression clearly, but I noticed that after a moment, he turned and walked back into the house.

chapter
11

WE organized our party into two groups: one group, led by me, to search the stable courts beyond the chapel wing; the other, headed by Mr. Churchill, to explore the chapel itself and the warren of rooms clustered around it. The men—no more than a dozen, none of whom I recognized—were eager to start.

I summoned half of the men, and, our lanterns alight, we set out for the colossal stableyard archway as Mr. Churchill and his group began their task of exploring the chapel wing.

As we reached the archway, Jamison appeared unexpectedly next to me. He had changed out of his livery into a simple shirt, sturdy wool trousers, and boots, and he was out of breath.

"What are you doing here, Jamison?" I asked.

"I couldn't stay away," he said, his voice low.

"We do not know what we shall find," I reminded him.

Jamison nodded, his head jerking at a peculiar angle, a haunted brightness to his eyes. He squeezed my arm. "Must get him," he said.

"Get who?" I asked.

"Him who did this to Emily," he said.

"We will try," I promised.

But Jamison was not listening. He shook his head violently, like an animal, and pulled me around to face him. The look in his eyes was wild, unbalanced. "He wouldn't stop, would he? He wouldn't leave

Emily alone." He started as if he had just heard a shot and yelled into the night, "She didn't know! She didn't know."

I tried to calm him. "We have enough men to search, Jamison. Go back inside and ask the others if they saw someone moving about the courtyard..."

Jamison shook his head vehemently. "Can't go back," he said. Instead of arguing further, he bolted from me shouting Emily's name and ran through a small door near the chapel and disappeared.

"Poor bastard," one of the men mumbled. "Thinks His Grace is up to his old tricks."

"What do you mean?" I asked.

The man shrugged. "Not for me to say. Only there's worse I seen at Blenheim than the duke, and that's the God's truth." He shook his head sadly and moved back into the crowd of men that waited for my direction.

Puzzled, I directed the men into the tunnellike vault to the stableyard. It was very dark, and our lanterns did little to pierce the inky blackness. Our shuffling steps sounded hollow as they bounced off the clammy walls, and I wondered for a moment if anyone had brought a gun.

I felt keenly the malice of Blenheim: It emanated from every brick, tainting anyone foolish enough to be enticed by the drama of this place. The house was as obdurate as the stones that built it; it was merciless, giving no quarter to anyone or anything. Blenheim, I realized, was a house devoid of sympathy and empty of faith. It was a very grand setting, but, like the velvet wall coverings in the bedchamber of the duchess, it concealed much. It was a splendid jewel box that stored a trove of dangerous secrets.

Once in the stableyard we broke into pairs and fanned out to begin our search. The men were thorough, working with diligence and purpose. Every door was opened, each stall scrutinized, all of the walls and floors examined carefully for some indication, a hint, that Emily was here. The horses observed us in silence—wondering, no doubt, what we mere humans were about so late in the evening. But nothing caught our notice. After some time, it became apparent that there was nothing to find. One of the men offered to help the others search the chapel wing—a suggestion I was quick to agree to.

We returned to the Great Court, and as the men made their way into the rooms on the ground floor around the chapel, I noticed Margaret standing at the top of the colonnade stairway with the duke, the duchess, and Mrs. Belmont. Her arms were crossed and she was frowning.

"So there you are, Vanbrugh," the duke said. Like Mr. Churchill, he was in his dressing gown, a less flamboyant but equally well-made garment of scarlet silk with the Marlborough crest embroidered in gold thread on the chest pocket. "Thought we had lost you, too."

"We were searching the stableyard," I said.

"So Mrs. Vanbrugh said, yes. Good man." He sniffed the air and put his hands in his pockets. "Marvelous night," he said. The duchess looked away.

"Have you discovered anything, Mr. Vanbrugh?" Mrs. Belmont asked.

"I am afraid not," I admitted.

"Bad luck," the duke said.

Margaret turned to me, looking concerned. "We are waiting for Mr. Moore to retrieve the key to the chapel."

"The key to the chapel? It was just open. We were in there only a little while ago."

"Yes, but the door has been closed and secured since then," Margaret said carefully.

This was perplexing news. "What could be the purpose of locking the chapel door in the middle of the night?" I asked.

The group fell silent, and Margaret looked at me, her eyes wide, as my old schoolmistress used to when drilling me on the rudiments of mathematics. It required but a moment to answer my own question. "Something is concealed in the chapel!" I exclaimed. "But surely there is a better place than the chapel to hide something," I said.

"Of course there is," the duchess said. "Hundreds of better places around Blenheim."

"But that is the point—" Mrs. Belmont expostulated, but she was interrupted by the return of the butler, who even at this late hour observed the dignity of his position by holding in his gloved hand a silver salver, upon which he had placed a small ring of keys. He presented the salver to the duchess, who took it without a word and selected a key.

"Pity you do not have your keys with you," Mrs. Belmont said to the duke.

"Yes," the duke replied. He peered into the dark sky.

The duchess pushed open the heavy wooden door. The reek of death had dissipated somewhat—as the high windows above the pews had been left open to air out the room—but it was still pronounced enough for the duchess and Mrs. Belmont to step back and place handkerchiefs to their noses.

I entered the chapel and stood for a moment on the stone landing. Moonlight from the windows fell dispiritedly on the monument to the first duke and duchess, who looked surprised to see us. After a moment the odor had dispersed somewhat as the air currents created by the open door carried away some of the stench.

"It is all right," I called out, "the smell has scattered."

"You had better be right, young man," Mrs. Belmont said from the colonnade. Tentatively, the women entered, filing past me and down the narrow, winding stairs. It was only after the switch had been located by the duchess and the chapel had been restored to light that I noticed the duke was not with us.

"Your Grace," I called, returning to the colonnade.

There was no one but the butler, who murmured, "His Grace has retired for the evening, sir." He walked past me to the chapel landing and inquired of the duchess, "Will there be anything else, Your Grace?"

The duchess looked up at him. "No, thank you," she said.

The butler nodded and disappeared into the night.

I joined the ladies at the bottom of the stairs. They stood hesitantly in the middle of the chapel.

"It is all right, Mother, the odor is tolerable," the duchess said.

Mrs. Belmont offered a muffled laugh but did not remove her handkerchief from her nose. "Perhaps for you," she said, "but I have always had a sensitive nose." She looked around the chamber. "What are we looking for?" she asked.

"Some indication that Emily is here," I said.

"Perhaps this is it," Margaret said from the corner of the room. She pointed to the floor. There, in front of her, was the trapdoor to the crypt. But far from being returned to its proper place to blend with the rest of the pattern, the lid had been rotated ninety degrees, so that this part of the design was out of kilter.

I looked at Margaret, who crumpled her handkerchief nervously against her bosom, and nodded.

"What? What is it?" the duchess asked.

"This trapdoor is askew. As if it had been replaced too quickly. Or in the dark."

The duchess blanched but said nothing. She turned to Mrs. Belmont and grasped her hand. After a moment she managed, "You think that Emily may be in there." She pointed downward. "In the crypt."

"I do not know, Your Grace. But I think that it is possible," I said.

The duchess closed her eyes for a moment and took a long, slow breath. When she opened them again and turned her gaze to me, her entire appearance had altered. She looked undone—outmaneuvered by what was before her.

"Mr. Vanbrugh, I wonder if you could collect some men and have them assist you. Mother, you, Mrs. Vanbrugh, and I will return to the house." The duchess took the arms of both Margaret and Mrs. Belmont and guided them to the stairs. Neither woman offered a protest. At the top of the flight the duchess said, "Please relay any news to me—whatever it may be."

"Of course."

After they had gone, I unlocked the lower door of the chapel, which opened onto the Great Court, and made my way back out into the night, where some of the men were milling about. Mr. Churchill, still in his dressing gown, and his group had just returned from the Kitchen Court and I acquainted him with what had happened.

He lowered his head so that his chin nearly touched his chest. In a confiding tone he asked, "The duchess has left the chapel, I hope."

"And Mrs. Belmont and my wife," I replied.

"Good." He nodded and turned his attention to the chapel door. "How many men will be required?"

"Not many. The trapdoor is not too heavy."

Mr. Churchill selected three men, one of whom held a crowbar, and they accompanied us into the chapel. The others followed us at a respectful distance and kept a vigil on the chapel landing and along the stair railing.

The men made short work of their preparation. They laid a thin gray blanket next to the trapdoor and one of them pried it up easily. The odor that emanated from the crypt, while pungent, was less overpowering than it had been earlier in the day. Still, it was acrid enough to induce Mr. Churchill to wrinkle his nose and glance at me, as if to appeal for relief.

"If you prefer, I will search for her," I said.

Mr. Churchill looked embarrassed and shook his head. He composed himself and, tightening his dressing gown around his stomach, kneeled down before the crypt. After a moment to steel himself, he took several deep breaths and, lantern in hand, leaned into the hole.

There was a long moment of frightened expectancy as we waited, suspended in a terrible uncertainty, for his report. As we waited, all we could see of him was the lurid, jeering dragon across the back of his dressing gown and his thin, hairless legs.

It seemed hours before he sat upright again. But when he did, his face was almost purple and he was coughing. No one spoke as we waited for him to recover himself.

"Did you find her?" I asked as his attack subsided.

"She is down there," he said. "God help us all." He wiped his mouth with the sleeve of his dressing gown.

The men murmured as Mr. Churchill directed three of the men down into the catacomb to retrieve the body. They made quick work of it, hauling Emily out of the crypt without fuss.

It was evident, even to a layman, that Emily had been dead for some time—and that she probably had been strangled. There were hideous bruises on both sides of her neck that could have been made only by another hand, and her eyes were bloodshot and bulging, frozen forever in a horrible, dreadful stare. Her mouth hung open, as if to scream a final agonized cry, and her hands were clenched into tight fists.

Looking down upon the poor creature, I was assailed by a crushing finality. Though I had seen others at rest, I had never been struck more profoundly by how fearful we humans are of death. We cling to life with a tenacity and a determination of purpose that defy rational judgment. How silly that is. Most of us lead such meager lives: Lonely and colorless, without joy or hope, with little to fill our bellies and even less to fill our souls. Yet we press forward to one more breath, one more heartbeat, toward a goal few of us know. What is the object of life? What is the point of it? And who is lucky enough to understand it—and embrace it? The duke in his palace? The beggar in the gutter? The minister in his pulpit? It was impossible to know. Perhaps it is a mystery whose solution is known only to God, who I suspect secretly snickers at our stupidity.

I looked away and shivered.

"Poor, stupid girl," Mr. Churchill said.

"She was not stupid," I said with more conviction than I intended.

Mr. Churchill turned to me, frowning. "She was foolish enough to get herself killed."

"That is not foolishness. That is a tragedy."

Mr. Churchill laughed. "A tragedy? I did not know that you were such a philosopher, Mr. Vanbrugh. I thought you were a practical man."

"I am practical. That is why I know Emily was not stupid. She understood exactly what was going on."

One of the laborers scowled at me but said nothing. "What *is* going on, Mr. Vanbrugh?" Mr. Churchill asked, sounding as contemptuous as the duke.

"I have no idea," I admitted. "But Emily did. And I will wager she told someone."

There was a rustle on the stairs as Jamison pushed his way into the chapel. "Did you find her?" he demanded. He elbowed his way through the crowd of men down the stairs and ran across the chapel floor, his mouth moving in a silent lament. Mr. Churchill moved forward to prevent him from seeing the body and warned, "Steady, old man." But Jamison was not to be deterred. He pushed Mr. Churchill aside and stumbled toward the body, which was now covered by part of the blanket. He knelt next to Emily and looked down at her shrouded form. "Where'd you find her?" he asked softly.

"Mr. Churchill found her in the crypt," I replied.

Jamison seemed bewildered by that but did not ask for an explanation. Instead he returned his attention to Emily, and gingerly drew back the cloth that covered her face and neck. When he saw Emily and the injuries that had been done to her, he gasped. He stared at her for an eternity, as if he were committing to memory every harm done to her. Then, with great tenderness, he traced the bruises on both sides of her neck, closed her eyes slowly, and pushed back from her face a strand of misbehaving hair. The silence was absolute. After a time, the butler and another footman came forward and, taking Jamison by both arms, pulled him back to his feet. "Come along, my boy, there's a good lad," the butler said kindly. Jamison pushed the men away and with a cry ran out of the chapel.

Mr. Churchill looked over at me. "Poor sod." He shook his head. "Come on, men," he said, his voice suddenly purposeful. "Let us remove this poor creature from this place."

Emily was taken to a room Mr. Churchill had already set aside in the Kitchen Court. We were a curious, solemn procession as we made our way slowly across the Great Court, navigating around the piles of stone and turf the workers had left. Most of the men accompanied us— an impromptu honor guard for a young woman many of them did not know. My gaze took in both colonnades, which in the deceptive light looked like two sides of a Roman arena—the Colosseum, perhaps, in which the emperors once stood to await the outcome of a contest be- tween a slave and a lion. As we passed the shallow stairway that was the twin to the colonnade stair just outside the chapel, I looked up and noticed the duke himself standing at the top of the stairway, watching me. Behind him, over his shoulder, was the looming presence of Monsignor Vay de Vaya. The monsignor made the sign of the cross as we passed by, but the duke observed us in steady, stately silence. I do not know if anyone else in our party observed their attention, but I could not shake a feeling of deep apprehension.

chapter
12

WHEN Mr. Churchill and I returned to the house, it was evident that news of our discovery had rushed through Blenheim. No one, it seemed, was asleep: The electric lamps had been relighted in the Great Hall, including the two oversized coach lanterns on either side of the front doors, and servants were up and about. The duke and duchess and their guests had assembled in the family dining room, in their dressing gowns and battered tweeds—whatever they happened to have thrown on. The duchess had ordered a cold supper, which was being arranged on the table and in the bow window at the far end of the room.

But we were a grim party and ate little. No one was inclined to conversation; we had seen too much this night. Everyone looked drained—the duchess in particular. She had dark circles under her lovely brown eyes, and seemed startled each time she reached for the pearls that normally circled her neck and did not find them. The duke sat still as stone, his expression guarded; he made no pretense at conviviality. Only Mr. Churchill looked remotely animated: He arranged a comfortable chair near an open window and ordered a bottle of champagne. As he settled in, he lighted a cigar and motioned me over to him as Margaret sat down at the table next to the duchess. Mr. Churchill offered me a glass of champagne, which I accepted gratefully. But as I took the slim flute, my hands shook.

"Does the poor girl have any family?" Mrs. Belmont asked.

"No," Margaret said.

"Mrs. Andrews tells me that she was an orphan," the duchess said.

"She was from Woodstock, I believe," Mr. Churchill added.

"Long Hanborough, actually," the duchess corrected.

I looked at Margaret in some surprise. She had not told me that Emily was from her village.

"Really," Mrs. Belmont said speculatively. "How interesting." The light from the chandelier caught her pince-nez and reflected off its lenses: From across the room they looked like two shining silver ovals. Cat's eyes.

The duchess turned to her mother. "How is it interesting?" she asked.

"Well, Mrs. Vanbrugh is from Long Hanborough," Mrs. Belmont said, nodding at Margaret.

Margaret frowned. "Yes. What of it?" she asked.

"Reverend Barton dined with us at Blenheim, Mother, and you know he is the vicar there," the duchess reminded Mrs. Belmont.

"I know who your dinner guests were, Consuelo." Mrs. Belmont took a sip of coffee and smacked her lips. "The reverend and I had a very pleasant talk. I had not known until this evening how closely linked the Barton family was to Long Hanborough."

Margaret said nothing, but a tension overtook the conversation. It was no longer idle prattle among houseguests; it had become something more treacherous.

"What are you trying to say, Mother?"

Mrs. Belmont put down her cup and arranged her dressing gown more tightly around her ample bosom. "I am not *trying* to say anything," she said deliberately. "I think it is very clear what I *am* saying."

The duchess looked at her mother. "Then do not be so coy."

"I am never coy," Mrs. Belmont said indignantly.

From across the room the duke said, "Alva is implying that Mrs. Vanbrugh and Emily knew each other."

"But that is not true," Margaret said after a moment, looking at me for support. "I did not know her at all, I assure you. I met her for the first time today. In my room."

"Of course you did not know her," I said.

The monsignor said, "You are very certain, Mr. Vanbrugh."

"I am certain that my wife would have admitted knowing Emily if she did." I made no effort to keep the exasperation from my voice. The monsignor and his rush to judgment irritated me.

"But I do not have to admit that I knew her, because I did not know her," Margaret insisted.

"I am aware of that," I snapped at Margaret. She glared at me but held her tongue. From where I stood, I could see she was trying to maintain her composure: Her lower lip quivered, and she struggled to keep from bursting into tears.

I should have felt some compassion, as I certainly was responsible for upsetting her. After all, as my wife, she deserved my respect and sympathy—at least in public. But the poisonous atmosphere in the room, in Blenheim itself, undermined my good intentions. It preyed upon me and my emotions: What had been bearable had suddenly become unendurable. The smallest aspect of her demeanor, the tiniest fault in her character, was magnified by our being in this huge, unmerciful house. Just as makeup exaggerates an actor's character onstage, Blenheim seemed to magnify Margaret's shortcomings.

Mrs. Belmont wiped her mouth with a napkin. "As I recollect," she said after a moment, "Long Hanborough is a very small village. Like Newport."

"Oh, good Lord, it is nothing like Newport, Mother," the duchess said.

Mrs. Belmont acted as if her daughter had not spoken. "It would be quite unusual to grow up in such a place and not be acquainted with everyone," she said.

"But not impossible," Mr. Sargent said quietly, his firm voice cutting through the air like a slender slicing knife.

Mr. Churchill chuckled. "In a world where the lame walk and the dead rise from the tomb, anything is possible," he said.

"I did not know that you were a man of faith," the monsignor replied, his eyes narrowing.

"Nor did I," Mr. Churchill replied.

"Winston is a man of ambition, not faith," the duke said.

"Ambition is but faith in oneself," the monsignor said. "It is not too great a leap from having faith in oneself to having faith in someone else. Mrs. Vanbrugh, for example."

"Faith in Mrs. Vanbrugh?" Mrs. Belmont said. "What are you saying?"

"I mean that, absent any other evidence to the contrary, we should believe what Mrs. Vanbrugh says," the monsignor said. "Our faith teaches us that we should be trusting. And to be trustworthy." He bowed slightly at Margaret, who turned away.

"Such trust can get one into trouble," the duchess said. "Oh, not with Mrs. Vanbrugh, of course," she said quickly, "but there are so many people in the world who want to lie, who live to lie."

"Or who lie to live," Mr. Sargent said.

"Yes," the duchess agreed. "It is their natural state. They emit deception and dishonesty, like an odor."

"My heavens, what a picture," said Miss Deacon from the doorway. "Why not throw ourselves from a window and end this misery?" She yawned and wandered into the room, her pointed departure a few hours ago apparently a forgotten memory. She wore a dressing gown of shimmering white satin that was cinched tightly at the waist; it clung to her form provocatively. She took no notice of the men's stares and the women's disapproval.

"Your timing is impeccable, my petal," Mr. Churchill said.

"Thank you, Winston," Miss Deacon said. She selected a grape from a bowl of fruit and popped it into her mouth. "Why are we all awake? Have I missed something shattering?" She looked from face to face. "Oh, I *have*. What is it? Did John propose to Alva? Or better yet— Alva proposed to Winston!" She grinned, happily certain of her wit.

"As a matter of fact, something shattering has happened," the duchess said.

"I knew it," Miss Deacon said. "Tell me instantly."

The room fell silent, each of us waiting for another to relay the unhappy news.

Finally the duchess said to the duke: "Perhaps you would care to tell Gladys what occurred this evening."

The duke grimaced. But after a moment, he complied. "One of the maids was found in the chapel crypt. She had been strangled." He took a large gulp of the whisky he was holding and frowned at the duchess, as if challenging her to find fault with what he had said.

Miss Deacon looked as if the wind had been knocked unexpectedly from her. The duchess indicated a chair and said, "Gladys, I think you had best sit down."

Miss Deacon looked at the seat as if she had never seen such a contraption. But she complied with the suggestion, her expression equal parts horror and disbelief. "Surely you are joking," she whispered when she had regained her voice.

"Sunny is speaking the truth, God help us," Winston answered.

Miss Deacon gripped the arms of her chair until her knuckles turned white. "How did..." she began, but stopped. She swallowed several times before trying to speak. "Who found her?"

"Mr. and Mrs. Vanbrugh," the duchess replied. "They came across her body buried under a pile of stones in the Great Court. One of her hands was visible. They alerted us, and when they returned to the body, it had been moved. It was found in the chapel crypt."

Miss Deacon rubbed her eyes with the palms of her hands, as a child might after a bout of crying. Without taking her hands away from her face she asked, "Which one?"

"Which one?" Mrs. Belmont repeated.

"Which maid?" Miss Deacon explained.

"Emily," the duchess said.

"Of course," Miss Deacon said softly. She placed her hands on the table and sat up straight. "What has been done?" she asked. It was clear she was addressing the duke.

"The body has been taken to a room off the Kitchen Court," he said.

"Has the constable been here?" she asked.

For the first time, the duke looked uneasy. "Not yet."

"Why not?" Miss Deacon demanded.

"There is no need to rush. The morning is soon enough," Winston said quietly. "No one can help the poor girl now."

"But Jamison will escape," Miss Deacon said.

Her statement electrified the room.

"What's that? What are you talking about?" the duke demanded.

"I said Jamison will escape if he is not caught."

"What does Jamison have to do with this?" the duchess asked.

"Jamison and Emily were sweethearts. They must have had a quarrel and he killed her in some kind of jealous fit," Miss Deacon said.

"That is preposterous," the duchess said. "Jamison would no more hurt Emily than he would the duke."

"I wouldn't put that past him," Mr. Churchill muttered.

"I will never believe it," the duchess insisted. "It is beyond impossible."

"Any man is capable of destroying the thing he loves most," the monsignor said. "We are all sons of Adam."

"Jamison is not like that," the duchess said.

"I am afraid he is," Mr. Churchill said suddenly.

The duke thrust out his jaw. "What do you mean, Winston?"

Mr. Churchill did not reply for a long moment. Then without emotion, his heavy face blank, his eyes unblinking, he said, "We saw Jamison in the courtyard, and he found us in the chapel when we found Emily's body. He was wild, consumed—an animal. He is possessed by a powerful emotion, I fear." He shook his head and sighed.

"That settles things," the duke said, ringing for a servant.

"It settles nothing," the duchess insisted.

"It is enough to try to find him," the duke said.

"But not to hang him for murder," the duchess shot back.

"Well, consider the alternative," the duke said. "Do you want to be murdered in your bed? Or whatever bed he happens to find you in?"

"See here," Mr. Sargent began, but fell silent as the butler appeared and the duke turned his attention to him.

"Jamison has strangled Emily and disappeared. Round up some men; he cannot have gotten far. And send someone to alert the constable at first light."

"Yes, Your Grace," the butler said.

As he departed, Miss Deacon added, "And hurry." The duke's words had energized her; her face, grave a few moments before, was now jubilant, as if the crucial piece to a particularly vexing puzzle had been found. "Yes, of course, Jamison is the man."

She reached across the table and clasped Margaret's hand. "My dear, this must be terrible for you. I am so very sorry."

Margaret looked at Miss Deacon in disbelief. "Are you?" she asked.

Mr. Churchill said, "Mrs. Vanbrugh has been a tower of strength."

"Very courageous," the monsignor agreed. He clasped his hands together and held them in a kind of benediction.

"You need not sound so surprised, Monsignor," Mrs. Belmont said. "Courage is not an attribute exclusive to men."

"As Mother will be the first to tell you. She has the heart of a lion," the duchess said.

"And the face to match," the duke mumbled—too softly for the women at the table to hear, but loud enough for the men in the bay to catch. Mr. Churchill snorted loudly but covered his laughter by an exaggerated coughing fit. The monsignor turned impassively to the window.

"What was that? What did you say?" Mrs. Belmont demanded.

"Nothing. I was clearing my throat," the duke said. "Come now, let's all go back to our beds. I am done in."

"An excellent suggestion," Mr. Churchill agreed.

"But the constable—" Miss Deacon said.

"I will leave instructions to be awakened when he arrives," the duke said. "Now run along."

The monsignor whispered something to the duke, who nodded.

Margaret came over to me. "I am sure I will have dreadful night-mares," she said. Her tone was frightened and petulant like a child demanding attention.

"You will sleep well," I said.

"It has been a very long time since I've done that." She looked down at her stomach as she reached for my hand.

Brushing her hand away, I plunged my fists into my jacket pockets. Margaret looked at me, hurt.

I met her gaze evenly. "What?" I demanded. "What else do you need?"

She sniffled and reached for her handkerchief. "I do not know how much more of this I can stand," she said, her voice quaking. She dabbed her nose several times for effect.

"How much more?" I repeated. "What have you done so far?" The memory of the lifeless hand in the Great Court flashed before me.

Margaret's eyes widened. "Why are you speaking to me this way, Van? I do not appreciate your accusing tone."

At that moment, Miss Deacon joined us and said, "Poor Reverend Barton."

I looked to Margaret for a reply, but she said nothing. Finally, I said, "What do you mean?"

"Only that he will be as saddened by the news as Margaret was," she said.

Margaret sniffed and turned to face Miss Deacon. "I do not understand." Her voice was low and deliberate.

Miss Deacon looked perplexed. "But surely you heard what Reverend Barton said tonight."

The monsignor appeared next to me. "What did Reverend Barton say?" he asked.

Miss Deacon frowned; two small lines creased the top of her nose. "Weren't you there, Monsignor? I thought you must have been. It was after dinner, on the terrace. Or was it when we were in the library? No, I remember now, it was while we were walking to the terrace that he mentioned it." She paused and looked at us, her expression cheerful. She was playing the coquette and clearly enjoyed the drama she was creating. "Yes, that was it." She smiled, which evolved into a yawn. "I am so sorry."

"Really, it is time for me to return to my room," Margaret said abruptly.

"A moment, Mrs. Vanbrugh," the monsignor said. "Miss Deacon, what was it that Reverend Barton said to you?"

"Oh, you did not hear him? He mentioned how strange it was, how unexpected, that Emily should be assigned"—she smiled at the word—"to his daughter while she was a guest here at Blenheim, since they had been friends as girls when they were growing up. In Long Hanborough."

The room fell still, like the moment after a clap of thunder rolled across the sky, paralyzing the world by the force of its sound. All of us were too stunned to speak; we could only stare at Margaret.

"Girlhood friends," the monsignor said.

"I believe the word he used was 'chums,'" Miss Deacon said. Her expression was exultant, pleased as a cat to show off the mouse she had cornered.

"No, we did not hear that, Miss Deacon," the monsignor said. "That was not what we gathered this evening. Most definitely not." He glanced at Margaret. "From anyone."

Margaret glared at the monsignor. I understood the dilemma in which she found herself: If she was to continue to deny the accusation Miss Deacon had made, she would publicly dispute what her father—a vicar—had said earlier. While Margaret wanted to contradict the slander, she could not without branding him a liar. And she would not do that—not at Blenheim, not in front of all of these people.

"Come along, we are all tired," I said. "If you will excuse us, I will take my wife upstairs now."

The duchess looked relieved at the suggestion. "A fine idea," she said.

"Oh, are you going upstairs? I will walk with you," Miss Deacon said, arranging her dressing gown.

Margaret looked at me in alarm, her eyes pleading.

"Oh, Gladys, I wonder, would you stay here for just a moment?" the duchess said quickly.

"Whatever for?" Miss Deacon asked.

The duchess did not reply, but the duke interjected, "You have done enough for tonight." He drew Miss Deacon back into the room. "Good night," he said to us, not unkindly.

I nodded to the duke, and with Margaret gripping my arm, we left the room and the other guests with as much dignity as we could muster. We walked sedately down the corridor, and at every step I could feel the rest of the party staring at us from the dining room. They said nothing, and their silence was as deafening—and as accusatory—as if shouts of "Liar" had been thrown at us.

Margaret held up through the Great Hall, but at the bottom of the stairway she faltered. "I cannot make it to my room," she whispered, falling against me.

I lifted her into my arms; despite her being pregnant, Margaret was still light, as weightless as a sunbeam. I carried her with no more effort than it would have taken me to convey an armful of wildflowers. Halfway to the first landing, Margaret snuggled her head against my shoulder. It brought back memories of more tender days, to our journey to England on the ship, when, as a newlywed, she fell asleep every night in my arms. I smiled at the memory, the gathering shadows consuming us as I climbed. Our days had been easier then; we knew less of each other, and every hopeful thing seemed possible.

I was now convinced that Miss Deacon had concocted the entire tumult to sow discord between Margaret and the duke and duchess. It was impossible to think otherwise: I had never known Margaret to lie. Nevertheless, I was no longer confident of anyone's motives: With Emily dead and Jamison her likely killer, I had even begun to wonder about Margaret. Her interest in Emily and her zeal to discover her remains were disquieting. Why had she been so firm in her desire to search for her? I very much wanted to know, as well as what Margaret thought Miss Deacon was attempting.

I opened the bedroom door and maneuvered around it carefully and lowered Margaret onto her bed. She asked me not to ring for Annie: "Please, Van, I do not want to see anyone else tonight. I am all in."

I nodded and helped her into her nightclothes. She was so subdued, so complying, that I became concerned; she had never been like this. She seemed defeated by Blenheim, beaten down by its deceptions. I arranged her pillows and drew a thin blanket over her, which she did not notice: She was asleep before the lamp on her night table had been extinguished. I do not think that she even heard me close the door between our rooms.

I undressed and, dousing the light, opened wide one of the windows. I pulled a comfortable chair over to the window and sat down in it, drinking in the fragrant night air. Clouds had moved in from the west and had obscured the moon, so it was difficult to make out the dark mounds of low trees that broke the horizon. The air was still warm, but a fitful breeze rustled the invisible leaves and promised rain.

My thoughts, jumbled and disordered, returned to Emily and her death. I could not conceive what the poor girl had done to merit such an appalling end, particularly in light of what I overhead her tell the duke about the sketchbook. Had she been killed for something as prosaic as a sketchbook? Or were there other, darker reasons? Circumstances, I was forced to admit, led me to agree that Jamison was the leading suspect. But if Emily told the duke the truth, wouldn't he have tried to protect her from Jamison—at least until she had located the sketchbook? Emily, unlike the duke, certainly could search for it all over the house without raising suspicion.

And what had my father-in-law said to Miss Deacon at dinner? He was such a sincere, uncomplicated man, I knew he would never willingly embroil his daughter in the unpleasant predicament she found herself in. But he had no notion of how Miss Deacon used words as weapons and her beauty as a shield; he was too easily convinced that a pretty face was an honest one. I resolved to contact my father-in-law early the next morning to get to the bottom of this problem.

My determination did not resolve anything, of course, but I felt a bit better for deciding on a course of action, even a modest one. It was the only avenue I could think that might allow me to escape, however briefly, from this living nightmare.

These troubled musings were cut short when I observed two specks of orange light moving through the darkness. As they came nearer, I realized that they were the burning ends of two cigars: one held by the duke, the other by Mr. Churchill. I hoped that they would not notice me as they proceeded down the gravel walk beneath my window, but I need not have worried: In the darkness I was as invisible to them as they were to me.

"Where did you put them?" the duke asked.

"Up on the terrace," Mr. Churchill said. "I will get them." One of the embers moved up the terrace stairway and disappeared behind a heavy pillar.

After a moment the duke demanded in a louder voice: "Where did you go?" His tone was anxious, like a little boy more frightened than he is willing to admit. "It is so bloody dark out here I cannot see where you are."

"Keep your voice down," Mr. Churchill said in an urgent whisper.

"Everyone is asleep, no one can hear us," the duke said defiantly, though he did as Mr. Churchill dictated.

"They will hear you if you continue to use that tone."

"Let them hear me," the duke said. "Fools." The embers of his cigar burned brighter as he puffed on it, and its aroma wafted to my window, making me realize just how near I was to them. The duke stood for some minutes in impatient silence, waiting for Mr. Churchill to reappear. When Mr. Churchill failed to return, the duke whispered angrily: "Winston, what the hell are you doing?"

Mr. Churchill did not reply.

"Winston!" the duke said more insistently.

"I am looking for the loose stone," Mr. Churchill said.

"You said you knew where it was," the duke said.

"Of course I know where it is," Mr. Churchill said. "But even you, Sunny, must admit that it is a trifle involving to locate one stone in utter darkness."

"Oh, very well," the duke replied peevishly. "Go ahead."

Mr. Churchill laughed. "You are too kind."

"Shut up and find it."

There was another pause as Mr. Churchill continued to look and the duke smoked. Then, after what seemed an age, a satisfied "Eureka" came out of the darkness.

"What? Did you locate them?"

"Yes," Mr. Churchill said. After a moment the other ember reappeared and moved like a firefly down the terrace steps.

"Where are you, dammit?" the duke burst out, his voice anxious. "Show yourself immediately." There was a stumbling sound. "Oh, careful, you oaf. That is my foot," he said.

"How kind of you to apologize for walking into me," Mr. Churchill said.

"Never mind that. Are you sure these are the originals?" the duke asked, his voice unsteady. There was a rustle of paper.

"I am certain," Mr. Churchill said. "I removed them from Consuelo's room myself."

"That was resourceful of you."

"It was self-preservation, not resourcefulness. I have just as much to lose as you do."

"I wonder," the duke said. His voice sounded suddenly faint and small.

"I am a Churchill, too, in case Your Grace has forgotten," Mr. Churchill said.

The duke recovered himself. "Yes, yes," he said. "But to discover that . . ." he stopped.

"That an unfortunate root was grafted onto the family tree two centuries ago?" Mr. Churchill offered. "It does tend to upset the digestion."

"Do not be so glib. If it gets about that both John Duke and the Earl of Sunderland were cuckolded by that damned Vanbrugh . . . I do not know what will happen," the duke said.

"It is not as if every Churchill has been above reproach," Mr. Churchill said. "As a family we have been known to misplace our morals from time to time."

"Yes, but that was their choice. They were the sinners, not the sinned against."

"It is not such a bad thing to be Duke of Marlborough, you know," Mr. Churchill said. "We cannot change the past."

"But we are forced to live with it," the duke said.

"What Anne did cannot be altered," Mr. Churchill said gently.

"True enough, but it can be ignored. We have to." The duke paused, and the end of his cigar burned brighter for a moment.

"You have no proof of any of this, Sunny, only a suspicion," Mr. Churchill cautioned.

"These letters make a very persuasive case," the duke said.

Mr. Churchill grunted but said nothing.

"The letters cannot get about."

"Amen," Mr. Churchill murmured. He crushed his cigar into the gravel, and the duke did the same.

"Amen," said another voice in the darkness.

"Who the devil is that?" the duke demanded.

"It is I," the monsignor said, joining them. His step made no sound on the gravel.

"You scared the wits out of me, Monsignor," the duke said. "We did not hear you come up."

"Yet I heard every word the two of you uttered," the monsignor murmured. "You have not been discreet."

"No one is awake, as you can see," Mr. Churchill said.

"I wonder," the monsignor said. I felt rather than saw his eyes scanning Blenheim's façade, searching for the slightest movement.

"Could you not sleep?" the duke asked.

"I was thinking of Jamison," the monsignor said.

"Don't tell me that you are afraid of him," the duke said.

"I am only frightened of him if he is not the killer of the servant girl," the monsignor replied. There was a Teutonic curtness to his declaration.

"What do you mean?" Mr. Churchill said.

"Does it not strike you as singular that Jamison has the least to gain from the death of this girl?"

"They were sweethearts. It was a crime of passion," the duke insisted.

"Perhaps. But what passion?"

"Lust, of course," Mr. Churchill said.

"Come now, Mr. Churchill, you can do better than that," the monsignor said in his most professorial tone. "Others in this house have much stronger motives to wish the servant girl dead. Mrs. Vanbrugh, for instance. Why is she so eager to deny that she knew the girl when they were young? And recall, it was she and Mr. Vanbrugh who found the body. Perhaps it was he who killed the girl to protect his wife's reputation. Pride is a much stronger emotion than lust."

"Pride," the duke repeated, considering.

"Yes. And the method in which the girl was killed is noteworthy. She was strangled, which indicates to me that she probably knew her murderer well—or well enough—for him or her to approach her without rousing her suspicions. Mrs. Belmont, for example. Or even the duchess. She was always a particular favorite of Her Grace's, as I understand. Or Mr. Churchill. Or even you, Your Grace."

"Me? What bloody nerve." The duke's voice bristled.

"I am not accusing you, only suggesting possibilities. When the constable arrives, it may not be so simple to convince him of Jamison's guilt. It is not a foregone conclusion—any of this. We know so little about what really occurred, or what burns within the heart of every man."

"Or woman," Mr. Churchill added.

"Indeed."

The three fell into silence as they digested what had just been said.

"Why are you warning us, Monsignor?" Mr. Churchill asked abruptly.

"I am a servant of the Lord," the monsignor replied enigmatically. And with a nearly silent step on the gravel, he stole away.

"What an extraordinary man," Mr. Churchill said after a moment.

"He's all right," the duke said. "When the chips are down, he'll be with us."

"Where is that, Sunny?" Mr. Churchill asked.

"Never mind. Come on, old boy," the duke said. "It is very late."

"What will you do with the letters?" Mr. Churchill asked.

A twig snapped over to one side of the house.

"What was that?" the duke demanded, ignoring Mr. Churchill's question.

"I heard nothing," Mr. Churchill said.

"I did. Near the shrubbery. I'll wager fifty pounds it's Jamison back for something. Come along." With that, they hurried along the gravel and disappeared into the night.

I was about to leave the window when the duchess appeared unexpectedly on the terrace, a lamp in her hand. She set it down on one of the tables and gazed out onto the lawn, rubbing her arms to keep away the evening chill. The soft light threw her profile into relief, and I was struck by how beautiful she was, even after the upsetting evening we had endured. She looked unimaginably fragile, her features finer and more delicate than ever. She called to mind those Italian paintings Margaret and I saw at the National Gallery.

I leaned out of the window to get a better look as Mr. Churchill returned. He was alone, and I must have attracted his notice, for he caught me watching the duchess.

I drew back into the room quickly as the duchess said, "What are you smiling about, Winston?"

"Your admirer."

"What are you talking about?" she asked.

"Up there."

"Where? No one is there. Everyone is asleep."

"Never mind. It is not important."

"Where is Sunny?" she asked.

"He is out looking for an intruder. He heard someone. Or thinks he did. The poor man."

"Yes, the poor man," she said, her voice tight.

"There, there, my dear. Everything will come right very soon, I am sure of it," Mr. Churchill said.

The duchess laughed. "With your help, of course," she said.

"With my help," Mr. Churchill said. His tone sent a chill down my spine.

THE duchess and Mr. Churchill went back inside and the night quiet enveloped me once again. I allowed myself to exhale fully: I had not realized how still I had been—and how anxious I was at being discovered. It was very late; the clock on the kitchen tower had struck two some time ago. Yawning, I stood up and stretched, nudging the chair away from the window. If I had any hope of contacting my father-in-law early tomorrow, I must get some rest.

I was almost asleep when I heard an ominous roil followed by a dull thud. It was not difficult for me to determine the first as the rumblings of an approaching thunderstorm, but the second sound proved trickier: I could not make out what it was or where it had come from. A few moments later I heard it again, louder this time—and it had come from the corridor. I jumped from bed and hurried to the door. I heard nothing; the passage was quiet. I threw on my dressing gown and opened the door just wide enough to poke my head out. It was darker there than it was in my room, but it was still light enough to see that no one was about. However, a narrow table that stood against one wall had been jostled. The carpet beneath it was askew, and the heavy candelabra that stood on the table was lying on the floor, one of the candles broken.

I stepped into the corridor and listened for a sign that others had heard the noise. But I saw no indication that anyone had been roused by the commotion. I set the table back against the wall and returned the candelabra to its place. Glancing around, I noticed that a chair at the top of the stairway had also been moved—and it appeared to have been bumped rather than intentionally repositioned. As I walked toward it, my bare feet stepped on several small, hard stones. I crouched down and moved my hands along the carpet until my fingers found what I had stepped on. They were small pieces of dried mud.

As I returned to my room, I observed that a door at the end of the passage—one I was certain had been closed when I carried Margaret up to bed—was now ajar. With a growing sense that something peculiar was unfolding, I picked up the broken candle, stopped at my room long enough to light it, and placed it in a small holder. I walked down the passage with it to the open door and peered behind it. To my surprise, it was not a room at all but another servants' stairway, full of tight, curving stone steps that hugged the sheer walls and circled up and down into obscurity. An oval-shaped skylight above allowed in just enough light for me to determine that the stairway ascended at least another story, but I could not tell how far down it went: The darkness was too thick.

Perhaps because of that, or perhaps because I concluded that no one could have descended these stairs without a source of light, which I would have seen, I began the climb to the floor above.

As soon as I gained the next story, I realized I had entered a different realm, a Blenheim altogether distinct from the floors below. This was intentional: Sir John designed Blenheim to appear from the ground as if it were only two stories. The main floor, which comprised all of the state rooms and the suites for the duke and duchess, was designed to impress, to amaze with its splendor. The second floor, while less striking, was commodious enough to lodge guests and the generations of Churchill children and their nurses, governesses, and tutors who used its endless corridors. But above the bedroom story was another floor, one obscured from view by the thick stone balustrades and the dozens of statues, ornaments, and finials that garnish the Blenheim roofline. This third floor was designed for utility, not grace; for the Churchills' servants, not the Churchill family. The dingy, narrow passages, which extended from the stairwell in two directions, were crowded with every manner of box, crate, trunk, fitting, and discarded object. Along the water-stained walls and in every dark cranny that could be found, debris from generations of Churchills was squirreled away. Planks of discarded, pitted timber were propped against a broken cane chair, a tangled pile of levers and pulleys overflowing from its seat. A discarded microscope peeked out from under the cracked glass of a hurricane lamp. Piles of oversized books were lined up along the floor, acting as supports for the inadvertent display of several un-distinguished landscapes and the grimy portrait of a disapproving cleric. A hinged screen decorated in the Chinese manner served as the final resting place for a burlap sack full of wine corks and a box of empty amber-colored bottles of something called Dr. Stephenson's Medicinal Improvement Elixir. A half-finished bust of a forgotten an-cestor, a dilapidated periwig resting uncomfortably upon its rough, un-polished head.

The clutter only added to the pervasive stuffiness of this wing, which, mingled with the lingering odor of overlooked chamber pots, gave Housemaids' Heights—for it could only be that—an oppressive, disagreeable air. The standards of cleanliness Mrs. Andrews imposed downstairs were relaxed—or overlooked—in this part of the house, it seemed.

This was the home, I knew, of the female house servants who kept Blenheim operating. Even from the top of the stairway, I could tell that the rooms had been inserted into any space that could be found, no matter how cramped or oddly shaped: around the myriad chimneys, supports, and beams that Blenheim required to remain standing. I re-called that the duchess had indicated that this floor had neither elec-tricity nor running water and that the duke had forbidden the addition of either. This part of Blenheim was just as it had been for nearly two centuries.

The passage was hushed and still, and all of the doors along it were closed. However, beyond the untidy muddle, I could make out, at the end of one corridor, a soft glow.

I crept toward it cautiously, not at all sure of who—or what—I would find. My bare feet were cold and damp on the floorboards, and the candle flame wavered. Gripping the holder more tightly, I pressed on toward the gray haze ahead of me. As I came to the end of the passage, a peal of thunder, stronger this time, rolled over Blenheim, and I realized that the light was coming from a small room on my left.

I reached it without calling attention to myself and looked in. There, kneeling next to the bed, his hands clasped against his face as if lost in prayer, was Jamison. His hair was wild, his trousers muddy.

"Jamison?" I whispered.

He shot up at me in surprise, a knife suddenly in his hand. When he recognized me, he relaxed and returned the knife to his waistband. "It is you," he said, his voice miserable.

I walked into the room and closed the door. It was neat but furnished simply, with a narrow bed tucked under the eaves. A small wardrobe to the right of the door contained two neatly hung aprons and a simple dress of gray wool; a pair of sensible black shoes stood beneath them. On the shelf next to it there was a tin of toffees, several small books (*Romeo and Juliet,* the poems of Lord Tennyson, a collection of stories by Edgar Allan Poe, *The Castle of Otranto*), and, in pride of place on the topmost shelf, a vividly colored silk scarf, neatly folded.

I sat down on a wooden chair near the open window and noticed that this room was wedged under the jutting roofline of the Great Hall, whose gigantic clerestory windows were only a few feet from the small porthole this room presented to the world.

"What are you doing here?" Jamison asked.

"I could ask you the same thing," I replied.

"This is where she lived," he said.

"Emily is gone, Jamison," I said.

"I know," he said, his voice broken.

"It is all very difficult...," I began, but there was nothing I could say to ease his suffering. "They are looking for you."

"I know. They'll never catch me, though. I can sneak my way through Blenheim better'n the rats."

"I am very sorry about all of this," I said. "Very sorry."

Jamison turned to me, his face cold and disbelieving. "What do you care? You never knew her," he said.

"No, but I have lost loved ones."

"Not your girl. Not when she told you she was up against it."

"What do you mean? Did Emily think she was in trouble?"

Jamison did not reply directly. "You lot. You're all alike. Heartless, that's what you are."

"I assure you I am not," I said quietly. "Sometimes I think I care too much."

Jamison looked unconvinced. "Except toward the missus, eh?"

"You are being absurd. What are you trying to say anyway?" I said after a moment, trying to sound affronted. But it was an unconvincing reply, and Jamison grasped this immediately. He managed a sly smile, and stood up, looking down at me, his eyes glimmering. "You aren't fooling anyone, and that's the truth of it," he said. " 'Course, it's no crime to admire Her Grace. You would hardly be a man if you didn't."

"I do not admire Her Grace," I said, my voice unsteady. "At least not in the way you mean."

Jamison chuckled. "As you say, sir. The wonder is that Mrs. Vanbrugh ha'n't noticed. She will, to be sure."

"She will do nothing of the kind because there is nothing to notice," I said.

Jamison turned away as a flash of lightning briefly lit up the sky, followed by a roll of thunder.

"Storm's brewing," he said.

"What is it that you are looking for up here?" I asked.

Jamison frowned and looked carefully around the sparsely furnished room. "I dunno," he admitted. He picked up the scarf and ran his fingers over it.

"Then what makes you believe something should be here?" I inquired.

"Emily told me. She said she was hiding something up in Housemaids' Heights. Something that cow wanted." The bitterness in his tone was raw, emphatic.

"Who is that?" I asked.

"Mrs. Andrews." He practically spat out the name.

I recalled Emily outside the sitting room door before her interview with the duchess and Mrs. Andrews. How frightened the girl had been, how vulnerable she was in that shadowy corridor. But she had been unexpectedly resolute, firm in her commitment, whatever it may have been.

"What does Mrs. Andrews have to do with this?" I inquired.

Jamison placed the scarf back on the shelf. "She had it in for Emily from the start, Mrs. Andrews did," he said.

"Why? Emily was competent enough."

"Emily was the best there is, and Mrs. Andrews knew it. Everyone did. It was because Her Grace *liked* Emily, and Mrs. Andrews is no friend to Her Grace. Hated her, ever since the day His Grace brought her to Blenheim from America. Mrs. Andrews never wanted to work for Her Grace and that's the truth of it. "She tried everything she could think of to get Emily to give her what she wanted. The monsignor did, too. The joke was, neither one was sure Emily actually had it."

I took a moment to digest this. "But what could the duke, the monsignor, and Mrs. Andrews all want?"

Jamison shrugged. "I dunno."

"Emily never told you?" I asked.

"She said she knew what it was but hadn't seen it."

A dull, throbbing ache began in my head. "But that is preposterous," I said.

Jamison smiled grimly. "She said she wouldn't look."

"Wouldn't look at what?"

"At what it was."

"Yes, I know, but why?" I demanded more loudly.

"For God's sake, keep your voice down," Jamison insisted.

I sighed in frustration. This was becoming more confusing by the minute. "Why would Emily not look at something she had in her possession?"

"She said it was personal."

"Personal to whom?"

"Personal to Her Grace," Jamison said, as if I should have understood this all along.

It took a moment to absorb his meaning. "Let me see if I understand you. Emily was hiding something that belonged to the duchess, which Mrs. Andrews and the monsignor wanted. For the duke?"

Jamison nodded.

"So Emily did not want either one of them to discover it, but she never looked at what was in her possession."

"Got it in one, you did," Jamison said.

"Extraordinary. But you did not find it in this room?"

"No."

"Did you examine the floor and the walls for any hiding places?"
Jamison nodded. "I did not find anything."

"Perhaps Mrs. Andrews or the monsignor found it after all."

"I don't think so. They are looking for it, as well."

"How do you know that?" I asked.

"I have my spies," Jamison said with some satisfaction.

"Perhaps Emily gave you a hint as to where she concealed it by the words she used," I said.

"What do you mean?" he asked.

"Did she say she had hidden it in this room, or just up here in Housemaids' Heights?"

"In her room," Jamison said firmly.

"Are you certain?" I pressed. "Think carefully."

Jamison scowled in concentration, and after a moment shook his head. "Ah, it's too hard to remember. All I knows is that she told me it was up here."

"In Housemaids' Heights," I said. "That is what you said."

"I did, didn't I," Jamison admitted. He looked about the tiny room. "Maybe it isn't in here after all."

"How did Emily come into the possession of this object?" I asked.
Jamison smiled. "She nicked it," he said.

"She stole it?"

"Oh, Emily's a Tartar, she is," Jamison said with spirit, and for a moment the image of the crumpled body beneath the pile of stones was replaced by the living Emily, alive again to both of us.

"Perhaps we should extend the search beyond this room, "I suggested "To all of Housemaids'—"

At that moment, Jamison clapped his hand over my mouth and in a blur extinguished the candles. He brought his mouth down very close to my ear and whispered: "Footsteps on the stair."

I nodded, and he slowly removed his hand from my mouth. We both strained to listen and in a moment we heard the same dull thump of a misstep taken in the darkness. Jamison motioned for me to follow him, and we climbed out of the window and onto the roof. As we did, a large bolt of lightning slashed across the sky, and another cascade of thunder helped cover any noise we made.

The rain began slowly, but soon it turned into an insistent summer downpour, soaking us to the skin as we made our way across the increasingly slippery roof.

The rooftops of Blenheim, obscured by the sodden blackness, were hazardous, as dangerous as something from one of the stories by Mr. Verne. The roof—parts of which were slate, parts of which were copper—angled confoundingly in all directions and was full of sharp edges and outcroppings. We were constantly tripping over serpentine drainpipes, navigating through unexpectedly deep arcades of chimneys, over oddly placed skylights, and around unexpected aviaries, startling dozens of birds. I gashed my foot against a leering stone gargoyle, which leapt out at me during a flash of lightning.

The most hazardous part of our escape, however, turned out to be a narrow catwalk along the edge of the roof that overlooks the Great Court. I was soaking wet and limping, cursing the night, the rain, and this demon of a house, when a scar of lightning and a clap of thunder fell upon us. Startled, I tripped and reached for the stone balustrade on my left for support. But it had been so weakened by time and weather that it crumbled away under my weight and a large piece of it plunged to the ground. I surely would have fallen with it, had not Jamison yanked my right arm roughly toward the roof so that I fell onto the slimy slates rather than onto the granite stones a hundred feet below.

"Got to take care up here," Jamison said as he assisted me to stand up. "Slippery place, it is."

"And frightening," I agreed, shaken.

Jamison offered a sudden, knowing smile. "Not to them that knows this place," he said. "To us, this is paradise. Or as close to it as we're to get here at Blenheim."

It certainly appeared that Jamison was well acquainted with the rooftops of Blenheim. Though the route he forged was labyrinthine, doubling back and forth all over the sprawling roof, he knew what he was about: When he paused so I could catch my breath—warning me to avoid the damp, slippery patches along the slates and the walls—he indicated that we had stopped at the clerestory window directly across the Great Hall from where we had set out. We could look through the window and observe—albeit imperfectly, for the panes were streaked with rain and grime—the window of the bedroom we had just quitted. I was impressed by the ease with which Jamison fixed our position, like a sea captain charting by the stars. But up here on the roof in the rain, there were no stars to use as guides; only a dizzying succession of eaves, chimneys, and statuary. It had the feel of a maze: I had become hopelessly lost, my sense of direction completely befuddled. But up here Jamison was in his element, composed and mindful.

I turned toward the window and peered across the cavernous Great Hall, now plunged into a darkness so complete, so unfathomable, that it looked like the mouth of hell. The window across the blackness was aglow with lamplight, and a figure was moving about the room, though we were too far away and the rain too insistent to identify who it was.

I tapped Jamison. "Look," I said, pointing. "There is someone in the room."

Jamison nodded. "Who is it?" he asked close to my ear, his voice a hoarse whisper.

"I cannot tell," I said.

Jamison rubbed the rain off one of the large panes and thrust his face close to the glass. He stared for a long moment and then turned to me, frowning as if he did not believe what he had just seen. He redirected his gaze back toward the room and stared at it for some time.

Finally, he stepped back and turned to me, his face full of wonder. "It looks like Mrs. Vanbrugh," he said.

I took an involuntary step back and lost my footing again on the slanting slates. Jamison grabbed me and kept me upright as I regained my balance. The look of concern on his face deepened when he said, "You'd better have a look, sir."

With my sleeve, I rubbed away as much of the rain and grit as I could, and, cupping my hands around my eyes, peered through the window. The figure was searching the room in much the way I had suggested to Jamison and for a moment turned toward the window to judge the strength of the storm. At that moment, the briefest flash of lightning illuminated the sky and the figure.

It was unquestionably Margaret.

I pitched forward, as if I had been struck in the stomach. Jamison watched with a hopeless fascination as I sought to make sense of what I had just seen.

"What could she be doing there? What could be her purpose?" I asked.

I struggled to my feet, soaked to the skin, my foot bleeding, my dressing gown ruined. But I barely noticed. All I could think of was Margaret in that window, caught in a flash of lightning, her face turned toward the sky. I did not know what to make of her presence, but a nameless fear began to take hold of me.

Though I did not want to, I willed myself to look toward the bedroom window again. I was just in time to observe Margaret collect her lamp and make her way out of the room. She closed the door behind her and once more the room was in darkness.

"She has just left," I said to Jamison.

"So should we," Jamison said. "Come along."

I followed him as we clambered up the roof and proceeded along the spine of the West Wing. With each step more questions flooded my exhausted brain.

What was Margaret doing in Emily's bedroom? What was she searching for? What of the protests she had made in the dining room? Had she not told the truth?

I felt light-headed, faint with a sickening sense that Margaret—difficult, querulous, reliable Margaret—knew more about Emily's death than I had imagined.

Jamison stopped at a narrow window and peered in quickly. Satisfied that the room was empty, he put both hands on the window and shook it gently. It popped open. Jamison smiled. "Loose bolt," he said. He pried the window wide and eased into the room, turning to assist me as soon as he was in.

Closing the window behind me, Jamison looked about. "There usually is—ah," he said as he located a candle on a delicate table next to the window. He pulled a match—miraculously still dry—from somewhere inside his clothes and struck it. He lighted the candle and held it above our heads so that we could survey the room and its contents.

The room was slightly larger than the others I had yet seen up in the Blenheim attics, but it was empty of all furnishings except for a chaise longue, a low chair, and a tall wooden stool, which stood under a skylight. A pile of loose papers was next to the chair.

"What kind of room is this?" I asked.

Jamison looked perplexed. "Used to be a trunk room, for Their Graces' traveling gear. Em and I used to sneak up here for a little time to ourselves. That's how I knew about the dodgy lock on the window. Haven't been up here for a while. I wonder where everything went," he said.

"And why," I added. "Jamison, what did Emily tell you about Mrs. Vanbrugh?"

"That they had been friends when they were girls. That she was to have a baby."

My heart had sunk to the pit of my stomach and could not catch my breath.

"So Miss Deacon was right," I said.

"About what?" Jamison asked.

"About Margaret. Miss Deacon said tonight that Margaret and Emily had known each other when they were young, in Long Hanborough. Margaret denied it, in front of the duchess, but it turns out to be true. What else is Margaret hiding from me?" I asked as the image of Emily's lifeless body once again appeared before my mind's eye.

chapter

14

JAMISON led us to another service stairway, and we descended to the bedroom story in silence, each to his own thoughts. I followed him to the main corridor, which was very dark. I hardly noticed; I was drenched, my spirits frayed. Blenheim had shattered me. As I reached my door, I turned to say good night to Jamison. But he had already gone, disappearing into the baffling drear of this place.

I removed my waterlogged dressing gown, leaving it in a soggy heap on the hearth rug, and toweled my hair dry. But before I staggered toward the bed, I crept quietly toward the door between my room and Margaret's and listened for a moment. I heard nothing. Carefully I turned the knob and opened the door. To my relief, Margaret was in bed. Perhaps my eyes had been wrong up on the roof; perhaps the rain and my own fatigue had tricked me into thinking that I had seen her there. As I moved closer, I heard her soft, even breathing. I said a prayer of thanksgiving into the darkness. As I turned to depart, I stepped on a loose floorboard, which creaked softly. Margaret started at the sound and pushed herself up from the bed, cried out, "What? What is it?"

Instantly I was by the bedside. "Nothing," I replied soothingly. "It is just a creaky floor. Go back to sleep."

Margaret looked at me in disgust. "For heaven's sake, put on some clothes," she said, falling back against her pillows. She rubbed her stomach absently, as if to calm the child within. "You frightened me."

"I only wanted to make certain you were comfortable," I said.

Margaret frowned and rolled away from me. "I *was*," she said, and made an elaborate show of arranging her disordered blanket.

"Go to sleep now," I murmured.

Margaret sighed. "If only it were that easy," she said.

"Do you want me to stay?"

"Good God, no," Margaret said, already easing back into slumber.

"All right, then. Good night," I said, relieved. I leaned down to kiss her, but thinking that I might startle her again, I stroked her head gently instead.

Her hair was damp to the touch.

"Your hair is wet," I said.

Margaret did not reply.

"Margaret," I repeated, more loudly this time. "Your hair."

"I am trying to sleep, Van," she said, an edge to her voice. "Please leave me."

"But your hair—"

"Please go. I am tired."

It is a sorry circumstance when a husband catches his wife in a lie—in a string of lies. I looked down at Margaret as if I were seeing her for the first time. I felt as if I had wandered into the room of a stranger whose habits and proclivities I did not know. Her behavior this evening had been mystifying, disturbing; it called into question everything I thought I believed about her.

I stumbled back to my room and threw myself into bed. I fell asleep almost immediately, grateful to lose myself in oblivion. But I slept fitfully: My dreams were full of Blenheim, one larger and more menacing than the original, and a vague but inescapable menace, and I awoke as weary as I was when I fell asleep.

My mood was improved considerably by the weather: The rain had passed. The day had dawned bright and clear, and there was a freshness, a purity, which lifted my spirits. I went to the window and opened it wide, breathing deeply of the fragrant air and savoring the fulsome green of the trees and the grass of the South Lawn and the rolling hills beyond. The sky was the color of a robin's egg, and the yellow sun moved gently up from the horizon, like a punter easing along the river. The birds in the trees and among the hedge-rows sounded happy, their high spirits celebrating the prospect of a lovely day.

It was still early and the house was quiet, so I waited a bit before ringing for a servant, using the time to pen a short note to my father-in-law, urging him to come to Blenheim to resolve an issue of great importance—before church, if possible. When I finished the letter, I rang the bell, but no servant came. I tugged on the bell again and checked the small clock on the mantelpiece. It was nearly seven-thirty. Early, perhaps, but the servants should certainly be up and about now.

Another few minutes passed and still no one appeared. Exasperated, I donned some clothes, picked up my shaving things, and ventured out to the bathroom. The room was colder than the corridor, so I washed and shaved quickly and returned to my room. As I closed the door to the corridor, Margaret called out.

I went in to see her. "I feel dreadful," she said, rubbing her forehead. "I must be catching cold."

I felt her forehead, which was cool. "Does your head ache?" I asked.

Margaret nodded. "And my throat, and my stomach," she said. She moaned softly. "I can barely move. I must stay in bed. Will you have someone send up some tea?" she asked.

"Of course," I said, moving toward the bell pull.

"And perhaps an egg," Margaret added after a moment. "And a bit of toast."

I paused. I was well aware how Margaret behaved when she fell ill: She could not stand even the aroma of food until she began to recover. I wondered—again—how truthful she was being.

"I shall send for a doctor," I said.

"No. I am sure I will feel better tomorrow. I just need to rest today."

"Are you certain?" I asked.

"Yes. I could not possibly get out of this bed. Yesterday was . . . too much."

I pulled a chair next to the bed and sat for a moment, neither of us speaking. After a while Margaret asked, "Did you ring the bell?"

"Yes," I said, "but no one seems to be answering this morning." I stood up. "I will go downstairs and have something sent up to you."

Margaret rolled away from me, groaning slightly. "All right. But hurry."

"I will," I promised.

The house was hushed and expectantly still; the other guests were not about. But as I descended the stairs, I felt rather than heard a low hum of activity, the kind one feels at the theater moments before the curtain is about to rise: a sense of great bustle and commotion just out of sight, all in preparation for the drama to come.

The front doors of Blenheim were wide open, as were the doors to the Saloon, which allowed a delightful breeze to blow through the house, scenting the rooms with the aroma of dewy grass and freshly cut flowers. I followed the inviting scents into the Saloon and noticed that the doors to the terrace had been opened, as well. On the majestic gilt and marble tables were two new large bouquets of flowers, which gave the room the feel of a splendidly opulent conservatory.

I stepped out onto the terrace between the tall pillars, thick as oaks, and stood in the sunlight. The atmosphere this morning was as unlike that of the previous night as could be imagined. The terrace then had felt like the last outpost against the intruding forces of the dark. But on this bright, promising day, it was a spacious quay from which to set sail out into the green sea of lawn that stretched out before me.

The tables were not set for a meal, but that did not trouble me: Since it was obvious that the staff was about, I would search out a servant to deliver Margaret her breakfast.

I went back into the house, and noticed that the doors along both sides of the Saloon were also open, communicating with the rooms next to it. The enfilade on either side looked impressive, even alluring; I had half a mind to explore the rooms.

I wandered into the room across the Saloon from where the duke had pointed out one of the tapestries to me. It was roughly twenty-five feet square, and was decorated in luxuriant green hues. The emerald silk wall covering and draperies were accented with gold urn-shaped designs that were woven through the fabric. The uphol-stered chairs and heavy sofas that dotted the large, square Oriental carpet were covered in a darker green damask and looked well against the wainscoting, which was painted a subdued ivory. The ceiling, a sumptuous design of right angles and half-circles, was also painted ivory, but had been embellished with intricate, deeply cut carvings that had been gilded. All of this splendor, however, was nothing to the artwork adorning the walls, particularly the enormous tapestry to the left of the chimneypiece, which portrayed John Duke on horseback, dressed in a scarlet coat, accepting the surrender of the French. A soldier in one corner of the weaving held the captured French flag, and behind him, in the background of the tapestry, were burning bridges and throngs of soldiers being driven into a distant river.

"Hideous, isn't it," a voice behind me said suddenly. "I do not understand why Consuelo allows these rugs to remain on display."

I whirled around in surprise. "Mrs. Belmont, you startled me," I said.

The lady was standing in one of the deep windows that opened out onto the South Lawn. She smiled at me good-naturedly, her pince-nez perched on her wide nose. "Good. That was my intent."

She was already dressed for the out-of-doors: a white blouse festooned with Brussels lace at the collar, a short dark jacket, a black skirt, sensible walking shoes, a small black hat with a dark veil folded away from her face. She carried a walking stick and a pair of gloves.

"Where did you come from?" I asked.

"From my room," she replied.

"Yes, of course. But I mean, have you eaten?"

"I breakfasted in my room." She looked puzzled. "Why?"

"Neither Mrs. Vanbrugh nor I have been able to rouse a servant this morning. My wife is indisposed and cannot come down to breakfast."

"I would imagine," Mrs. Belmont said dryly.

"You should imagine nothing of the sort," I retorted. "She has a chill."

"As you say," she said. She began to put on her gloves. "Do you like the tapestry?" she asked, nodding her head toward it crisply.

"It is very well executed," I admitted.

She shook her head. "You men are all alike. War is a perfectly acceptable subject for art for the lot of you."

"You are too harsh, I think," I said.

"Nonsense. No woman would dream of commissioning tapestries

of all these battlefields and casualties and then hang them on her drawing room walls for everyone to admire. Only a man would do that." She straightened her jacket. "This is a house built on war. That is why no happiness can survive here."

She looked at me in challenge, provoking me to disagree. But I held my tongue, for I had reached the same conclusion. There was no happiness here. There was something about this place that triggered our darker impulses: prevarication, dishonesty, melancholy. Man was insignificant here; Blenheim's shadows were too long to escape from.

"Do you agree with me?" Mrs. Belmont asked.

My finger traced the outline of a red lion rampant in the tapestry—the same lion I had seen in the family crest. "It is not important what I think, Mrs. Belmont."

"I know that. But do you *agree*?" she demanded.

But I was fixed on not answering her directly. "Surely it is the opinion of the duchess that matters most, since she lives here."

"So does the duke," Mrs. Belmont said.

"Yes, but he was born here. It is a different matter entirely to be brought to a house than it is to grow up in one. This is the place the duke knows best. He is part of it; he understands it in a way no one else can."

"Oh, he understands it, all right," Mrs. Belmont said.

"Perhaps he even loves the place. But it is different with the duchess. Tell me, does she find happiness here?"

She smile at me impertinently. "I should ask you that question."

"What do you mean?" I asked.

Mrs. Belmont said with remarkable calm, "My daughter and I have no secrets from one another, Mr. Vanbrugh. She has told me everything."

The thought turned my blood to ice.

"There is no need to be ashamed," Mrs. Belmont said. "Consuelo was quite amused by it all."

"Amused?" I repeated, instantly angry.

"Oh, do not act the injured lover. That is not what life is all about."

"And what, pray, is life all about?" I said with hostile precision.

Mrs. Belmont looked around the room. "Do you see that portrait over there? The one next to the fireplace?" She indicated a portrait of a young man in a long, well-tended wig who wore a chest plate of polished gray armor, a small flutter of white lace peeking out at the neck. His left hand rested confidently on his hip, and he met the gaze of the viewer squarely, sure of his abilities and his future.

"That is the first duke, at the height of his powers," Mrs. Belmont said. "The duke once told me that when the first duke was old and infirm, he came across this painting and said, 'This was once a man.'" She shook her head slowly. "You see, even the first duke had regrets." She looked at me, a knowing expression on her plain, hard-featured face.

It was more than I could bear. "Mrs. Belmont, if you are trying to say something, be plain. I am not a sophisticate."

The old woman frowned and puffed out her wrinkled cheeks. "You disapprove of me, Mr. Vanbrugh."

"No, Mrs. Belmont, I have to care about you to disapprove."

My intent was to shock her, to propel her to the truth. Instead, it prompted a laugh—a loud chortle of appreciation.

"Good for you," she said, taking my arm. "Good for you." Her gloved hand curled around my sleeve. "Walk with me a moment," she said as she guided me back into the Saloon.

"But my wife wants her breakfast," I protested.

"Oh, yes." At that moment she caught sight of a footman walking hurriedly across the Great Hall. "You there, boy," she said, snapping her fingers at the young man, who stopped dead in his tracks. He turned a fearful face toward us. "Send breakfast up to Mrs. Vanbrugh immediately."

"Certainly, Mrs. Belmont," the servant said, frozen in his tracks.

"Quickly, man, she is waiting."

The poor footman scurried away like a mouse relieved at having been spared by the housecat.

"There, you see? She shall have her breakfast in a moment. Now, let us take a walk around the courtyard."

I stopped short. "I do not think that is a good idea," I said.

"Why not?" she asked. "Oh, yes, that girl." She uttered this with indifference, as if the events of last night had been a mere trifle. "Mr. Barton will be here today, I believe, since the girl was from Long Hanborough. Then we shall content ourselves with the lake."

We exited the house through the Saloon and headed down the gravel path toward the lake. At first neither one of us spoke: Mrs. Belmont seemed to be in a peculiar kind of brown study, and though I was relieved that my father-in-law would arrive soon, I had no intention of initiating a conversation with this disagreeable woman.

We rounded a bend in the path and came upon a small, duff-colored stone temple with a seat carved into its rear wall. It had a pleasant view of the lake and stood atop a gentle slope of trees and wildflowers that stretched gently toward the water.

"Let us rest here a moment," Mrs. Belmont said as she sat down. She patted the stone seat next to her as if it were the most comfortable spot in the world. "I have something to ask you."

I complied and prayed to heaven that this purgatory would not last long.

Idly Mrs. Belmont played with the pearl buttons on her gloves. "Mr. Vanbrugh," she began, "do you believe it is possible for a person to love too strongly?"

I replied carefully, "We are all capable of excess, I suppose. Even in love."

"Do not be glib. I am asking you a serious question."

"Madam, that was a serious answer."

She turned her attention to the handle of her cane, a sturdy piece of polished ebony topped by an elaborately engraved crown of silver. "What I am really asking, I suppose, is: Can a mother love her child too much?"

I was determined to keep this conversation impersonal. "I have never been a mother, so I am hardly an authority," I said.

"But you are soon to be a father," Mrs. Belmont pressed, "and I think you have the glimmer of an idea of what I am asking."

"I assure you, Mrs. Belmont, I cannot answer your question the way you want me to," I said.

"What a prig you are. I was wrong about you."

"What I am, what I do, is no concern of yours, Mrs. Belmont." I stood up.

"Oh, sit down, we are not finished," she said.

"I am."

"*Please* sit down." She said this emphatically.

I hesitated a moment, then against my better judgment I sat down next to her and waited.

Mrs. Belmont looked at me gravely, then turned away. A herd of sheep was making its way slowly across the hill on the other side of the lake; occasionally one of them would bleat loudly enough for us to hear. Behind them, in the distance over the treetops, was the sturdy tower of the Woodstock church. It was a peaceful vista—a far cry from the conversation I was trapped in.

"It is quite beautiful here," she said. "Quite beautiful and quite dull." She sighed. When she began to speak again, her tone had shifted: It was subdued, even sad.

"I received a letter yesterday from a friend of mine, in America. We have known each other for years, since we were children. She is from the South, too—Virginia. Big Stone Gap. She is a woman who has always harbored great ambitions, both for herself and for her child, a daughter. From an early age my friend was determined to marry a very wealthy man. And so she did—richer than Croesus. He was in coal. When she had a daughter, she was determined to secure an even more spectacular match for her than she had for herself. She had met the Duke of Marlborough and his wife, my son-in-law's father, you see, when they visited Virginia years ago, and had gotten the notion into her head. She succeeded beyond her wildest dreams. She prevailed upon her daughter to accept the hand of the man her mother had chosen for her, a ... foreign prince. She lives on the Continent now, in a drafty castle." She paused and twisted her cane slowly. "It has not been a happy marriage, either for my friend or for her daughter. My friend divorced her husband, and after a time married a man more sympathetic to her ..."

"Ambitions?" I offered.

"If you like. But my friend now sees how unhappy her daughter is and wonders if she was right to compel her daughter to agree to such a connection."

"It was never a love match?" I asked.

"No."

I was beginning to understand the point of her story. "Very few marriages among foreign princes are, I believe."

"Ah, but the *daughter* was not a foreign prince. She was a simple

American girl who had ambitions for herself and her life—ambitions to marry a man who was completely unsuitable, I understand, but with whom she might have been happy."

"So this foreign princess is unhappy," I said.

"She has made the best of things, as women usually do. She wants for nothing and bears her mother no ill will—which is far more charitable than I would have been in her place, believe me." Mrs. Belmont grimaced, as if in pain, which made her homely face more disagreeable. "Tell me, do you think it is possible for a mother to be too ambitious for her child? Could her reason be displaced by her desire to see her daughter exalted?"

I looked at Mrs. Belmont and saw, in the slightest flicker of her small, shrewd eyes, a glimpse of the remorse she—not her friend—felt.

I leaned forward and stared out at the placid lake. Several swans slipped gracefully, silently, into the water. "As I said, Mrs. Belmont, with love, anything is possible."

Mrs. Belmont considered this. She sighed. "I suppose all that a mother can do is to make amends. We are very hard on our daughters—harder than their fathers ever are. We see ourselves in them, just as you will in any son you have. Let me give you a piece of advice: If Mrs. Vanbrugh births a girl, make certain that she never forces her child to marry against her wishes."

"Mrs. Belmont, why are you telling me all this?" I asked.

She looked surprised at such a question. "I would have thought that was obvious," she said. "It is because you are in love with my daughter." She said this without rancor or distaste, as if it were a perfectly normal disclosure to make on a mild summer morning in the English countryside.

I felt my face redden and I jumped to my feet. "Mrs. Belmont, that is . . . that is . . . ," I said, willing my voice to steady.

"Why, you are embarrassed," Mrs. Belmont replied, smiling as if she were amused by my reaction. "There is nothing to be ashamed about, I assure you."

"I assure you, there is. I have nothing but the highest regard for the duchess—"

"Apparently," Mrs. Belmont said.

"—but I have known Her Grace scarcely two days."

"Two days is long enough to know," Mrs. Belmont said, clutching her stick.

"And ten minutes can be an eternity. Good morning, madam." I bowed slightly and turned to leave.

"Wait—do not go. I did not say you had done anything improper. I only indicated what is obvious to all of us: You are in love with Consuelo."

I turned back to face this gnome of a woman. "In my morality, Mrs. Belmont, it is improper for a married man to love a woman who is not his wife, no matter how exalted the woman may be," I said.

Mrs. Belmont sat up straight and twisted her walking stick into the stone floor. "What a hypocrite you are. It is too late to talk about morality."

"I beg your pardon?" I said, affronted.

"Do you honestly expect me to believe that you would deny the feelings you have for my daughter while pretending to remain faithful to that silly wife of yours?" Mrs. Belmont asked.

Dumbfounded, I stepped back and stumbled off the temple step onto the gravel path, which only angered me further. "What you believe, madam, is your own affair, and I have no interest in knowing any more about it. I beg you to leave me out of your schemes. You have already ruined one life with your meddling; I refuse to let you ruin mine."

"I think you have done that quite well all by yourself, Mr. Vanbrugh. You require no assistance from me."

"What are you talking about?" I demanded.

"Only that it was not I who dallied with another woman while my wife was in the same house uncovering the body of a childhood friend she denies ever knowing." She smiled with such satisfaction that for a moment I wondered if she had lured me out here with the purpose of laying this out before me. I stared at her, unsure of what I should say. She looked at me placidly, as a cow might, her bulbous eyes unblinking.

"Very well, have it your way, Mr. Vanbrugh. We will speak no more of it," she said. "For the moment."

"I think it is time we returned to the house," I said.

"I believe I will stay here a while longer."

"As you wish," I replied.

As I turned to go Mrs. Belmont noted: "Do not think it has passed my notice that you denied none of this."

I did not credit this comment with a response. Instead, I headed toward the house as hastily as I could. As I walked away, Mrs. Belmont called after me. "You should work for the Catholics. The monsignor could put you and your casuistry to good use."

It was a struggle to remain composed; my heart was pounding hard, and my thoughts were hopelessly jumbled. To my relief, I encountered no one along the path back to the house.

This was the second time in as many days that such a bold statement had been expressed about my feelings for the duchess. I greatly feared that the others had been discussing this, too—toying with the idea, debating its finer points, passing judgment, perhaps even laughing at its folly. I shook my head, trying to throw off the growing panic I felt. Had my feelings been so obvious, so evident, that they were apparent to everyone in the house? Even the duke? And what of Margaret—did she observe it, as well? Had I betrayed my feelings? Had Margaret betrayed me about Emily? What else about her did I not know?

I headed for my room, resolved to collect myself in privacy. But as I drew closer to my bedroom door, I faltered: I did not want to face any questions from Margaret, no matter how innocuous they might be. I needed some time truly alone. My gaze fell on the door to the service stairway, now closed. I headed for it and the roof.

The attics were quiet, and I encountered no one as I retraced my steps to the room Emily once occupied. In the morning light, the room was cheerful and welcoming. I unfastened the window without difficulty and climbed out onto the roof.

In the bright sunshine, the roofs were much different in mood than they had been the night before. No longer a swamp of slime-covered slate, they reminded me of the rocky shores of New England where I spent my summers as a child. The dormers, flues, stairs, and statuary broke the smooth line of the horizon the way the boulders and rocks jutted up from the gray, cold Atlantic.

A refreshing breeze blew along the roof ridges, and on an impulse I clambered up to the highest gable I could manage. From this peak, I looked out over the entire estate: the sweeping, well-tended lawns; the peaceful lakes traversed by the elegant stone bridge, like a knot between the bows in a neatly tied ribbon; the quiet square of stone lakeside that identified Rosamond's Well; and the imposing obelisk, set on the crest of the opposite hill, which proclaimed the greatness of John Duke. There were people about, Lilliputian when seen from this height, traversing the stable yard, leading animals to graze, even one bicycling along the path from Long Hanborough. The effect was restful and uncomplicated, peaceful and clear as only the countryside can be.

In the tranquillity this aerie afforded, I decided that Margaret and I should return to London as soon as it was polite to depart. We were not meant for this place; the dramas unfolding around us were unfamiliar, even dangerous. Blenheim was not a welcoming place, and the people here for this weekend were not, either.

Relieved at my decision, I retraced my steps of the night before, climbing up and over the Great Hall until at last I arrived at the unused room that Jamison had shown me. To my surprise, the window was open, and a murmur of voices reached my ears, punctuated by a low, throaty laugh.

I crept toward the window and before I reached it noticed that a trick of the light had turned the open window into a kind of mirror: Its angle reflected the goings-on in the room itself. This was a blessing, for if I had actually stolen a glance into the room without being prepared for what I would see, I am certain I would have screamed.

The reflection revealed the duchess, unclothed except for a thin scarf of mauve silk that circled her throat and fell between her breasts, was lounging unashamed in the low chair. Her white arms were stretched behind her head in a languid pose, and her legs stretched out provocatively before her. She was speaking quietly to someone.

"This is much pleasanter than Tite Street," she said to someone I could not see.

"And what is wrong with Chelsea?" another voice—Mr. Sargent's—asked.

"It is much too noisy, one cannot open the windows," the duchess replied.

"Oh, that is not the reason."

"Then what is?" the duchess asked.

"It is much less thrilling there. There is no risk."

"There is no risk here," she said.

"May I remind you where we are," Mr. Sargent said.

"Sunny has not been in the attics once in the last ten years. Besides, he has his own distractions."

Mr. Sargent chuckled. "Be careful with Gladys. If she has her way, she will sit across the table from the duke at dinner."

"Would that she could," the duchess said.

"Do you mean that? Would you divorce Sunny?" Mr. Sargent asked.

The duchess moved a hand down to her breast and felt the scarf in her hand. "When I do leave Blenheim, it will be on my terms, not Sunny's," she said, her voice low but firm. In a lighter tone she continued: "I cannot leave yet. You have not yet completed the painting. Sunny must gloat over it a while and point it out to everyone."

"I would not complete it if I had to paint Gladys Deacon. I would sooner move to Italy."

The duchess laughed, her breasts swaying with the movement. "Have you decided what you will paint me in?" she asked.

"Nothing at all. I am going to paint you just as you are."

"No, I am serious, John. What have you determined?"

There was a pause, and Mr. Sargent walked over to her. To my horror, he was also naked, his hair tousled. His shoulders and arms were smudged with blue paint—there was even paint on his hip. He gazed down on the duchess with obvious relish. "I am going to paint you in a dark gown with long sleeves cut up to your elbow lined with rose satin, the color of your luscious skin." This prompted another laugh from the duchess and Mr. Sargent fell upon her, taking her into his arms.

I looked away and fell to my knees, revolted and infuriated by what I had seen. I lurched away on all fours as quickly as I could, without a care for the commotion I was making. It did not matter: I was too overcome.

I had been duped, played for a fool by a woman I admired and who, I thought, returned my regard. This naïve American architect from Boston, Massachusetts, had been gulled into believing that the glorious Duchess of Marlborough thought well of him—well enough to seduce him with her body and her words.

How foolish I had been, how completely ridiculous. I should never have been so trusting, so willing to let my feelings cloud my judgment. I had *presumed* in a world I did not understand, to which I did not belong, and I was paying the price.

I began to cry, the sobs breaking out of me in ragged outbursts, the tears scalding my cheeks. Behind me I heard laughter—mocking, exultant laughter. It sounded inhuman, otherworldly, as if the palace itself were taking pleasure in my despondence.

chapter

15

I made my way over several roofs before plunging headlong into the first open window I happened upon. The room was empty, but I hardly noticed. I made my way into the corridor—another narrow, cluttered passage I did not recognize—and managed to locate another stairway and return to the bedroom floor without being detected.

I accomplished all of this without close attention to my surroundings, for with each step, my heart sank deeper into a jealousy so acute, so encompassing, that I could scarcely breathe. I could not dispel the shocking, scandalous memory of the duchess and Mr. Sargent, together in that room. It haunted me, consuming me like a dry twig in a forest fire.

I felt betrayed—stunned that the duchess would disregard my feelings and what had happened between us. And while her husband was in the palace! I would never have believed that she could be so cruel, so manipulative, to me.

But my feelings ran deeper than that. She had been unjust, which struck me like a harsh slap across a cheek unused to such severity. I had been raised in a respectable family that honored its pledges, repaid its debts, and believed that the world is founded on a set of rules that support the entire structure of polite society—of civilization itself. That is how order is preserved. It is like architecture in that way: If the foundations are sound, then the upper floors will stand. If they are not, then the building surely will collapse. So it was with the duchess,

I thought. I believed her to be a young woman of integrity, an American of exceptional gifts who understood the virtues of true love and finding a soul mate to treasure. Yet in this liaison with Mr. Sargent, she had shown herself to be just like the rest of the self-indulgent rich, convinced that honesty toward others who opened to their hearts to her had no place in her life. The sin of disregard for the honest feelings of another did not stain her soul, it seemed. I was heartily disappointed in her and equally disgusted with myself for believing her better than she was.

Gripped by an overpowering need to escape the suffocating confines of Blenheim, I headed toward the stairway. Miss Deacon, dressed soberly for the day in a coat and skirt of light gray, was leaving her room. I must have looked as distraught as I felt, for her smooth smile of greeting dissolved into an expression of concern.

"Why, Mr. Vanbrugh, you look done in," she said, placing a gloved hand on my forearm.

I drew my arm away quickly, suspicious.

"It is nothing," I replied unconvincingly in a voice that was not my own. I brushed past her toward the stair. But she was not one to be so easily put off.

"It is certainly not nothing," she said, catching up with me. "What has occurred? Is it Margaret? Is this her doing?"

I ignored the question and began my slow, unsteady descent. But with each step, my legs grew weaker, so to maintain my balance I clutched the balustrade with both hands. I managed to reach the landing without incident, only to trip on a worn spot in the plum-colored carpet. I nearly fell, which prompted a small scream from Miss Deacon, who observed me from above. But by gripping the balustrade more tightly, I caught myself in time and held on. I leaned against the wall to catch my breath. As I did I heard: "Mr. Vanbrugh, you are frightening me. For heaven's sake, tell me what is wrong."

I looked up and saw Miss Deacon peering down at me like a puzzled deity troubled by the actions of a mortal.

"Nothing is wrong," I said. I struggled down the rest of the stairs and hobbled across the Great Hall toward the open front doors as I heard Miss Deacon behind me, in a tone that grew louder and more insistent, "Mr. Vanbrugh! Mr. Vanbrugh!"

I reached the front door just as the figure I had seen on the roof making his way toward Blenheim on a bicycle wended his way carefully around the piles of stone in the courtyard. It was my father-in-law. Relief flooded me, and I called out his name as I hurried down the steps. I managed to meet him in the middle of the Great Court, where I hugged him warmly, thanking Providence for the unerring goodness of this man.

"That is quite a greeting," Mr. Barton laughed.

"It is a relief to see you," I replied. "We have had a bad time of it."

The expression on his face darkened. "Margaret is not ill. Is the baby all right?" He looked up at the house. "You should have sent for me."

"I was going to," I said, feeling my note still in my pocket. "The baby is fine, but Margaret is being hounded. By Miss Deacon."

Mr. Barton looked startled. "Hounded? For what purpose?"

"The woman who served Margaret here as a maid disappeared yesterday before dinner. She was discovered last night over there"— I pointed to the site—"under a pile of stones. She had been strangled."

The normally rosy cheeks of my father-in-law drained of color, and his jaw went slack. He seized my arm and looked as if he might collapse. I wrapped an arm around his shoulder for support and said, "There, there."

He shook his head sadly. "Merciful heavens," he said, his voice empty of his usual optimism. "Does . . . does anyone know how this all came about?"

I shook my head. "No. But there are suspicions."

His eyes grew wide. "You think it was someone here, at Blenheim," Mr. Barton whispered. I did not reply, but he understood instantly. "Preserve us," he said. He drew a deep breath. "Who found the girl?" he asked after a time.

"Margaret and I," I said.

"Poor child," he murmured.

"There is more," I warned.

"What more can there be?" he asked, his frown deepening.

I considered how to say what I knew had to be told.

"After we found the body, Miss Deacon circulated the story that

Margaret had known the girl when they were younger. Margaret made it very clear it was not true. But no one believed her."

"Miss Deacon said that the girl was from Long Hanborough, did she?" Mr. Barton said, his voice drifting. "What was her name?"

"Emily."

"Yes. Emily. There was an Emily, the niece of old Mrs. Parker. She was a good girl, went into service. She came here." He frowned. "And Margaret said that she did not know Emily?"

"Yes."

"I see," he said carefully. "And who brought up that she did?"

"Miss Deacon and Mrs. Belmont."

"And how did they come by this particular piece of intelligence?"

"Miss Deacon said that you had told her this at dinner. But Margaret explained that she had never known Emily, it was all Margaret could do to keep herself together before she left the room. I had to take her to her bed, where she is still."

"I see," Mr. Barton said again, more quietly this time. He removed his battered watch from its pocket and checked the time. "Has the constable been summoned?" he asked.

"The duke said last night that he would send for him this morning."

My father-in-law cocked his head in surprise. "That is unusual, even for His Grace." He looked poised to offer a further opinion, but he held back. Instead, he spent a considerable time wiping the watch lens, winding the mechanism carefully and placing it back into his pocket, patting it flat against his round stomach. When at last he spoke again, it was in a reflective tone.

"I remember something that the old duke once said. I was a young curate at the time and had come to Blenheim to attend a fête—a fair or bazaar or some such function, I cannot recall—at which the duke was expected. He was very late, abominably so, and when he did arrive, he did not even attempt to apologize—did not even attempt it. I was with a group of people who were standing with his wife—by then he was married to his second wife, not the mother of the present duke. Her Grace chided him a bit for his ill manners. And he said, 'The Churchills have never produced a gentleman. We were begat by a rogue and have been cads ever since.' He was quite unemotional about it, the duke, as if he were proud of this particular feature of family

history. We laughed at the remark, all of us, more out of embarrassment than anything else. But his wife did not. The duchess looked at
him with an expression of such bitter regret that it gave me gooseflesh.
Still, I was young then, and had not seen much of the world, so perhaps
I would react differently today." Barton offered me a rueful, grin and
patted my arm.

He turned toward Blenheim, whose façade, even in the soft sunlight, loomed unforgiving and combative against the bright sky. To my
dismay, Miss Deacon appeared on the portico. My father-in-law waved
briskly at her and directed in a low voice: "Wave to her, Van."

I grunted. "She does not deserve such civility."

As he waved he replied, "Mark my word, she knows more about
this than she wants you to know."

"What makes you say that?" I asked.

My father-in-law took my arm and carefully climbed the stairs.
"Miss Deacon has a notable understanding of cads."

As he climbed the steps to the front door—passing the cannon
engraved with the Churchill coat of arms and the stone sculptures of
Roman armor, flags, a drum, an axe, and cannonballs, which stood
sentinel on either side of the steps—my father-in-law gathered speed.
He reached the landing smiling and only slightly out of breath. "My
dear Miss Deacon, how well you look, given the horrors of what happened last night. Van was just telling me about the poor girl."

Miss Deacon had removed her coat and was dressed in a blouse of
buttery yellow with a narrow green belt. She looked at my father-in-
law a moment, considering. "Come into the house, Mr. Barton. The
duke would like to speak with you."

We entered the Great Hall and there, at bottom of the stairs, stood
the duke and Mr. Churchill, talking quietly. Miss Deacon led us to
them. When we reached the bottom of the stairs, we stood awkwardly,
waiting for the two men to finish. Miss Deacon said to the two Churchills, "Mr. Barton has arrived."

"Ah, Barton," the duke said, as if we had just appeared. "Perhaps
now we can have a little peace around here."

"There is always peace for the pure of heart," my father-in-law said
amiably. Our host flushed and looked away. Mr. Churchill said, "Too
true, Barton," and warmly took his hand.

"We have something to discuss," Miss Deacon cut in, her tone stern.

"Oh, yes, the service," Barton replied as he pulled from an inner pocket a small worn Bible bound in brown leather. "I received Her Grace's note. I have a few texts that I thought would—"

"No, not the service, your daughter," Miss Deacon interrupted, cutting him off.

My father-in-law did not look startled at this. With a great deal of care, he returned the Bible to his pocket and adjusted his spectacles. "What about my daughter do we need to discuss?" he asked, his voice quiet.

Miss Deacon suddenly seemed to lose her nerve. She turned to the duke. "I believe His Grace has something to say," she said.

Without preamble, the duke said, "Yes, yes. About this housemaid who died last night. Emily."

"What about her?" Mr. Barton asked.

"She knew her. Your daughter, I mean."

"And Mrs. Vanbrugh denied that she knew her," Miss Deacon interjected. "She lied. In front of all of us."

His Grace nodded as Mr. Churchill looked up the stairs as the monsignor descended them and joined us. "I do not take such impertinence lightly," the duke said. He tried to look affronted, but it did not wash: His ire sounded forced, as if he were an indifferent actor who had been poorly coached.

Mr. Barton cocked his head and looked thoughtful. "I find it difficult to believe that these walls have never heard an untruth, or a fib, or a tall tale," he said.

"Yes, but that is not the point," His Grace replied.

"What is the point, Your Grace?" my father-in-law asked.

The duke was bewildered by the question. He opened his mouth but nothing came out of it.

"The point is," Miss Deacon said, "Emily was strangled last night, and that your daughter denied knowing her."

There was a small silence, which my father-in-law broke.

"I am just a country vicar, Miss Deacon, so I am not clear what I am to make of all this."

"Miss Deacon means to accuse Margaret of murdering the housemaid," the monsignor said.

The baldness of the statement caught everyone off guard.

"Is that it, Miss Deacon? Would you care to accuse Margaret of strangling Emily? If you do, I would very much like to hear it directly from your lips."

Miss Deacon turned to the duke for support. His Grace colored and his eyes bulged a bit more. "See here, Barton, the fact of the matter is, well . . ."

"Miss Deacon believes Emily died at Mrs. Vanbrugh's hands," the monsignor interrupted. "But that does not mean that others share her suspicion. Other names have been suggested."

"By whom?" the duke demanded.

"By other interested parties," the monsignor said. "Mr. Churchill, for example."

"I? That is unlikely, surely," Mr. Churchill said with a laugh.

"Unlikely does not mean impossible," the monsignor said. "When the constable arrives, he will want to question all of us as to our location last night and who might have had a grudge against Emily."

"No one had a grudge against her; she was only a silly housemaid," Miss Deacon said.

"Then she must have been murdered for something she owned or had in her possession. Or knew," the monsignor said. He looked at each of us carefully.

"Oh, why will no one say that the duke thought Emily knew where Mr. Sargent's sketchbook was hidden," I cried, tired of talking around the issue.

"How do you know that?" the monsignor asked.

"I heard the duke and Emily arguing about it," I said.

"You were eavesdropping," the duke shouted.

"You were hardly discreet. The windows were open," I shot back.

The duke smoothed his hair against the side of his head. "Well, I certainly didn't kill the girl, if that's what you're suggesting."

"Then who did?" I asked.

"Jamison," the duke said obstinately.

"They were in love," I said.

"A lover's spat," the duke said.

"He had nothing to gain by killing her and everything to lose."

The duke looked at me angrily and clenched his fists.

"Yes, what would someone gain by . . . removing Emily from Blenheim?" the monsignor asked.

From far away, a door closed decisively.

"It is the wise man who recognizes that," Mr. Churchill intoned.

"And what of the wise woman?" Miss Deacon demanded.

"Yes, what of her, Miss Deacon?" Mr. Barton asked. "I admit I am at a loss when I encounter one, quite at a loss." His eyes shone in quiet amusement.

Miss Deacon looked confused, but recovered herself. She turned to the duke, who looked bewildered by the conversation he was witnessing. "Would you say, Mr. Barton, that it was wise of Margaret to lie about her friendship with Emily?"

"I have no idea," Mr. Barton admitted. "Perhaps you could ask her yourself." He looked up the stairway and smiled. To my astonishment, Margaret was descending it, accompanied by the duchess. They were both dressed simply but appropriately for a Sunday morning, the duchess in a long, draping dress of pink pleated silk, with a high ruffled collar, Margaret in her light blue skirt and blouse with a matching jacket of royal-blue linen trimmed with lace.

"Good morning, my dears," Mr. Churchill said, taking the hands of both Margaret and the duchess as they stepped off the last step. "How well you both look."

"Thank you, Winston," the duchess said. "I slept very well."

I cringed, dumbfounded by the ease with which the duchess faced her husband and her guests. How could she remain so poised, so relaxed?

My heart was pounding so hard I was certain that others could hear it as they stood in a circle, waiting for someone to make the next move in a game whose rules I did not know.

It was Miss Deacon, finally, who took the initiative. "Margaret, we were just speaking about what we had discussed last night."

"Oh?" Margaret said, her voice high and tight.

"You must recall," Miss Deacon said.

"I am afraid I do not. I have been unwell, as you may know," Margaret said.

"Of course we will not speak of it," the duchess said—her voice firm.

"But we must, Consuelo," Miss Deacon insisted.

The duchess stared at Miss Deacon. "Not now, Gladys. I think some of us need a bit of breakfast."

Mr. Churchill grunted in assent. "Excellent. I am dying of hunger," he said.

"That would be a blessing," Miss Deacon muttered, her eyes flashing at Mr. Churchill.

"Gladys," the duke said in rebuke.

"I cannot believe that you are going to let her get away with this," Miss Deacon said, pointing to Margaret.

"Get away with what?" Mr. Churchill asked.

"With killing Emily, of course."

"No one accuses my daughter of murder, Miss Deacon," Mr. Barton said.

"And why not? It could have been her," she cried.

"It most certainly was not," I said angrily.

"Yes, it was. I saw her."

At that, Margaret fell against the duchess, who held her upright long enough for Mr. Churchill and I to come to her aid. I directed Margaret to a nearby chair and set her into it. I offered to fetch her some water but she shook her head. She watched Miss Deacon clearly, fascinated but repelled.

"Do you have any evidence on which to base such a claim?" the monsignor asked, standing before Miss Deacon like an inquisitor, his slim shoulders straight.

"I saw her," she repeated, her tone reckless. "Margaret strangled Emily out behind the chapel yesterday afternoon and hid her body first under the stones and then in the crypt."

"That is not true," the duchess said.

"Then why did Margaret lie about knowing Emily in Long Hanborough?" Miss Deacon demanded.

All eyes turned to Margaret, who after a long, dreadful hush, confounded us all by asking Miss Deacon, "How did you know?"

Miss Deacon looked triumphant. "When I walked by your room yesterday, you and Emily were talking about how you used to float paper boats in the pond down the lane from the vicarage. It sounded quite idyllic."

"It was," Mr. Barton agreed. "But it does not follow that Margaret strangled Emily."

"It signifies that Margaret denied knowing the dead girl," the duke said.

"That proves nothing," the duchess said.

"I did not strangle Emily," Margaret said.

"Well, then, perhaps you can explain how this happened to be in the possession of Mrs. Vanbrugh." Miss Deacon opened her fist and the kerchief she held in her hand fell open. Inside was a thin silver ring.

"It is a ring," Mr. Barton said.

Miss Deacon smiled. "Yes. It is the ring Emily wore."

Margaret gave a small cry. "No!"

"How did you come upon this?" Mr. Churchill asked, more curious than accusing.

"From Margaret. I removed it from the drawer of her bed table. I observed her putting it there last night."

"That is ridiculous," the duchess said.

"You are taking sides against Gladys?" the duke demanded.

"I have never had this ring in my possession, I swear it," Margaret cried.

"First she denies knowing Emily, then she denies having this ring, then Consuelo comes to her aid against me," Miss Deacon said. "There is no need to lie further, Margaret. I observed you from the passage."

"No, it is not true," Margaret said, overcome by the enormity of what Miss Deacon was alleging.

The duchess took command. "Mr. Barton, take Mrs. Vanbrugh upstairs. Winston, help Mr. Vanbrugh. Gladys, come with me." Miss Deacon in tow, the duchess took one of my arms, Mr. Churchill the other, and guided us into the Green Writing Room. We were followed by the duke and the monsignor. I was settled into a low settee with a high back next to the white marble fireplace and sat facing them, who stood before me like a tribunal.

"Gladys, the time for evasions is over," the duchess began without preamble.

"This is no evasion," Miss Deacon replied, her eyes determined.

The duchess crossed her arms. "All right, have it your way. But if you will not be plain, then I will be. I know you are lying, Gladys Deacon. I know you never saw poor Mrs. Vanbrugh take that ring and hide it in her room. I know she did not strangle the servant girl."

Miss Deacon laughed bitterly. "How certain you are."

"I am—very. Because I know that you cannot see the bed or the table in Mrs. Vanbrugh's room from the passage. You see, I arranged that room for Winston's mother, at her request. She always occupies that room when she visits." Mr. Churchill gasped. "Yes, Winston knows the room. Remember? Jennie asked that the bed be placed *behind* the door, so that she would have at least a little privacy. She is a clever woman. I once thought you were like her, Gladys," the duchess said.

Miss Deacon looked confused. "That is ridiculous," she began, but stopped short when her gaze fell upon Mr. Churchill, who stared at her, his face growing red with anger.

"What the hell is this all about, Gladys?" he growled.

Miss Deacon stared in sullen silence at the tapestry of Marlborough accepting the French surrender.

"What has possessed you so these last days?" the duchess asked.

Miss Deacon's jaw hardened. When she did speak again, her voice was thick, choked with feeling.

"It is my turn, Consuelo," she said. "It is my turn."

"Not yet," the duchess said. She cast a quick glance at the duke. "I am not finished yet."

Miss Deacon opened her mouth to reply but thought better of it. Instead, she ran from the room. The duke followed her.

"Well, that was pleasant," the duchess said, her voice tired.

"You understand what she intends," the monsignor said, falling into a chair opposite the duchess.

"Yes," the duchess said. She rubbed her eyes with her long fingers.

"It could get disagreeable," Mr. Churchill said.

"No doubt it will."

"You will be discreet, I hope, my dear," Mr. Churchill said.

"You and your precious family, Winston. I hope whatever poor soul you trick into marrying you will treasure the Churchill name as dearly as you seem to. You are the personification of the family motto."

" '*Fiel pero Desdichado*,' " Mr. Churchill intoned, then chuckled. "Faithful but unfortunate. An apt motto for a flawed family," he said, his expression once again impish.

"Each of us is flawed in his own way," the monsignor said.

"Just not as spectacularly," Mr. Churchill said, "if you take my meaning."

"I do not," I said. "I do not understand why Miss Deacon is hounding my wife."

The duchess nodded. "It does seem queer. But that is the way with Gladys. She disrupts in order to make her point."

"But what is her point?" I asked in exasperation.

"Why, to take my place," the duchess said.

"Do you mean that she really wants to be duchess? To replace you?"

"Yes."

"But that is unheard of," I said.

"Hardly. There are many ways to lose a duchess. And death is not always the easiest one to pull off. Gladys is getting ready to accuse me of murdering poor Emily, Mr. Vanbrugh. She accused Margaret and failed because she did not think through her plan of attack. That is the way with Gladys. She has a deadly instinct for the jugular but terrible aim. Her intelligence lacks patience. If living in this house has taught me anything, it is that success is equal parts intelligence and patience. Would you not agree, Your Grace?" she asked the figure of John Duke in the tapestry.

"Gladys may not plan as carefully as you do, Consuelo, but she is a quick study. She will be cleverer the next time. I hope you are prepared," Mr. Churchill said.

The duchess crossed her arms. "I will know what to do," she said.

"Good," Mr. Churchill said. "I would not like to see you lay down your coronet."

"Nor I," the monsignor said with more emotion than I thought possible. He held her hand for a moment.

"At least not until I am ready," the duchess replied. "The sooner

Sunny and Gladys realize that, the sooner calm will return to Blenheim." She patted Mr. Churchill on the shoulder. "If it ever can."

"But first we must collect evidence against the person who strangled Emily," Mr. Churchill said. "Or force a confession. That should not be too difficult. We are all so frightened, the guilty one is bound to reveal the truth. Perhaps it is already here among us, only waiting for one of us to notice."

A S soon as I was able, I excused myself and made my way upstairs to ensure that Margaret had been made comfortable in her room. I was halfway up the first flight when I heard the the duchess behind me.

"Mr. Vanbrugh," she said, halting my progress. "May I join you?"

The duchess climbed toward me, delicately holding up her skirts.

"I would rather you didn't," I said bluntly.

She hurried up toward me. "Please, I insist," she said, drawing alongside me. She glanced at me as she climbed and said, "This has not been the most pleasant weekend you have spent in the country."

"No." I looked away, ashamed and angry.

"Blenheim is not usually like this, you know," she said.

"Blenheim is not the primary difficulty."

The duchess gave a regretful laugh. "How true. It is us, of course. We are the difficulty."

"Yes, you are."

The plain fact was, the behavior of our hosts and their guests *had* been more than a mere difficulty—*they* were responsible for our distress, our disillusionment, for the murder of that poor girl. I had never encountered such appalling conduct, least of all from people the world would deem my superiors. They had shown themselves to be beyond honor, beyond propriety, beyond humanity. They were wild animals, lurking in a jungle made of stone, waiting to prey upon the weak.

"You must pardon us, Mr. Vanbrugh, for this horrible weekend," the duchess said as we reached the landing.

"It is unpardonable. It is beyond redemption."

"Surely not that."

"We are in hell, Your Grace. And the worst of it is, we have brought all of this upon ourselves."

The duchess looked grave. She reached for her pearl choker, which even at this early hour adorned her slender neck, and tapped the pearls lightly.

"We shall make it up to you," she said.

"That is impossible," I said.

"Why?"

My heart sank. I knew then that she would never understand.

"The fact that I have to explain that to you is proof enough."

"Proof enough of what? Please tell me. I would very much like to know."

"Never mind. Mrs. Vanbrugh and I will leave for London as soon as possible."

"Mr. Barton is conducting the service this morning," she said.

"Then we will wait until after the service."

"There is not a train from Woodstock until the afternoon," the duchess said.

"Then that is the train we will take," I insisted.

We reached the door to Margaret's room, which stood ajar. I pushed it open and saw, standing across the room in front of the window, Mr. Barton and the duke. My father-in-law nodded to us but the duke turned away. I walked into the room and went directly to Margaret, who was lying on the bed, a damp cloth over her forehead. I took her hand gently, and she gripped mine.

Though the sun was by now well up, the room was still cool; the warm morning air had done little to dissipate the chilly atmosphere in the room.

"She is feeling better, I think," Mr. Barton said, his manner intentionally cheerful.

"Well enough to speak when she is spoken to," the duke said sharply.

The duchess came over to the bed and looked down at Margaret. "We should not overexcite her," she said. "She must rest."

"Yes, you would like me to leave her alone," the duke snapped.

The duchess turned to him. "It is best," she said.

"For you, too, of course," the duke said.

The duchess stiffened. "As you say, my lord," she said, her tone icy.

I was grateful that I was facing away from them, so I did not have to witness this exchange. My father-in-law, however, was in the thick of it. "Yes, well," he said uneasily, "let us see what we shall see." He came toward me and asked, "How is the cloth, Van? Do you need another?"

"No, it is still cool," I said.

"Are you certain? I can locate another," he offered.

"No, thank you."

Margaret squeezed my hand. "Van," she whispered, "tell them to go away."

"I will." I turned away from her and faced the others. "She wants to be left alone."

"Why?" the duke demanded.

"Of course, we will leave immediately," the duchess said.

But the duke was not so amenable. "I am not leaving this room until she has answered my questions."

Margaret whimpered and rolled toward the wall. "I cannot help him," she said, her voice muffled by the bedclothes. I thought of what Emily had said to the duke and shivered.

"Come along, there will be plenty of time to bully Mrs. Vanbrugh when she is feeling better," the duchess said.

The duke stared at his wife with a mixture of fury and contempt. "That would suit you, I am sure, to put this off. To delay the inevitable."

"All I am delaying is your rudeness," the duchess replied. "Our guest has expressed a desire to be alone. I am trying to prepare for church and must finish dressing before I collect Mama. It is fortunate, Mr. Barton, that you are ready. Do you know if the monsignor will be joining us?"

"The monsignor will remain in his room," the duke said.

My father-in-law coughed. "Actually, Your Grace, the monsignor inquired if I would have any objection to his attending the service this morning. I was delighted, of course, and told him he was most welcome." He frowned. "That is, if Your Grace has no objection."

"Good God, how could I object?" the duke said with feeling. "I am only the Duke of Marlborough. No one listens to me. I have no say in any of the goings-on here; they slip like sand through my fingers. I have poisonous letters peeling off the walls, a dead servant girl in the courtyard, and a house full of uncooperative guests. A Catholic priest who wants to attend a Church of England service in my chapel? Why not? Perhaps it will even become the fashion. I hope to heaven the pope does not find out. He will want us to invite him next." He gave a hollow laugh. "The world is falling apart around me; why should a priest in my chapel concern me?" He shook his head and stared out the window. With a start, he paused, like a pointer homing in on a bird. "Good Lord," he muttered, and without another word hurried from the room.

The atmosphere lightened considerably at his departure. Even though I could not see Margaret's face, I felt her relax a little. The duchess emitted a long sigh. "Mr. Vanbrugh, will you be joining us for the service?" she asked.

"I will stay here with Mrs. Vanbrugh," I said.

The duchess nodded and turned to my father-in-law—who was looking at the window. "Mr. Barton, would you mind walking with me a bit? I value your opinions on the hymns Mr. Sharp is planning."

"Of course, Your Grace, of course," my father-in-law said; there were few subjects he embraced as enthusiastically as the details of a Sunday service. He followed the duchess out of the room and, passing by me, whispered the word "Jamison" as he patted my back. "Goodbye, my dear," he called to Margaret as he closed the door behind him. Immediately Margaret turned to face me.

I stood up sluggishly, already worn out, and moved to the window, wondering what my father-in-law had meant by the mention of Jamison.

The green lawn, as supple as a piece of velvet, folded out before me, bordered by dense groves of beeches, cedars, and oaks. Two figures stood under the lowering branches of the copper beech closest to the house, and one of them darted further into the shadows as the duke appeared on the lawn, yelling something I could not hear. The remaining figure walked out from under the tree to meet the duke, and I noticed that it was Mrs. Belmont. They spoke quietly for a moment, the duke pointing toward the trees, Mrs. Belmont shaking her head. They then returned to the house, talking animatedly.

"Thank heaven they have left," Margaret said, sitting up slowly. "I do not think I could have withstood any more of their jabbering."

"They were hardly jabbering, Margaret," I said.

"Well, whatever it was, it was driving me to distraction." She tucked an errant strand of hair behind an ear. "I must look a fright," she said, fishing for a compliment. But I did not have the energy to be polite. I returned to the bed and sat down on it. I looked straight into Margaret's eyes and said quietly, "It is time for the truth."

Margaret colored and played with the blanket.

"Margaret, you cannot expect your father or me to defend you if you will not tell the truth," I said. "Why in the world did you lie about knowing Emily?"

She shuddered and looked around the room as if she might come across an excuse hidden behind a painting or under a chair. With a great deal of reluctance, she realized that she had no other recourse. "She asked me to," she said. "Emily, I mean."

"What benefit would that serve?" I asked.

"She felt that if it was known that she and I had grown up together, it would put her in jeopardy."

"So she felt she was in danger," I said slowly.

"Oh, yes." Margaret said. "She said that the duke was bullying her."

"For what purpose?" I asked.

Margaret discharged a long breath. "I am not supposed to say. I promised her I would not."

"Emily is dead because of what she knew. If you know what she did, or if someone suspects that you do, you are in very grave danger, as well. You must tell me all you know."

My logic was not as clear as it could have been, but Margaret saw the wisdom of it in any case. "All right, Van. But I do not know very much, really." She moved off the bed and crept quietly to the door.

With a swift, silent flourish, she threw it open, trying to catch out anyone who might have been eavesdropping. But the corridor was empty. Satisfied, Margaret returned to the bedside and sat next to me.

"I hardly know where to begin," Margaret said. "It is all so strange." She placed a hand on her breast to calm herself.

"Emily and I recognized each other immediately, of course, but did not say anything to anyone. Emily said that Mrs. Andrews did not like her and did not want her associating with the guests."

"But she was not associating with us," I objected.

Margaret nodded. "You are right, of course, but Emily said that Mrs. Andrews was growing suspicious of her, because of her friendliness with the duchess. Emily said that Mrs. Andrews thought Emily was singled out by the duchess for special consideration—she was her pet.

"It sounded to me as if Mrs. Andrews may have been jealous of Emily."

"It would appear so," I agreed.

"Emily said that the duchess had confided in her a bit about several..." Here Margaret paused to choose her words carefully. "Personal details."

My mind leapt to the sordid scene that I had witnessed earlier. I forced myself to ask, "What sort of personal details?"

Margaret pressed both hands to her breast and struggled to remain composed. "That...well, that the duke had strayed from his marital vows."

"The duke was involved with another woman? Miss Deacon, I suppose."

"Yes," Margaret said, looking surprised. "How did you know?"

"Everyone knows," I said.

"Then all of the stories she recounted during our walk were true."

"Emily corroborated them?" I asked.

"Well, no," Margaret admitted. "But Emily told me that the duchess was aware of these indiscretions—some of which happened right here at Blenheim, under her very nose. Imagine!" Margaret said this with such astonishment that I did not have the heart to explain that the duchess was as guilty as her husband. "Emily said that the duchess even came upon them one evening, down by the lake. They did not see her, and the duchess did not confront them, I understand, but they were definitely observed." I felt a twinge of pity for the duchess; it must be a shock for any wife to discover that your husband has not remained true.

"Did Emily know how the duchess prevailed upon the duke to break off the affair?" I asked.

"That is just it, Van. It is still going on—right here while we are at Blenheim," Margaret exclaimed. Any sign of her previous indisposition had disappeared: Her eyes once again were bright, her cheeks pink with color, her hands expressive.

"What is more," Margaret added, inclining her head toward me, "the duke does not know that the duchess is aware of the relationship." She nodded, like a weary observer accustomed to the world's sinful schemings. There is nothing like a morsel of thrilling gossip to revive a certain kind of woman.

"I find that difficult to believe," I said.

Margaret stared at me. "Why?"

"The duke may not be as clever as he thinks he is, but he is cleverer than the duchess believes him to be."

Margaret frowned. "What do you mean?" she demanded.

"I think it is very likely that the duke realizes the duchess knows of his affair with Miss Deacon. And that the duchess has decided to do nothing about it."

Margaret looked horrified at this; her eyes widened in alarm. "You know something," she said.

"Perhaps."

"Well, what is it?"

"First tell me what else Emily said to you."

Margaret considered. "Emily said that the duchess was worried about the letters—the letters you found. What was in them?"

I hesitated, unsure whether Margaret should be privy to information I promised to keep confidential. She noticed my indecision and said, "I am not a child, Van. I am perfectly able to grasp what is happening."

"Very well," I agreed, as a large cloud obscured the sun. The room fell into sudden shadow, and a chilly breeze blew about the room. Margaret shivered, and got up to close the window. When she had seated herself back onto the bed, I began.

"The letters I found are love letters between Duchess Sarah and Sir John Vanbrugh."

"The Blenheim architect?"

"Yes."

"Were they lovers?"

I nodded. "One of the letters accuses Sir John of carrying on an affair with Anne, one of the daughters of Duchess Sarah. Anne was the Countess of Sunderland, and all of the subsequent Dukes of Marlborough descend from her. The last letter I found accuses Sir John of fathering Anne's son, the baby boy who became the third duke."

Margaret pressed her hands together, as if in prayer, and brought them to her lips. She held them there for a long moment, not speaking.

"If it were true, the duke and I could be related. Distant cousins perhaps, my pauper to his prince. But when the original letters disappeared and Emily was murdered, it began to seem that this was more important than just a footnote in the Churchill family history."

"You can never breathe a word of this," Margaret whispered. "You must hold your tongue. So must we all."

"The duke will hold his tongue, but I think he is frightened that the secret will slip out somehow. I think Miss Deacon knows about the letters—"

"Miss Deacon," Margaret exclaimed in dismay.

"I will bet she wheedled it out of the duke. Perhaps she threatened to reveal everything unless the duke marries her."

"But that is unthinkable," Margaret said. "Oh, the poor man." There was genuine sadness in her voice. "He suffered through all of the scandals his father brought upon the family, and now it appears he will have to suffer through more. It is too awful."

While I understood her sentiment, I did not share her empathy; after all, the duke had brought this trouble upon himself.

"I wonder how the sketchbook is connected to all of this," Margaret said.

"The sketchbook Mr. Sargent is looking for?" I asked.

"I do not know, and Emily did not, either. But the duchess directed Emily to pinch it. She was most insistent. She directed Emily to wait for a sign from her and that when Emily received it, she was to go to a room in the attic she had never been to before to fetch the book and to conceal it. And under no circumstances was she to look through it."

"Where was she to hide it?" I asked.

"That is the most extraordinary thing," Margaret said. "Emily told me that the duchess was very particular that Emily not tell her where she had hidden the book. She also said that if Mr. Sargent asked for the book, she was to say that she had not seen it. But the duchess said that there might come a time when she would have to retrieve it, so Emily was to stow it someplace that she could explain to the duchess easily, if that became necessary. So one night Emily was directed to a part of the attic she had never been to before and, to her surprise, came across a large sketchbook leaning against the wall. She scooped it up and hurried back to her room. She was sorely tempted to look through the book, she said, but she did not."

"That is what she told you," I said.

"I believe her, Van," Margaret said. "She was a truthful girl."

"The same was said of you until yesterday," I replied.

Margaret blushed but refused to be provoked. Her self-possession was convincing and made me believe that she was speaking the truth.

"So Emily had no notion of what was in the sketchbook or why the duchess wanted it removed," I said.

"No, none," she said.

"Did Emily say where she had hidden it? Did she give any hint at all?"

Margaret smiled and looked pleased with herself, like a cat that had just cornered a bird and was relishing the pursuit.

"She said she hid it with other books," Margaret said.

"Of course, the library," I said. "What a clever girl. It is the ideal place to hide a book, among thousands of others."

"That is just what Emily said," Margaret agreed. "She told me that she concealed it nearby, but that it was in the midst of other books so she was certain it would not be discovered."

"Have you tried to locate it?" I asked.

"No."

"Come along, then," I exhorted, "and we will see what we can find."

We nearly sprinted to the Long Library, hurrying down the stairway and across the Great Hall. We had almost crossed the hall when the bell signaling the beginning of Sunday service began to toll. As the mournful peals echoed through the house, engulfing us in their cold, numbing cadence, Margaret and I slowed our steps to match the rhythm of the bell, and as we walked the passage past the busts of dukes and duchesses long dead, I thought of Emily, a poor neighborhood girl who never imagined that her fate would be to die within earshot of the Blenheim bells. I wondered if she knew of the dalliance between the duchess and Mr. Sargent, or the one between the duke and Miss Deacon. Did she ever confide in Mrs. Belmont? That did not seem likely. But she might have in Mr. Churchill. And what of the monsignor, his cold, all-seeing eye turned on everything at Blenheim?

The library was mellow with light; its west-facing windows did not yet have the full sun on them.

"Oh, help," Margaret murmured as her eyes took in the towering shelves of books encased behind gilt-latticed doors that hugged three of the walls. "Where should we begin?"

"You begin with the shelves to the left of the door, I will do the same on the right," I suggested. This tactic seemed logical and Margaret could offer no alternative, so the idea was adopted. As Margaret began her search, I cautioned, "Remember, it may be hidden behind larger books, so look closely."

We began with great diligence, taking meticulous care to return each book to its proper place on the shelf. Such attentiveness demanded that we explore every inch of each bookcase, even the highest shelves, which entailed climbing a set of unsteady library stairs. It was tedious work, made more so by our growing realization that our time was limited: We had less than an hour until the service was over and the household would parade through the door at the end of the library and our secret would be out.

Conversation died quickly as we became engrossed in our task. I paid no attention to anything except the books before me, so it was with some surprise that after a considerable time my eye noticed, hanging just above one of the cases, a life-sized portrait of Anne, the Countess of Sunderland, by a painter named Kneller. It was a startling portrait: If the likeness were true, she was indeed captivating. She had a handsome oval face, a straight nose, a rosy complexion, rich, dark hair, and a full, puckish mouth. She was dressed in a gown of the lightest gray, which seemed to shimmer in the light, and wore over her shoulders a cape of crimson velvet trimmed with ermine. The painter had arranged her leaning against a table and she held a small crown—the ducal coronet of the Marlboroughs, I guessed. Despite the distinction of her attire, there was a sadness in her expression, and in the intelligent brown eyes the painter had captured a lingering sorrow, a sense of hope that had been lost forever, which suited this house and this family. I could understand why Sir John found Anne so bewitching, and, if the letters were true, why she looked so poignant, so desolate, so *alone.*

Two of the bookcases were locked, which disturbed me at first, as I had no key. However, upon examining the locks, I discovered how easy they were to pick. With a small penknife, I opened both cases without difficulty and continued searching. It was then that I concluded that even if I had the means to open these doors, the odds were that Emily did not—a Blenheim housemaid, after all, does not normally carry keys to the library cases.

My spirits flagged as I neared the end of my search. I had uncovered nothing to indicate that any of these books had been read or disturbed within the last year, never mind the last few days. Dust had collected along many of the bindings, particularly on the higher shelves, indicating that they had not been removed in a long while, and all of the books were pressed hard against the backs of the shelves.

It occurred to me that there might be a hidden compartment somewhere in one of the cases, but an examination of them—and, later, of those Margaret had gone through—revealed nothing.

I looked down the long room toward Margaret, who was also at the end of her search. She was staring at the cases, slumped in defeat.

"Did you find anything?" I called out.

"Nothing at all," she answered, dispirited.

"It is not here," I said.

From a low sofa facing toward the towering bow window came the booming voice of Mr. Churchill: "What in the hell are you two looking for?"

Margaret cried out in surprise and demanded, "How long have you been here?"

"A trifle longer than you have," he said, rousing himself to peer at us over the back of the sofa. "I always read in here on Sunday mornings, whenever I am in residence."

"You should have identified yourself to us sooner," I said.

"It was perfectly clear that you did not wish to be disturbed," Mr. Churchill explained, beckoning us toward him. We complied reluctantly.

"You were spying," Margaret said.

Mr. Churchill smiled. "I am a man of considerable skill, Mrs. Vanbrugh, but even I have my limits. I cannot take on the task of intelligence gathering if I do not know what I should be gathering intelligence *about*." He looked upon us kindly and rose from the sofa. Though wrinkled, his attire was handsome: dark wool pants and a tailored white shirt, a maroon smoking jacket, the black satin lapels—clear, for once, of any ash or debris—his bare feet encased in black velvet slippers. For once he was not smoking, and he held a small book in one hand.

Margaret responded with a candor that was as remarkable for what it disclosed as what it concealed. "We are searching for a particular book, but it does not appear to be here," she said.

Mr. Churchill looked interested. "This library is the inside of my soul. Tell me what you are looking for and I will point it out to you."

"It is of no consequence, the book is not here," Margaret said.

"How can you be so certain? There are thousands of volumes in this room. Surely you have not had the opportunity to peruse them all. Tell me the title of the book and I will wager that I can find it for you."

"This is not the kind of book that is expected to be in the Blenheim library," I said.

Mr. Churchill looked at us but said only, "I see."

"Why are you not at church?" Margaret inquired suddenly.

"The same question could be directed toward you," he said.

Margaret considered him, taking his measure. After a long moment she replied, without embarrassment, "I am unwell. I have taken to my bed."

Mr. Churchill laughed—an expansive, bellowing yelp of appreciation that rollicked through the room like a piece of Bach happily played on the organ.

"Bravo, Mrs. Vanbrugh, that was first-class," Mr. Churchill said appreciatively when he had recovered himself.

"Thank you," Margaret replied. Her eyes fell on the book in his hand. "What holds your interest today?" she asked. *The Prince*? Or Locke perhaps."

"Neither one, as a matter of fact. I am becoming better acquainted with one of your countrymen, Mr. Vanbrugh. Mr. E. A. Poe." Mr. Churchill turned a fixed gaze at me. "Are you familiar with him?"

"I am, a little," I admitted. "It has been many years since I have read his tales. I hope you are enjoying him," I replied after a moment, uncertain.

Mr. Churchill shrugged his heavy shoulders with the studied indifference the well-bred Englishman employs to pass judgment on the world. "His logic is spotty and his motivations are suspect, but his poetry is not revolting to the ear," he said.

I was poised to offer a remark about his magnanimity, but my comment froze on my lips when I took a closer look at the book Mr. Churchill held in his hand. Its spine reminded me very much of the one I saw earlier, the volume of Poe stories I had seen on Emily's shelf.

"May I see your book a moment?" I asked.

Mr. Churchill looked surprised, but complied.

As I held the slender volume in my hand, it fell open to a page whose corner had been folded over. It appeared to be in the middle of one of the stories. There was a deliberate dot next to the phrase "the Minister had resorted to the comprehensive and sagacious expedient of not attempting to conceal it at all." I looked at Mr. Churchill and knew immediately that this was the book Emily had kept in her room.

"Where did you find this?" I inquired.

"That is an odd question to ask in a library," Mr. Churchill said, frowning, the lines around his mouth deepening.

"I have seen a volume of Poe like this quite recently," I said.

"I am certain you have. They are cheaply made and easily found in London, I believe," he said.

"No, I saw this here, at Blenheim," I insisted.

"Did you?" Mr. Churchill replied, trying to sound uninterested, but there was a new tension to his voice.

"And this is not the kind of book one is apt to find in this library."

"There are many books here that might surprise you," Mr. Churchill said. "The fifth duke was a great collector of extraordinary books. And common women."

"Does the library have many artists' sketchbooks?" Margaret asked abruptly.

Mr. Churchill glowered. I was poised to press the point when the bell began to toll again, this time more happily. The service was over.

The door from the colonnade opened moments later and a steady stream of servants poured hurriedly into the room, straightening their coats and removing their Sunday hats. They were surprised to encounter us, but they bowed and curtsied to us as they filed past. Mr. Churchill spoke to several of the older servants, who returned his greeting with shy, delighted smiles. He clearly was a favorite of the Blenheim staff.

Mrs. Belmont came through next, walking between Mr. Sargent and the monsignor. She was scowling, her small, suspicious eyes narrowed to slits and her jaw tight with vexation. When she saw Margaret, she said, in a tone of deep mistrust, "I was led to understand that you were ill."

"I was, Mrs. Belmont," she said.

The lady's frown deepened, and she peered up at Margaret through her pince-nez. "You have recovered remarkably fast," she said, the wattle of her neck shaking.

Mr. Sargent interjected politely, "I am glad to see it. It is far too pleasant a morning to be indisposed."

"It is I who have cured her, Alva," Mr. Churchill said to lighten the mood. "My charms are a restorative to women."

"The only thing you restore in women is a renewed appreciation for the muzzle," Mrs. Belmont said.

Mr. Churchill looked puzzled, as if he did not expect such a response. "Madam, you slander me."

But Mrs. Belmont was not to be cajoled into a better humor so easily. Frowning more deeply, Mrs. Belmont said, "I was under the impression that in England it was not slander to speak the truth. Or have you men changed this law while we were at church?"

"If they had, I am certain they would not have consulted me," Mr. Churchill said, smiling.

"Well, that is honest at least," Mrs. Belmont said.

"Mrs. Belmont has a great respect for honesty," the monsignor said.

The older woman turned to him with disdain. "I have a great respect for what is right, something you Catholics know very little about, it seems to me."

"Does it, madam? How little you know of Catholics," the monsignor said, his voice as hard as the diamond in the center of the crucifix he wore.

The colonnade door flew open then, and the duke stormed into the room, gripping tightly a fistful of paper. He was accompanied by Miss Deacon, who looked fearful as she struggled to keep up. Ignoring all of us, he made straight for the service bell next to the fireplace and pushed it savagely several times. He seemed to be in the grip of a terrible, thundering rage he could scarcely control. As he waited for a servant to respond, he paced before the large, deep fireplace. It was almost as tall as he, and the firebox was decorated with fleurs-de-lys along its slanting sides and the family crest pressed into the iron against its deep rear wall. The black marble columns on both sides, carved in the Doric style, supported a heavy chimneypiece, upon which stood nothing but a delicate alabaster bust of the duchess. Her head was turned to one side, her long, delicate neck curving in a graceful arc, as if her attention had just been caught by an unheard voice. The sculptor had captured an introspective expression, as if she were imagining another time.

The bust caught the attention of the duke, who with one hand yanked it down. He stared at it, his protuberant eyes red and his jaw clenched tight. He held the bust in one hand, the papers in the other, as if he were weighing the two. He seemed to come to a decision and, with a small smile on his face, flung the bust into the fireplace, where it smashed against the rear of the fireplace, shattering into thousands of small pieces.

The sound of stone against metal, shrill and reluctant, echoed through the room.

No one uttered a sound, though Miss Deacon flinched as the bust struck the heavy iron. Mrs. Belmont, her fleshy face immobile, watched her son-in-law intently but did not offer a word of protest.

The duke took no notice of us; in truth, he seemed unaware of our presence. It did not enter his reason that he had witnesses.

After a long, terrible silence, Mr. Churchill said quietly, "I never cared for that bust myself."

The duke looked up at the sound but did not reply, for at that moment the butler arrived. "Have this fire lighted at once," the duke commanded.

Mr. Moore looked at the fireplace and noticed the pieces of the bust. "Yes, Your Grace. I will send a footman," he murmured, bending down quickly to retrieve a piece from the hearth rug.

"Touch any of that and I will sack you," the duke snapped, his anger lashing across the butler like a whip.

The servant froze and without changing his expression stood upright. He offered a correct bow to the duke and departed as quietly as he had come. Even in the face of the quivering anger of his employer, the butler had adhered to the strict protocol at Blenheim: His duties did not include lighting a fire—even one that had already been lain, as this one was. That was a task to be carried out by a footman.

"Oh, damn it, I will light it myself," the duke said in exasperation moments after the butler departed. He pulled from the pocket of his morning coat a small box of matches and, extracting one, struck it. It ignited quickly and the duke threw it onto the wood, setting the dry kindling ablaze. The duke lighted several more parts of the kindling and watched it for a time until he was satisfied that the fire would catch. It was only then that he turned to us, registering our presence for the first time.

Even if none of us in the Long Library on that Sunday morning had been acquainted with His Grace, Charles Richard John Spencer-Churchill, ninth Duke of Marlborough, it would have been obvious that he was angry—livid beyond description. He seemed devoured by a molten wrath unchecked by either courtesy or refinement.

"Excellent. An audience. That will make this more enjoyable," he said with a chilling, corrosive calmness.

No one was quite sure what to say. Mr. Churchill finally asked, "What has occurred, Sunny?"

The duke snickered—a hollow, airless chuckle. "If only it were that simple," he replied as he toyed with his signet ring.

"Very well," Mr. Churchill agreed. "What has transpired to prompt such emotion in you?"

The duke pulled himself to his full height and, eyeing me, said clearly, "The reputation of my family has been attacked. In my own chapel."

"I would hardly call it an attack," the duchess said quietly. Her voice startled us, as no one had detected her arrival or that of Mr. Sargent and my father-in-law, so caught up were we by the duke's fiery theatrics.

His Grace turned to his wife and in a voice quivering with undisguised fury said: "You are hardly in a position to judge. When you are the subject of an indictment from your own bloody pulpit, then you may quibble with me. Until then, I have no interest whatever in anything you wish to say on the subject."

The duchess trembled and turned to Mr. Sargent, her dark eyes appealing. But it was not from Mr. Sargent that a defense came, it was from my father-in-law.

"Your Grace, the duchess does not merit such a denunciation, no, she does not," Mr. Barton said. "If anyone is to blame, it is I. But when I spoke of the fleeting glories of this world, I was not referring to you or to your family. I would never make so bold, so heedless, a statement. *Never.* I have nothing but the highest regard for your family. I would never be so discourteous, in public or in private."

But the duke was not swayed by this appeal. "Do you take me for a fool, Barton? Do you think I did not hear the sniggers behind me— from my own servants? Good God, this world has come to a pretty pass when *my* footmen and *my* housemaids and *my* undercooks, whom I keep and feed and clothe, jeer at me in church. I will not allow it. Not in my house or on my estate."

He looked around the room and his eyes fell on the duchess. His expression intensified. "I have been slack; I have forgiven too easily. But not now. Never again. I have too much to lose. I have too much at risk." He broke his gaze from the duchess and turned his attention to his fist of paper. Loosening his grip on them, he opened his hand and stared at them as if he were seeing them for the first time. It seemed to quiet him, for after a moment he continued, his voice steadier, "I should have done this as soon as you found these bloody letters, Vanbrugh. They were the beginning." He glanced at me, and just for an instant his anger was replaced by fear, the haunted look of an animal hounded by a predator I did not see.

The duchess stepped toward the duke. "Do not destroy those letters," she said.

"Consuelo, *wife*"—he enunciated the latter with great bitterness—"they are no more a part of this house than you are."

The duchess looked stung. "That is not true," she said, but the duke would not hear any more—from her or anyone.

"What is true at Blenheim is whatever I say it is," he shouted, his high, thin voice bouncing off the ceiling of fine ornamental stuccowork that trimmed the low domes in the ceiling. "If you do not believe me, look at those bloody tapestries hanging in the state rooms. They were not concocted by the French, you may be sure."

"Sunny, that is not in dispute," Mr. Churchill said. He sidled up to his cousin and took his elbow gently and tried to guide him to the door.

But the duke was not to be persuaded so easily. He wrenched his arm away from Mr. Churchill and bellowed in great indignation, "Keep your hands off me, you swine, or I swear to God I will strike you down."

Mr. Churchill stepped back, bewildered by the vehemence of the words.

"I am the Duke of Marlborough," the duke cried, his passion equal parts fury and anguish. "Do you have any notion of what that signifies? I am the master of Blenheim. My wife is one of the richest heiresses in America. My lot should be happy; I should be content. I should be content!"

Red-faced, his body tense, his eyes bloodshot, the duke looked like a cornered animal, a beast caught in a trap. Breathing heavily, his forehead creased with lines, he jerked his head up at the portrait of John Duke over the chimney piece and contemplated it. When he spoke again, it was to that painting, as if John Duke were a spectator to this unfolding tragedy.

"Let me be plain," the duke said, his voice low. "I will not allow that truth, *my* truth, slip away because of some inconsequential correspondence." He held up the letters. "Any man who desired these for the purpose of circulating them is a scoundrel who deserves the worst fate that can befall him." With that, he tossed the letters into the flames, and all of us stood transfixed as the paper curled and blackened in the consuming fire.

"*Omnes vulnerant, ultima nerat.*" Mr. Churchill intoned.

"What did you say, Winston?" the duke asked.

"Just a benediction of my own." He turned from the fire.

"That is that," the duchess said quietly.

"Did you hear me, Sargent?" the duke demanded. "Did you hear what I said?"

Mr. Sargent stood very still and, in a voice of discouragement, replied. "Yes, Your Grace. You were very clear."

The duke sighed and stretched his shoulders, as if to loosen them after laying down a particularly heavy burden. A smile playing about his lips, he said, "Now all I have to do is locate that sketchbook, my dear, and all will be well." His voice sounded newly confident, almost exultant, and after a moment I understood why. By burning the letters, by making such a public spectacle of it, he was able to deflate their power to affect him. He was like a child who was surprised to discover that he had secured all of the toys for himself and that his nanny had suddenly disappeared: He now had everything. The duchess had lost in her attempt to seize the upper hand at Blenheim. The duke, once again, reigned supreme.

The butler reappeared quietly and said with the appropriate solemnity, "The constable from Woodstock is here, Your Grace."

"I will see him in my room," the duke said, and left the Long Library without another word. As the door closed behind him, Mrs. Belmont asked the monsignor, "What was it Winston said?"

"It is a Latin phrase. It means, 'All wound, the last kills,' " the monsignor said.

chapter
17

"M R. and Mrs. Vanbrugh, I wonder, do you have a moment?" Mr. Sargent asked, his voice gentle.

Margaret looked up at the painter, her expression wary. The histrionics the duke had exhibited a few moments before had disturbed her: Her face was empty of color, and her hands were icy. She had no wish to join Mrs. Belmont in scrutinizing the behavior we had just witnessed, which that lady embarked upon immediately after the duke left the room. Still, the inquiry from Mr. Sargent was not completely welcome, for its purpose was unclear.

"I will not take much of your time," Mr. Sargent promised, looking around the room. "If we could find a quiet place to talk . . . ?"

Margaret studied him for a moment, as if she were considering his studious green eyes or the shape of his jaw under his dark, well-trimmed beard. What she saw seemed to satisfy her, for she nodded almost imperceptibly. "Very well," she agreed, matching his confidential tone.

"Perhaps one of the state rooms?" I suggested.

Mr. Sargent arched an eyebrow in disappointment. "I thought, if you were both amenable, we might take a short turn in the park," he said.

Margaret wilted perceptibly: She had no desire to do anything of the sort. However, when he indicated the colonnade door, she followed him, and we slipped out of the library just as Miss Deacon called out, "Where are the three of you off to?"

Before any of us had the opportunity to reply, Mr. Sargent closed the door firmly behind us. "There," he said with relief. "That is about all of Miss Deacon I can abide for the present. The Lord gave us one day in seven to rest, but He overlooked one day of rest from the likes of Gladys Deacon. That would truly be a blessing."

His tone was buoyant and he smiled, but there was a determination to his voice that belied the lightness of his tone.

Mr. Sargent led us along the colonnade past the chapel door and down the shallow steps to the Great Court, which we proceeded across in silence. He led us away from the house toward the main gate, an impressive wall of tall, spearlike iron spikes, their points painted gold. When he reached to disengage the latch, his coat sleeve was pulled back and I caught a glimpse of his wrist, upon which was a small but noticeable spot of blue paint—the same teal he was painting with this morning. I shuddered and turned away, angry again at the way the duchess had toyed with me. I shut my eyes and willed the recollection back to oblivion. When I opened them moments later, Margaret and Mr. Sargent were on the other side of the gate, watching me curiously. I followed them, but it was as if another presence had joined us during that interlude, the ethereal spirit of the duchess, who hovered about Mr. Sargent as . . . what? A protector? A judge? A soul mate? It was impossible to tell.

We continued down the drive and headed toward the Column of Victory, crossing the bridge as we progressed. I made several attempts to engage Mr. Sargent in conversation, which he acknowledged with civil, one-word replies but nothing else. After a time I simply gave up.

On the far side of the bridge the paths divided, with the road itself curving left as a grass path continued a slow ascent up the hill toward the column, running between two long rows of young but sturdy elms, which in this fine weather looked robust and amaranthine. But instead of selecting that path Mr. Sargent indicated a grass path on our left and suggested: "Let us wander down there. I believe there is a bench Mrs. Vanbrugh can rest upon."

We followed him and descended to a flat, marshy area near the lake. There, tucked between two ancient, knotted beeches, their branches heavy with new leaves, was a small square pool fed by a tiny waterfall that cascaded from a stone wall set into the hill. Facing the pool was an iron bench, to which Sargent led Margaret. He offered me the spot next to her. When I was seated, he nodded in approval as if we were compliant subjects for his next portrait and lighted one of his cigarettes. He smoked in silence for a full minute, gazing back across the lake at the silhouette of Blenheim, obdurate and mysterious even from a distance.

"It is a curious thing about Blenheim," he said, pointing his cigarette at the house. "It is a marvel from all angles." I understood what he meant: Its monstrous square towers and commanding arcades gave the palace a romantic, medieval air, as if it were a fortress from ancient myth, perched high on a cliff over the Rhine or along the road to Damascus. "From here it looks like a backdrop for an opera. Or perhaps a music hall sketch. *The Marlborough Follies* or some such nonsense." He did not smile. Instead, he threw his cigarette, only half-smoked, into the reeds, frightening a frog into the water. "And we are merely performers." He leaned over and picked from the ground a thick, knotty stick and paced before us, at odd intervals jamming the stick into the soft earth. "It is a travesty, you know, what is happening up there," he said. He glanced up at the house, as if he half expected it to disappear when he was not looking. He seemed to be waiting for something.

"Do you know what this place is?" he asked suddenly.

"Of course," Margaret said. "This is Rosamond's Well."

Mr. Sargent began to bore a hole into the ground with his stick. "Rather modest to be the stuff of legend."

"Perhaps it was not always like this," Margaret replied.

"Perhaps not, Mrs. Vanbrugh. Mr. Vanbrugh, are you at all familiar with the fables surrounding this well?"

"If Aesop did not write it, then I am not familiar with it," I said.

Mr. Sargent grinned and peered into the clear pool and listened to the soothing murmur of water falling into water. "Henry the Second had an estate here he used to visit for the hunting. During his travels in Wales, he met a young girl, name of Rosamond Clifford, the story goes, and installed her here, away from the prying eyes of his wife, Queen Eleanor. Legend has it that this is the spring in which she used to bathe." He twisted his twig into the ground with some energy—so forcefully, in fact, that it snapped in two. "But the queen caught wind of this Rosamond anyway and had her poisoned—perhaps on this very spot. That seems more in keeping with the spirit of Blenheim, doesn't it?" With one hand he smoothed his moustache. "The duke informed me that this is the oldest part of the estate. Everything else here has been built since Queen Anne deeded the land to the Churchills in the eighteenth century. This spring was here long before any of this was built, and will be here long after all the rest is rubble." He used the remaining part of the stick as a wand, directing it over our heads across the horizon toward the bridge, the palace, and the outbuildings. "Decidedly this is the most romantic spot at Blenheim."

"They say this place is haunted," Margaret said.

"So you have heard that story, too. One of the coachmen told me that on some nights people hear a woman screaming in agony. They say it is Rosamond in her death throes. When they investigate, they can never find anyone."

I shifted in my seat. "Mr. Sargent, why did you bring us here?"

"I thought it might provide a little perspective," he replied.

"I am not sure I know about the kind of perspective you are referring to," I said.

"But you do, I am certain of it," he insisted. "They really are all different parts of the same whole. When I paint a portrait, or when you design a building, or when Sir John wrote a play, we contrive to force the viewer to see what we want him to see. But that is what is so extraordinary about people: They—we—never quite do what we are supposed to. We see what *we* want to see. But what artists and architects forget sometimes is that a painting or a building can be enjoyed from many angles, many perspectives." He looked at me, his eyes animated. "Do you understand?"

I did, but I certainly was not going to be lectured to by this pompous bore. Still, I had the feeling that we were unwitting and wholly unprepared actors in a drama whose denouement we could only guess at. It was deeply unsettling.

"You are going to have to be plainer," I said. "We must return to the house soon. We are leaving on the afternoon train to London." Margaret squeezed my hand in relief.

Mr. Sargent frowned. "But you must help us."

I shook my head. "We are not the best people to assist you, Mr. Sargent."

Mr. Sargent looked grave as I heard a noise over my shoulder. I turned, and was startled to see the duchess making her way toward us. She was dressed as she was when we left her, but had donned a smart, tight-fitting jacket of blue wool and a small straw hat with a veil of light gauze. She carried a parasol to fend off the sun, but her shoes were not sturdy enough to negotiate the footpath. She was having difficulty keeping her balance, and Mr. Sargent hastened to assist her in her final steps. I rose and offered her my seat, which she accepted gratefully.

"I had forgotten how perilous these shoes are," she admitted as she sat down, poking the toe of one of them with her parasol. "The last time I wore them, I slipped down the stairs and landed at the feet of one of the footmen. The poor man did not know what to do, so he fell to his knees." She chuckled and looked around, sighing. "This really is a lovely spot. I used to come here in the afternoons before the children were born. Sometimes I would have tea down here." She leaned toward Margaret and said, "People say that the water here has miraculous powers. When we were first married, my husband had the water tested by a professor we know at Oxford, but he could find nothing extraordinary in it. Still, Mullins, one of the gardeners, swears it cured his arthritis, and the fourth duke thought bathing here lessened the pain of his gout."

Mr. Sargent stood next to the duchess and placed his hand gently against her back as he leaned down to speak. There was nothing vulgar in the gesture, but it was done with no thought to its propriety. It clearly was not exceptional.

"Mr. Vanbrugh has indicated that he and Mrs. Vanbrugh are returning to London this afternoon," Mr. Sargent said. "I was about to explain how imperative it is that they stay a little longer."

The duchess leaned forward on her parasol and looked from Margaret to me. In that attitude, she looked very much as her mother did when she confronted me in the Temple of Diana. A strange expression played about her eyes, shrewd and calculating, as if she were playing a hand of bridge and knew her only chance of winning was to play a bold game.

"How . . . specific have you been?" the duchess asked Mr. Sargent.

"Not very," he admitted.

The duchess picked an invisible piece of lint off her lap. "I am sorry you have been treated so poorly here. Sorrier than I can ever say. We have been exceedingly careless of your feelings—I as much as anyone." I moved to interrupt, but the duchess held up her hand in appeal. "Please, Mr. Vanbrugh. Allow me the dignity to admit when I have erred."

"All right," I agreed.

She inclined her head in an appreciative nod. "Thank you. I want to atone, to make certain that both of you understand how much I value your acquaintance and hope very much that we can be friends." She offered a dazzling, hypocritical smile at both of us. "It is no secret that the duke and I are not the most well suited of couples. We are not of one mind, as the two of you so obviously are. We married very young, and had different expectations of what life together would be."

"You do not owe us any explanation for your behavior, Your Grace," I said.

She turned up to look at me, surprised. "But I do. Or at least I feel as if I do. I have not been at all open about what is happening with the duke and me. But I must, I *must*," she said with feeling, tightening her hands around the parasol.

I held my breath, praying that she would not admit her infidelity with Mr. Sargent in front of Margaret.

The duchess pressed on, her voice subdued. "The duke believes that Mr. Sargent and I are . . . involved," she said.

Margaret looked puzzled. "Involved?" she repeated. She turned from the duchess to me, searching for clarification. The duchess chose not to reply at once. Instead, she watched Margaret carefully for a sign that she grasped her meaning without forcing the duchess to resort to a more explicit detailing. Her perseverance was rewarded: In a trice Margaret understood, shrinking back onto the bench. She blushed deeply and turned away from the duchess, mumbling, "Oh, yes . . . I, of course . . . yes . . . I understand."

The duchess reached for one of Margaret's hands and clutched it. "It is not true, Mrs. Vanbrugh, you must believe me," the duchess professed. "It is completely false. Mr. Sargent and I are firm friends, nothing more. In fact, we have only become acquainted since the duke commissioned a portrait from Mr. Sargent."

She looked to Mr. Sargent for confirmation, and he nodded solemnly.

"Indeed, yes," he said. "There has been nothing improper in my dealings with Her Grace."

I was stunned—shocked beyond the power of speech. The audacity of the duchess—to attempt to convince us that the truth was other than what I knew it to be—was staggering, as daring as it was unforgivable.

That she was lying so that she could continue an affair with Mr. Sargent was breathtakingly arrogant. But I should not have been so taken aback: she was not aware that I knew of their relationship, and was under no inclination to admit it, least of all to two near strangers. But there was a small part of me that yearned to believe that the duchess was still capable of fidelity, if not to her husband, then at least to the truth. I half hoped that in a moment she would confess all— that they both would.

"Please, Mrs. Vanbrugh, tell me that you do not believe such stories," the duchess entreated. "Nothing could be less true."

Margaret ventured, "Why would the duke propose such a horrible story?"

"Sometimes my husband can be distrustful," the duchess said.

"He is a jealous man, but he has nothing to be jealous about," Mr. Sargent explained.

Margaret looked carefully at both of them. She made no sign that she felt the necessity of canvassing my opinion. Nor did I offer one; I knew by now that it was too late, that Margaret's desire for the truth from the duchess had died, so I remained silent.

After a terrible moment of indecision, Margaret said: "I am very glad to hear it, Your Grace. I own that I did not know what to think when you said . . ." she drifted off into silence.

"You are very good, Mrs. Vanbrugh," the duchess said, embracing her quickly. She turned to me and smiled, her eyes gleaming with elation. "You both are."

"Hear, hear," Mr. Sargent agreed, offering his hand to me.

I shook it without comment, feeling ashamed and utterly alone.

"But I do not understand how the duke could be so unkind," Margaret said.

The duchess smiled. "My dear, you are so gentle that you find it difficult to understand when others are not," she said. "Emily was right about you."

"Emily? What did she say?" I demanded.

"Only that Mrs. Vanbrugh had been her lifelong friend and that she had always been treated very well by her," the duchess replied.

I frowned. "Why were the two of you talking about Margaret? What could Emily have meant by that?"

The duchess did not answer. Instead, she rose and suggested, "Let us make a wish."

"Yes," Mr. Sargent said agreeably. He extracted a leather pocketbook from his coat and, selecting four coins from it, handed each of us a penny.

"Toss the penny into the pool and make a wish," the duchess directed. "It will come true."

I shook my head. "I do not believe in magic."

The duchess looked distressed. "I have never known Rosamond's Well to disappoint," she said. As if to demonstrate, she approached the edge of the pool and closing her eyes and taking a deep breath, dropped her penny into the pool. It sank quickly to the bottom. She was followed in quick succession by Mr. Sargent and Margaret, who giggled at the childishness of it all.

"Come along, Van," Margaret said. "Do not be such a stick."

"I am being nothing of the kind," I said, throwing the penny into the water. "I just find all of this preposterous." The coin skittered across the surface to the shadiest corner of the pool, where it disappeared under the dark water.

"You do not believe in wishes?" Mr. Sargent asked.

"I believe in what I see," I said.

"That was what Saint Thomas said," Margaret said, "and remember where his skepticism got him."

I had no rejoinder, which the duchess observed. "Mr. Vanbrugh cannot dispute that. Shall we return to the house?" she asked, pointing with her parasol toward the path.

We began our trip back in silence, climbing the hill in single file, Mr. Sargent assisting the duchess while I guided Margaret. When we had regained the bridge, the duchess turned to me.

"I was thinking of your comment about only believing what you see, Mr. Vanbrugh," she said. "It prompted me to recall the visit my husband and I made to Egypt while on our honeymoon. I was very young, hardly more than a girl, and one morning the duke determined that we should venture out to Giza to see the Pyramids. I was terribly excited: I had been fascinated by them ever since I was young, and I was eager to see them for myself. When I first saw them across the desert, they were magnificent—colossal and unyielding. There was a purity, an elemental grace, to their strict geometry that impressed me greatly. Oh, they were remarkable." She smiled briefly at the memory. When she spoke again, her tone had turned grave, even sad.

"But as we rode closer, their flaws became evident. The smooth top layer was gone—it had been stripped away years before, I was told— and the blocky stones underneath, which were huge and rough, had been pitted and scarred by centuries of wind and sun. I could see where the stone had crumbled or had been hacked off and carted away. As I stood there, in the heat and the stench of the camels, I came to a strange, unhappy awareness: From afar, the Pyramids were a marvel. From up close, the mystery was how they stood for four thousand years." The duchess looked embarrassed. "I know I am chattering away. But you do understand, I hope?"

"I understand you perfectly," I replied sarcastically.

But if the duchess noticed the irritation in my voice, she did not acknowledge it. Instead, she pressed her point. "I am sure you will think this odd, but as I stood there, I thought about how a marriage can appear to the world. From afar, it can look sturdy and smooth. But from up close, one can make out the fissures and blemishes." The duchess looked at us slyly, unsure of what response her rambling tale was eliciting.

I could muster no sympathy for her; I had had my fill of ducal deceit. I was readying a withering reply when Margaret, with great gentleness, put her hand on the duchess's forearm and nodded slowly, her eyes brimming. The duchess seemed overcome by this. Her expression was transformed from unease to relief. She hugged Margaret quickly and whispered, "Thank you, oh, thank you, my dear." Both ladies began to weep quietly, and after several moments caught themselves, giggling at the absurdity of their emotions. Mr. Sargent offered handkerchiefs to both women, which they accepted. Then arm in arm, they continued on to the palace, Mr. Sargent and I behind them.

All of this mystified me no end, but Mr. Sargent looked satisfied, as if he had expected such an outcome.

When we reached the main gate a cloud moved in front of the sun, dulling the gold-tipped spikes somewhat so that they seemed hostile rather than decorative. Before Mr. Sargent reached for the latch, the duchess turned and asked me, "Mr. Vanbrugh, what is wrong? You seem out of sorts."

"I believe more than ever that it is time for us to return to London," I said.

"Oh," Margaret said, her voice full of genuine regret.

"Of course, you may leave if you wish," the duchess said. "I can certainly understand why you would want to. But before you depart, I wonder if you would allow me to ask Mrs. Vanbrugh and you for one final favor?"

Immediately I was on my guard.

"Would the two of you assist Mr. Sargent in trying to locate his missing sketchbook?"

Without hesitation Margaret said, "We would be pleased to."

The duchess smiled and embraced Margaret again as the cloud moved directly in front of the sun, throwing a shadow across all of Blenheim. I understood then how adeptly we had been managed. The visit to Rosamond's Well, the shared intimacies, the meandering yarn about the Pyramids—all had been a carefully arranged scene, a set piece to provoke a response. The entire purpose of this outing was to engage Margaret in helping to locate the sketchbook. And Mr. Sargent was as culpable as the duchess; he was as much a part of the scheme as his mistress. But did the duchess think that Margaret knew where Emily had hidden the sketchbook? If she did, she was in for an unfortunate shock.

"Do not try to influence Margaret. I won't allow it," I said.

"What are you talking about?" the duchess asked.

"This whole farce you and Mr. Sargent concocted, to get us to help you, it will not work. I *know*, you see. I know everything about you. The two of you."

The duchess looked quickly at Mr. Sargent, whose eyes narrowed. "Exactly what do you know, Mr. Vanbrugh?" he asked carefully.

I opened my mouth, poised to reveal all that I knew about their tawdry relationship, but at the last moment I could not utter the words my heart so wanted me to. I was afraid of upsetting Margaret; I had treated her badly enough during our visit, I did not want to distress her further.

"You know perfectly well what I'm talking about," I replied.

Mr. Sargent stared at me in surprise. "No, I do not," he said after a time.

"Very well, then. I will be happy to tell you. In private."

"No, John, don't," the duchess said to Mr. Sargent, a sudden fear in her voice.

"Listen to Her Grace," I warned. "She understands this is not a ploy."

Mr. Sargent stared at me, as if to consider what to do. "Do not be a fool, Vanbrugh," he said.

"I'm not the fool here," I said.

The duchess shuddered as Margaret said, "Calm down, Van. I do not mind helping to search for the sketchbook."

"But I do," I said.

Margaret patted my arm. "It will be all right. Trust me."

She looked at me so imploringly that the fight in me disappeared. I could not argue with her anymore.

Mr. Sargent relaxed at that and as we passed through the gate, he spoke. "I feel I should warn you, Mrs. Vanbrugh, that the book is very personal. It has work in it that is for no other eyes but my own. If you do find it, I beg of you not to peruse it."

"I would not dream of such a thing," Margaret said.

"But how will she know if she has found the sketchbook if she cannot look in it?" I asked.

"All of my sketchbooks are embossed with my initials," Mr. Sargent explained. "It is a vanity, I know, but my parents began the practice when I was a young student and I have continued it ever since."

"How charming," Margaret said. "It should make it much easier to locate."

"I hope so," he agreed.

We advanced toward the palace as the sun reemerged, its rays catching the gaunt, emphatic figure of Pallas Minerva, the goddess of victory, which perched atop the heavy carved pediment like a vulture over a carcass. Her aspect, like the house she watched over, was stead-fast and merciless, unyielding even in triumph. Behind her, positioned precariously along the edge of the pediment, were statues of two cap-tured slaves, their arms shackled behind them. How like them I felt.

"Where have you searched for the book?" Margaret asked Sargent.

"All over the house," he said. "Everywhere we thought Emily might have concealed it."

"Have you investigated the library?" Margaret asked as we entered the palace.

"The Long Library?" Mr. Sargent frowned. "I have, a little. But that was not really the part of Blenheim that Emily frequented."

"Perhaps, but..." Margaret paused, scanning the hall for eaves-droppers. When she was sure that there were none, she continued in a more confidential tone: "Emily told me that she had concealed it with other books."

"She did? How extraordinary," the duchess said. "Did she say any-thing else more explicit?"

Margaret shook her head. "No, but do you not find that revealing?"

"I do, Mrs. Vanbrugh," Mr. Sargent said.

"But we have searched there already and found nothing," I said.

"When did you look?" Mr. Sargent asked.

"This morning, while you and the others were in the chapel," Mar-garet explained. That was why we were there when you arrived."

"Mr. Sargent nodded. "I see."

The duchess inquired, "Did you find anything in the library that you thought was unusual? Perhaps that might be a hint to look else-where."

"No, nothing," Margaret admitted. "And we searched quite thoroughly." She turned to me for confirmation, but I looked away. I was determined not to be a party to any of this macabre deception.

"Perhaps another pair of eyes might see something your excellent ones did not," Mr. Sargent said with new resolve. "I am willing to take another look through the library. Consuelo?"

"I will help you," the duchess agreed, looking inquiringly at Margaret and me.

"As will I," Margaret agreed.

I was not so obliging. "If we are to leave this afternoon, Your Grace, I have several tasks to do before then," I said.

The duchess looked at me a moment. She did not frown, but pressed her lips together in disapproval. "Is this not one of the tasks?" she asked.

"No, Your Grace," I replied evenly.

"Very well, let us go about our business," the duchess said. "Perhaps Mr. Vanbrugh will change his mind."

The three of them set off for the library while I headed for my room, certain that they were embarking on a fool's errand. I did not understand why the duchess and Mr. Sargent felt the need to include Margaret in their hunt, other than that she might recollect a piece of intelligence she had not heretofore done. But I thought that unlikely. Margaret was not the most observant of souls, at least in the way that the duchess and Mr. Sargent hoped. It was not in her nature to pay much attention to the subtleties of things. That was much more my expertise than hers; my mind worked that way. Whenever we entered a room together, I was the one who noted the details of the space: the dimensions, the moldings, the placement of the windows and lamps, the furniture and its embellishments. By contrast, Margaret was more likely to notice the people and what they sounded like and how they—

I stopped cold on the stair. A detail I had observed in Emily's room popped out of the sea of my memory suddenly, like a long-submerged buoy. It was a small point, but of if what it made me think was borne out, I might be able to find the sketchbook that the duchess and Mr. Sargent were so eager to recover. And the sketchbook, I realized, was the key to the murder.

chapter
18

I headed for Housemaids' Heights. But this time, instead of creeping to it furtively, I rushed for it, like a hound trailing a fox. I held my breath as I leapt up the service stairs two at a time, not to keep quiet—for I was making no attempt to disguise my progress—but because I was so eager to reach the room and test my hypothesis that I scarcely remembered to breathe.

I threw myself down the attic passage, bumping into all manner of items along the way. The corridor seemed narrower, more cluttered with castoffs, than I recalled. But I paid it no mind: Achieving the room consumed my full attention.

When I reached the door, I paused, listening carefully for any sound behind it. To my relief, there was none. I turned the knob slowly and pushed at the door.

To my shock, it stood firm. It had been locked.

I uttered an oath I had not heard since a sailor aboard ship shouted it when he lost control of a length of rope and burned his hand. I pounded loudly on the door, as if to rouse the slumberer within, to no avail, which only frustrated me further. I was so angered by this unexpected turn that it took me a moment to determine that if I could not gain entrance through the door, the only other alternative was through the window.

I tried the knobs of several nearby doors, and found that they were also locked. Puzzled, I checked thoroughly every door along the passage, and discovered to my growing alarm, that each had been secured. Shaken and angry, I veered down a passage I had not explored before. It was dingier and more cluttered than the others, as if it had been forgotten. There were fewer rooms along it, and many of their doors lay ignored behind broken furniture and dilapidated trunks from another time.

After a good deal of shifting and shuffling, I happened upon a door that was not locked. It opened into a space that was not really a room at all, but rather a niche which once had stored linen. There was a narrow window at the far end—so thin, in fact, that I did not know if I could maneuver myself through it. However, after several false starts I managed to open it, and eased myself through it by leaning out the window on my right side and then turning to the left.

The way back to Emily's room obliged me to scale several roofs and crawl around a handful of oddly protruding gables. As I straddled the crest of one of the wings, the peaceful countryside spread out below me, bathed in happy sunlight. I had the sensation that I was astride a breaching whale. I felt suspended, hanging in the air a moment before the enormous creature I was riding—and which I could not control—plunged back into the depths of the unfathomable ocean.

After two failed attempts to locate the room—for the roofs of Blenheim were as confusing as the rooms they covered—I reached the window I was seeking. To my relief, its latch had not been fastened tight; I was able to open it as Jamison had.

The room was as I had left it: simple and neatly arranged. I went immediately to the small bookshelf and looked for the volume of stories by Edgar Allan Poe. It was not there, I noted with a grim nod of approval. No doubt Mr. Churchill still had it.

I am neither an admirer nor a critic of Mr. Poe; I have never been drawn to his grim stories or moved by his poetry. However, as a child, I recall reading several of his detection stories and enjoyed their ingenuity, particularly the one that deciphered a code—"The Gold Bug" I believe its name is. Another story I read had at its heart the retrieval of an important letter which had been placed cleverly in plain view but had been arranged so cunningly that even the most attentive eye took no notice of it. I did not remember the name of the story, but given that someone had drawn attention to this particular stratagem in the volume of Poe I had seen—had it been Emily? Or Mr. Churchill?—I concluded that this was the method Emily had adopted to conceal the sketchbook.

I looked around the room apprehensively. If only there were anything in this room! It was so simply furnished—everything was easily reached, and the room was so little ornamented that no article could be hidden. Yet I reexamined every piece of furniture, every personal item I could find, and after a few minutes I was forced to conclude again that the sketchbook was not here.

I unlocked the door from the inside and stood in the passage. I tried to imagine what it must have been like for Emily to live in this room, how soothing it must have been compared to the disarray just outside her door. The contrast was remarkable: Inside all was calm, while outside in the passage were all manner of discarded furniture, paintings supported by piles of books, broken mirrors, old trunks—

Books.

There, along the corridor, a few steps from Emily's door, under several undistinguished landscapes, was a pile of heavy, thick, dark books.

I hurried to the pile and moved the paintings, drawing out the books one by one. I examined each one carefully. They were old stewards' ledgers from times past, full of fading figures on yellowed pages.

My keenness waned as the pile got smaller, and with a growing sense of despair I plucked the last book but one from the pile. As soon as I held it, I knew it was different, and my heart leapt when I noticed the discreet initials of JSS embossed in the bottom corner of the cover.

I had found the sketchbook Mr. Sargent had been searching for so eagerly.

I gripped the book tightly, scarcely able to believe my good fortune, and covered the embossed gold initials with my thumb. I was sorely tempted to inspect it right then, but I thought better of the idea. Instead, I returned the books to the pile—trying to prevent them from appearing as if they had been disturbed—and returned to Emily's room with the book in my hand.

I closed and locked the door behind me and sat in the small chair by the window, the sketchbook on my lap. With a growing apprehension, I opened the book.

Perhaps it was because my mind fills with the details of a building before it becomes whole, but for a moment I did not recognize the images I beheld. I saw a series of charcoal lines, dark and supple, circling and arcing across the pages. It took a moment for me to realize that these graceful lines were, in fact, drawings of the exposed torso, arms, legs, breasts, and nether regions of a beautiful woman—the Duchess of Marlborough—captured by Mr. Sargent in his distinctive style.

The duchess had allowed herself to be drawn, stripped of all covering and adornment, in a variety of poses. In some of them she was relaxed, carefree; in others she was provocative, even wanton. In all of them there was a total lack of shame to her aspect.

The illustrations seemed to be divided into three categories. At the beginning of the book were small, precise studies of particular parts of her physiognomy. The supple hollow where the shoulder meets the neck. A leg bent at the knee. An expressive hand caught in mid-gesture, the fingers beckoning. While drawn with great proficiency and very much *à la mode,* these illustrations had a tentativeness, an uncertainty, about them that the later sketches did not. They were much less confident than the larger, more complex studies Mr. Sargent had drawn in the middle section of the book. They concentrated on the body itself, and were bolder, more daring, more explicit, but they were also more tender: There was a longing to them that the earlier ones lacked.

But it was the handful of sketches toward the end of the book that took away my breath: They were the most arousing of all. They set my blood racing, these full-figure studies, effected in great, specific detail. The duchess standing against a chair, her knee on the seat. The duchess arching her back, her eyes closed. And the duchess drying herself with a towel. These drawings were so sensual, so alluring, so *alive,* they exuded the confidence that comes only from a communion of souls. The relationship between Mr. Sargent and the duchess clearly had moved far beyond that of artist and model. A union of spirits had been fused. The duchess appeared unafraid in all of these—untroubled by modesty or fear, shame or regret. She had a shocking unconcern for her reputation and for restraint: In fact, there was no discretion in any of these final sketches. They were almost debauched in their rapturous celebration of the physical: One could almost feel the artist embrace this woman.

I closed the book and shook my head. "What in the name of God were you thinking?" I whispered. The words hung in the air as if expecting an answer.

Now I understood why the duke was so eager to locate this book. If he possessed this, he would have the upper hand in any dealings with the duchess. Her standing, her character, her very independence could be checked by his threatening to release this book to the world. And it was also apparent why Mr. Sargent wanted this book back so desperately: It was as much a chronicle of his love—and his affair with a married woman—as it was a book of sketches. For I knew that these images would never be transmitted to canvas. They were too precious to share with the world. They had been drawn by a man to celebrate the woman he loves. They were not meant for others to see.

With a finger, I wiped away as much dust as I could from the spine as the clock in the kitchen tower began to toll eleven o'clock. The bell sounded crisp up here; it had fewer impediments to reach the ear. The tolling distracted me a bit, so I did not hear the approaching footsteps or the slight scratching of the key in the lock. So I was more than startled when I saw the doorknob turn and Miss Deacon entered. She was as caught unawares by my presence as I was of hers.

"Good God, Mr. Vanbrugh," Miss Deacon said, stepping back into the passage.

"I did not expect a locked door to open so suddenly," I said.

Once Miss Deacon recovered her composure, her eyes fell upon the book in my lap. Not raising her eyes from it, she asked, "What brings you to a locked room in Housemaids' Heights?"

"The same thing that drew you here, I would imagine," I replied. "Tell me, how did you manage to locate the key?"

She turned her gaze from the sketchbook to my face. "The duke gave it to me," she said.

"Of course. It was resourceful of him to think of locking this door."

"Not really. It was my suggestion."

I nodded. "There is nothing much of any particular interest here, either to find or to preserve," I said.

"Is that a fact?" Miss Deacon said, looking again at the sketchbook.

I did not reply.

"I think the resourceful one is you, for finding a way in." She glanced at the window. "I see we must be more cautious."

"There is no need for new precautions on my account," I said.

"Of course not. You have found the sketchbook."

"No, I mean that Mrs. Vanbrugh and I are leaving Blenheim today."

Miss Deacon raised her elegant eyebrows in surprise. "So soon? We were just getting to know each other."

"We have overstayed our welcome."

"That is not possible. No one is welcome here," Miss Deacon said. "This is the least hospitable house in England."

"Not even for you?"

"I am particularly unwelcome."

As I looked at her, considering, I marveled at her courage. She stood before me, poised and self-assured, as confident standing in a servant's room trying to wrangle a book from a stranger as she was at terrifying Margaret with stories about the duke. She had the self-possession that springs from the inner certainty that in the end, she will prevail.

"I am certain the duchess will be sorry to see you go, with your task unfinished," she said.

"Task?"

"Her rooms."

"Oh, that is nothing. I have no doubt that she can find another architect with a great deal more experience than I."

"Perhaps. But not anyone with more character."

I laughed hollowly. "Character is hardly what is called for here."

"Oh, really?" Miss Deacon said. "I would have thought that character was exactly what is called for."

"You are being arch, Miss Deacon," I said.

"I am being nothing of the kind, Mr. Vanbrugh," Miss Deacon lied, blushing a little at being caught. "But I do think that Consuelo genuinely believes in you."

"That is flattering to hear, but what she asked me to do is beyond my abilities. Now if you will excuse me, I must go downstairs and see to our luggage."

Rather than give way, Miss Deacon moved into the doorway to block it. "But we are not done here."

"Done?"

"You have not given me the sketchbook," she said. She put out a hand.

"And I will not."

Her eyes narrowed. In a cooler tone she said, "May I ask why?"

"Because it is not mine to give you."

"But you found it."

"It does not belong to me. It belongs to Mr. Sargent."

"Yes, but—" she began, then stopped as she grasped the import of my words. "You are not saying that you are going to give this sketchbook back to John Sargent," she said in disbelief.

"That is exactly what I am saying," I replied.

Miss Deacon looked at me in astonishment.

"All right, then," she said after she had recovered. "Just give me the book and I will see that it is returned to him." She took a step toward me and held out her hand.

"I prefer to give it to him myself."

She paused. "I cannot let you do that," she said.

"You cannot?" I repeated. "Miss Deacon, you have no say in this."

"But I do," she insisted. She looked around the room speculatively, as one might who was furnishing a flat. "You see, that book can be of extraordinary value to me."

"But it is not yours," I said.

"That should not matter," she said, then: "That does not matter."

"I believe it does."

Miss Deacon replied quickly: "Mr. Vanbrugh, this is not America. This is not even London. You are at Blenheim. The Duke of Marlborough rules here."

"The last time I noticed, you were not the duke, Miss Deacon," I said. "Or even the duchess."

She scowled. "I speak for the duke in this," she said.

Her words chilled me, for I felt their potency. Still, I would not submit so easily.

"That may be, Miss Deacon, but I will not hand over something that belongs to another just because you say you speak for the duke."

"Be careful, Mr. Vanbrugh," Miss Deacon warned.

"Be careful of what? Be careful, or I will end up with the duke angrier at me than he already is? Be careful, or you will assail me with more stories about Margaret, or the duchess, or the monsignor, or whoever else you want to destroy? Be careful, or I will end up dead, like poor Emily? You seem not to understand, Miss Deacon, that I do not want this life. It is only a façade—a false front. Tricked up and highly decorated, to be sure, but there is nothing behind it. It is privilege without merit, honor without duty. You would feel that way, too, if you still had a drop of democratic blood left in you."

"What I feel is none of your business," Miss Deacon replied, annoyed.

"And what I feel is none of yours. But since we are leaving Blenheim this afternoon, Margaret and I, I no longer have to witness your deceit. That you wish the duke to divorce his wife and marry you is one thing—reprehensible, but a private matter among the three of you. But that you are willing to put all of us through this, this *game* to satisfy your desire to become the Duchess of Marlborough is outrageous."

"You pathetic man, you know nothing of outrage," Miss Deacon sneered.

"Maybe not, but I know a prostitute when I see one."

Miss Deacon lunged forward and slapped me hard across the face. The force of her blow threw me backward, but when I brought my hand to my cheek, I felt no pain, only a rising awareness of the peculiar sort of astonishment that comes from an unexpected reaction. "You see it, too," I said in a whisper of wonder.

"I see nothing of the kind," Miss Deacon said. "The duke and I are in love and intend to marry, as soon as he is free."

"The Duke is the stupidest man in England, you said so yourself," I said. "You cannot be in love with him."

"I am," Miss Deacon said, her voice raw and defiant.

"Then you are more foolish than I thought you were."

Miss Deacon lunged at me again and demanded, "Give me the book." She had the element of surprise on her side, and her grip was unexpectedly firm—her long, hard fingers wormed their way under my palms—so it was with considerable effort and only after a brief, almost comical tug-of-war that I wrested it back from her. Yanking the book threw her off balance and she fell to the floor. As I stood above her, a horrible truth engulfed me, as cold and certain as death itself.

"It was you. You strangled Emily," I said, conviction and awe in my voice.

Miss Deacon made no effort to rise. She sat on the floor, her legs splayed in front of her, her breathing ragged. She looked like a child caught in a lie: flabbergasted and humiliated at being found out. But rather than rebut my assertion, she looked down at her hands, as if she were unsure they were hers. After a moment she spoke again, but her voice was disengaged, empty—hollowed out by the secret she had held so close. "Sunny needed me to. She would not give him what he wanted."

Her admission was straightforward, even simple, but its import was monstrous, as overpowering as Blenheim itself. Her words provoked a shudder of revulsion in me that racked my soul.

"Miss Deacon, that is not good enough," I managed after a moment.

"He kept insisting, but she would not tell him. He knew Consuelo had given Emily the book: Mrs. Andrews overheard the duchess and Emily and told him all about it. I was so afraid that Sunny would frighten Emily so much that she would return the sketchbook to Consuelo." She looked up at me suddenly, as if she did not recognize who I was or where we were. Her expression was thoughtful, as if she understood something now she had not before. Then, without warning, while still seated in the corridor, she began to scream. Her cries, strident and shrill, pierced the air like needles through fabric, filling the house with noise.

She made no effort to detain me as I stepped over her and ran down the passage toward the stair, the sketchbook firmly in my hands.

I ran from Miss Deacon and her angry shrieks, certain I could get away from them. But the noise pursued me: It seemed to grow louder as I hurried down the narrow stairs, reverberating through the stairwell so that when I reached the bedroom floor landing, a voice on the stairs below me demanded, "Who is screaming like a banshee?" It was Mrs. Belmont.

I halted, the skin on my neck tingling. I did not want her to detect my presence.

"It is only a servant," the monsignor said from behind her.

"A servant? Where is Consuelo? She must put a stop to this," Mrs. Belmont said.

"Perhaps she is trying to locate the poor creature now," the monsignor said.

Mrs. Belmont listened a moment and then drew a quick, surprised breath. "I declare, that is Gladys screaming," she said.

"Miss Deacon?" the monsignor repeated, his voice alert. "What is wrong?"

"It is Gladys," Mrs. Belmont repeated with more conviction and began to climb the stairs.

I eased out of the stairwell and stole down the bedroom corridor as quickly as I could to my room. The passage, which yesterday—only yesterday?—I had found dark and claustrophobic now seemed immensely bright and exposed. Panic began to simmer within me, and I felt suddenly hot.

The route led me across the high, narrow balcony that overlooks the Great Hall. I approached it with great apprehension, for its position and prospect exposed me to anyone who was standing in the hall. As I drew closer, I heard the duke directing several servants and I cursed my rotten luck. I fell to my knees, pressed myself against the stone wall, and crawled slowly toward a shallow niche in the center of the balcony in which was hung a large portrait of Queen Anne. Such a position offered me the luxury of an obstructed view of the duke and, I prayed, a decent chance of remaining undetected.

The duchess and Mr. Sargent appeared from the library corridor and stopped, uncertain. I wondered where Margaret had gotten to.

"There you two are," the duke said.

"What is that?" Mr. Sargent said, putting his hands over his ears as Miss Deacon began another round of shrieks.

Raising her voice to be heard above the din, the duchess asked, "Why is Gladys carrying on?"

"I will wager that it has something to do with you," the duke said. "And him," he said, cocking his head toward Mr. Sargent.

"He has a name," the duchess replied tartly.

"So do you," the duke barked. "And as I recall, it is mine."

Mr. Sargent lurched toward the duke, his fists clenched.

The duchess restrained him. "John, it *does not matter*," she said. "It does not matter."

The duke did not move: He stared at Mr. Sargent as if to provoke him into striking. But Mr. Sargent thought better of it. After a moment, he pulled his arm away from the duchess and said, "I am going to my room," leaving the Marlboroughs standing in the middle of the suddenly silent Hall.

"Your friend has a nerve," the duke said—loud enough for Mr. Sargent to overhear. But Mr. Sargent said nothing.

The duchess waited until the painter was out of hearing before she asked her husband, "Do you honestly believe Gladys will treat you any better than I have?"

"Gladys loves me, and I her," the duke said, with the arrogance of a man who is more conceited than perceptive. "The strongest emotion you have ever bestowed on me is polite indifference."

"That is not true," the duchess said. "It was you who first admitted you did not love me. When you proposed." She shook her head at the recollection. "How greedy you are, like a child: You always want whatever you do not have."

Anger exploded from the duke like gunfire. "Do not judge me. I will not tolerate it," he shouted.

"You tolerate so little, it is a wonder you can survive the day," the duchess said.

"I am so tired of you," the duke said, his voice venomous.

The duchess shrugged a shoulder in indifference. "What did the constable say?"

"What I wanted him to say," the duke said. "What a tragedy, how terrible for you, Your Grace, we will work to catch this criminal quickly. I told him the likeliest culprit is that shiftless footman, Jamison."

"Will he help keep this quiet?"

"Of course."

Miss Deacon emitted another loud, lingering scream. "Gladys is especially dramatic today," the duchess said.

"She will be finished soon enough, I expect," the duke said. "Silly cow." He sighed. "Perhaps she has news."

"What news would she have?" the duchess asked.

"About the sketchbook."

"I think she may be disappointed in that."

The duke frowned. "You are awfully sanguine."

"I have known Gladys longer than you," the duchess replied. "She was my friend before she became your mistress."

That admission, delivered so impassively, was almost more than I could endure. I had heard enough. As slowly as I could, I crawled along the floor, as near to the wall as I could get. I was nearly across the balcony when the duke demanded, "What was that?"

"What?" the duchess asked.

"Up on the balcony. I saw something move," the duke insisted.

I willed myself to be as still as the stones around me.

"There is nothing on the balcony," the duchess said. "It must have been a shadow."

"A shadow? I did not see a shadow. I have never mistaken anything for a shadow in my life," the duke said indignantly. "Hey! You! Up there," he called. "Show yourself at once."

I was certain that I had been discovered, and was only moments away from a humiliating confrontation with the duke.

At that moment there was a commotion at the end of the passage. The footmen had located Miss Deacon, and were escorting her down from Housemaids' Heights. Far from being satisfied with being discovered—which I had concluded was her goal—Miss Deacon seemed more frenzied than when I left her. Her cries and screamed orders were earsplitting even from the balcony, so I knew that the footmen were having a difficult time of it. They did not stop on the bedroom floor, where Miss Deacon had begun a new round of wailing, but conveyed her to the main floor.

The tumult she was causing distracted the duke, for when Miss Deacon appeared in the Great Hall, she was in a state of near hysteria, crying incoherently and attempting to say something through strangled sobs.

"Take her into one of the state rooms," the duchess directed. The footmen complied, and I heard the steps of the duke and duchess follow them through the Saloon. Seizing my chance, I got to my feet and ran as swiftly and as quietly as I could to my bedroom. But as I reached the door, another scheme suggested itself. Rather than retreat to where I was sure to be discovered, I must find a place where no one would think of looking for me—at least for the moment. I tried to recall the plan of Blenheim that Mr. Churchill had showed me. How foolish I was not to have examined in the more detail the plans for the wings—the stables, the kitchens, the orangery. They would have excellent hiding places there. But then again, they were also hundreds of yards from where I was standing—a continent away—and I would not get there unobserved. I must content myself with someplace in the main house, someplace forgotten, or abandoned, or out of date, or—

I smiled at the idea that occurred to me. Without another thought I again headed for the service stair and, taking care that I heard no one, descended to the main floor, making my way surreptitiously toward the bedroom of the duchess, where this muddle began.

The shortest route to her suite took me through the rooms that the duke occupied. They were quiet; there was always the chance that the servants would be about, but I met no one when I passed through them and arrived at the family dining room.

The dining room was full of light. The long table was sleek with polish, its surface satin-smooth, mirroring the immaculate silver centerpiece of Louis XIV on horseback, burnished and gleaming with the luster of centuries of attention. Even the haughty portrait of John Duke above the mantel improved markedly in the sunshine: He looked pleased to see me again, as if he approved of my plan to outwit his descendant—or, if I were to believe the letters, my distant cousin. I smiled at the old rogue.

As I drew closer to the door that separated the dining room from the rooms the duchess occupied, I observed that it was not quite latched. Someone had been in this room recently—perhaps was in there even now—and had been careless about concealing his traces.

I listened at the door for voices on the other side, for a hint at how I should proceed. But it was quiet. Perhaps it was safe to enter the room after all. I pushed at the door gently, and it opened before me.

The room was much as I had left it, but still I entered the room cautiously, trying to determine if anyone had been here.

I tried to shake the despair that was threatening to strangle me. From the far corner of the room, on the far side of the bed, came a dull groan. I whirled around and saw emerging from the pile of fabric the disheveled form of Jamison. He crawled out from the velvet like a bear leaving his cave, yawned, and lumbered toward the fireplace. He crouched down and inspected the coals, as if he were preparing to light it. After a moment, he stood up and gazed at me, without surprise or fear.

"What time is it?" he asked.

"After eleven," I replied, my voice steady. "How long have you been here?"

"Since last night," he said.

"I thought you had run away."

He shook his head and for a moment a rueful grin hovered about his lips. "Not yet," he said.

"What possessed you to conceal yourself in here?" I asked.

"I knew Her Grace had moved. No one'd be about."

That was true enough, but I marveled that he could reenter the house and find his way to this room without being discovered. "You could have used your room."

Jamison shuddered. "I would have been sacked, I would, if anyone had seen me," he said simply.

"But surely you cannot think—" I began, but checked myself.

"I know. I am as good as gone. But I cannot leave Blenheim. Leastways, not right now." His dark eyes clouded, and he snuffled, rubbing his dirty sleeve across his nose. From a pocket, he extracted a box of matches. He kneeled before the fire and, after arranging the coals, lighted it quickly, so that in a moment there was a merry glow. "There, that's better," he said, standing up and rubbing his hands together.

"Surely you cannot be cold," I remarked.

"Since Emily was found in the courtyard, I've been gripped with a chill I can't get rid of," he said. His voice brimmed with a weary sorrow.

"Do you have any warmer clothes?" I asked.

Jamison did not reply. His eyes fell on the sketchbook. "Is that the book?" he asked.

"Yes."

He stood up straighter and asked formally, "May I see it, sir?"

I shook my head. "I'm sorry, Jamison, but it is private."

He frowned. "Perhaps it is," he admitted after a moment. "But I would like to have seen what Emily was killed for." He shivered, and extended his hands toward the coals. "If I may ask, sir, where did you find it? I searched her room right enough."

"It was not in her room. It was out in the corridor, amid a pile of books."

Jamison raised his eyebrows. "Emily was a shrewd one, she was."

"Look here," I said. "Where will you go?"

"I expect to London, or maybe Bristol."

"Do you have any money?"

"A little," he admitted.

I pulled out my pocketbook and handed him as much money as I could prudently spare. "Here. Take this."

Jamison looked at the notes gravely, but shook his head. "I am obliged to you, but I cannot take your money," he said. "Emily wouldn't allow it."

"Emily is gone, Jamison," I said, pressing the notes on him.

He stepped back and pulled his hands away, as if just the touch of the money would sully him. "Not from me," he said. He thrust his hands in his pockets and closed his eyes, repeating, "Not from me."

I stood before him, in awe of his love for a woman he would never see again. "Of course, if that is what you wish," I said. I returned the notes to my pocketbook. "I am sorry, Jamison," I said.

"No, sir, it is I who should apologize to you. When you and the missus first arrived here at Blenheim, I . . . Well, I looked down at you, I did, since you didn't have no valet of your own to see to you and no white tie for dinner. But . . ." He paused, falling into silence.

"All of that is true enough," I agreed.

Jamison smiled quickly—pleased but shy about our moment of good will. "Here now, I almost forgot," Jamison said roughly. "I found something odd," he said. "Leastways, I believe I did."

"What is it?"

"I found it underneath Her Grace's pillow. I borrowed it last night, and when I picked it up I found this book under it and a piece of paper fell out."

Jamison handed me a letter and the book, a recent copy of *The Provok'd Wife* by Sir John Vanbrugh. I opened the letter, which looked just like the others, and with a growing sense of disbelief read:

Van—

I wrte in grate haste, for 'tis of great moment. Ere long, & I will be a widow, may God forgive me. I sent the maid to Coop'r & akwir'd the potions from him. I drop'd them meself into J's wine, as I vow'd I wou'd—and yu, who thought me n'er wou'd have the courage. But women who love have ten times the heart of they'r men. J tasted naught, but soon enough he fell into a slumber, & now scarcely breathes. I cringe at the hor'or of waking up besid a dead man, bt, my hart sings at being w/you always. He grones

soft & is weekr by the minute. I shudder in fear, & joy, & Yr love,
etc.

Then, scrawled at the bottom of the letter was an additional line, which chilled me as nothing had ever before:

He lives! He knows! My love for you, 'tis ruin'd me.

My hand trembled, and I shivered as a sudden breeze blew through the room. I glanced at the windows and to my surprise observed that they were closed.

What I had read was impossible, it could never have been. But through miscalculation, or divine intervention, or a simple accident, I had come to understand that the letters I had found in the duchess's rooms were a complete fabrication, one more example of Blenheim's sleight-of-hand. If Jamison had not shown me a copy of the play, I would have believed the entire charade.

"This cannot be," I murmured several times, but there were enough similarities to the other correspondence to disturb me. It was indisputable that this letter was written in the same hand as the others had been; I would swear to it. I was being forced to conclude that the letter had been addressed to Sir John by Duchess Sarah: This was a letter from a woman overcome by her emotions and misguided by desire. If the contents of this letter were ever revealed, and it became known that Duchess Sarah had tried to poison John Duke for the love of Sir John, the response, even two hundred years later, could be disastrous for the duke and his family.

The only problem was it was a lie. They all were. All created by the—

Jamison was staring at me, his open face worried. "You look all done in," he said. "Is it the letter?"

I coughed and attempted to look unperturbed. "In a manner of speaking. Tell me, have there been any workmen in this room recently?"

Jamison thought. "A fortnight ago, the duchess came down from London with a workman or two. They were here all day, and then they left. I don't know what they were doing."

I refolded the piece of paper and slipped it into my pocket as the door opened and Mr. Churchill strolled in.

"Ah, yes, I thought you might be here," he said, a satisfied smirk settling about his mouth.

"Are you speaking to Jamison or to me?" I asked.

"You, of course. Sunny has been searching high and low for you." Mr. Churchill's eyes flickered as they fell upon the sketchbook, which I hugged to my chest.

"I thought he would be," I admitted, not moving.

"You have something he has been looking for," Mr. Churchill said.

"Perhaps," I replied.

For the first time, Mr. Churchill acknowledged Jamison. "Hallo, Jamison. Back again, I see."

"Yes, sir," Jamison said, looking toward the door to the dining room. "I'll be on my way, then," he said.

"A first-rate suggestion," Mr. Churchill said heartily, as if a glass of champagne had just been offered. "Mr. Vanbrugh and I have something to discuss."

"In point of fact, I have nothing to say to you, Mr. Churchill," I said. "Margaret and I are preparing to catch the afternoon train to London, so I will say good morning."

"Not so fast," Mr. Churchill replied, stepping forward. "You have something His Grace is very keen to have."

"But I am not eager for him to have it, as I told Miss Deacon," I said, stepping away from him. "So if you will excuse me—"

I heard a flurry of footsteps and suddenly the duke was standing next to Mr. Churchill. He looked very tired: He was pale, his dry lips cracked and colorless, his heavy jaw slack. But his small blue eyes shone with a feverish satisfaction when they fell upon the sketchbook. "Excellent, Vanbrugh," the duke said. He advanced toward me like a cat. "If you please," he said, holding out his hand expectantly—as if I would willingly give him something which his mistress had killed for.

I glanced at Jamison, who understood immediately the predicament I found myself in. He nodded.

I turned my attention to the duke. "Not today, Your Grace," I said, as I bolted through the open dining room door as Jamison threw himself at the duke, pushing him into the fireplace.

As I ran through the enfilade toward the Duke's Cabinet, the angry howl of His Grace and the unexpected sound of shattering glass reached my ears—and, I would conjecture, those of every other soul at Blenheim.

chapter
20

"VANBRUGH! Halt right there!" Mr. Churchill shouted, running after me.

The Grand Cabinet, when I reached it, was dark, but this time there was the hope of light: The draperies, still closed, could not keep all of the morning sun from peeking around their edges. I closed the door behind me and ran through to the Green Drawing Room: My plan, hastily formed, was to escape to the gardens through the Saloon. But quickly I pulled up short: Scurrying toward me from the Long Library, his cassock straining with each stride, was the monsignor, his heavy gold crucifix in one hand to keep it from bouncing onto his chest. His expression was determined, inexorable—and frightening.

With the monsignor only several rooms away and Mr. Churchill gaining on me, I felt more like a pawn than a man; a bishop and a knight are formidable adversaries. I slammed the doors to both the Grand Cabinet and the Red Drawing Room and maneuvered some of the heavy furniture against both sets. I would not be able to block the progress of either man forever; my hope was to impede it long enough to escape.

I stole out into the main corridor. I had only a moment to devise another plan for dodging Mr. Churchill and the monsignor, and no doubt other members of the household who would be collecting at their cries; I could already hear a growing chorus of voices accompanying the thumping on doors that the two men had begun moments before. I had only a few minutes—

"Why, Mr. Vanbrugh, what are you doing in here?" Annie asked in bewilderment, her flat country voice echoing through the passage. The girl was holding a basket of bed linen and was headed upstairs, but her simple face puckered in alarm at my unexpected appearance.

She had emerged from the service stair, which was just outside the Green Drawing Room door, and I went to it gratefully, putting two fingers to my lips and whispering, "Softly, Annie, please."

Eyes wide with fright, Annie froze.

"Is anyone belowstairs?" I asked.

She swallowed loudly. "Yes, sir. We all are."

"How about upstairs? Do you know if there is anyone about?"

"I can't say, sir. But I believe everyone has breakfasted. Except for you, sir." She stared at me, a look of panic growing in her eyes. "What's wrong, sir? Has there been another murder?"

"No, Annie, nothing like that. It is just that Mr. Churchill and the monsignor are trying to get their hands on this book."

Annie peered at the book, as if it were a poorly behaved dog. "Why, sir?" she asked.

"It is not theirs, and the duchess gave it to Emily for safekeeping. I believe this is what Emily was killed for, Annie."

Annie stared at the sketchbook, a combination of fear, excitement, and revulsion playing across her face. "It belongs to Her Grace, then," she said, her voice reverent.

"Not precisely. It belongs to Mr. Sargent." There was a low thud, and I knew that the Green Drawing Room had been breached. "Annie," I said quickly. "I am going upstairs to see if I can find Mrs. Vanbrugh. Be a good girl and tell Mr. Churchill that you saw me run toward the library. Do you understand?"

The girl nodded. "The library. Yes, sir."

"Good." I started up the curving stone steps.

As I reached the bedroom corridor, the duchess was at the top of the main stairs. She looked down the corridor at me, unsure at first who I was. When she realized it was me, her anxious expression melted and she hurried toward me.

"Mr. Vanbrugh, you do not know how pleased I am to see you," she said.

"I have found the sketchbook."

The duchess broke into a relieved smile as the door to Margaret's room opened, and the duke stuck his head out into the passage. Her Grace froze, immobilized at the sight of him, and clutched her hands tightly to her chest.

"Ah, Vanbrugh, I knew you'd come up here," the duke said easily. "I was just telling your wife that you found the sketchbook. She was expressing great surprise at the news." He pulled Margaret out into the corridor, and she obliged him reluctantly. He was not hurting her, but there was a firmness to his direction. "We were having quite a nice chat about it."

"How is your burn, Your Grace?" I asked.

"Oh, a trifle—hardly worth mentioning. It is nothing to concern yourself with," he said. "Jamison no doubt is in much worse shape than I am. He jumped out a window and disappeared. No doubt he is bleeding in a hedgerow somewhere. I have my men out looking for him." The duke looked immensely satisfied.

"For what purpose?" the duchess asked.

"Why, to arrest him for the murder of that servant girl."

"That is a monstrous lie," I said.

The duke narrowed his eyes. "I would not say that, Mr. Vanbrugh. These things happen, and that is an end to it. Lovers have a falling-out. Passion fades and is replaced by . . ." He stopped and inspected his fingernails. "Something more destructive."

"Jamison did not kill Emily," I said. "I will swear to it."

The duke shrugged. "Well, the constable thinks it very likely that he did."

"No doubt because you told him what to think," I said.

"I told him the truth," the duke said, calmly smoothing his moustache. "And that you and Mrs. Vanbrugh discovered her body. No doubt he will want to speak with the two of you, as well. Which means you will not be able to return to London this afternoon." He smiled. "Besides, we have a little matter to resolve first."

"Van," Margaret said, her voice a warning—but of what? I did not wait to find out. I turned and ran back to the service stairs, and threw myself up the flight to the attic story, the duke in pursuit.

I flew blindly down a corridor, which was lighted only by a grimy window at its far end, and struggled to heave as many impediments in the way I could find: empty picture frames, moth-eaten carpets, a cracked earthenware jug, a teetering tower of decrepit dining chairs, their leather seats long ago rotted away, several croquet balls, a forgotten fire bucket, a bath chair with one of its wheels missing, an old-fashioned wooden wine cooler, a pair of discarded andirons. The sounds these made crashing against the floor and each other were tremendous, but the shouts and snarling oaths they provoked in the duke were oddly satisfying.

I reached the end of the passage unsure of what to do. I had settled on breaking the window glass and climbing out onto the roof when I noticed an unobtrusive door in the right wall, which had a simple doorknob and no lock. I pushed open the door and with great, rusty reluctance, it opened. I entered the dark room quickly, slammed the door behind me and looked about. I was in a box room, dim and dusty, full of forgotten trunks and the accrued detritus of generations. I dragged two heavy chests in front of the door and stacked them snugly against it, just as the duke and, to my surprise, Mr. Churchill began to pound on it, demanding to be let in.

I ignored the duke and his condemnations as my eyes cast about for an escape. The room was long and narrow, rather like a fissure in a rock, with an eave that cut low across its entire length, so that there was very little space in which a person of my height could stand upright. To my alarm, I found no other door—nor was there a window. However, halfway down the slanted ceiling there was a small skylight that was just large enough for a man to crawl through.

I maneuvered three small chests underneath the skylight and placed them one on top of the other. I scaled them and examined the skylight closely. It was quite old and its simple hinges were rusty with disuse. There was no other recourse but to break the glass. I glanced behind me toward the door: The chests teetered unsteadily as someone on the other side of the door pushed against them.

Holding the sketchbook tightly in both hands, I plunged it through the glass with a swift, sharp stab, like the lunge of a saber. The old glass shattered easily, and pieces of it cascaded down upon me. I drew back in the hope that I could avoid injury, and was lucky that only my hand was cut. I removed my coat quickly and with it wiped the remaining shards from the frame. With my hands still wrapped, I threw the sketchbook out onto the roof and pulled myself up through the skylight onto the roof just as one of the chests fell to the floor and the duke and Mr. Churchill eased themselves into the room.

I picked up the sketchbook and ran over the roofs wildly, my only object to elude my pursuers. The sun was almost completely over-head—it was nearly noon—and there were very few shadows among the dormers, eaves, spouts, and statuary of the Blenheim rooftop. Everything up there had been thrown into harsh relief by the bright, unforgiving sunlight. There were no surprises here, no tricks of the eye, no false perspectives. Up here, away from the contrivances and flourishes, the scale was human: erratic and practical, straightforward and unadorned.

I thought that I could navigate my way to a part of the roof I was familiar with and reenter the house. Yet nothing was familiar; every-thing had been turned around somehow, twisted and warped into a world I did not recognize. Twice I was forced to double back when it became clear that I was headed into a blank, unscalable wall or crum-bling balustrade. It was as if the house itself was conspiring against me, rearranging the rooftop to confound my escape. I was as much a stranger up here as I was among the state rooms below, a perplexed observer of a world I did not understand. My only consolation was that I had slipped away from both the duke and Mr. Churchill, but I feared my ingenuity would not outsmart them.

My wandering brought me to the high square tower that stood at one corner of the Great Courtyard, above the rooms occupied by the duchess and overlooking the curving colonnade that accommodated the triangular room Mr. Churchill had commandeered. As an element of the Blenheim design, the tower was an essential, even crucial, piece, anchoring the palace and connecting the main house with the kitchen wing. It was a huge, heavy piece of architecture: strong and stout and stately, and even from this height imparted the feeling of being both an ancient castle and a military outpost. The tower was higher than any other part of the house except the central roof of the Great Hall, and at the tower's summit was a heavy stone arcade whose piercing verticality was emphasized by four attenuated carved pinnacles that stood at each corner. A mild scent of burning coal indicated that the flue to the duchess's bedroom was nearby—snaking inside one of the stone piers.

I peered into the arcade and to my surprise saw that it was roofed, creating a diminutive belvedere that offered a stunning vista across the courtyard to the lake and obelisk. It was remarkably neat and well swept, and there was even a small chair arranged advantageously to face the view, as if its occupant had recently departed. At the far side was a narrow stairway with a rusty iron railing that led up to a closed trapdoor in the roof, while across from me was a dark wedge of slate that faced away from me and thrust itself up from the roof itself. I moved to see if it might be some sort of access to the attics when a door in it flew open and out stepped the duke, Mr. Churchill, and the duchess, each of them as startled at encountering me as I was of seeing them.

"There you are," the duke said, as if I were a fractious child who had been lost in the park.

"You gave us quite a scare," Mr. Churchill said, breathing heavily.

Desperately, unthinkingly, I made for the narrow stair and hurried up it, throwing my weight against the trapdoor. It opened grudgingly and I emerged out onto a shallow, cone-shaped metal roof perhaps twenty feet in diameter that looked out onto the Kitchen Court, the Oxford road, and the village of Woodstock beyond. I turned to close the trapdoor behind me, but the duke proved too quick: He struck my leg with his fist and threw me off balance, tossing me to the metal roof and sending the sketchbook flying out of my hands onto the other side of the shallow cone. Fear clutched me as I realized that there was no balustrade up here; only a low ridge the height of one brick stood between me and oblivion. I crawled over to the book as quickly as I could and clutched it tight as the duke, Mr. Churchill, and the duchess joined me on the promontory.

"I am not giving you anything," I said. I stood up and tried to ignore the dull ache in my right arm where it had broken my fall.

The duke took no notice of me—or, indeed, any of us. Instead, he breathed deep and looked about him, mesmerized by the prospect. "I had forgotten that you can see two faces of the kitchen clock from here," he said. He reached for the immense stone finial that decorated a corner of the arcade and rubbed his palm over the huge pitted coronet and scrolls that supported the heavy orb above. "Splendid," he murmured. The duke and said thoughtfully, as if he had not just pursued me through the house, "I used to come here when Grandfather was alive, to get away from Mama." He smiled at the memory. "It was the only place where no one ever found me."

He turned his attention to a small spot of dust on his pant leg and rubbed it briskly. When it had been wiped away, he looked at me. His face was set and stern; we had reached the last redoubt. "The time has come, Mr. Vanbrugh, for you to cease these temper tantrums. You are disrupting my household."

"That was never my intent."

"Your intent is beside the point, man," the duke said, but stopped abruptly, as if he had resolved to hold his temper. In a calmer voice he added, "It is rather more complicated than that."

"My position is very simple," I replied. "I will return this book to Mr. Sargent. It belongs to him; it does not belong to you."

"Mr. Sargent is not on this roof, Mr. Vanbrugh," Mr. Churchill said. "He is being managed by the monsignor downstairs."

"I am sure he is."

"You have nothing to fear from us," the duke said, his mouth a thin line that parroted a smile.

"I am not afraid of you," I replied. "I am only interested in what is right."

"What is *right*?" The duke laughed. "How absurd you Americans are. So misguided about what is right." He glanced, for the briefest moment, at the duchess, and in that instant an expression of deep, infinite grief passed across his weak face. In that flicker, I understood something I had not before: Standing before me was a man who had never been without pain, who bore fear on his unimpressive shoulders that would cripple others, who withstood unimaginable burdens. He was a man whose constant companion was not his family but the history of it; who was as ignorant of love as he was of the life of a common man. Being the Duke of Marlborough, far from allowing him to relish the joys this earthly life can offer had enervated Charles

Spencer-Churchill's spirit, draining him of all hope. His only recourse was to press on, to muddle through the endless night of his private misery.

"Well?" the duke said, turning to the duchess.

"Well what?" she asked.

"Are you going to allow your American architect to behave this way in my home?" he asked.

"Mr. Vanbrugh can speak for himself," she said.

Mr. Churchill shook his head. "Sunny, you are off the point," he said. "Mr. Vanbrugh, you have found yourself in the midst of a private family matter, a perplexity from which, I am certain, you would like to retire. Am I correct?"

"Yes, of course."

"Excellent," Mr. Churchill said. "Then please allow me to offer myself as a go-between—an ambassador, if you will. If you would be so good as to hand me the sketchbook, I will ensure that it reaches the proper hands." He offered a pallid smile and held out a chubby hand. "You have my word."

"Oh, Winston," the duchess whispered, her hands to her mouth, as if she were afraid she would say too much.

Mr. Churchill thrust out his jaw, and in that attitude he looked much like his cousin. He took a step toward the duke, and in that simple, perhaps uncalculated gesture, he made his true allegiance known.

The duchess closed her eyes and she let her hands fall to her sides. When she opened them again, her face overflowed with shame; she was powerless before the three men who would determine her fate. She lifted her gaze to my face, her large brown eyes anxious, all confidence gone. The sparkling, assured American duchess with whom I had been infatuated was no more. In her place was a frightened, disappointed young woman who, I imagined, would never trust again.

"Mr. Churchill, I am not a fool," I said. "Why do you believe that you can deceive me with such an absurd promise?"

"I do not know what you mean," he said.

"What you consider 'the proper hands,' as you call them, is most assuredly not what I would consider the best course of action. Would you, as a Member of Parliament, deny a man his property?"

Mr. Churchill looked at the duke but did not reply. The silence lingered about us, growing more ominous with each moment.

"Mr. Sargent is not a British subject, he is an American," the duke said.

"Well, Mr. Churchill?" I asked. "Would you do that?"

Still he did not speak.

"What are you doing, Winston?" the duke demanded, his voice flustered, strident. "Are you mad?" He pointed to me. "You cannot allow this nonentity simply to walk away from here with that book and return it to the scoundrel who drew—"

The sound of footsteps running across the rooftop below us distracted him—an opportunity I seized to head for the stairway.

"He is escaping," the duke shrieked, panic seizing him. He threw himself at me, but I had expected that and was prepared: My fist clenched, I hit him squarely across the jaw. His fatuous eyes bulged even further, and he fell back onto the slanting roof with a satisfying grunt, sliding toward the edge. As he struggled to regain his feet, I ran to the stairs. But Mr. Churchill was too quick: He tripped me and I fell forward, still clutching the sketchbook. He lunged for it but I recovered myself quickly enough to roll away from him toward one of the chimney flues. "Stay where you are, or I swear to God I will throw this book down the chimney," I yelled.

The duke looked stunned. "You would not do such a thing."

I held the book directly above the flue. "Shall we see?"

"No," the duke cried.

"Who killed Emily?" I demanded. "Did you?"

"You bastard," he growled.

I moved the book closer to the top of the flue.

"No!" the duke cried.

"I said, who killed Emily?" I wanted to hear it from his own lips.

The duke looked at me irresolutely. After a terrifying moment of uncertainty, he said quietly, "Gladys did. She strangled her."

"Good Lord," Mr. Churchill said.

So it was true. "Why?" I demanded.

The duke hung his head and wiped a bit of blood from the side of his mouth. "Because she was afraid Emily would give the sketchbook back."

"Did you carry Emily to the chapel and put her in the crypt?"

The duke nodded.

"Why?"

"You found her unexpectedly," he said simply. "Before we could dispose of her."

The duchess began to weep—slowly at first, then quickly turned into huge, wracking sobs that consumed her.

"But why would Gladys do to such a thing?" I asked.

"The title," the duke said, his voice low. "She wants the title."

I remembered the conversation with Miss Deacon when she made it very plain that her ambition was to be Duchess of Marlborough. Ambition that naked, that ruthless, would attempt anything.

"You are a disgrace," I said.

The duke slapped my face hard, with the back of his hand. I did not expect such an attack, and stepped back against the slanting roof, which loosened my grip on the sketchbook just enough for the duke to snatch it from me.

"I have it," he exulted, raising the book above his head.

I scrambled back to my feet and threw myself at him. As I did, I heard footsteps on the stair and from below Margaret appeared. "Van!" she screamed. "What is happening?"

"The duke," I shouted, as we scuffled.

With a strangled cry, Margaret threw herself on top of the duke, pulling at the sketchbook with as much energy as she could muster.

"Get them off me," the duke snarled as Mr. Churchill grabbed Margaret around her waist and tried to pull her from the duke. Margaret made one last frantic grab for the book and with a cry of triumph wrenched it from the duke's arms just as Mr. Churchill wrenched her from the mêlée.

When the duke realized he no longer held the book, he became a man possessed, lashing out at Margaret with a savagery I had never witnessed. He was too far away from her to hit her, so he began to kick her so ferociously that Margaret lost her footing and tumbled backward. The force of her fall was so strong and so startling that the low brick wall could not break her fall. In one horrible, shocking motion, she rolled down the slanting roof and over the ledge, the sketchbook still in her hands.

She did not cry out—nor did anyone else; it all happened too quickly. We froze, stupefied by what we had witnessed. There was no sound until her body hit the newly placed stones of granite in the Great Court below.

I have no clear memory of how or when I left the roof. All I do recall is running across the courtyard to the end of the arcade beneath the corner tower and stopping short to avoid falling over the unwieldy figure of Mrs. Belmont. She was kneeling over Margaret, talking to her quietly. When I appeared she rose with some difficulty and, taking my hand, said quietly, "She is still alive, but barely."

"Do you ...?" I began, but could not continue.

"She fell and hit the stone balustrade of the arcade before she landed. The monsignor has gone to summon a doctor," Mrs. Belmont said.

"Let us carry her into the house," I said.

"Leave her be," Mrs. Belmont directed. "The monsignor believes her spine is injured. You may do more harm than good by moving her."

"We are to leave her here?" I asked.

"For the time being," she said, not unkindly. "It is for the best, my boy."

I looked down at Margaret, who was lying on her back, her hands at her sides. She was absolutely still; nothing moved save her eyes. Though her face was pale, the expression she wore was peaceful, and she did not appear to be in pain. She smiled a little when she saw me but did not speak.

I took one of her hands and held it tenderly. "Oh, Meg," I whispered. I wanted to say more, but I could not; I was lost.

Margaret closed her eyes and ran her tongue over her lips. She was still for so long and her breathing became so shallow that I was certain death had come.

"How did it happen?" Mrs. Belmont asked.

I opened my mouth, but the words would not come. The events were simply too gruesome, too horrible, to relate. All I could manage was a choking moan. Mrs. Belmont gripped my shoulder firmly, both in support and in admonition. "There, there," she said, her voice husky, "Margaret needs you to be strong."

The others appeared then, like specters in a dream. The duke and duchess, Mr. Churchill and Mr. Sargent were suddenly about, talking in low, urgent voices.

"How did this happen?" Mr. Sargent asked.

There was a tense moment, which was broken by the duke.

"She slipped on the roof," he said quietly.

I stared at him in astonishment. "She did no such thing," I said, my voice returning.

The duke looked down at me, his face cool. "She slipped on the roof, Mr. Vanbrugh," he said.

"That is not true," I said, standing up. "You kicked her. I *saw* you."

The duke looked away for a moment, embarrassed. He turned to Mr. Churchill and said, "Winston, perhaps you could explain."

Mr. Churchill frowned and crossed his arms. "She fell from the roof," he said, his voice thick. He cleared his throat and said, "Mrs. Vanbrugh lost her balance and fell."

"The poor creature," Mrs. Belmont murmured.

"That is not what happened," I exclaimed, stunned by his words. I turned to the duchess. "You were there, you were a witness," I said. "You saw him"—I pointed to the duke—"kick Margaret like a dog he did not want around. Tell the truth. Tell everyone the truth."

The duchess frowned and did not speak.

"Tell them!" I insisted, my voice rising, the words resounding off the façade of Blenheim. In the distance a lamb bleated.

The duchess looked down at Margaret, whose eyes were still closed. When she finally spoke, her voice was clear, unruffled—strangely at odds with the terrible lie she was to tell.

"Mrs. Vanbrugh tripped. She turned too quickly and lost her footing," the duchess said. At that moment, the clock in the kitchen tower began to toll noon, its somber peals ringing out across the estate, as my father-in-law ran toward us, accompanied by the monsignor and Miss Deacon.

Mr. Barton was hatless, his face red from concern and exertion. He knelt down next to Margaret and stared at her, his face a study of parental distress. He glanced inquiringly at the duchess.

"Margaret fell from the roof. The monsignor has called for Dr. Foster," she said. "I am so sorry."

"The roof?" Mr. Barton asked, puzzled. "What was she doing up there, Van?" he asked. A solitary tear ran down his mottled cheek.

I could not answer; the deception that was unfolding before me was monstrous, beyond any evil I had ever witnessed. That the duke, the duchess, and Mr. Churchill would willfully lie about what had occurred on the roof to prevent the messy questions the duke would have to answer was almost as horrible as Margaret's fall.

I looked at the duchess, revulsion filling my soul. That I had so recently longed for her now seemed unimaginable. Once I would have thought that she would defend the virtues of honesty and truth above all else, even at the expense of her husband and his precious family name. But I had been mistaken—as misguided in my faith in her as I had been about nothing else in my life.

"Mrs. Vanbrugh was trying to retrieve the sketchbook that Mr. Sargent had lost," the duchess said carefully.

"She found it?" Miss Deacon asked.

"It has been found," the duchess said, as she glanced quickly at me.

Miss Deacon looked inquiringly at the duke. "But where is it?" she asked.

Mr. Churchill turned away, his shoulders hunched. "Gladys, you have the delicacy of a rhinoceros," he said, his voice overflowing with disgust.

Miss Deacon turned to Mr. Sargent. "You do not have it again, do you, John?" she asked.

"If I did, I would never tell you," he said.

"Why on earth not?"

Mr. Sargent stared at her, incredulous.

"Good God, Gladys, do shut up," the duke exclaimed.

"But I do not understand this at all," Miss Deacon persisted. "If the sketchbook has been found, then who has it?"

There was a strained pause as, indeed, the four of us who witnessed Margaret fall from the roof with the volume in her hand looked about, wondering exactly where the book had landed.

As if she read our thoughts, Mrs. Belmont said, "There was no book here when the monsignor and I came upon Mrs. Vanbrugh."

"That is correct," the monsignor agreed.

The duke murmured something to the duchess, who shook her head. We were saved from further contemplation of this by Dr. Foster, who arrived in a small carriage, clattering through the archway with a great deal of commotion. His arrival returned our attention to Margaret, from which it never strayed.

"What happened?" he asked.

"She fell from the tower," the duke said.

The doctor looked at him doubtfully but said nothing. He had brought a pallet with him, and directed us how to transfer Margaret onto it with a minimum of disruption to her spine. After she was settled securely, we carried her into the house and to a small bedroom along the passage to the Long Library, where the doctor performed a more detailed examination.

I stayed with Dr. Foster during the procedure, as did my father-in-law, and it quickly became apparent that Margaret had sustained very severe injuries. The doctor wore a grim expression, which seemed to grow more pronounced as time passed. After his examination, he called us into a small room next to the bedroom.

"It is very serious," he said quietly. "She has been paralyzed by the fall, and cannot move her arms or legs without assistance. I believe that there are extensive injuries to her internal organs, as well, and nothing more can be done except to make her comfortable and wait for the inevitable."

"Do you mean that she will die?" I asked, horrified.

"I am afraid so," Dr. Foster said.

"But she is pregnant," I whispered.

The doctor wiped his brow and shook his head. "Then it is a double tragedy," he said.

"How long until the end?" Mr. Barton asked.

The doctor folded his large red hands. "It is difficult to say," he replied, "but I believe within the hour."

My father-in-law and I looked quickly at each other, and we both had the same thought. "Then we must get her to Long Hanborough as quickly as possible," I said.

"Yes, that would be best," Mr. Barton agreed.

Dr. Foster began to object, but he could offer no argument to Mr. Barton and his simple demand: "I will not have my daughter die at Blenheim."

I went searching for the duke to ask his permission to use one of his larger carriages to transport Margaret to the vicarage. I headed for the Long Library, where I heard voices.

I slammed the door behind me, and had the satisfaction of observing the startled faces of the others as they turned toward me.

"Oh, Mr. Vanbrugh," the duchess said, walking toward me.

"Stay right where you are," I ordered, my voice curt. "I do not want any more of your sympathy." All thought of preserving civility evaporated as I saw clearly for the first time the Duchess of Marlborough and the people around her for what they truly were.

"Oh, do not say that," the duchess said softly.

I could not keep the derision from my voice. "How could I say anything but that? You have destroyed whatever good opinion I held of you—all of you—which I know is of little consequence, you have made that very clear. And I assure you, I can tolerate being disparaged by the likes of the Churchills: it is easy to ignore the opinion of people you hold in so little regard. But your duplicity, your willingness to arrange the truth like a fashionable hat, that is intolerable. And unforgivable."

"That is outrageous, Mr. Vanbrugh," Mr. Churchill grumbled. "You are not fair."

"Not fair?" I repeated. "Mr. Churchill, a servant girl is *dead* at the hands of a guest of this house. Margaret was pushed off the roof by your cousin." Miss Deacon and the duke began to protest, but I shouted over them, silencing their objections by my fury. "Is no one at Blenheim willing to admit what really happens in this house? Is the truth something that bends to the caprice of Their Graces?"

The room had fallen deathly still, like the silence that follows the fading whistle of a train in the night. But a certain rancor had taken hold, too: The people grew quiet but wary, like hunters waiting to trap a skittish, unpredictable animal.

"I thought that the truth is a compass that always points north; it may sway from its particulars, but it always recovers," I said. I looked at the duchess and continued, my voice icy and clear: "If I had known that honor vanished at the gate of this ridiculous pile of stones, I never would have gotten out of the carriage."

"You do not understand—" the duchess began.

"I understand that you are indifferent to the truth, to what is right. You have destroyed my life to save your precious reputations. You are despicable cannibals and I cannot stand the lot of you."

I turned to leave.

"You are just going to let him walk away?" Mrs. Belmont said suddenly.

"Shut up, Alva," the duke said, his voice weary.

Mr. Barton and I prevailed upon Dr. Foster to assist us in transporting Margaret to Long Hanborough. Even in the short time I had been away from her, her condition had worsened considerably; Dr. Foster had grown more worried that she might die en route to the vicarage.

None of us spoke as the horses stepped away from the main steps, and yet just before we entered the archway that led to the Kitchen Courtyard, I caught very clearly the startling sounds of a satisfied chuckle. I turned around and caught a final glimpse of the Great Court. No one was about; indeed, all that I could see was the fierce, belligerent face of Blenheim, the afternoon shadows advancing across its bulk.

epilogue

SUMMER 1933

MADAME Balsan opened the parcel in her lap guardedly, as if chary of its contents. When the top piece of paper had been folded away and the faded black leather was revealed, she emitted a small gasp of surprise. In a flurry, she threw the paper and twine aside so that, for the first time in more than a quarter of a century, she held the sketchbook of John Singer Sargent.

She placed the book on her lap so that the small gold initials in one corner of the cover, dull but still legible, were upright. "JSS," Madame whispered, her intelligent eyes bright as she traced the letters with a long, speculative finger. For a moment, Madame Balsan was transported to a glen of memory nearly forgotten by the present, to the world of a young woman who had loved unwisely and trusted her own abilities too completely.

"How did you come to this?" she asked.

"Mr. Barton had it," I replied.

Madame frowned. "Mr. Barton? That is impossible."

"I have included a letter." I indicated the sketchbook.

Madame opened the book and found on its first page a single piece of paper, covered on both sides with the small, precise handwriting of my father-in-law.

> *My dear Van—*
> *I hope this parcel reaches you. We have seen so little of each other these past years and have been out of touch for so long, that*

I must trust in God and His Majesty's Mail that this will get to you in good order.

You will perceive what this is immediately, I am confident. But you may not know how it came to be in my possession.

It was several days after we buried poor Margaret, after you had quitted Long Hanborough, that I was visited by little Annie, the housemaid who had waited upon Margaret after the death of Emily. Annie had an extraordinary story to relate—so unbelievable, in fact, that I scarcely could have given credence to any of it were it not for the simple truth that Annie could not have conjured such a tale on her own.

On the terrible day that Margaret died, Annie was cleaning the bedroom corridor just above the duchess's rooms. The tall windows were open to take advantage of the fine weather, and they gave out onto the roof of the curving wing that winds between the main house and the tower. Annie told me that she heard voices that sounded as if they were far away then a sudden sound, just outside the window at the end of the corridor, like the clapping of a pair of hands. She ran to the window and came across this very book lying on the roof right in front of her very eyes. She had no notion of what it was, she said, but thought it might have been one of the books Mr. Churchill was studying, so she picked it up and thumbed through it. What she saw shook her to the very marrow.

Annie did not know what to make of this, but had the wit to realize that this must be the sketchbook which the household was so intent upon locating.

Her first thought was to return it to Mr. Sargent directly, but the drawings were of such an alarming, personal nature that she then fixed upon presenting it directly to Her Grace. But then Annie recalled how insistent His Grace had been to recover this book that she was not at all sure but that she should present this to the duke—who was, after all, the head of the house.

The poor girl was in a dreadful muddle, but she had the presence of mind to conceal the book while she determined the correct course of action. At that moment, the household alarm was raised:

Margaret had fallen from the roof—an event the poor girl had not witnessed, thank heaven. But Annie was a girl of resources, and during the hubbub she managed to include the book (along with instructions not to open it) in a parcel of discarded linen bound that day for her mother, a seamstress in Woodstock. On her next day off, Annie went to her mother's cottage and the two of them determined that I was the best person to establish what should be done with this.

She brought it to me, and I swore Annie to secrecy and told her that I would have to work out what to do with this. But the more I pondered it, the more fixed I became to keep it in my possession and say nothing of it to anyone, at least at present. The book had caused nothing but strife and misfortune for the people who desired it; that was undeniable. And I was less confident that its return to Mr. Sargent, or its turning over to Their Graces, would stem the tide of enmity and bitterness that followed this slim volume. Better, I decided, for everyone to believe that it had been lost forever—in all probability destroyed.

By rights I should have burnt this book. But God forgive me, I could not. The drawings were too beautiful—they were full of tenderness and devotion. These drawings were more than just scribblings; they were the earthly expression of a divine love. To destroy them would be a blasphemy.

Days turned into weeks, then months, and as each one passed I expected to hear from Her Grace—a letter of condolence, perhaps, or even an invitation to tea. But nothing ever came. I gathered that the family had quitted Blenheim shortly after you and I departed, and had not returned together in quite some time. Later, of course, I was as saddened as the rest of the world to hear that the duke and duchess had secured a formal separation, and that the duchess had settled permanently in London. Perhaps it turned out for the best: The two were like oil and water—they did not mix well for long. And later, of course, I read in the newspapers that the duke and duchess had divorced—what a scandal! Were you in England for that unpleasantness? I fancy I was more surprised that the duke had converted to Catholicism than that he married Miss Deacon. The duchess, of course, is married to that French aviator—Balsan, I believe his name is, and went to France to live. I pray that they will be happy, for she certainly was not when she lived at Blenheim.

I hope I was not wrong in keeping this book from you, my

*boy. I have waited a time to dispatch it—too long, perhaps. I
cannot account for the reason; I am not certain of it myself. I think
it is likely that I was afraid that you had not yet forgiven the
parties involved. You are too loyal a soul to ignore your commit-
ments to another—to Margaret most of all. But as I have grown
older, turning into a doddering old man who has outlived his use-
fulness, I have come to know that in this life forgiveness is more
important than loyalty. We have so little time here, we should not
waste a moment being unwilling to forgive. It is hard work, hating.
It requires far too much attention and energy—effort we can de-
vote to other, pleasanter, pastimes.*

*I have forgiven the duke, and the duchess, and Mr. Churchill
for what happened to Margaret on that roof all those years ago.
It would please me no end if you could, too.*

*I have always lived within a short ride of Blenheim, and I
have been acquainted with three generations of Churchills. And
while I was never on as intimate terms with them as you were, I
do believe that they—*

Madame Balsan looked up at me. "Is that all?"

"That is all that I found."

"Found?" Madame asked, perplexed.

"Yes. My father-in-law died last month. In Long Hanborough."

Madame pressed her lips together but said nothing.

"His heart just gave out, I understand."

"His lion heart," the duchess murmured.

"I am surprised your son did not tell you. The Marquis of Bland-
ford."

"We are not as close as we once were."

I nodded. "Neither were Mr. Barton and I. Still, he bequeathed all
of his possessions to me. A very generous spirit. I came upon this book
in his bedroom, in a small desk he used."

Madame Balsan frowned. "But he writes of his sending it to you."

"Yes. But he never did," I said.

"And he never finished the letter. That is curious." She said this as
if she did not truly believe me.

"So much of life is curious," I said.

The duchess closed the book. She wanted to ask me a question, I
was certain, and was working up the nerve.

"Are you still in touch with Miss Deacon?" I asked. "Or should I say, Duchess Gladys?"

"Not for years—before the Flood, as you bloody well know," she snapped. The ghost of a smile played about her lips. "I understand that the paraffin wax she had had injected into her face to preserve her beauty has begun to sag. They say her face looks like a bowl of boiled turnip. So now her outside resembles her insides."

"Would that were true for everyone," I said.

The duchess looked startled at that but said nothing. She ran her hand along the binding of the sketchbook. "Have you looked through this?" she asked, her voice a whisper.

"I thought you'd never ask."

"What do you mean?" she said, her voice cross. "Does that mean you have or you haven't?"

"It means, Madame, that you do not know me nearly as well as you think you do."

She gazed out into the garden, her attention captured by a swan, its long neck curved in a graceful arc, as it swam silently across the moat. "What did you think of the drawings?" she asked finally.

"I think the artist who drew them was very much in love," I said.

The duchess smiled slowly, remembering. "What fools we were," she said.

"Yes," I agreed.

"The finished painting is quite remarkable," she said, satisfied.

"It is ridiculous," I said. "A piece of propaganda."

The duchess looked startled. "Have you seen it?" she asked.

I nodded. "I visited Blenheim a while back, on one of the visitor days. Just before the duke closed it up."

"Well, Sargent is out of fashion now," she said.

"Oh, he is much worse than that. He is a liar. That painting is a complete distortion of the truth. The duke looks almost noble in it. And your sons, he painted them as if they were little girls, dressed in those ridiculous costumes."

"Ivor wrote me to say that when Sunny finally threw Gladys out of Blenheim, she hired a van, loaded up the Monets and Cézannes she had hung everywhere and those dreadful dogs, and simply drove away." Madame Balsan puckered her mouth, as if she were not certain of the vintage she was tasting. She took a sip of coffee, put down the cup carefully, then played with an invisible wrinkle in her dress. "And what of the duchess in the painting?" she asked.

I knew she would ask this. Her vanity could not resist. "She is the most ridiculous of all."

Madame cringed. "Mr. Vanbrugh, that is rather bitter."

"I am much, much more than bitter," I said, my voice rasping with emotion.

"You quite frighten me."

"Excellent. That was precisely my intent." I gazed at the quiet maturity of her face and figure. She had settled comfortably into her middle years, but I managed to catch the briefest glimpse of the young beauty who had once excited the passion of an artist and the ardor of a young, foolish man who knew nothing of life. Sitting with her, in this elegant room in the quiet French countryside, I realized that for the duchess, the death of Margaret was simply a nightmare forgotten long ago, a disagreeable, inconvenient memory that was best ignored and never spoken of.

"Tell me, did the stories about Mr. Sargent and all of his young men bother you?"

The duchess blanched at the suggestion. "I—"

"Never mind. To see you shocked is enough." I reached into my coat pocket and withdrew the last letter from Duchess Sarah I had found. I held it delicately in my hands, staring at its yellowed vulnerability.

"What do you have there?" she asked after a moment, trying to change the subject. "Is it something else for me?"

I handed it to her. "It is the last letter of Duchess Sarah's you wrote to dupe me. To dupe us all."

Before my eyes Madame deflated. She took the letter but did not open it. "How long have you known?" she asked.

"Since the day Margaret was killed. You were afraid the duke would recognize your handwriting so you ensured I made copies of the letters and that the duke saw those, not the originals."

"Where did you find the letter?"

"Jamison found it in a copy of *The Provok'd Wife* under your pillow. Rather prophetic title, wouldn't you say?"

She crumpled at the final piece of evidence of her treachery. "I only wanted the upper hand over Sunny," she said.

"So you used me, an unknown draftsman whose only sin was a celebrated name. I was a pawn, used by the queen to check the king. The ploy failed. How foolhardy." I stood up. "I think it is time for me to go."

"So soon?" she said, but it was an empty inquiry; she wanted no more of me.

"I must return to Paris this evening. I have been promised the newspapers from London. By special courier, in fact."

"Why? Is there some news we simple folk in the countryside should be aware of?" the duchess asked, trying to sound arch.

"Perhaps. The art critics are passing judgment on several sketches by Mr. Sargent that have come to light recently."

The duchess looked wary. "Oh?"

"It really is an astonishing story. They were discovered in the desk of a country vicar. Can you imagine? Four original Sargents sitting in a cubbyhole, undetected all these years. What on earth would a clergyman be doing with sketches by Sargent?"

Her lower lip quivered as her face, that once striking face, went white. She reached for the sketchbook and opened it quickly. In a matter of moments she had located the spots where the four drawings—the four audacious, exquisitely rendered nude studies of the young Duchess of Marlborough—had been removed by someone who was adept at cutting paper—a draftsman, perhaps.

"I do not believe it," she whispered.

"I told you when I arrived that I had news, Madame," I said. "And so I do." I walked to the door in silence, as Madame Balsan, the former Duchess of Marlborough, struggled to make sense of the calamity that was about to shatter her world. "I have made arrangements for copies of the newspapers to be delivered to you here, since I imagine that you are not planning on venturing out for the time being."

I bowed slightly. "This visit has been a pleasure, Your Grace," I said as I closed the door behind me. I did not look back.

Author's note

A *Weekend at Blenheim* is a work of fiction, but most of its settings and characters are based on actual places and people.

Blenheim Palace, one of the largest private homes in England, has been the seat of the Dukes of Marlborough since Sir John Vanbrugh designed it and oversaw its construction in the early eighteenth century. The ninth Duke of Marlborough, a descendant of the first duke, did marry the American heiress Consuelo Vanderbilt in 1895 and brought her to England as his duchess. In 1905, the duke engaged John Singer Sargent, the most popular portrait painter of his day and an American, to paint a complement to the large portrait of the fourth duke's family that hangs in one of Blenheim's staterooms. He agreed, and today the two paintings hang across from one another in the Red Drawing Room, competing somberly for attention.

The house party chronicled here is a complete invention (as is the novel's narrator), though it is certainly plausible that Winston Churchill, Gladys Deacon, Alva Vanderbilt Belmont, and Monsignor Vay de Vaya could have strolled the corridors and gardens of Blenheim together. But what they say—and perhaps more important, what prompts them to act—are my invention.